AN UNEXPECTED PARADISE

CHELSEA CURTO

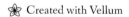

To everyone who's never found their Happily Ever After depicted in a romance novel before, this one is for you. It might not fit the traditional mold, and it might look a little different, but it's still just as special. You are just as special.

CONTENT WARNINGS

This book contains items that might be triggering to read. I've included a list below.

-Mention of self harm, a miscarriage, the loss of a parent and abuse from a past significant other (none of which are depicted on page)

-OCD behavior (checking locks on doors)

-A scene involving a spiked drink at a bar. No on page assault occurs, and the male main character is not the one who performs the drink spiking.

ONE

JO

Today is either going to be the day I get fired or the day I commit a murder.

I'm not sure which one I'd prefer more.

What I *do* know is the murder is definitely going to happen first.

The idea of inflicting violence flashes through my head at the sight of my workplace rival and the bane of my existence, Jack Lancaster, loitering outside the entrance to our office building, fingers deftly typing away on his caseless iPhone.

He's positioned himself right in the middle of the bustling sidewalk during the morning rush hour, not a care in the world as pedestrians meander around him to avoid a head-on collision. They're far nicer than me; I would elbow him as I passed, right below the ribs, and let him know precisely how much of an inconsiderate prick I think he is.

My eyes narrow and my pace slows to almost a crawl as I approach him, grip tightening on the two cardboard trays of coffee I'm juggling like a circus performer, stacked tall with six drinks each. The late autumn wind propels me down the sidewalk alongside a pile of crunchy, freshly fallen leaves, whipping my unruly red hair into my face and pushing me closer to a conversation I certainly do not want to have. He spots me approaching before sliding his phone away in his pocket and tossing a signature scowl my way.

"Josephine," the dreaded baritone voice drawls, meeting my contemptuous gaze with a scornful look of his own.

I suppress an involuntary shudder. I'm never prepared for how my name sounds coming out of Jack's mouth, a mix of trepidation and unexplained, unprovoked warmth slithering from the top of my spine to the small of my back with that single, calamitous word.

No one in my life calls me Josephine. Except him. I go by *Jo*. Just Jo.

It's how I introduce myself to anyone I meet and how I sign every company email. It's also how my coworkers, family, and friends refer to me. Jack, however, refuses to adhere to my hopeless plea to shorten the word and continues to call me Josephine, much to my chagrin. It's always spoken so bitterly, dripping with disdain and agitation, as if my mere existence ruins his pompous, self-important life.

"Jack," I reply cooly, powering past him and not bothering to stop for pleasantries. We don't *do* pleasantries. I balance the trays with practiced ease, lean forward to scan my ID, and pull open the glass door. He offers no help, not even a polite word of encouragement or round of applause as I accomplish the laborious task alone, cups almost spilling onto the sidewalk and turning it a murky brown. It turns out, folks, chivalry is dead; brought down by the man next to me. I refuse to ask for his help, though, not quite reaching *that* level of desperation. He'd hold it over my head from now until the end of time, delighting in my momentary lapse of weakness.

I'm tempted to slam the door shut in his face, a nod back to our first encounter, but I take the high road instead, propping it open with the heel of my black flat. He grunts what I decipher as a non-verbal, meager *thank you* but could also be construed as a patronizing *fuck you*. It's hard to tell with him. Some people in the office interpret his quiet demeanor as diffidence or antisocial behavior. I know the true story; Jack Lancaster is a grumpy, crotchety, and irritable man, destined to be unhappy for the rest of his life.

My eyes dart over as he falls in step next to me and we stroll across the tiled lobby floor. He's wearing a navy-blue suit today and his face is flushed, which means he went to the gym this morning. On Tuesdays, Thursdays, and Fridays, his cheeks appear colored when he berates me, a light rosy pink overtaking the usual golden tan.

We part at the elevator, me striding in with attempted poise and him hovering on the other side as if crossing the threshold to join me is equivalent to scaling a mountain in the dead of winter.

"Enjoy your elevator ride," Jack says, words flippant and clipped, dismissing and banishing me to the vestibule. I take a breath, steeling myself and shaking off the interaction. We'll have another round upstairs in a few minutes, and I'm grateful for the pause in our bickering.

It's hard to pinpoint when the animosity between us began. I'm willing to venture a guess and say it was the very first day we met, over two years ago. A dreary mist and light rain blanketed the world in shades of gray that fateful morning, no sun to be found.

Fitting, right?

I had been at Itrix, the tech company where we work, for a week, and I was running late. As a people-pleaser and Enneagram two, I get immense joy out of helping others. Showing up behind schedule when people are counting on me is my idea of hell. That being said, I'm *never* late. I prefer to arrive to my destination excessively early and read in a corner rather than pushing the time limits and rushing to a commitment.

It also happened to be the morning of my first presentation in my new role as the head of marketing and advertising, making me more flustered than usual thanks to a late train and dreary weather. After sprinting across the lobby floor, I slid into the cramped elevator in full disaster mode, complete with frizzy hair, a mis-buttoned shirt, and my messenger bag dragging on the floor, buckles scratching like nails on a chalkboard. I repeatedly pushed the button to close the doors and start moving the car, blatantly shutting out and ignoring a man who hollered for me to hold the elevator. The man, I learned shortly thereafter, was Jack Lancaster, Head of Software Development and my brand-new colleague I hadn't had the pleasure of meeting yet. Surprise!

Look, it wasn't intentional.

Did I hear him yell *"WAIT"*?

Yeah, I did. The space wasn't buzzing with raised voices and cheery conversation. It was as quiet as the dead of night, not a peep coming from the other occupants. I closed the doors anyway, rage and shock etched between his furrowed eyebrows and disgruntled mouth.

Did I feel guilty the whole ride up to the fourth floor, wondering what bad karma I would be forced to endure thanks to my ruthless act? Disgustingly so. I'm not a door-closer. I'm a *door-holder*, and to this day, I'm still unsure what possessed me to act so callously.

I knew I'd pay for my sins eventually. I just didn't expect for it to be a short twenty minutes later, the same man barging in and interrupting my presentation.

He was livid.

Actually, livid might be the understatement of the century.

For the rest of my hour-long speech, he proceeded to give me the cold shoulder in addition to disregarding my slideshow, holding personal conversations in the middle of the question-and-answer session and incessantly typing on his laptop, fingers *tap, tap tapping* away, the clickity-clack sound causing my eye to twitch for hours after.

He cornered me at the end of my talk, informing me in a not-so-kind manner that he thought what I did was *"elementary"* and *"unnecessary,"* citing a decline in the talent level of recent hires and an increase in frivolous spending. I truly thought he was being facetious and funny, and I laughed in his face while waiting for a joke that never arrived.

Here we are years later, hostility festering with a vengeance, no peace treaty in sight. Our weekly encounters include disparaging comments and callous interactions. He calls me loud and ostentatious, while I like to point out his lack of emotional connection with anyone in the office. The man *never* attends company social events or happy hours, nor have I seen him hang out with another human being.

He shoves into my chair while I'm writing, a large streak overtaking my page of notes. I send all email correspondence to him in a ridiculously large font so he can never claim he didn't read a memo, no matter how hard he tries to evade my communication. Some days when I walk into a room he's inhabiting, he'll look at me, lips pursing like he's eating a lemon, then end his conversation and leave without so much as a sidelong glance my way.

He's switched sugar with salt, causing my afternoon tea to taste disgusting. I leave his drink at the farthest end of the conference table, forcing him to get up and walk all the way around to retrieve it. When I have computer issues, he refuses to help me, delighting in my apparent incompetence and asking me questions such as, *"Did you try turning it off and back on? Sounds like a user error."*

It's a blessing we only see each other once a week. The hour-long interdepartmental company meetings on Tuesdays I have to suffer through with him push my patience to the brink. The other four days, we pretend the other doesn't exist and live in perfect harmony.

The elevator doors open and I exit onto the fourth floor, heading for the conference room where our meetings occur. Sometimes I'm amazed the high-rise skyscraper is still standing. The other tenants should be grateful that our individual offices have two floors of separation; otherwise, this concrete cylinder would have turned into debris months ago.

"Morning, Jo," my friend Tyler exclaims brightly as he walks into the room.

"Hey, Ty," I answer, beaming at him as I delicately slide the trays off my arms and onto the oval wooden table. "I got you an extra shot of espresso. Thought you might need it."

Tyler and his husband Alan adopted twin girls a few months ago and he looks more haggard with each passing day. He gives me an appreciative, albeit tired, smile.

"You're an angel. Oh, hey, Jack," he says, greeting the cloud of gloom who has joined us in the room, darkness following closely behind.

"Morning, Tyler."

Sure, the greeting isn't downright polite and there's not a hint of excitement behind the four monotone syllables. Still, it's a heck of a lot kinder than how he greets *me*.

Jack sifts through the drinks before extracting one, letting out a huff. I love trying to decipher the noises he emits. This one appears to be a mix of irritated and contrived.

As the person who lives the closest to the best small business coffee shop in town, I've been designated the coffee delivery gal on meeting days, using the company credit card to provide liquid gold to my fellow colleagues and wake them from their sleep-induced haze in the early hours of the day. An idea of a rotating schedule was tossed around so I didn't bear the brunt of the work, but I enjoy the extra steps outside. I don't own a car and rely on my legs and the train for transportation, frequently opting to walk. It's my exercise and an excuse to bypass getting a gym membership. The perks of city-living.

"Grumpy? That's what we're going with today? Your insults are fading, Josephine. Frankly, I'm disappointed. You can do much better."

"Good thing I don't live my life for your approval. I was in a rush this morning, so that's all you get. Sorry to ruin your day."

We both know I'm not sorry. Writing everyone's name on the individual drinks so they can differentiate between the beverages is a necessity when tired hands grab for the first source of caffeine, orders often becoming flip-flopped and switched. I don't offer the same courtesy to Jack, assigning him an array of phrases and nicknames that are far from cordial.

I had nothing new or witty to put on his cup today, and Google hasn't been much help as of late. Typing *insults to put on your office nemesis' coffee cups besides their name because you can't stand them* into the search bar doesn't yield a plethora of results, believe it or not.

"This tastes like decaf."

I can hear the frown in his voice without seeing his face. Jack is always frowning, lips perpetually downturned and alternating from a half-scowl to a half-grimace. It's a miracle they haven't gotten stuck in that position.

And a shame.

Carla, our office administrator, vehemently claims she once saw him crack a smile in the communal kitchen when telling a joke. No one believes her. His happiness is akin to seeing a unicorn: rare and nonexistent.

"I asked for your usual. Black coffee. Pretentious and asshole-ish to match your soul and shining personality."

"This isn't a regular black coffee. I think you messed up the order," Jack says sharply.

"You think I purposely gave you the wrong drink? I went out of my way to ask the barista to specially ruin your order, and your drink order alone? Are you delusional?"

"I wouldn't put it past you. It's not hard to get right. Perhaps if you put your useless social media apps down, the drinks would arrive correctly."

I rise from my chair, facing the thorn in my side head-on.

He's not a towering, imposing man who takes up a lot of space; quite the opposite, actually. On the days I don't wear heels, our heights are nearly identical. It varies who nudges out who; sometimes I slouch too much and the advantage goes to him. Other times when he's crabby (re: every hour of every live-long day), shoulders hunched and curved in on himself, I'm awarded a handful of prideful inches. Those days I stand over him, relishing in my victory. Today's shoe choice causes our noses to be almost aligned, eyes parallel, and I concede to a temporary tie in the height game.

I'd be remiss if I didn't begrudgingly acknowledge the most devastating part about Jack Lancaster. It's his damn eyes. It was the first thing I noticed about him as the elevator doors closed in his face. I almost pried the steel apart so I could stare a little longer, mesmerized by the luminous orbs.

They're sapphire blue, the same way the sky looks on a hot summer day; no trace of clouds to be seen and you're begging for any source of shade to be shielded away from the unforgiving sun. They rival the color of the ocean off the coast of an uninhabited island in Southern Europe. Vibrant. Resonant.

Alluring. A contrast so vastly different from the dark and prickly interior of their owner, I'm not sure they're even real. Women and men have probably written sonnets about how ensnaring they are. *Wars* could start because of those blasted things.

One day when I threw a particularly snarky comment his way before a meeting, they twinkled briefly, awakened from their normal moody slumber, a bear out of hibernation after a long winter. I must have imagined it, though, because I haven't seen the sparkle since.

We might be self-proclaimed mortal enemies—his choice of words, not mine—but I can still appreciate the fact that he's an attractive man even on the days he annoys the ever-loving fuck out of me. I would never admit that to him, of course. Absolutely not. We don't share personal anecdotes with each other, and I'm certainly not going to boast about his good looks and stroke his ego.

But, yeah.

He's hot.

And I hate him a little more because of it.

"You know I didn't pour the coffee, right? I simply collected the drink. Perhaps if you have such a grievance with the way it tastes you could be on permanent delivery duty from now on. Or better yet, invest in an at-home coffee maker and eliminate all future complaints."

Feeling bold, I pluck the warm cup from his grasp and bring it to my lips. My gaze remains on him as I take a sip. His mouth parts and his eyes widen as he follows my motions. Swallowing the bitterness down is nearly impossible, and I try not to wince at the terrible flavor. I hate coffee, and coffee with nothing in it is vile.

A borderline serial-killer order.

When they do interviews about all the famous capital

murderers, I'm sure if asked what they liked to drink, *black coffee* would be a common response.

"Tastes fine to me."

My fingers itch to take a swig of my sweetened tea to wash away the lingering residue. I wouldn't be able to tell the difference between decaf and regular if my life depended on it, but it's fun to watch him get worked up.

He blinks, four quick flutters of his eyelashes. His mouth still hasn't closed and the hand which formerly held the drink in question dangles in the air, limp, awkward, and without a purpose. I help him out, gleefully shoving the cup back to its rightful owner and being the one to dismiss *him* for a change.

"You are unbelievable," he mutters, snapping out of the speechless trance and shuffling to his usual spot at the opposite end of the table. He takes the coffee with him, grumbling gruffly under his breath.

Minor victories!

"Have you heard the rumor circulating that Jensen is announcing something important at the meeting today?" Tyler asks, drawing my attention to him and away from the grizzly bear moving out of sight. "Andy in sales thinks we might get bought out."

It's not an illogical hypothesis; we're a flourishing, small-name, tech company competing heavily with some of the upper-tier powerhouses. The website my team and I poured hundreds of hours into revamping went live five days ago and is already showing an uptick in revenue. Itrix keeps getting bigger and bigger, pulling in clients who are leaving big conglomerates to give *us* their business.

"I thought today might be the day I lose my job. It probably has to do with the new software update we're about to announce. I'm sure it's a totally boring, not at all exciting announcement."

"You're probably right. Maybe we're finally getting a Nespresso machine!"

"You'd prefer more caffeine supplies over a paycheck," I laugh, shaking my head. "Unlimited PTO would be a cool addition to our benefits."

"Oh! We can work from home once a week!"

"Bring our dogs to work!"

The rest of my colleagues trickle in, voicing their thanks for the provided coffees that get drowned out by my boss, Jensen, entering the room.

"Morning, folks," they say, standing in front of the small group. Our meetings only involve the ten department heads who then pass on any pertinent and time-sensitive information to the rest of their large teams. "I have a busy morning, so I'm going to keep this short. No, this isn't a bad gathering, so cool your jets. I've heard the rumblings around the office, and I promise it's not anything detrimental to your careers.

"We'll talk about this next week in more detail as concrete numbers roll in, but based on initial data our website relaunch has been massively successful. Big shoutout to the entire marketing, advertising, and softdev teams! This new overhaul will keep us competitive."

There's a round of applause, and Tyler squeezes my shoulder in congratulations. I smile, proud of my team and their hard work.

"Now, the fun part of today," Jensen continues. "We received two invitations to the Tech Development Seminar being held in Key West this year. After a careful review process, the board and I selected our two attendees based on a few criteria: recent work performances, contributions to the company, and the overall role they have here at the office. If I could send everyone, I would. These two individuals are an asset to Itrix and have demonstrated their skills time and time again. We'll be represented well."

They pause for dramatic effect, amused eyes dancing around the room while we all sit on the edge of our seats, curious to see who the lucky two are. Anticipation cackles and fills the pregnant pause, stretching longer than necessary.

"Jack and Jo, you're going to be our attendees!"

TWO

JO

Time around me stops. It's quiet for a moment, a sliver of solitude and peace as I process Jensen's enthusiastic words. They sink in slowly, stabbing and pricking my body like tiny needles as the solitude morphs to panic. Worry. Nervousness. I laugh out loud, humorless and sharp, unsure of how else to react.

"Wait, what?" I ask, my heart racing in my chest, a runner charging for a finish line with a last-minute burst of energy. "The two of us? Me and... Jack? Together? On a trip? I don't... That's not..." I stammer, struggling to find the correct words to convey how very, very *wrong* this situation is.

Jensen shrugs, unperturbed by their announcement and how it's sending me spiraling.

"It's perfect timing with the marketing changes we're undergoing and the website relaunch. You can talk with other advertising folks and maybe find a partnership or collaboration."

"Great," I say feebly, voice trembling.

This isn't great. It's pretty freaking horrible, if you ask me. Catastrophic, even.

I shuck off my blazer in a frenzy, skin turning clammy and

damp. I expect to find Jack glowering as he gets ready to protest the decision and present a PowerPoint about all the reasons I shouldn't be going to a prestigious event. A quick glance down the table reveals there's no recognition he's even bothering to listen to the discussion at all. His eyes are focused on the table while his hand twirls a pen absentmindedly, ignoring everyone.

He looks pained.

That might not be the right word.

He doesn't seem mad, and that's what I find most concerning.

"Great! The conference is in three weeks, so I'll forward you two the information later today. That's all I've got, everyone. See you next week!"

"Are you okay?" Tyler asks quietly when we're the only two left in the room.

"Okay? Am I *okay*? No, I'm so far from okay! I can't go to a conference with him!" I inhale deeply, holding the breath for three seconds before releasing it.

"Is it really that bad? How much are you going to see him? One night at some mixer while you drink cheap wine and sweat to death? You're not sharing a room with the man. The conference will have a lot of networking potential, Jo, and you'll meet new people. I love working with you, but maybe there's something better out there." He reaches forward and squeezes my hand. "I know you've been researching positions outside of Itrix."

"You're right. This is a phenomenal opportunity. But... I feel like an imposter. I didn't do the work on my own, and who's saying I deserve to go over anyone else on my team?"

"Oh sweetie, I know you're a humble person and would never brag about an accomplishment, but you've helped change the face of Itrix. We were so sad before you came along. Do you remember the old website that used clip art from Windows 95 up until last week? In 2022? Enough said. Sales are at an all-time high since you've taken over the marketing department. Morale is up, and we have exciting social events every other month. People love working here, and our company is thriving. You've played a huge role in that."

"You're trying to be nice," I mumble, stacking the empty cardboard trays on top of each other and throwing them into the recycling bin as I stand from the table. "You're obligated to say that as my work husband."

"I wouldn't lie to you," he says, walking down the hall beside me.

No, he wouldn't. Once, when I wore a new sweater, Tyler took one look at it and told me it belonged in a nursing home or morgue. He lovingly refers to it as the *cardicant*. The poor Banana Republic item has never seen the light of day again.

"Okay," I sigh, a block of dread still prevalent in my spine. "I will go to Key West and try not to hate it. Wow, that sentence sounded pretentious, I'm sorry."

"And I'll do my best to not be infinitely jealous when you're tanning on the beach and I'm covered in baby spit-up."

"That's cute. You know they say baby spit-up is all the rage right now," I call over my shoulder, entering my office and closing the door firmly behind me. I collapse into my leather desk chair, needing an uninterrupted minute—or twenty—to breathe in silence and process what the hell is going on.

There's no denying that attending the TDS would be beneficial. We've never received an invitation before, and now we've been presented with two. Rejecting my spot is an insult to Jensen, their opinion of me, and the painstakingly diligent work I've put into the website project. I may not feel like my skill set is up to the caliber of an important conference, but others do. And that's what matters.

It's also going to be an opportunity to discuss strategies that have been successful for other companies and potentially open doors to help nudge me toward figuring out what I want to do career-wise. On a whim, I applied to a position outside Itrix out in Colorado a few months ago, thinking a change might be in order. I did an interview over the phone, but I have heard nothing since. It's safe to assume they selected another candidate.

Which is fine. It's just, for a while now... I've felt stuck. Unsure of what to do next.

I'm not unhappy here; far from it. I enjoy coming to work every day and I love what I do. I'm close to my family and best friend. A piece is missing, though, and I can't put my finger on what, exactly, it is.

I often find myself simply going through the motions of work and life without a lot of joy. And I've always been a firm advocate in experiencing joy every day, even in small quantities and doses. Lately, my days have become a little dull. A little dimmer. They aren't *bad* per se. They're just... fine. Okay. Average. I'm searching for that spark and passion again. Maybe this conference will strike a new match of excitement.

I pinch the bridge of my nose, contemplating my options. Do the pros of attending this conference outweigh the cons? The one lonely, minuscule, tinyyyyy hard-to-miss item in the con column is Jack Lancaster. It's immature to consider not going because of him. We're adults, and we can handle this like adults.

Hopefully.

The door to my office opens abruptly without an invitation, and my eyes jerk up, only to be met with *him* standing before me.

"Josephine," Jack says, his arms crossing over his chest as he stands in the doorway. He's ditched his suit jacket in the five minutes since I last saw him, looking almost naked without the outer layer. Is this visit his idea of extending an olive branch amidst our current predicament? A soldier of war without his armor, coming in the name of peace and tranquility?

"Yes?" I ask, a flash of optimism sparking in me. Hope blooms like a flower, thinking we're going to discuss this civilly, and I offer him a tentative smile that goes unreturned. He strides to my desk, stopping directly in front of me, his thighs almost pressing against the wooden barrier.

"Are you feeling all right?"

"What?"

"Are you feeling all right?" he repeats verbatim, no change in the inflection.

"I'm fine." I blink, bewildered by the weirdly considerate question. The side of his jaw relaxes fractionally at my answer and he nods once. Upon further reflection, nod might be a generous exaggeration. It's more of an awkward sideways jerk of his head, similar to what one would experience with a neck spasm.

Is *he* feeling all right?

"Good. I wanted to let you know I'll be attending the conference. I'm not sure what that means for you."

He runs his hands through his hair while he speaks, the natural waves falling across his forehead and nearly shielding his face from view. He doesn't have the mess I deal with daily, and if I had to give his hairstyle a name, Casual Surfer would be appropriate.

The color is stuck somewhere between blonde and brown, sunshine yellow and auburn, mixing like paint on an artist's palette and forming a perfect shade of bronze. Outside in the morning light, under hues of orange and red, it looks more blonde; soft, golden locks pushed away from his face, sharp cheekbones on full display. In the afternoon dullness under artificial lighting, however, it seems more brown, matching the first falling leaves of autumn that currently litter the sidewalk outside.

"What does that mean for me? I'll be attending, too. Obviously."

His eyes narrow, and I know an obtuse comment is on the tip of his tongue, waiting to spill out.

"Are you? We should give the attendees a heads up you'll be coming. They'll want to say goodbye to their loved ones since you're going to bore them to death with your graphs and nonsensical information about useless social media sites. Believe it or not, companies can survive without the grandeur of an Instagram page. I, for one, think we should allocate our budget elsewhere, in more important projects. Not on *you*."

"My graphs? You think that will be their issue? They'll be begging me for death; it'll be a grateful, welcomed blessing after hearing your ramblings on numbers and codes no one cares about, using fancy words us lowly, uneducated peasants can't comprehend. I know you do it intentionally, hoping to appear smarter than you are. It doesn't work on me. I see straight through your bullshit. What a team we'd make."

The corner of his lip turns up imperceptibly, barely rising an inch. It causes me to pause; the movement looks positively asinine.

I think he's trying to smile? Maybe? I can't be certain because it kindaaaa looks like a fishing hook is lodged in his mouth, stretching the muscles unwillingly. It's a pathetic attempt, yet somehow it's the closest he's ever come to displaying any form of jovial emotion.

A for effort, I guess?

I rise from my chair and lean across my desk. Jack takes a step closer, mirroring my actions.

"Is there a reason you're here, Lancaster, or are you harassing me for the fun of it?"

Our faces are close. I could kiss him if I really wanted to. Which I don't, but all it would take is another lean forward and my mouth would be on his. I watch, transfixed, as his eyes scour my face before fixating on my lips. I swallow, cheeks flushing under his scrutinizing gaze. He hasn't broken eye contact yet, and I refuse to be the first to crack.

"Verbally sparring with you is the highlight of my day, Josephine." The comment sounds like a growl, low and throaty. The tone does something remarkable to me; it's like cool silk running tenderly against my cheek and down my neck to the rest of my warming body. Heat stirs at the pit of my stomach, swirling like a deadly whirlpool and ravishing my insides. My senses raise in awareness and I swear there aren't any other sounds in the room except his voice. His sultry, captivating voice.

"Maybe I seek you out to annoy you on purpose," Jack continues. "I enjoy watching the way your face contorts into a frown whenever you see me. Your bottom lip sticks out when you're thinking hard about an insult to throw my way. Did you know your eyes shift from rich, emerald green when you're passionate about something to..." He stops mid-sentence, terror evident in his own eyes.

His tongue escapes his mouth, darting across his lips. The sensual maneuver snaps me back to reality. I draw in a staggered breath, looking away and severing whatever charged bond has formed between us in the last thirty seconds, hurling it out the window, never to be seen again.

What the hell?

"I really dislike you," I mutter, putting much, much, *much* needed distance between us. The desk doesn't offer nearly enough separation. I know his goal. I know what game he's trying to play. He's trying to pressure me into backing out of the conference. Asshole.

"I can assure you, the feeling is mutual," he snaps, mask back on as the normal, icy facade settles into place. With that, he leaves my office, slamming the door behind him.

It isn't until I'm packing up my purse for the night that I realize not only does Jack know the specific shade of my eyes, but he seemed positively petrified to admit it to me.

THREE

JACK

That couldn't have gone any worse.

Honestly. What the hell was I thinking?

It's not even noon and the entire day has gone to shit. I should have realized the rain pattering against my window when I woke up would foreshadow the Tuesday mood.

As if being forced to attend a conference with the woman who drives me up a wall every time we interact isn't enough torture, I had to go and let it slip when I was accosting her I know the color of her eyes, thanks to my big fucking mouth.

Her eyes that change depending on her moods. Emerald green when she's fired up and speaking passionately. Freshly cut grass green when she's talking about what makes her happy, wearing a wistful expression.

These are things I shouldn't notice as a coworker-slash-enemy, but I do.

It's a problem. And it has been for two long, forlorn years.

I wasn't thinking clearly in her office and got caught up in the moment. She was in my space, crowding me, and fighting back with sarcastic remarks and a ferocious intensity synonymous with *her*.

She nearly made me smile in public with her quip about my job and the duo we'd make. I had to actively bite my lip to stifle the reaction and not show the small thread of emotion slowly unraveling from the spool that sits tucked away inside, never letting the world see an ounce of my happiness.

Not that I have a lot of happiness to display. The tank is pretty freaking low these days.

The whole encounter stemmed from wanting to make sure she was okay. When Jensen announced we would be the ones attending the conference, panic practically seeped from her pores. I could sense her discomfort from the other side of the room. Everyone could. She tried to hide the way her breathing became labored while also looking like she was on the verge of a breakdown.

I get it. She's distraught about having to go somewhere with *me*, no buffer of Tyler or our other colleagues around. That recognition really set her off, and my chest felt tight and inexplicably painful when I realized I was the source of her blatant uncomfortableness. After the meeting was adjourned, I bolted from the room, confused by the sensation that was crippling me, making it difficult to focus on anything but Josephine.

It's the reason why I charged into her office a few minutes later, a *need* to check on her persistently hollering in my brain with every step I took. A small, feeble part of me wanted to ask her if she'd like a hug then wrap her in a soothing embrace. Instead of being a decent human being with a backbone and a drop of kindness, however, I interrupted her day, belittled her, and pushed her even further away. Par for the course with the two of us.

Great. We're off to a good fucking start, and we still have three weeks to go.

Dammit, dammit, dammit.

I pull my phone out of my pocket and type out a message to my group of best friends.

JL: 911BC. Please.
JL: Mickey's at 7.

NR: Might be a few late, but count me in.
HD: Anything that needs our attention right now, J?
Are you okay?
PW: It's open house night at our school, so I'll be there ASAP.
NL: Any hot, single moms going?
PW: Jesus, Neil, STFU.
NL: It's an important question!

JL: No. It can wait. I'm freaking out.
JL: But not time sensitive.

NR: Deep breaths, man.
NR: Whatever it is, it'll be okay. We've got you.
HD: Text if it changes to Threat Level Midnight. <3
NL: But for real. Hot single moms? MILFs?
PW: NEIL. You have a girlfriend you don't deserve.
HR: Someone block him for the rest of the afternoon.

Despite the tension that's crawled its way up my back, nestling between my shoulder blades like a squatter who refuses to leave, I let out a sigh of relief and a huff of laughter. When I moved to the city over two years ago, I didn't know anyone. It wasn't ideal, but anything was better than *there*. There holds too many memories.

Too many ghosts.

Too many screwups and mistakes I hopelessly needed to escape. I took the first job I could find and landed here, right outside Boston.

After reluctantly agreeing to join a recreational baseball league to have social interaction and physical exertion thanks to the persuasion of a friend of a friend, I met Henry Dawson, another guy on the team. He took one look at me, saw how pathetic I was, and invited me out for a beer with his group of guys. They welcomed me with open arms and I fit in perfectly. Now I have the four best friends in the world.

Our group chat is always busy, and when I haven't checked my phone in a while thanks to work and becoming immersed on my computer, I'm left scrolling through 100 missed messages, ranging from the best Taylor Swift song (I'm partial to "Bad Blood") to life advice. We came up with the 911 Bro Call (I hate the name, but it works) to distinguish between an actual crisis that needs immediate attention and the best margarita recipes to impress a woman on Taco Tuesday.

I don't partake in the recipe swaps. I have no women to impress, unlike Henry and Noah, two of the most eligible bachelors in the city. My nights involve sitting on my couch and watching *Jeopardy!* alone. Titillating, I know.

When we enact the 911 Bro Call, the group convenes as quickly as possible to discuss a heavy and important topic without judgmental questions or comments. I think finding out I'm going to be attending a conference with *Josephine* is pretty fucking important.

Groaning, I pick up the now lukewarm coffee on my desk and chug it back, cringing at the temperature. I can't prove it, but it's definitely decaf and tastes abysmal. I still don't believe she didn't slip-up on purpose, and there will be laxatives in my drink next week for sure. The icing on the cake of this absolute shit morning.

It's too late to go back and change the past, and we're unwilling to repair the rocky road we've traversed so far, the reason for our disdain and dislike deeply rooted. I declared us public enemies two years ago. Besides her closing those elevator doors in my face—a grudge that I've gotten over but enjoy bringing up to hear her try to defend herself—I'm insanely irritated by how hard-headed she is. It's her way or the highway, and she never backs down from something she feels passionate about. Which pairs spectacularly with my innate compulsion to always be right.

Neither one of us likes to be the first to cave so we always clash, butting heads over the most unessential topics.

Topics like whether black or blue ink is more professional when signing a formal document. I prefer blue, which she calls distracting.

Which font is best, Times New Roman or Arial, when submitting a proposal to investors. Her pick is Arial, citing how "stuffy" and "uptight" TNR appears.

Whether a company needs a social media division to be successful. News flash: It doesn't.

We're two vastly different people.

She's the day. Sunshine. Brightness. All-encompassing warmth. Lending a hand wherever needed. Someone people look to for solace, joy and comfort.

I'm the night. Colder. Darker. Uninviting. Someone people rarely offer more than a passing second or two of attention to, eagerly searching for the bright colors of a new dawn.

I prefer it this way; keeping to myself and staying in my office, away from the hustle and bustle of a get together or social events where I have to pretend to have fun. Too many people can be difficult for me, a constant reminder that my social skills have wavered over the past few years, hesitant to give anyone any insight into who I am and unwilling to trust so freely.

Josephine, however, thrives in social settings, comfortable talking with anyone and everyone, never nervous about meeting new people. She enjoys getting to know someone, and genuinely cares about them once a bond is formed.

She's also exceedingly over-the-top nice, helping others even when they don't deserve it. She extends deadlines, stays late, and puts others before herself. I see her leave the office as late as I do sometimes, her body curved over itself after another long, exhausting day of lending helping hand after helping hand.

I fall within the infinitesimal percentage of the population that she doesn't award her kindness to. I know it's my doing, but it still irks me, making me feel like I have a ticket to hell, courtesy of the apparent angel that is Josephine Bowen. She Who Can Do No Wrong.

Her emails might be the worst part. I know we go at it verbally, a fun tennis match of volleyed words lobbed back and forth, but the condescending tone on my computer screen prickles at old memories and wounds, a far-cry from the border-line comical insults she throws directly at my face.

Memories and words that have plagued me for years.

"Maybe you could try a little harder."

"I'm the only one putting in any effort into this relationship, Jack."

"Why don't you ever pull your weight?"

I idly scratch the scar on my inner wrist, attempting to dissociate from the past and focus on the problem in front of me.

The massive train wreck of a problem.

I know how revered the TDS is. I've worked in software development for almost a decade and it's the pinnacle of conferences in our nerdy little world. Jensen wrangling two spots is impressive; it's a selective process and invitations aren't handed out to everyone. Itrix has been successful as of late, but I didn't know we had elevated ourselves to the level of being invited to the TDS.

When Jensen announced that I would get to go, I was elated. How could I not be? Career-wise, this is important. It helps Itrix and could also help me down the road. I'm not giving up any potential future opportunities because *she* is going. Contrary to what she thinks, I can survive a few days with her.

Attending the conference isn't the problem. That'll be easy.

The worst part isn't that she makes me want to yell until my voice is hoarse out of frustration. That's part of my routine when interacting with her, and I regularly grit my teeth when she speaks, tabling the snarky comments I want to make.

It's more awful and humiliating than the annoyances.

It's her fiery red hair haunting my thoughts in the late afternoon hours when the sun fades into the sky, bleeding through the clouds like a wildfire in a dry forest, the color matching those curls I want to wrap around my fist and yank.

It's the coffee cups with half-hearted insults scribbled on them that give me fucking butterflies, a gaggle of wings fluttering in my stomach while a stupid ass smile tugs at my lips in the lonely confines of my office.

It's never giving *her* any hint that she's the only one who slowly chips away at my stoic facade with her chisel of kindness, another piece crumbling each day, without even realizing it.

Here, without an audience, my fingers trace over the loopy letters of her elegant handwriting, one by one, committing them to memory and wondering what was going through her head when she wrote them.

Simply put, I can't stop thinking about *her*.

I've tried.

Really fucking hard.

She hates me and thinks the feeling is mutual. It kind of is, no matter what pathetic games my heart wants to play.

She can't bear to be around me either, and I expeditiously remove myself from any room she's occupying out of fear I'll babble like an idiot and begin telling her things.

Stupid things.

Things she would never believe.

The most horrible, fucked up part of all of this is... I don't want to stop thinking about her.

Not for a second.

I'm not sure if that makes me want to laugh, cry, or scream.

Probably a mixture of all three.

Goddammit.

I'm so fucked.

FOUR
JO

After uttering every expletive under the sun for the entirety of my afternoon, I'm finally sliding onto a well-loved barstool with ripped leather next to my best friend, Abby at Mickey's, a local dive bar in town and the spot of our weekly meetups.

It's dark and dingy in here; certainly not a place you'd pull over if you were passing through town and searching for a bite to eat based on aesthetics alone. I'm not sure it's listed on Yelp, and a lighted neon letter out front has been burned out for over a year. No one appears in a rush to fix it, perfectly content with the flickering Ickey's as the temporary name. Lackluster design and curb appeal aside, the beer is cheap, the staff is friendly, and we haven't gotten food poisoning yet.

"I need a drink," I say grumpily, bypassing a formal greeting and resisting the urge to bang my head against the sticky wooden counter.

Abby raises her eyebrows at the blunt statement. "Rough day?"

I smile as Esmerelda, our favorite bartender, hands me a beer and places a vodka cranberry in front of Abby. Nodding my thanks, I grab the bottle and take a long sip before letting out a groan.

"You have no idea."

"Start talking," Abby says, crossing her legs and looking at me, patiently waiting for details.

After 16 years of friendship, she knows me better than I know myself. We met in high school after sitting next to each other in chemistry class. What started as awkward conversations over our Bunsen burners about homework and class schedules transitioned to sleepovers, beach trips, and secret-sharing. She's picked me up at my lowest lows and celebrated my highest highs.

"Jensen announced Itrix scored two invitations to the annual tech conference being held in Key West. Guess who gets to go? Me."

"Holy shit, a trip!? Congratulations! That's incredible! I've never been to Florida! Our educational seminars are in places like Podunk, Missouri. There's not even a McDonald's nearby!"

I hold up a hand to halt her premature excitement. "Yes, it's awesome, hooray for palm trees, the ocean and a lawless state. The other invitation, unfortunately, is going to Jack."

"Ohhhh. That makes things interesting." She's well aware of Jack and our exasperating coexistence. I've spent many hours in this very bar complaining and lamenting about him. She always takes my side, nodding emphatically in agreement whenever I call him an uncultured pillock. "Wait." She frowns, pausing for a moment before continuing. "Is this the TDS conference?"

"Uh, yeah?"

"The same conference Greg attends every year?" Abby asks quietly, and my stomach plummets to my Converse-covered feet like I'm flying down the hill of an intense roller coaster.

Greg. My ex-boyfriend. The one we *never, ever* talk about. The one part of my life where, if I ever ended up in an accident and lost parts of my memory, *he* would be the one and only thing I'd want to forget. I'll take reliving my first period every day for the rest of my life over him.

We used to work together and, against my better judgment, had a relationship for the better part of two years. Until he straight-up ghosted me, saying he needed to be with someone who had a more productive job than "sitting on Twitter all day" and he wanted "some space to think" because we were moving "too quickly" even after dozens of months together.

I vaguely remember him attending the conference. When I mentioned it would be interesting to go, Greg laughed in my face, telling me I didn't fall into the category of qualified people who were invited.

Hindsight is 20/20, and it's clear now what an asshat he was.

Is.

I doubt much has changed. Love makes you believe idiotic, moronic things, like the man of your dreams can be the same one who consistently verbally berates you, or the way to get over a breakup is a dramatic haircut. Neither are accurate. Trust me.

"Oh, fuck me, it is," I curse, putting my head in my hands. "Now I really can't go."

"Let's talk about this logically. Greg might be there. Maybe he's fallen off a building if we're lucky. Chances are he hasn't. And Jack will be there too, which sucks, I know. What about the good parts? I know you like your job, minus you-know-who, of course, but didn't you say after you finished the website launch you were going to pursue something else? See what else is out there? You even applied for other positions!"

"Yeah. You're right. I need to get serious about my next steps. I'm always looking for a new challenge, and I don't want to feel stagnant and frozen in my career. That's happening now, and I think I've reached the natural conclusion of my time at Itrix."

"Exactly. This conference is going to be a chance to share your redesign of the company's social media presence and marketing strategy, which is important because I know how much time and effort you put into the project. Imagine getting to show off that success to others! It could open some interesting doors. So what if the loser of the century is going to attend?"

"Are you referring to Greg or Jack?"

"You know they're nowhere near the same."

No, they're not. For all the juvenile verbal feuds Jack and I engage in, there's a clear-cut line separating him from men like Greg.

"I haven't thought about him in years."

"More reason to go! Show him how successful you've become *and* how great you look. It'll be a networking event and a revenge tour."

We flag down Esmerelda and order a large basket of fries to split.

"I wish I had someone to take with me, you know? To prove I'm finally happy and I've moved on."

"You are happy and you've moved on, right?"

"While I have nothing to show for it besides failed Tinder dates, I'm not hung up on him. I can assure you, that ship has sailed, and hopefully his hits an iceberg."

She giggles. "Speaking of Tinder, why not use the app? I hear it's the spot for guys wanting a hookup. Maybe you could find a date on there," she suggests, reaching for the fresh fries that arrive. "That's what the young people at work say. Oh! And do not swipe if their first picture involves a fish. Or a group photo!"

"When did we migrate out of the young people's category?" I groan. "I'm not a statistician, but men holding fish have proven to be exceedingly douchier than men *not* holding fish. That's Online Dating 101."

"I feel so out of the dating game. I wish I had better advice."

Abby and Raul, her husband, met our senior year of high school. She ran into him on her way to the track and yelled at him for being in the way. He apologized profusely, asked to make it up to her over dinner, and they've been together ever since. Those two are endgame.

"That's what happens when you marry your high school sweetheart. The same person who was in your Top 8 friends on Myspace in 2007 is still sleeping by your side, fifteen years later. We aren't all as lucky as you. Dating apps aren't full of fairy tales anymore. They're a weird place; too many unsolicited dick pics or offers to sit on someone's face and not enough time. I'm also stuck in the awkward age range where I could date a dude or his dad, and both would be perfectly acceptable."

"Oh, daddy, huh?"

"Hey, I'll try anything once. Maybe older men have their shit together."

"Did you know men don't reach emotional maturity until they're 43 years old?"

"I have to put up with dick pics and vapid communication for another *decade*? That's horrifying."

"The unsolicited dick pics are foul," she agrees, wrinkling her nose as she grabs a fry, watching it dangle in front of her. The perfect metaphor. Limp. Unwanted. No, thank you. "A dick isn't even that hot, you know? Especially in a text message when you're asking someone what they do for a living. How do they think that makes sense? 'Yeah, I work in insurance. By the way, here's a picture of my junk you didn't ask for. Enjoy!'"

"Nowhere in my life did I get prepped for seeing a photo of a dick at two in the afternoon on a Thursday come across my screen. That was not part of the public-school curriculum. We bypassed dick-etiquette and went straight for SAT prep."

"I bet it came across. Maybe the private school kids got the special lecture?"

I cackle. "Do you know what someone said to me the other day when we were chatting? 'Cereal. Soup. Josephine. All things I'd like to spoon.'"

"Wait. That's kind of funny."

"It's horrible! I shouldn't be spending my time answering what five emojis best describe me. The answer is the taco one and the exhausted smiley." I take a handful of fries and shove them into my mouth. "I'm perfectly content being a party of one."

"What about Jack? Can he do it?"

"Do what, exactly?"

"Be your fake boyfriend! You know, pretend while you're around people. That's my favorite trope in a book! I doubt it would be *that* hard. Ooh, is he hot? I'm a little disappointed I haven't seen a photo of him. It could be perfect! You two already know each other!"

"Pardon?" I choke. "Hang on. Slow down. What does hotness have to do with anything? You haven't seen a photo of him because he's antisocial. Truly, I think all he does is go to work, go home, and sit in his house, staring at the walls until another day begins. Knowing him, it's probably a dark cave somewhere. Maybe he's a vampire. That would explain the surly attitude."

"Are vampires surly? They're just misunderstood. Wasn't the guy in *Twilight* nice?"

"We are not having a conversation about Robert Pattinson right now. I need adequate visual aids to talk about him properly when I'm not all fired up. As I was saying, a mutual disdain and quest to piss off the other is a great foundation for any healthy adult relationship. It's shocking we're not already married."

"You haven't given me a good reason why you two shouldn't be a couple."

"When did we decide I was going to use a fake boyfriend?! It would never work!"

"Is he hot?" Abby asks again, diverting our discussion again, as if I didn't hear her the first time.

I did. Loud and clear. And maybe I'm afraid to admit to her that hell yes, he's really freaking hot, one of those men you look at and think, *"gee, he'd never be interested in a plebeian like me,"* because I try not to dwell on it myself. The less time I think about Jack, the better.

"If he is, I don't see what the problem is," she continues. "You two need to bang it out, get rid of the tension, and have a harmonious fake relationship that possibly, probably will turn into something real."

"Bang it out," I repeat, before bursting out in laughter. "I'm sorry. Jack strikes me as a guy who greedily gets off first, then rolls over and falls asleep while you're lying there, unsatisfied and forgotten, wanting more than he can provide. He's selfish, self-centered, and moody. My vibrator can do a better job."

I say it with as much conviction as I can muster, but my traitorous mind wanders.

To Jack. In a bed. Naked. Sheets pooled around a toned waist, bronze hair laid out like a halo against a satin pillow, a sexy, devilish grin on his face as he reaches out his hand, fingers meeting mine in some longing, aching caress. Or in the office on the conference room table, not bothering to take off his pants, too desperate and needy to worry about clothing. He simply lowers his zipper and goes to town.

I cough loudly, shaking my head and dispelling the erotic

images. *No, no, no, no, NO.* Why did I have to go down this road?

"So he is hot," Abby grins. "I knew it."

"Who's hot?" a voice from behind us interjects.

I almost drop the fries I'm holding in my lap, familiar with the source of the question. Whipping around, I'm met face-to-face with Jack Lancaster, an arrogant smirk on his face.

"What are you doing here?" I sputter, staring at him in disbelief. I've never seen him outside of work in a social setting, but he's right in front of me wearing dark jeans, a white V-neck shirt that shows a smattering of light chest hair, and clean sneakers. I can't help but look him up and down, surprised by his presence and outfit choice. Shocked would be an adequate adjective for how I'm feeling.

Transfixed, even.

Also mind-blown, because holy shit, he wears casual clothes way too well.

I'm beginning to think this man isn't real; he's a cyborg sent to earth to cause the downfall of mankind, starting with me. I can't stop staring. *Oh my god, Jo, look the fuck away!*

"I'm enjoying a night out with friends at an establishment I frequent and enjoy. Is that a problem?" Jack asks, crossing his arms over his chest. "You don't get to control everything, Josephine. I'm allowed to be here. It's a neutral zone in the Lancaster-Bowen war."

Bare forearms, a part of his body I've never seen before thanks to his uniform of fully buttoned shirts and wickedly formal suit jackets in all climates—even the dead of summer—capture my attention. I briefly ignore his jab, zeroing in on what might become my kryptonite.

Those. Damn. Forearms. Have. VEINS.

Veins that protrude above his skin and twist from the back

of his hand, winding past his elbow and disappearing under the sleeves of his shirt.

Shit. I didn't know arms could do that.

You learn something new every day.

He catches me staring and another smirk skirts across his lips.

"You must be Jack," Abby says, reaching out her hand and betraying our best friend alliance. "I've heard so much about you."

"Probably all terrible things, if Josephine is the one sharing them," he replies, shaking her hand and giving her a rare, full smile, a sight I've never witnessed before.

Oh, dear god. He has a dimple.

Right there, on his left cheek, a deep indentation that's impossible to miss and is now on full display.

That... That is extremely problematic. I wish I had never seen the damn thing.

"Don't believe any of it," he continues breezily. "I'm not nearly as horrible as she makes me out to be. Abigail, right? She's mentioned you to other people in the office, it's a pleasure to meet you."

"The pleasure is all mine," Abby counters. "When Jo talks about you, I have a different image in my head. I like this version better."

"What were you two discussing?" Jack asks curiously, his arms still crossed over his stupid chest as his shirt stretches across his stupid shoulders. I notice a small scar on his left wrist, a jagged, uneven white line contrasting against his tan skin. He subtly shifts his hands, the mark disappearing from view.

"Congratulations on being selected to attend the TDS. That's a high honor!"

"Thanks. I'm pretty excited."

"Jo was saying she hopes to find someone to accompany her

to Key West, since her ex will be there," Abby adds casually, and I jerk my head to stare at her. She smiles brightly, ignoring my glare. If looks could kill, I'd be doing 25 to life with no remorse. Not a single iota. "Have you heard about the him? He's a Grade-A asshole. I loathe him. Anyway, we were talking about a fake boyfriend thing, where you're not actually together but only appear to be dating when certain people are around," she explains. "How convenient that you'll be there too!"

"Convenient indeed," Jack agrees, like he's seconds away from volunteering his services. It's time to shut this down before it gets out of hand.

"I'd rather be alone and look miserable than pretend to be dating *you*," I hiss. His faint smile falters and the dimple vanishes from sight as he scowls in return.

"Trust me, I certainly wasn't offering. This has been enough interaction with you, and my friends are waiting. Goodbye." He reaches past my shoulder and grabs five beers, holding all of them in one hand by the neck.

Jack walks a few steps away before turning his head, peering at me over his shoulder, our gazes colliding. Time for one parting shot, I suppose.

"Oh, and Josephine?" He tips his head to the side, the slightest inclination, while his eyes beckon me forward.

I'm not sure what spell he casts or what possesses my body to slide off the barstool and move toward him, but I do, shuffling ungracefully across the floor until I'm directly in front of him.

He's taller than me tonight and he tilts his neck, lips landing above my ear. The surrounding sounds have silenced and we've teleported away. Out of Mickey's. Out of this universe. It's only me and him, not another soul around. A lock of his hair brushes against my forehead and I shiver at the contact.

"I always let the woman finish first," he says huskily, soft enough for only me to hear. "No one leaves unsatisfied."

His words are a match to spilled oil, lighting me ablaze.

He pulls back, breaking our private interlude, eyes hooded and pouring into my soul. The bright, vibrant blue has morphed into inky pools of seduction and desire, coaxing and urging me to jump into the dangerous deep end headfirst.

I should walk away. I should hurl a drink in his face and scream that I'm filing an H.R. complaint. What insane thing do I do instead?

I gasp. In shock. In surprise. In intrigue. In... something deeper and darker and more visceral.

I want to hear *more*.

FIVE
JACK

Josephine gasps in response to my brazen statement, a sound so shocking and intoxicating I freeze when I hear it, limbs heavy like I've spent the night downing shots of cheap vodka, drunk off alcohol and *her*.

A drink being hurled at my face in retaliation for the unfiltered, inappropriate comment is what I expect to happen, if we're being honest. Or, at the very least, a punch to my arm and a threat to ruin my career. It would be well-deserved.

What I *didn't* account for is the sultry noise and sharp inhale. The way time seems to stop as she holds her breath for four seconds before releasing it in a stuttered exhale that acts as an autumn breeze flittering across my chin and cooling my rapidly heating skin.

She's leaning closer, her body pressing into mine and causing our chests to almost fuse together, worlds colliding. Her mouth parts, silent words on the tip of her tongue as shallow breathing begins to ring in my ears, forming the sweetest, sexiest melody known to man. Josephine is the conductor, the noises she's emitting are the notes from a beautiful orchestra, and I'm in the audience, on the edge of my seat, anxious to hear what she does next.

Good god. Is this really happening?

There's no way.

It physically hurts to walk away as I shuffle backwards and run into a table, praying to every deity in the universe that my jeans don't begin to tighten like a high schooler looking at a *Playboy* magazine for the first time.

This is bad.

The thin, fragile line between disdain and attraction I've refused to let myself imagine or believe is becoming skewed and harder to distinguish the longer I stand here gaping at her. Who would have thought a single sound might be the driving force that catapults us over the ledge I've so carefully avoided for so many years?

Before this moment, I was perfectly content knowing she had zero interest in me. We made it crystal clear we weren't going to acknowledge the fact that we're both two young professionals who share the same work environment and the tension that encapsulates us with every interaction.

Yeah, she's freaking gorgeous. You'd have to be an idiot to not see her beauty. And, sure, I've had one or two fleeting visions of her in the shower after a long day of working on her website project, but I've never, ever had a physical reaction to her for the entire duration of our tenure together. Especially in her presence. That's weird. And creepy. And unacceptable.

A hot sensation claws at my insides, ripping all the boundaries and normalcy to mutilated shreds and leaving me thoroughly confused and borderline overwhelmed. I clear my throat, doing my absolute best to not appear like a total fucking mindless idiot as I inch away from the pair as stealthily and quickly as possible.

Too late. I'm an imbecile.

"Abigail, it was great to meet you. Have a good rest of your night." I raise the bottles in their direction and hurry back to my booth and friends, collapsing onto the leather when I arrive.

"Where'd you go to get the beers, man? New York?" Henry asks, laughing as I distribute the drinks.

"She's here," I say through gritted teeth.

"She? She who?" Patrick, another buddy, asks.

"Josephine."

"Holy shit, where?!"

All four of them crane their necks toward the bar in tandem.

"Redhead. Jeans. High-top Converse."

Patrick whistles. "She's really pretty."

"Like, effortlessly pretty," Henry agrees.

"I know," I grumble, taking a sip of my drink.

"So is her friend," Noah adds.

"Married. Don't even think about it."

"Prettier than—" Neil starts to say, but I stop him from speaking any further with a grunt.

"We're not playing the comparison game. Women's looks are not a competition, and no matter what happened in my past, I'm not pitting people against each other." They nod in agreement, and the subject gets dropped.

"Jack. Dude! Did you talk to her?"

"We exchanged a handful of words."

"Like, your phone number?"

"I walked up as she was talking to her friend about..." My lips twitch and I rub my hand over my face to halt the smile. "My bedroom habits."

"Shut the fuck up." Henry grins. "What did she say?!"

"That I'm selfish and probably leave the woman unsatisfied. So, I corrected her statement and let her know I always let the woman finish first. Which I do."

Fuck.

Did I really say that?

What was I thinking? How did she not punch me straight in the face?!

"You *didn't*," Noah says, sounding impressed. "And?!"

"She... gasped. Whatever that means."

"Holy shit! She's thinking about you two doing it!" Henry exclaims excitedly. "Now *I'm* thinking about you two doing it. And I'm here for it! Hot people having hot sex. Sign me up!"

I choke on a sip of beer. "I can assure you, she's not. More like plotting ways to stab me to death."

"That's kinky. She gasped. That's a telltale sign."

I arch my eyebrow and stare at Henry. "And you're suddenly the expert on women, Mr. Refuses To Have A Relationship?"

"Just because I don't have a relationship doesn't mean I don't know how to *read* women," he scoffs. "In fact, out of all of us, I'm probably the expert in that area. Did she move closer to you after you said it?"

"Yes..."

"Her eyes probably got wide."

"I'm not answering that."

"Breathing changed."

"No comment."

"AHA! I knew it. See, case and point."

"Objection, your honor. She's never heard me talk about something so personal, and I caught her off guard. I'd have the same reaction if she said it to me."

"Because you also would think about you two doing it."

"Oh my god." I rub my temples in exasperation. "I should have kept my mouth shut."

"You're pushing past his boundaries, Henry, so kindly shut the fuck up," Noah says, coming to my rescue.

"Thank you."

"Are you going to tell us about the 911BC? I've been worried about you all day," Patrick says kindly.

I really don't deserve these guys as friends. Even with the incessant teasing and jokes, I never want to imagine life without them.

"It's fitting she's here tonight. I got invited to this big conference. It's a prestigious event in our industry."

"Okay..." Noah says. "That's a good thing, right? We should celebrate!"

"Josephine's also going. Which can only mean disaster is going to ensue since we do—"

"YES!" Henry yelps, leaping out of his seat. I stare at him as he punches the air. "Holy shit, it's happening!"

"It's about time!" Patrick adds, jumping up to join him in the middle of the bar.

I gawk at their behavior as they hug each other and bounce around before shooting daggers at Noah, embarrassed on their behalf. They don't seem to care about the scene they're causing. "Can you please stop them?"

"Stop them? Hell no! This is great news!"

"Jack and Josephine, sitting in a tree," Neil sings next to me, and I bury my face in my hands.

"I hate all of you," I groan. "This is a real problem."

"Please enlighten us how you going on a trip with the woman you have a crush on is a problem?"

"It's not a crush," I mumble, ignoring their pointed looks. "It's not," I repeat firmly.

"Maybe if you say it three more times, you'll believe it. Like the Bloody Mary curse," Henry interjects, and I roll my eyes.

"I'm serious when I say she irritates the shit out of me. Besides, she could never like me back, so it's futile what the feeling *actually* is. I'm 32 and unable to communicate my emotions like an adult. No one's taught me how, and after last time..." I trail off, shoving the wounding memory far away. "It's a big fucking problem, because she's bright and kind and nice and beautiful and *nothing* like the broken, messed up, unwanted piece of scraps I am," I almost shout, my chest heaving with exertion.

The four of them become silent.

"The thought of spending any amount of time with her terrifies the hell out of me because I'm inevitably going to screw up. That's what I do. I *ruin* things, and I don't want to ruin her. Why bother trying to be anything but an asshole? It's worked just fine for the last two years."

"Shit," Henry mutters, sliding back into the booth and clapping my shoulder tightly, the charged energy from a few seconds ago evaporating. "First, you do not ruin things."

"Yeah, man. Look at us. You've made our group better," Patrick agrees.

"You might be broken," Noah adds. "We all are, in a way. There's nothing wrong with that because you're slowly repairing yourself, and *that* matters. Being broken, however, does not equate to being unwanted. Or a piece of scrap or a leftover. You can't change the past. No one can. What you can control is the future."

"I wish I understood what it means to be around her. She drives me up a fucking wall, day after day. We're always five seconds away from having a huge screaming match. I also want to push her against said wall, devour her mouth, hold her hand, and..."

"Fuck her?" Neil asks, and I scowl at him.

"You're too crass," Henry exclaims, throwing a napkin at him from across the table. "I'm going to exile you."

"You talked about them doing it!"

"It was called for in the moment. Read the room. Now isn't the time or the place."

"If you had let me finish, you would have heard that I want to apologize for every argument I've started. It doesn't matter, though. What's important is we're going to this conference. Together. And I need to figure out how to navigate my behavior correctly so I don't expose myself as an asshole to everyone else there."

"Okay, let's think about this logically," Patrick begins. "I suggest initiating a truce with her. You can move forward as adults."

"Good idea," Noah agrees. "She'll probably think it's a trap, so you'll have to prove to her you're invested in keeping things civil and mature between you."

"Who knows? Maybe the time you spend together will help you sort out your feelings," Henry adds.

"I don't need to sort out any feelings. Nothing is going to happen."

"Even if she likes you, too?" Neil asks.

I contemplate the question. Josephine possibly liking me back, even as a friend, is too far-fetched to bother validating. We'll always be two people who don't get along.

But that *gasp*.

I can't stop thinking about it. It's playing on a loop in my head, again and again, amplified through a loudspeaker in a crowded football stadium, loud enough for the whole world to hear but meant only for me.

The sound went straight through me, a bolt of lightning from my brain to my heart to my dick, annihilating every organ along the way.

Her throat bobbed as she swallowed, hesitant eyes meeting mine.

Maybe...

Maybe she's confused, too? Lost on the gamut of like and dislike, weaving between the two with our interactions.

"I guess I can try to be nice to her. At least until we get back from the trip."

"Thatta boy. Fewer scowls. More smiles. It makes you less intimidating, and you, my friend, are borderline menacing. It wouldn't hurt you to laugh now and then, too," Noah jokes, poking my side, and I wince.

"Okay. I can do that. I think."

"Let it happen naturally," Henry says. "If you run into her, a simple 'Hey, how's it going?' will go a long way. That might get her to call you a name besides.... What did she use the other day on your cup?"

"A dimwitted dingus." My fingers peel the label off my beer and I bite my lip to keep from grinning. I liked that one. Even laughed at it. Not in front of her, of course. "I never thought I'd be taking advice about women from you all. It appears I am out of options and hell is freezing over."

"You know how in *Beauty and the Beast* they help the Beast to not be an asshole? That's what we'll do, too," Henry says, rubbing his hands together. "I call dibs on Mrs. Potts!"

"I want Chip!"

"I don't want to get stuck with the candlestick," Noah groans. "I don't know any French."

"We need to get him a library with lots of books!" Neil adds thoughtfully. "Get your singing voices ready, lads."

Ah. I guess they've committed to this plan, then.

"To Team Jock! Wait. No. Hate it. Team Josephack!" Patrick announces, raising his beer in the air.

"Both are horrible. Please stop. There's no need for relationship names given there is no relationship. There never will be. I motion to amend it to Team Jack Attempts to be a Decent Human," I suggest.

"Yes! To TJATBADH!"

My smile comes naturally now as my eyes drift across the

room to the bar where Josephine is talking animatedly to Abigail, head titling back as she laughs. She's so freaking happy. All the time.

I wonder what it's like to go through life seeing only the good and never the bad. To wake up excited for another day, eager to sprinkle goodness onto others like pixie dust from a child's fairytale.

I can try to be a decent human being.

For her.

SIX

JO

Our office is suffering from a sugar shortage. A few days ago, Jack smugly paraded around the building taking drink requests from every employee. Except one. Any guesses who? When I went to make myself a drink, because *fuck him*, I discovered the lack of sugar. He appeared out of nowhere, drinking out of a hysterically accurate mug that read *World's Okayest Coworker,* proudly smirking that he used the last in Tyler's beverage. Not a single grain remained, and Jack simply shrugged when I asked if he intentionally ostracized me. He insisted that he only wanted to be nice and bring something to each of his friends, which is a category I do not fall into.

I'm aware the two of us will be nothing more than hostile coworkers. The gesture and words stung, but for the first time, his actions *hurt*. What he did was purposeful. I hated that day.

As I pour the beverage into my favorite cup, refusing to reminisce further, I start the walk back to my office to prepare for my afternoon meeting with a potential advertising investor, silently running through all the talking points I want to hit.

Profit. Margins. Website traffic.

Profit. Margins. Website traffic.

Repeating the words, I'm admittedly distracted as I turn the corner out of the kitchen and run straight into a tall, firm body. The mug I'm holding tumbles out of my grasp and spills down the front of my shirt, landing on the floor. It bounces and rolls away, leaving a trail of tea in its wake.

Staring at the mess slowly seeping into the carpet, I see scuff-free black leather shoes and laces tied into perfect small knots. I realize I'm pressing myself against Jack without seeing his face. Which, to be honest, is slightly worrisome that I have his shoes memorized.

"Of course it's you," I hiss, jerking my gaze up to glower at him.

"Maybe you should watch where you're going," he snaps. "It's not that difficult to pay attention."

"You ran into me!" I exclaim. Liquid dots his forehead like splattered paint. I think there are a few drops hanging from his hair, too.

"Yes, well, maybe I wouldn't have if you weren't in the way. Would you believe that you're not the only one in the world, Josephine? Other people roam these hallways. How was I supposed to know you would come around the corner? I didn't do it on purpose."

"Of course you didn't," I answer sarcastically, storming back to the kitchen. Jack trails behind me, his footsteps heavy. "You never do it on purpose, do you?"

"I'm sorry," he says, the two words lacking any sort of genuine apology, and I turn to face him.

"Are you sorry, Jack? We play these stupid games day after fucking day. And that's only the days you can bear to be in the same room as me! Half the time when I enter a space, you *stop speaking* and leave. Do you know how that feels?

"I'm sick of it. We aren't friends. Your drink parade solidi-fied the fact that you truly dislike me, and it hurt like hell. How can I ever believe anything you say is real when all we do is treat each other like shit? I know I'm as guilty as you are, trust me, but I'm done playing games. You win. The white flag is being waved. I can't do this anymore. I wish... I wish we could go back to the very beginning and start over. Or, better yet, I wish I never met you at all." Unexpected tears prickle my eyes and I bat the drops away before they can fall and he can figure out I'm mourning the loss of a friendship that was dead on arrival and never existed.

"Josephine," he whispers, a quiet juxtaposition from his earlier tone. "I'm so sorry. It was an accident, and I wasn't paying attention. I was reading an email that put me in a bad mood. I should have been looking where I was going, not down at my phone. It's entirely my fault. I took things too far the other day, and for that, I sincerely apologize. I didn't look at it from your point of view. The last thing I ever want to do is cause you pain, which I've clearly done, time and time again.

"I don't want to play games with you," he continues. "I don't want to win. I don't know why it keeps happening, but it does, and for that, I'm sorry. Give me another chance. Please."

Please. It sounds foreign coming from Jack, oddly sweet and sincere. I weigh his words for a moment before tilting my chin up half an inch, eyes raking over his face. He looks distraught and hasn't bothered to wipe the residual liquid away. His mouth pulls down in a frown that's different from his usual moody grimaces. This one is full of repentance.

The ask... The plea seems real. Authentic. Honest. More true than any other half-ass apology he's given me in the past, and I'm inclined to believe him.

"Maybe... Maybe this can be the start of a truce? Or something different from what we've had before. Because I can't keep going down this path with you. It's exhausting. And I'm so tired."

"I'm tired, too. If you want a truce, you get a truce. Anything you want, Josephine. Anything at all." He clears his throat and shifts on his feet. "The first order of business is letting you know that I have a spare shirt in my office."

"I'm happy for you." The stain has grown, covering my entire chest and half my stomach. I have exactly thirty minutes until my meeting begins. The man I'm seeing is the son of a *billionaire*. I'm not sure soiled blouses are part of the dress code.

"You can borrow it."

"Don't you need to change?"

"No. Take it. Please."

That word again. Zipping up my spine at supersonic speed and causing a shiver as it captivates me, wrapping me in a tight embrace. "Only if it's not orange."

The corner of his mouth notches up the smallest degree. I think if he were to smile with his whole being, he'd be the most beautiful person in the world.

"It's white, so it won't look any different from what you have on. It'll just be a little baggier, and, well, not covered in brown liquid."

I can't help the giggle that escapes no matter how hard I try, and Jack perks up at the sound.

"Okay, fine. Orange would clash horribly with this mess of hair, but anything will look better than brown liquid. Thank you for offering."

He leads us out of the kitchen and to the elevator. We ride up to the sixth floor in silence. When we enter his space, he closes the door behind me and my eyes sweep over the room I've never stepped foot in before.

"Wow, love what you've done with the place," I say flatly, taking in the drab environment. It's devoid of any personal touches. No pictures are present, and the eggshell white walls are bare, barren of any posters, diplomas, or certificates. An old wooden bookshelf sits off to the side, empty save for the stacks of papers on the bottom two shelves. A bookshelf without books. Makes sense.

"Smart-ass," he mutters.

"I'm not changing in front of you," I laugh nervously, my back pressing against the wooden door. Our encounter at Mickey's last week trickles into my vision. No, I certainly haven't been repeating the eleven words he said to me as I fall asleep at night, his gravelly voice tickling my ears as I cover my face with a pillow and scream at the way he's taken over my mind.

Absolutely not.

He must be recalling the exchange too. A slow pink color crawls across his face, settling on his sharp cheekbones while his eyes skirt away from mine. "That's not what I was implying. The shirt is hanging on the door. Um, behind you." He reaches past me, arm grazing mine before displaying a hanger with a long-sleeved white shirt.

"You don't have an extra woman's skirt around here, do you? In an 8? Maybe a 10 if the company is inconsistent with their sizing, as most are?"

"Believe it or not, I don't. There's no rush to return it. Take it home so you don't smell..." He trails off, finger tapping on his chin contemplatively for a handful of seconds before continuing. "*Totaltea* like a spilled beverage."

I pause, digesting his remark as I stare at him, mouth agape in surprise. "Did you make a joke?" I ask, unconvinced by what I heard.

His mouth twitches again, raising half an inch in the corner as his head tilts to the side, arms unraveling from their defensive position.

"Yeah," he replies. "I think I did."

I can't help the laugh that tumbles out of my mouth. My

shoulders shake and I keel over, clutching my under-used abdominal muscles as they constrict.

My laughter fuels him. A full-on smile erupts this time, wide and bright.

Holy cow.

I acknowledged his attractiveness in his brooding, grumpy state, but with a grin like that, he's positively devastating.

An unknowing assassin, wielding smiles as his weapon of choice.

I freaking knew it.

"That was so stupid," I get out, gasping for air and clutching the cramp developing on my side.

"It made you laugh, didn't it?"

"I didn't think you were capable of—"

"Being funny?" he finishes, eyebrow quirking amusedly.

"Exhibiting any sort of human emotion," I correct. That earns me a chuckle, a heavy exhale of air that he follows up with a clearing of his throat, a neutral, stoic veil replacing the quick slip into a carefree persona.

"Has enough time passed where I'm allowed to share that I've been holding onto that pathetic joke since the elevator to diffuse the tension and problems I caused?" The faint, rare twinkle in his eyes winks at me, appearing like the North Star in the night sky.

"It's working. I'm also glad to see you haven't combusted after being in a room with me for so long! It's a miracle!"

Jack sighs, heaviness nudging away the airiness of complacency. "Josephine."

I hold up my hand, stopping him from continuing. "Let's quit while we're ahead, yeah? Thank you for the shirt."

"I'm sorry, again, for causing you to spill."

"To be fair, I can be a little clumsy myself," I confess. "That must have been one hell of an email."

"You have no idea." He breaks our eye contact, looking remorseful, a heartbreaking story lingering behind the expression. Silence, our usual companion, settles between us again, leaving little opportunity for further questions, no matter how curious I might be.

I take that as my cue to leave, refusing to overstep my time in this new realm we've established.

"Have a good day, Jack." I turn for the door.

"You, too. Oh, and Josephine? This goes without saying, but you deserve to hear it. You look good in everything. Even bright orange. Good luck at your meeting."

I swallow the compliment down, unfamiliar with how the affectionate words feel coming from *him*. I'm not in the right headspace to decipher the validity behind his statement, so I push his kindness far away, to a place I can't spend hours obsessing over it, and throw away the key. Hustling to the elevator and back down to my floor, I slip the stained blouse off and throw it behind the fake plant sitting in the corner of my office. As I button up the garment, my nose lingers near the fabric, getting a waft of Jack's signature scents I've only ever experienced in passing; quick inhales of smells I haven't been able to discern until today.

Coffee. Citrus. Clean.

I shouldn't wrap my arms around myself, nestling into his clothing like it's my own, but I do. The fabric is warm. Soft. Inviting. Is the shirt a representation of what Jack could be if he really and truly tried?

This truce will end sooner rather than later. It has to. It's us. The trajectory has already been charted and we're unable to sustain this weird kindness. For a moment, though, I want to remember what it's like when we act like friends. For a moment, I have hope.

Jack's shirt might be my new lucky charm. When I presented our sales numbers to the investor, his eyes lit up, full of money signs, and he shook my hand excitedly, telling me he'll be in touch.

It's rewarding to know my contribution is going to help the financial success of Itrix. More investors and advertisers mean more money and job security. Sure, dreaming of a bigger paycheck is nice, but I think about how nailing a simple meeting can add an extra $400 a month into Tyler and Alan's baby college fund account. Or how the additional money can offer Haley, a girl on my team juggling two jobs, more assistance to pay for her mom's hospice stay. I couldn't care less about my payout. This is for them, and that brings me a little extra joy today.

I'm grinning like an idiot as I walk past reception after escorting the man out. How can I not?

"I like the oversized blouse look on you, Jo," Carla comments. "That look is kind of in right now. It's pretty sexy!"

"Thanks! I had a slight wardrobe malfunction, and Jack let me borrow a spare shirt."

"That was nice of him. Speaking of nice, someone left a present for you."

Occasionally I'll receive small sample products from up-and-coming companies, hoping for a website ad partnership or collaboration. I wasn't expecting anything today, though, so I'm intrigued.

"What is it?"

"A ten-pound bag of sugar." She stands up, placing the family-sized package on the top of her desk. I gape at it, perplexed.

"What in the world? Who left it?"

"It was here when I got back from lunch. There was a note attached."

There's no way to sugarcoat this. You are sweet, and I am not.

I'm sorry. For so many things.

-JL

I process the scrawly handwriting before breaking out into another shit-eating grin.

"Do you know who it's from?"

"Yup! Thanks for holding this for me." I lift the deceivingly heavy bag off her desk and bring it back to my office, vowing to pick up a set of weights and workout this weekend.

Or next.

I place the sugar in the chair across from me and shake my head at the absurdity of what's staring back at me as I try to focus on work.

Hours later, my computer pings with a new email.

To: Josephine Bowen
From: Jack Lancaster
Subject: Meeting
6:20 p.m.

How'd the meeting go?

Jack Lancaster
He/Him
Princeton '12
Harvard ALM '15
Head of Software Development, Itrix

I read the message twice. Jack *never* emails me so casually. Most of the time he fervently refuses to correspond by email at all. Taking advantage of the unusual dynamic of today, I fire back a quick reply, changing my signature before hitting send.

To: Jack Lancaster
From: Josephine Bowen
Subject: Re: Meeting
6:25 p.m.

Really well! I think the shirt won him over. Thanks again!

Jo (not Josephine) Bowen
She/Her
Did Not Attend Princeton '12
Yale AND Harvard Valedictorian '15 (at the same time and faster than you)
Queen of the World

His answer comes back seconds later.

To: Josephine Bowen
From: Jack Lancaster
Subject: Re: Re: Meeting
6:28 p.m.

You're welcome. I expect a cut of the profits. It pains me to admit this, but you're kind of funny. On very rare occasions. Don't let it go to your head.

Jack Lancaster
You're Right, It Sounds Douchey
Don't Ruin That Shirt
It's My Favorite
Just Kidding I Have 10 More Of The Same One

Chuckling at his reply, I power down my computer and retrieve my stained shirt from its hiding spot, shoving it into my bag. I walk to the elevator, scrolling through my phone and catching up on social media while I wait. When I hear the ding, I look up.

"Oh, hello again," I say to the only other occupant in the elevator. Jack.

"Hi," he responds, peeling his eyes away from his phone.

He stares at his clothing on my body, mumbling something incoherent under his breath that sounds suspiciously like an expletive-laced string of words. I tug on the rolled-up sleeves nervously.

"Looks like the shirt worked out," he finally says, pulling at the collar of his own button-up.

"Indeed. I'll wash it and get it back to you on Monday."

"No rush."

"Any fun plans this weekend?"

"Not really, no."

"Do you do anything besides work?" I ask curiously as the elevator doors open and we file out.

"I do plenty of things."

"That sounds mysterious."

"Maybe I like to be elusive."

"It is part of your charm."

We're standing in the middle of the lobby, people maneuvering around us as they exit the building for the night, but neither one of us moves.

"What about you?" he asks.

"I'll probably sit around and bake 1,000 pies for an entire village, since I've recently come into possession of an obscenely large bag of sugar, and then apply to *The Great British Bake Off* so Paul Hollywood can tell me how abysmal my crust is. Thank you for the gift, by the way."

"I have no clue what you're talking about. I'm glad we have remedied the sugar shortage; I shudder to think of how the office would survive without your graphs and emails if we lost you to a caffeine deficientea."

"Multiple jokes on the same day, Lancaster? Are you ill?"

"I assure you, I have zero ulterior motives. We have a truce, remember? This is the start of a new path for us. What's that poem about the road less traveled?"

"That's it, huh? Two years of animosity and bitterness gone, and now we're best friends? All I had to do was let you see me cry and burn my skin?"

"Did I hurt you?" he asks sternly, gaze sweeping over my face and quickly studying every inch. "Where?"

"N-no. I'm fine. It was a joke. The tea only got on my clothes. Your face took the brunt of the damage."

He nods, placated and relieved. "Slow down there, Bowen. I never mentioned friendship. We're simply amending our title to amicable colleagues who don't violently lash out. We're not making bracelets and braiding each other's hair. Fair?"

"Fair. For the record, you'd rock the hell out of a fishtail."

"What in the world is a fishtail?"

"Never mind. When I'm 82 and using the same bag of sugar, I'll think fondly of you and wonder if you still have a stick up your ass. Have a good weekend being mysterious, Jack. Stay out of trouble." I head for the door, walking backwards so I can give him a valiant salute.

"Enjoy your pies. And Josephine?"

"Yeah?"

"No more games. No more jokes." He looks at me, *really* looks at me, a calculated stare that causes me to fidget, an awareness of being stealthily studied and *seen* developing in my lower abdomen. "From now on, it's you and me, and I really want to try. Deal?"

"Deal," I breathe out.

He tilts his head to the side, lips curling into a small smile, one dimple on display in the fading sunlight. "Good."

I try not to stumble over my feet as I evacuate the building, gulping down the fresh air greeting me on the other side. The parting declaration threw me off balance; Jack's willingness to try, to make an effort, to be better is disarming. It's also an action I've selfishly wanted to initiate over the course of the last two years, but kept finding myself too afraid time and time again to take the first leap and shift our well-established routine upside down.

It's safe to say we've graduated from spiteful, conniving coworkers who disagree constantly to... What? Adult pen pals who share emails, shoot the shit in the elevator, and lend each other clothes?

How in the world did we get here? Did our antipathy disintegrate after one honest conversation where I laid out my frustrations and regrets? Was it that easy? Or was it the bag of sugar, the culmination of every half-assed *I'm sorry,* and arguments from our past forgotten with a handwritten note and sweet package?

Jack said no more battles. No armor or weapons.

It's just us. Exactly as we are.

Wanting to show my true self to him should frighten me.

The idea of learning more about him, casting away the misconceptions I've built up in my head should have me running for the hills.

Should, should, should.

I'm not running. I'm not scared.

Instead, a tiny tingle runs up my body, stopping on the left side of my chest directly adjacent to my heart, giving an optimistic, curious tug.

What does *that* mean?

SEVEN
JO

Abby sent me a spontaneous text asking to meet at Mickey's tonight. After another long week of work and the conference looming past this weekend, my mind is frazzled, racing to worst-case scenarios. She never likes to go out on Fridays, so, naturally, being the over-worrier I am, I've been envisioning Final Destination shit all afternoon.

The bar is busy when we arrive—bodies are crammed against each other and it's standing room only. The smell of alcohol permeates through the air and half of the overhead lights flicker ominously, the room appearing darker than normal. We're lucky to find two seats at the counter bar, and I can hardly hear the bartender when he asks us if we want anything to drink.

"Are you ready for your trip?" Abby asks loudly over the commotion, taking a sip of her vodka cranberry when it arrives a few minutes later.

"Believe it or not, I am. Since we enacted our truce, Jack and I have had some pleasant exchanges lately. Last week was the bag of sugar. This week was a polite nod when taking his cup of coffee, no mumbled snarky comments directed my way. I'm cautiously hopeful this new mutual understanding is here to stay. It's better for everyone long term. Work is more bearable. I have fewer headaches and my emails are answered in a matter of seconds. I used to have to wait hours for a one-word reply. As long as this behavior can last through the conference next week, I think we'll be in good shape."

"He's turning over a new leaf. That's promising!"

"Still doesn't explain the whole leaving-the-room-when-I-enter thing. We could be friends if we tried hard enough, but neither of us has fully committed, so we're in a weird limbo of being cordial humans. It's hard to explain."

"If you two become friends, our lives will be so boring. What would we talk about?"

"I'm sure we'd find a topic or two we enjoy. We could enrich our minds and talk about current events, or how to end world hunger and poverty."

"As much as I appreciate the sentiment, I think world hunger is a little out of our reach, given we're sitting in a shitty bar, drinking beer, and we have zero political platforms."

"Okay. Fair," I concede. "Switching topics, I'm buying new bathing suits on Monday, then we leave early Wednesday morning."

"Oooh, are you doing one-piece suits or bikinis?"

"To be determined, but I'm leaning toward one-pieces. Classy, and my boobs won't pop out unexpectedly if I see anyone at the pool. Shopping is stressful enough, and then you put on a bathing suit in the fitting room with artificial lighting and poorly angled mirrors that showcase every wrinkle and patch of cellulite and it's game over. Whatever doesn't make me want to cry will be the winner."

Abby laughs in agreement, clinking her glass against mine. "Ain't that the truth? Have you thought about Greg anymore?"

"No. To be honest, I simply don't care. Why should I be

ashamed about being single? Having a partner does not define a woman. Or a man. And, sure, yes, would it be nice to have a hot guy by my side? Of course. But I'm fine. It'll all work out."

"Wow. That's very mature of you."

"You're the one who told me we're not young anymore. I had to wise up at some point! Speaking of young, you've been taking years off my life by making me wait to hear why you wanted to meet up. I know for a fact you prefer to watch housewives on Friday night over drinking. So, spill."

A smile sits on her face. "There's no point drawing this out. You know how bad I am at keeping secrets from you! This might be the last time I'm drinking for a while."

"What?" I look between the drink sitting on the bar, then her stomach, immediately connecting the dots.

"We're going to try for a baby!" Abby squeals and I yelp in response, reaching forward and engulfing her in an enormous hug.

Abby and Raul experienced two heartbreaking miscarriages early in their marriage. They wanted to wait before trying again, not only for Abby's physical health, but for their mental health, too. I still remember when Raul called me in the middle of the night and told me I needed to come over immediately, his words coming out in choked sobs.

The image of Abby sitting on the bathroom floor, tears staining her cheeks and hands covered in blood will forever be etched in my memory. I sat with her as she cried, rocking her back and forth, stroking her hair and attempting to find words that conveyed my sympathy for the gravity of the heartbreak she was experiencing.

"This is so exciting! I'm so happy for you! When? When are you going to start?"

"Oh, *now* the boring married people's sex life is interesting," she jokes, wiping her eyes, and I swat her shoulder. "Next week.

We're ready. Therapy has been really helpful, especially couples' counseling. Work is going well for Raul, and our relationship is thriving. We're opening up more and sharing our fears and hesitations. We're nervous and anxious. Excited. So freaking ready. It's reassuring to know we're on the same page. I'm hopeful this time, Jo," she whispers.

"So am I," I agree, lacing her hand in mine. "No one is more deserving than you two. I can't wait to be Aunt Jo!"

"You already are Aunt Jo! Don't forget about your niece and nephew; the ones who are related to you!"

"Yeah, yeah, I love them dearly. I meant I can't wait to be Aunt Jo to *your* baby. That's going to be so freaking cool! You're going to be the best mom."

"It's going to be incredible." Her smile is wide now, the happiest I've ever seen her throughout our friendship. It makes my heart swell with joy. Her phone buzzes on the bar, and she reads the screen, her smile growing. "It's Raul. He finished work early. I told him I was going out with you."

"Go home and be with your baby daddy!" I shoo her away.

"We've been here for 10 minutes! I'm not abandoning you!"

"Go," I repeat firmly. "Mickey's will always be here."

"Will you be okay by yourself?"

I pat her arm. "I'm fine, I promise. One more and I'm heading home, too. I'll text you when I leave. Go see your man."

She leans forward and kisses my cheek, and I squeeze her shoulder in return. "Think you'll have time to hang out on Tuesday before you leave?"

"I should! Have fun." I wink at her before turning back to the bar, gesturing for another drink. The bartender sets a fresh glass in front of me and I smile.

"Hey, beautiful," an unfamiliar voice says, sliding into Abby's vacant seat. I'm greeted with the sight of a man in his early forties wearing a suit and sporting a receding hairline. Great, a creep I don't want to talk to.

"Hello." I peer over my shoulder, wondering how quickly I can make my escape. A $4 beer isn't worth the harassment from some sleazeball.

"Are you here alone?"

"Nope. I'm meeting a friend and my boyfriend. They're running a few minutes late but should be here soon." The lie slips out easily and I reach into my purse for my cell phone. A blank screen shows me it's dead. *Dammit.* I must have forgotten to charge it at work. "If you'll excuse me." I bring the beer to my lips and take a swig, hoping this dude gets the not-so-subtle hints I'm dropping about kicking him to the curb. He has about 20 seconds to back off, or I may knee him in the nuts.

"I can keep you company while you wait." His hand inches dangerously close from the leather of the barstool to my bare thigh. The blazer he's wearing is too short on his arms and his fingers are stubby and round, reminding me of the Vienna sausages my parents used to give us for lunch growing up. I want to break them off one by one, hairy knuckle by hairy knuckle.

"I said I was fine. When will men understand that no means *fucking no*?" I ask in an icy tone.

"Have you ever been with two guys at the same time? My friend Mark over there said he'd be interested if you are." He gestures to another man sitting nearby, who raises his drink in my direction. These two are giving off *seriously* weird vibes.

I mean, sure, every woman has fantasized about being with two men once in her life, but it usually involves buff, hot dudes from superhero movies or sexy men with wings from the fantasy novels I like to read. Not the sketchy businessman in town for some conference I couldn't care less about.

"It's going to be you and your hand tonight, buddy. And you

might not even have that if you don't back the fuck up." I turn away from him, taking another sip of my beer, grateful the bartender has made his way over to my side of the bar.

"Enjoy that drink, bitch," the man snaps, walking away.

"Are you okay? Sorry it took me so long to get over here. I saw he was harassing you," the bartender says, offering me an apologetic smile.

"I'm fine. Thanks for checking."

"Dude's a creep."

"That's for sure."

"Let me know if you need anything else. I'm Austin, by the way. It's my first night."

"Thanks, Austin. Whenever you get a minute, I'll take my check. I know it's crazy in here, so no rush." I spin around on the stool to survey the crowd and make sure Dickbag 1 and Dickbag 2 have left. As I scan the room, a flash of familiar bronze hair captures my attention as it ducks around a corner toward the bathrooms. I frown, checking the area again.

For a second, I thought it was...

There's no way. Either it was a trick of the light or this beer is going to my head way too quickly. I'm ashamed to admit I'm disappointed my findings reveal no one I know.

After chugging the rest of my drink and signing the bill, I rise off the stool. My legs feel heavy and my ankles roll to the sides like I'm wearing heels and struggling to walk. Which is odd, because I distinctly remember putting on sandals tonight.

"Whoa," I mutter, gripping the bar tightly for support. The edge of the wood feels slippery under my grasp and it's difficult to hold myself up. I try to wipe my hand on the discarded napkin sitting near me to establish a firmer grip, but it takes too much effort.

"You okay, baby?" The creepy voice is back, closer than before.

"I'm fine," I mumble, bringing a hand to my forehead. Sweat is forming near my hairline and my skin is on fire like I've been running outside in the middle of summer.

"You sure don't look fine. Why don't you sit back down and rest for a second?"

I nod and climb back onto the stool, my head lolling forward. Sitting is nice. Sitting is easy.

"I'm fine."

"You're more than fine." An ice-cold hand lands on my thigh, clutching it, fingers pressing painfully into my skin. I want to bat it away, but the idea takes too much energy and brainpower. Another hand lands on my arm. "We can take care of you." A finger trails down my neck.

"No. No."

Sounds mix around me, an indeterminable blend of noises at an ear-splitting decibel. I think I faintly hear my name laced amongst the deafening resonance. I can't be sure.

"Can you open up?" That slimy voice again.

"No," I try to repeat, unsure if the word makes it out of my mouth.

Everything is fuzzy and I can only make out a few inches in front of my face; I'm underwater without goggles, unable to see anything. A glass shatters next to me and a spray of wet liquid clings to my clothes. Close raised voices hurt my ears and I squeeze my eyes shut, willing everything to cease.

Then, the world goes black.

EIGHT
JO

The pounding in my head is incessant and almost unbearable. Someone is taking a hammer and repeatedly beating my skull into concrete; unrelenting pain radiates through my entire body. It's the first thing I notice when I gain consciousness.

I'm also not in my own bed. It's the second thing I'm aware of. I can tell right away; the sheets currently burritoing me are silky and cool—much smoother than my old, worn bedding that typically encompasses my sleeping body. My clothes are uncomfortable and tight, like I'm in a straitjacket and can't escape. I open my eyes timidly, trying to ignore the ache pulsing across my forehead and migrating down my face.

A quiet voice drifts in from beyond the cracked door. I squint at the intrusion of light threatening to seep through the partly drawn curtains. It's already bright, and the warmth flooding the room tells me it's well past early morning.

I blink at my surroundings and take in the room inch by inch, trying to deduce where, exactly, I am. It's not Abby's house. The window in her guest room is behind the bed, not next to it like this one. A noise from out in the hallway deters me from finding any more answers. I push up onto my elbows, wincing at the effort it takes.

"You're awake." I stare at the figure in the doorway. Jack. Standing a few feet away from me. With a black eye? His cheek is red, and a fresh bruise snakes its way up to his forehead.

"How are you feeling?"

This has to be a dream. Or I'm hallucinating and truly losing all sense of reality.

That would explain why I'm face to face with my colleague in a bedroom that is certainly not mine.

"Um. What am I doing here?" Panic creeps up my spine, vertebrae by vertebrae. Something isn't right.

"Do you remember anything from last night?" His voice is hushed, and I can barely hear him over the chirping birds outside the window.

Holy shit, did we sleep together? That's definitely an event I would remember, right? I pause, gathering my thoughts. The strain makes the ache in my head feel like a roar. I want to cover my ears and scream.

"Um, not a whole lot. I remember being at Mickey's with Abby. She left, then I was alone. After that, everything gets foggy. There are gaps in the night." I try to play through the memories in my head. The visions blur together and I can't find a clear stream of events. "Don't take this the wrong way, but please tell me we didn't hook up or have sex. If I threw myself at you, I don't remember it. It wasn't intentional."

He pushes the door open with his foot. Moving to the wooden dresser, he pulls out a clean shirt and athletic shorts. Setting the clothing on the edge of the bed, out of my reach, he looks down at me, face solemn. I've never seen him so serious. Now I'm really panicking.

"Someone spiked your drink at the bar last night, Josephine."

That was the last thing I expected to hear. Bile rises in my throat.

"W-what? How? Who?"

"I got to the bar around eight. You were sitting alone, and I assumed whoever you were meeting hadn't arrived yet. I didn't want to interrupt your night out. When I saw you again, I knew something was wrong. You were having difficulty standing. Some guy kept talking to you and touching you, even after you told him to get off." His eyes narrow to slits. The bright blue is dark and angry; dangerous, stormy waves replace the calm seas, threatening to destroy everything in their wake. "When the guys tried to get you to leave with them, I intervened and got decked in the face."

"Fuck," I exhale, my hands trembling. "How did I end up here? C-can you fill me in on the parts I'm missing?" My voice quivers with fear, afraid to learn what he's withholding.

"Your phone was dead when I tried to get in to call Abigail or a family member, and I sure as hell wasn't putting you in a car with someone I didn't know after what I witnessed. I talked to an emergency room nurse who said the smart thing to do would be to bring you in, but I was afraid they wouldn't let me stay with you since we're not related or married. I didn't want you to wake up alone or confused, so I acted recklessly and brought you to my house, going against her advice. She told me to closely monitor you throughout the night, and if things got worse, I was instructed to bring you in right away, which I promised to adhere to. You slept in my bed, and I slept on the couch. I stayed there except for when I came in to check on you. It seemed like a huge overstep to change you, so I apologize you're still in those clothes."

He glances down at his phone and the new, unobstructed angle magnifies the severity of the bruise. It's practically glowing, and I wince.

"You've been out for about 12 hours, and thankfully didn't get worse as the night progressed. I couldn't think of anything else to do and I... I was really fucking scared and didn't want to leave you alone." His voice cracks at the end of the sentence and it pierces my soul, a poisoned-laced arrow straight to my core. "I'm sorry. I'm so sorry. I know I probably crossed a line, and you can hate me on Monday, Josephine, but I couldn't... I had to do *something*."

"Oh." It's the only word I can articulate. I hesitantly look up at him leaning against the dresser, arms crossed tightly over his chest. His entire body is rigid, face taut with worry. He's aged since I last saw him yet he is still hauntingly beautiful under the obvious fatigue. The bags under his eyes are puffy and pronounced. A faint stubble lines his cheeks. His clothes are wrinkled and there's dried blood on his t-shirt, just under the collar. His face is pale, drained of any color. My heart thumps erratically in my chest, revelations barreling into me, one after another. "Thank you."

The magnitude of what he's done for me shakes my being like a seismograph recording an earthquake, and I know those two tiny words are hardly adequate in the attempt to convey my gratitude to him. My appreciation.

He took a punch to the *face*.

For *me*.

It's suddenly almost impossible to breathe, and I'm nearly suffocating.

"Is someone else here?" I ask, desperately clinging to any sort of normalcy. "I heard voices."

"No." He runs his hand through his bronze hair. It's disheveled and askew this morning, sticking up at odd angles, so different from the gussied waves I'm used to seeing at work. "That was Rebecca, the nurse I spoke to earlier on the phone."

"Rebecca."

"My buddy's girlfriend. I called her directly at the hospital and she broke close to ten protocols to talk to me."

"What did she say?"

"Symptoms generally last about twelve hours but could persist longer, so hopefully you're on the mend. She said to keep monitoring you today. How are you feeling? That's the only thing I care about. Fuck everything else."

"My head is killing me. I'm nauseous and hungry at the same time. My body aches. I feel weird. Like I'm here, but not fully here, if that makes any sense. It's hard to describe, and thinking is difficult right now."

"Rebecca said that might be a lingering effect. I put some water and Advil there for you to alleviate any lingering aches or pains." He gestures to the bedside table. "You can take a shower or bath and change into some fresh clothes. I figure they'd probably be more comfortable than what you're wearing."

"You don't keep a closet full of women's clothing for people to change into?" I joke weakly, reaching for the oversized shirt and shorts. I see a glint of relief dash through his eyes at my attempted humor.

"Believe it or not, I don't. Breakfast will be ready soon. It's not my place to tell you what to do, so please yell at me to shut up at any point. I know you're quite fond of that." Fresh pain rushes through my head as I attempt to snort. Grabbing the pill bottle, I take two, chugging half the glass of water down.

"I think you should stay here tonight," Jack continues, talking faster now, his demeanor changing, worry fading into an obvious desire to be helpful.

He's trying to find the right things to say, weighing words before speaking and making sure they're not overpowering. It's hard to keep up when he's going 100 miles an hour and I'm barely crawling along at a snail's pace. "I can drive you back home tomorrow or to your car. Or to Abigail's. Once you eat, you'll probably be in a better position to decide."

"Okay. Let me think about it."

Now he's the one who winces at my short, staccato answer. I think he was expecting more pushback. More of a fight. More of... *us* and our usual selves.

Nothing about *this* is normal and usual.

"I'm sorry. I'm dominating this conversation and screwing up. Forgive me. The adrenaline is finally settling down."

"You're not screwing anything up," I say, the heavy pressure still lodged in my chest, settled by his presence. "You're right. After I eat, I'll be functioning better. Have you seen my phone? I need to call Abby."

"It's in your purse. In hindsight, I should have plugged it in, but my head was all over the place. There's a charger next to the bed."

"Thanks." I dig my phone out, plugging it into the charger and watching the battery appear on the screen. "May I use your restroom and shower?"

Discovering I slept in Jack's bed after he saved my life has shifted my world on its axis. It's not like we hooked up and I have to do an awkward walk of shame. Yet, it's strangely intimate to be sprawled out on the mattress where he sleeps, about to put on his clothes, when we've never been physically intimate. Or touched at all.

"Of course. It's right through there." Jack points to the closed door across the room. "Take as long as you need. I'm going to stay out of your way and get some breakfast going. Do you need any help to get in there?"

"Let me see." I swing my legs to the side of the bed lethargically and push myself up, feet sinking into the plush blue rug. The motion uses the entire bar of my remaining energy and I stumble, losing balance.

He's there in a second before I can blink, his right arm draping around my waist and catching the fall as he slowly guides us to the bathroom. My independent ass wants to yell *"I'm perfectly fine"* and *"self-sufficient."* Instead, I give in, leaning into his steadying embrace, forgoing an argument with him for the first time in my life.

Not today. Not after what he's done.

He doesn't deserve the anger sizzling at my fingertips and the scream perched on the tip of my tongue. Not when he's the one helping. Guiding. Keeping me upright and alive, a stable rock withstanding the hurricane churning within me.

"Is this all right? Please tell me if you're uncomfortable and I'll stop touching you." His gaze darts to where we're joined at the hip, then back to my face, assessing for any hesitancy. I nod, conveying my grateful approval. "I've never taken a bath in here, so feel free to christen it if you desire."

"Not a fan of bubble baths?"

"Only if there are battleships and rubber ducks," Jack replies, leading me to the closed toilet seat and gently setting me down. The porcelain is frigid under my thighs and I shiver. "And sadly, I have neither." He turns on the water, a trail of coffee and citrus filling my nose. It's a comforting combination I never expected to calm my heart rate until this very moment. My body and brain relax into the safety of his familiarity. "Bath or shower?"

"Shower."

"Final answer?"

"Yeah."

"Let me grab you a few things." He squeezes past me, opening a squeaky cabinet as he withdraws a large white towel, a washcloth, and a new bar of soap. He opens the box, placing the soap inside the shower, leaving the towel on the vanity to my right. Small droplets of water coat his arms, but he either doesn't notice or doesn't care. "I'm going to leave the door cracked. I won't come in, I promise, but I'm only giving you ten minutes before I check on you. Got it?"

"Yes," I agree, before adding, "You're bossy."

"Good. When it comes to your well-being, Josephine, I'm going to be as bossy as I want. That is non-negotiable."

He leaves the steaming room, keeping the door slightly ajar. I peel off my clothing from last night, smelling like beer and sweat. They can burn in hell for all I care. I shudder as I step under the warm water, groaning as the heat engulfs me. Rolling my shoulders, the water cascades down my back and chest.

Our trips to Mickey's normally involve two beers and pizza or fries; hardly enough to do any drunken damage. I'm so fucking enraged someone tried to take advantage of me. I'm also so thankful nothing worse happened, knowing that thousands of women aren't so lucky.

The more ferociously I scrub my skin clean of the memory of last night, the quicker a small part of me returns. Tears fall down my cheeks, mixing with the soapy water draining away.

"Josephine? Doing okay?" Jack's voice comes from the other side of the door.

"Yeah, I'm finishing up."

"Take your time. I just wanted to check."

My body is red and flushed from the heat. Knowing I can't stay in here forever, I turn off the shower and reach for the fluffy white towel waiting for me, wrapping it securely around my body. Padding back to his bedroom, I close the door to the hallway to give myself some privacy as I pull on the shirt and shorts Jack left out, not bothering with a bra or underwear.

I dry my hair as best I can before hanging the towel on the hook in the bathroom next to what I'm assuming is Jack's. Walking down the hall, I follow the aromas coming from the kitchen.

NINE
JO

I'm not sure what I expected to find when I turn the corner, but it certainly isn't Jack standing over the stove, a slew of plates piled around him, creating a miniature disaster zone. A patterned dish towel hangs loosely from the back pocket of his ripped jeans, a hair's breadth away from falling onto the light hardwood floor.

"Can I help?" I ask, and he whips around. He's holding a flowered spatula in one hand and he looks me up and down, his assiduous assessment causing me to wring my hands together anxiously. He exhales when he finishes his perusal, seemingly satisfied with whatever he finds, eyes drifting to the ceiling briefly before letting his shoulders sag away from his ears.

"Nope. You can sit and relax. There's tea and orange juice set up." He turns to the stove, and I take a seat at the square table. I add one cream and one sugar into the steaming mug, bringing the cup to my lips and savoring the sweet taste against my tongue.

"What are you making?"

"A bit of everything." He brings two plates over, both filled with eggs, bacon, a pancake the size of my face, bright fruit, and breakfast potatoes complete with peppers and onions. I look up at him in disbelief and he shrugs, giving me a sheepish smile. "I might have gone overboard."

"*Might?* You could invite the entire neighborhood over and there would be plenty of leftovers."

"You don't have to eat all of it. I wasn't sure how your stomach would be acting this morning, nor do I know your breakfast food preferences. So. Here we are."

I hum, taking the plate from his outstretched hand. "Potatoes. In any form. And pancakes. Carbs are my love language." I wait until he sits across from me before digging into the eggs, unexpectedly ravenous.

"Favorite potato?"

"Simple question. Mashed."

"Hash browns seem like an underrepresented option. They don't get a lot of love."

"That *would* be your pick. They're, like, bottom of the pyramid and only marginally better than scalloped potatoes. There's a whole hierarchy."

"That's not a thing."

"I'm making it a thing!"

"You're something else."

"And you're an excellent cook." I polish off my eggs, grimacing slightly as Jack douses his with ketchup, ready to take the compliment back. "That, however, is revolting."

"Hush, Josephine. There's no need to insult my food choices with your closed-mindedness. Don't knock it until you've tried it. I worked in a hospital kitchen when I was younger for some extra cash, so I learned the basics. The rest I picked up along the way. Cooking can be cathartic for me sometimes, which I know is weird."

"I don't think that's weird at all." I cut my massive pancake into smaller pieces as quickly as possible, my fork and knife working in unison. "It's good to have an outlet. Reading is cathartic for me."

He doesn't answer, and when I look up, I notice his eyes are on me. Jack blinks, a drop of syrup dangling off the corner of his mouth. I have the strange and sudden urge to lick it away.

That's a recent development.

"What are you doing?"

"Pardon?"

"You cut all your food."

I flush, temporarily forgetting I'm in front of someone who isn't accustomed to how I eat. "It's a habit of mine. I have to cut my food before taking a single bite of that item. Steak. Chicken. Pancakes. I've always been this way. People notice, and it makes going out with a date super fun."

"I'm sorry. I didn't mean to call you out or draw attention to it."

"No worries. It's how my mom used to eat, too. The trait runs in the family."

"Does she still eat that way?"

"She passed away when I was 12."

The words are out of my mouth before I can think twice, not realizing what I've shared. All the air leaves the room and Jack's eyes widen in horror.

"Shit," he curses, slowly putting down his silverware. "I'm so sorry. I didn't know."

"How would you? We're not friends, and we've never shared life details with each other. It's been a long time. It still hurts, but the grief comes in waves. I'm fine. Please don't make this a thing."

"That may be true, but I'm still sorry." There's an emotion on his face that wasn't there before.

Pity. I hate that look. I've gotten *that look* for years; from teachers at open houses, friends, parents of my teammates. It's usually accompanied by them placing their hand over their heart and offering their condolences, as if their apologies are going to bring her back. Nope. Nineteen years later, and it still hasn't worked.

"How are you feeling?" he asks, changing the subject. "Do my potatoes have magical healing powers?"

I push a piece of pancake into the syrup puddle, grateful for the shift. "Better. This might be skewed data, though. I skipped dinner last night before the bar, so I'm not sure how accurate my rankings of your potatoes might be."

He stills. "When was the last time you ate a full meal?"

"Breakfast yesterday morning. A Pop-Tart. I had a meeting during lunch, then I was late to meet Abby at Mickey's, so I got sidetracked."

I watch Jack's expression shift. "Josephine." My name tumbles from his mouth, deafening in the quiet room. I swallow hard and look away. The sarcasm that normally fills his words is now laced with reverence. I hate that my skin prickles at the thought of *Jack* feeling compassionate toward me. "You're kind to a lot of people. Who takes care of you and makes sure *you're* okay?"

"Besides my family and Abby? No one. I don't have anyone," I say bitterly, shoving the rest of my pancake into my mouth.

We aren't going down that road; my inability to connect with a man as a romantic partner. My reluctance to let someone see me—*all* of me—especially after the catastrophe of last time. The flaws and mistakes and the messy parts. I'm aimlessly stuck between fine and settled, trying to catch up to my peers without knowing what or where the finish line is.

As we finish our meal, Jack and I share a handful of small comments, an amiable conversation never teetering back into personal information territory.

When I stand to take my plate to the sink, he stops me, his hand gently touching my elbow. I jump at the contact, a torpedo of shock racing through my body.

"I can do that," he says.

"You cooked. I can clean a dish."

"You should rest."

"I'm not as fragile as you think," I snap, turning on the faucet.

The water lands on the discarded plates at an awkward angle, splashing onto my face and causing droplets to run down my nose. Jack snorts, and it takes a lot of self-control to not grab the faucet and spray him in retaliation. I ignore his stares, rinsing, cleaning, and putting leftovers away in the fridge, aware of his eyes watching my every move. When I finish the tasks, I sigh, hanging my head, embarrassed by my rudeness.

"I'm sorry. You're trying to help, and you've been wonderful so far. I shouldn't take my frustration out on you."

"Why are you apologizing? Something horrible happened to you. You're allowed to feel the emotions associated with it, even if that includes anger toward me. Besides, I like when you get snippy. It reassures me you're still in there."

"I am." Then I add, whispering, "Thanks to you."

"I have some work I need to do. You're more than welcome to the couch in the living room or my bed. Anywhere, really. I imagine the last thing you want is a man hanging around. I'm going to stay out of your way the best I can. If you need me, I'll be down the hall."

"Do you have a roommate?" I ask.

"No. I live alone. What about you? Do you have a roommate? A boyfriend that can come pick you up?"

"Boyfriend? Please. I had a terrible date the other day, and that was enough for me."

"Oh? Want to share?"

I groan, burying my face in my hands. "It was horrible. He was shorter than his profile said. Height and age differences don't matter to me, but be honest about it, you know?"

"I think it's pretty obvious when someone isn't 6'2". As a proud member of the barely 5'10" club, I know lying about your height is pointless."

"Exactly. We went to Olive Garden, which isn't the worst Italian food I've ever eaten. I can get behind some never-ending breadsticks for sure. But he tried to kiss me when he greeted me. On the mouth! Then he tried to sit on the same side of the booth as me, was rude to the waitress, made horribly racist jokes, and implied he scams people out of money for work. I left halfway through the dinner because he asked if I believed in soulmates and tried to lick my cheek. My *cheek!*"

Jack chuckles softly. "The oldest cliché in the book. I'm sure if you had said yes to the soulmate question, he would have made some comment about you being his. Bright side, at least he wasn't married?"

"Wow, cynical Jack Lancaster finding a bright side to an awful experience? How the tables have turned."

"How many breadsticks did you eat before you escaped?"

"Six! Six breadsticks in twenty minutes, all so I could keep my mouth shut and not go off on a tirade."

"That might be a world record for breadstick consumption. What was his name?"

"Paul."

"It's Paul's loss. All right, it's time for me to be productive and time for you to rest." Jack guides me down the hall, depositing me back in his room before leaving without another word.

Now that I'm showered, fed, and aware of my surroundings, the bedroom looks different. The walls are a light canary yellow with white, billowy curtains covering three windows. There's a desk in the corner that has stacks of papers and writing utensils on it. Framed photos hang on the wall between two large book-shelves overflowing with books.

Ah.

There are the books.

I move toward them, reading the spines and appreciating how diverse his collection is. My eyes gravitate to a photograph showcasing a large group of two dozen people. I find Jack right away; he's hard to miss. He looks much younger, his youthful smile bright and eyes sparkling, wearing a graduation cap and gown. His arm is around the shoulder of a beautiful blonde, and she's leaning into him, nestled in his neck, gaze focused lovingly on his face while the surrounding group claps and grins at the camera. She's wearing a graduation robe as well, and they focus their attention only on each other, not a care in the world for the rest of the people with them.

I wonder who she is. The photo looks like a wonderful memory, taken at a happier time. Was it his college graduation? High school graduation? Is this his family? Or the family of a significant other? I feel disconcerted, like I'm intruding on a personal moment no one should see, the intimacy between the couple noticeable even through a weathered photograph. Pushing the thought away, I reach for my charged cell phone, ten messages popping up. Tapping the screen, I open Abby's contact info. The phone rings once before she answers.

"Jo?"

"Abby," I exhale, climbing onto the bed.

"Thank fuck. I was about two minutes away from coming to your house and breaking down the door."

"Well, it wouldn't have mattered since I'm not there. Someone spiked my drink last night. I passed out. Jack was there and brought me back to his place."

"Roofied? At *Mickey's*? That shit never happens there. Who? How? Fuck, forget that. Are you okay?"

"I can't remember a lot. Some creep kept trying to talk to me after you left. I brushed him off. He got pissed and called me a bitch. After that, everything gets fuzzy. I guess Jack got involved? Physically, I'm okay. I just feel so stupid."

"Sweetie, you didn't do anything wrong."

"Didn't I? I shouldn't have stayed out by myself. I should have kept my eyes on my drink."

"Jo," she says firmly. "This is not your fault. Staying out by yourself does not warrant getting drugged or assaulted. Stop that."

"I'm sorry. I'm trying to understand this whole mess. I'm sorry I didn't call you right away. My phone was dead."

"Don't apologize."

"Jack said he thought it would be a good idea to stay here today."

"You shouldn't be alone. Do you need anything? Do you feel safe? I can come pick you up and bring you here."

"Yes, I feel safe."

"Can I talk to him?"

"Who?"

"Jack."

"What?" I sputter.

"Yeah. If it's not too much trouble."

"He said he was going to do some work. Let me see if I can find him." Padding into the hallway, I see a door open on the left side. I knock, not wanting to burst into his private space unannounced.

"Come in," he says, and I push into the room. "Josephine." He shifts in his chair, blocking part of his desk from view. The movement is subtle, but it catches my attention. "What's wrong? Are you okay?"

"I'm fine. This is kind of weird, but Abby is on the phone. She wants to talk to you."

"Of course." He stands and walks toward me, taking the phone from my hand. "Hello, Abigail. I was wondering when I would hear from you. Sorry. Abby." He's quiet, listening to her intently. "Yes. Mhm. I agree." His eyes dart over to me. "Right. I do, too. I understand." Another nod. "Sure. It's 2618 Woodwind Street. Tomorrow morning. Just the one. No, the couch." He laughs at something she says, light and genuine. "You got it. I will. Here she is."

"What the hell was that about?" I ask Abby once he hands the phone over.

"I wanted him to know what would happen if he tried anything stupid. And now I have his location. I trust him."

"He said four things to you! And I'm pretty sure they were all one word!"

"I can tell these things about people, Jo. Text me and keep me updated."

"I will. I promise. Love you."

"Love you too. So much. I'm so glad you're safe."

I hang up the phone, shuffling my feet on the carpet.

"Abby is nice. She made some comment about only one bed. Am I supposed to understand what that means?"

"Oh, good grief," I mumble. "Ignore her. It's not important. I'm going to head back to your room if that's okay. The room, uh, where I was before."

"Of course that's okay. You know where I'll be."

I inch my way out of his office, closing the door behind me. Crawling back into his bed, I pull the covers over my head, welcoming the surrounding darkness. I could hide out forever in this cave of sheets I've made—warm, safe, and tucked away from the rest of the word. It's not my space, but it's still comfortable and peaceful. It's almost like the bed knows I belong here.

———

Jack's soft voice rouses me from the slumber I don't remember embarking on.

"How are you feeling?" he asks quietly. I pull the sheets off my head to find him standing with a fresh cup of water in his hands. I sit up groggily, my head throbbing less than before.

"Not any worse." I take the cup from him and bring it to my lips, the cool liquid gloriously refreshing my parched throat.

"Do you mind if I sit for a minute?" He gestures to the end of the bed.

I nod, thankful for his kindness and recognizing I don't want to feel crowded or trapped. For all the insulting names I've called him and the scores of fights we've had, I've never once considered him callous or purposely malicious. Yeah, he's been an asshole on many, many, *many* occasions. Watching him be exceedingly attentive and cautious, however, is a new personality trait. I don't hate it; it's just going to take some getting used to.

"Sure. Can I ask you a question or two about last night? There's still a few things I don't understand."

"Of course," he replies, practically falling off the mattress and onto the floor. "I'll do my best to answer them honestly."

"How did you get the bruise on your face? I know you said you intervened and got punched."

"It's a blur. I told the two guys to leave you alone and they decided not to listen. One called you a handful of derogatory names I would never dare repeat. So, I went for his throat, and he punched me in the face."

"You went for his *throat*?"

"Mhm."

"Like... choked him?"

"I tried. As soon as I got a good grip, his asshole friend decked me from the side."

"You did that for me?"

"I would do that for any woman, Josephine, but I would do far worse than pathetically try to grab a guy's throat to protect *you*. So, to answer your question, yes, I did that for you. And I'd do it again."

I let out a gasp at the startling words. The thought of Jack ripping out someone's throat for hurting me shouldn't be hot, but alarmingly, it is.

"When you make that sound it's very difficult for me to concentrate," he whispers.

I swallow thickly, throat scratchy like sandpaper, attempting to calm down. This is totally normal. The man who disliked me up until two weeks ago tried to kill someone and got injured in the process. And he'd take a second punch to protect me. Yup. Nothing to see here, folks.

"What is this bruise from?" I hike up the borrowed shorts I'm wearing and point to the handprint-shaped outline on my inner thigh.

A curse tumbles out of his mouth. "They... He... I..." His fists clench in fury. "Give me a minute."

"I-I get kind of demanding when I'm drunk. You said we didn't sleep together, but clearly I did something stupid." I cover my face in shame. "If I threw myself at you or propositioned you in any way, I'm sorry."

Jack's next to me in a flash, kneeling on the floor next to the bed and prying my hands away from my wet cheeks. "Josephine." I sniff, staring at the sheets. "Josephine," he says again, voice rougher. "Look at me." I obey him, and when I meet his eyes, there's not a trace of glee or humor. Rage, sadness, disappointment, and grief are all prevalent, combining to make Jack seem like a madman on a mission.

"What?" I whisper. Our joined hands hover together in front of me, his grip feather-light.

"You were not drunk. They drugged you. You did not proposition me for anything, nor would I ever engage in behavior like that when you're not in control of your body or actions. No matter what your sexual preferences are, that does not correlate to how you want to be treated when you can't give consent. The bruise is from those men. They tried to hold you down. That's when I got involved. I couldn't take it anymore, watching you tell them no over and over again. They wouldn't let go of you, so I took matters into my own hands."

"Does it hurt?" I ask, snaking my right hand out of his grasp and touching the swollen mark on his face delicately. The bruise is larger than I thought it would be, a nasty shade of faded red with flecks of purple. Jack's long eyelashes flutter closed at the contact. He tilts his cheek into my palm and my thumb rubs over the spot. It's warm and slightly raised above his otherwise flawless skin.

"I'm fine," he answers, low and raspy. It sends a shiver down my spine. His free hand lightly grazes my arm, sweeping up to my shoulder and down to my fingertips. "I don't care about me. What can I do to help you?"

"You've done enough. More than enough. I can never repay you."

"I would never dream of asking for anything in return." He pulls away, severing our contact. I miss him instantly.

"What happened to the men? Did they get caught?"

"I talked to the bar owner this morning. They used cash to pay, bolted after you dropped your glass and I got my hands on them, and there are no cameras inside. Someone thinks they remember seeing a company logo on one of their shirts, so the police are going to follow up on the lead. The best they can do at this point is cite them for trespassing. They deserve far fucking worse, but it's better than nothing."

"Trespassing. When they could have hurt me or another woman however they wanted. How is that fair?"

"It's not," he agrees firmly. "My friend is a lawyer. He said those guys are long gone. There's no way to see what else they possessed. Even if the cops chase them down, they will have dumped whatever they were carrying. The amount they put in your drink was enough to knock you out, but not enough to show up on a test."

"Bullshit," I whisper. "It's not their first time."

"Probably not. And it might not be their last. Maybe they got spooked. Unfortunately, there are some heinous men out there. I'm so sorry you were subjected to their behavior. I gave the cop my number, and he said he'd let me know if anything turns up, but to not hold my breath."

"Thanks for following up. It means a lot."

"Trust me, Josephine. If I had it my way, those two losers would be tied up in a chair, face beat to a bloody pulp. I need to go on a run and work some of this anger out. Your clothes are in the washer, and I'll switch them over when I get back. I'm going to clean the sheets, too."

"You didn't have to do that."

"I wanted to. When it comes to you, it seems I want to do a lot of things. I'll be back soon. Make yourself at home."

ELEVEN
JO

I'm a curious individual by nature, always wanting to learn about others. How do they fold their towels? Do they rinse their dishes completely before putting them in the dishwasher, or do they forgo the appliance altogether? Are there nightlights in their hallway? Are they a morning person or a night owl?

It makes sense that I can't help but throw back the covers of the large bed after Jack leaves and make my way through his quiet, empty house, wanting to investigate the living space of someone I've worked with for two years and know nothing about.

I'm very curious about him.

He's given me free rein over the Kingdom of Lancaster and I'm going to use it to my advantage.

Perhaps in the back of his closet under piles of coats and rarely used clothes he has a weathered and ancient shoebox packed full of old love letters he looks at on rainy afternoons, yearningly remembering better days with a partner he once loved more than life itself.

Maybe there are mementos from his childhood stacked up, like certificates of achievement and vocabulary tests with backwards letters. A yearbook with unfortunate class photos and bowl cuts. Folded notes from middle school and beaded keychains. A picture from prom of him in an ill-fitting suit, accompanied by a date who's name he's long since forgotten.

It's strangely disorienting while simultaneously thrilling being here, unchaperoned outside the confines of our regimented office and roles. I'm excited and nervous as I begin my investigation, afraid of what I might find and how what I find might change my opinion of him.

All the furniture is curvilinear and welcoming with bright colors, comfortable fabric, and sleek finishes, not appearing like the sparse bachelor pad setup or dark, gloomy cave dwelling I envisioned. The king bed I've almost made my own has a headboard of deep mahogany and the coffee table has multiple coasters that look used, rings staining the aged wood. Dishtowels hang from the cabinet below the sink, and a key rack sits by the door. There's a vase of fresh flowers, pink daisies to be exact, on the kitchen counter right under the large bay window, and I wonder where—or who—they're from.

It's a well-loved space, that much is obvious. It's a sanctuary for him—a respite from the 9-5 corporate grind—that shows small glimmers into his mystifying personality. Minute indications of the man Jack truly is become more and more real the harder I look.

The rogue blue and white argyle sock hanging limply out of the laundry basket, not quite in the hamper but not escaping onto the floor.

The cedar-scented candles in the living room on the entertainment unit, wicks half-melted down.

A pile of historical fiction novels sitting on the end table, a bookmark peeking out of three of them, all in assorted stages of completion.

The far side of the couch that dips slightly deeper than the one closer to the door, cushions exhibiting an indentation from overuse.

The row of various men's shoes neatly lined up in a row against the wall in the foyer by the front door, my pair of sandals next to them. I smile at the sight.

I can't help but wonder if there's someone else in his life I haven't met yet. A girlfriend. A boyfriend. A partner he doesn't speak about due to his private nature. This house is warm. Welcoming. Inviting and becoming. Does he live here alone? Is he happy? Or does he walk the halls at night bereft, wishing he had someone by his side, the usual bitterness transfiguring to sorrow and loneliness?

And who's the mysterious woman from the photo on his wall? I can't stop thinking about her, and the way she makes— made—Jack happy, an entirely different human exhibited in the photo. Does she make him laugh? What does she have that my coworkers and I don't?

I *really* want to know more.

After finishing my tour of the living room and kitchen—and learning his fridge is full of proper food and not just cases of beer—I walk back to his office. I notice a dozen Post-It notes attached to his desk, looking like a rainbow of paper with green, blue, pink, and orange pieces dangling from the edge. Frowning, I approach the colored surface, picking one up, trying to decipher the messy handwriting taking over every inch of the square.

12:32 a.m.: 85 bpm (any higher—ER)
2:07 a.m.: 67 bpm
3:12 a.m.: 58 bpm (sleeping on side)
4:02 a.m.: 52 bpm (skin less clammy)
~~Fever~~
~~Vomit~~

unresponsive to talking (told a dumb story—I'd stay asleep too)
5:06 a.m.: 49 bpm. Called Reb—should be ok w/ no doc

My hands shake as I pick up another one.

I'm sorry. I'm sorry. I'm sorry. I'm sor
6:37 a.m.: 48 bpm (skin less pale—sleeping on back)
~~*Awake?*~~ *Still asleep @ 7:04 a.m. (& unresponsive to talking)*
~~*Blue lips*~~
~~*Shakes*~~ *(kicked off blanket)*
8:32 a.m.: Reb called. Should wake up soon. Monitor symp.
Google—long-term effects?

It's the same handwriting from the bag of sugar Jack gave me a few weeks ago. The penmanship starts to become illegible the closer to morning the notations get, letters too close together and getting smaller and smaller. Finally, a lightbulb goes off in my brain and the realization sinks in.

These notes are about *me* and last night. Now his exhaustion and dirty shirt makes more sense; it wasn't a rough night of tossing and turning. He didn't sleep. At all. He stayed awake, checking on me every hour, making sure I was breathing and doing okay, meticulously taking notes to keep tabs on me.

He talked to me while I slept, trying to wake me up. Printed off symptoms and side effects and figured out which ones I had and which ones I didn't. Called his friend multiple times to give updates and ask what else needed to be done.

My eyes fill with tears and I quickly wipe them away, not wanting to spill any traces of my presence onto the papers. Reattaching the sticky notes to the desk, I swallow, wanting to give Jack the biggest hug in the world.

This kindness is earth-shattering. He didn't just intervene and yell at some guys harassing a woman and bring me back to his house to let me sleep off what feels like a bad hangover. He saved my life and sacrificed his own health and well-being to take care of me. My chest aches and I have a deep desire to be with him right now. To thank him over and over again, letting him know I never considered him a villain in our story; he's a hero. He always has been. Last night proved that.

As I move away and try to regain my composure, a stack of paper cups next to the monitors catches my attention. I didn't notice them at first, too curious about the Post-Its. They're in the same spot he blocked from my view earlier when he spoke to Abby. I freeze when I read the bottom one, feet halting on the carpet, stuck in quicksand.

Grumpy

It's my handwriting, clear as day.
Holy shit.
I pick up the cups and pull them apart frantically, one by one. Some are months old, dating back to early last year.

Boomer (after someone explained to him what Snapchat was)
Life Ruiner (for the first few months after he interrupted my presentation)
Insufferable Know It All (no explanation needed)
Salt Ba(n)e Of My Existence (after he put salt in my tea—I'm proud of that one)
Lint Licker (just because)

I gawk at the scene spread out like a Starbucks assembly line. Over a dozen cups sit before me, taunting me. Cups that I gave him at our weekly meetings, insult after insult on display. My heart rate accelerates, another drop of knowledge about Jack Lancaster being presented in front of me.

He keeps the cups.

Okay. Yes.

But what does it *mean?*

I'm sure if I looked hard enough, I'd find souvenirs from other colleagues scattered around. There might be a Post-It note from Tyler somewhere with a silly joke or funny story. Or one of the #FunFridayFacts emails Carla sends out, which range from facts about animals to Guinness world records. Is this Jack's way of connecting with people, preferring a small token over social interaction?

I feel guilty about stumbling upon this facet of his life. Yeah, I want to know more about him, but I also don't want to do anything that will remotely piss him off. Like go searching for more clues and insights. His generosity over the last eighteen hours has been unfathomable. I won't ruin the momentum we've gained because I'm nosy, and I'm certainly not going to ask him to explain the reasoning behind holding onto the souvenirs.

It can't be just me, can it?

There's no way.

Unless...

When he sees me approaching the office building, he scowls so fiercely it's surprising he doesn't have wrinkles around his mouth or deep rivets between his eyebrows.

He refuses my company-wide social outing invitations, *blocking* the emails so they return undeliverable.

In meetings, when I speak, he pays me no attention, unwilling to participate in the interactive parts of my discussions.

I'm supposed to believe he really likes coffee cups?

Not plausible.

And why the hell did he deliberately move, shielding them from view?

Is he embarrassed? Does he think I'd make fun of him? The cups have always been my way of expressing my frustrations with him in a pathetically comedic way to avoid stabbing him in the chest with the closest sharp object.

I didn't think he enjoyed them or looked forward to receiving the graffitied beverages.

Slowly, I return the cups to their proper order, fighting back a grin.

There's something going on here. I'm going to find out what it is.

He's maddening, sure.

Antagonizing and obnoxious, too.

I think somewhere under that prickly, rough exterior, there might be a different Jack.

A man who is sentimental.

Kind.

What made him this way, so angry with the world and all of its occupants? *Who* made him this way?

I've seen flashes of what he could be. What he used to be.

The small, infrequent smiles buried under tense, angry expressions.

The crinkles in the corner of his eyes that fade away to smooth skin before you can blink.

The dimple that's shown itself a handful of times, begging to be released into the open for good.

The way he stood up for me and protected me.

How he makes sure I'm comfortable before doing anything out of our ordinary element.

I don't think it's a make-believe version of him. It's one he's kept hidden away, a shell of the man he once was.

I would never, ever try to change him. Or fix him.

People aren't projects we bend and mold, shaping them to some higher ideal of a perfect human. Jack is no exception to that. But I am determined to bring more happiness into his life from this point forward.

And if that means more stupid cups with stupid jabs written on them, so be it. I'll bring him a new one every day if he wants.

"Josephine?" Jack's voice travels down the hall, and I falter at the sound. Dashing away from the desk, I smile at the door, hoping I don't look too suspicious or guilty. "There you are." He stands in the entryway, and I watch his eyes slide from me to the desk, widening slightly.

"Hi! How was your run?" I ask, overly bright, attempting to compensate for my snooping, feigning ignorance that the bright colors of the squares and the high stack of cups aren't in plain sight.

"Not bad. What are you doing?"

"Sorry! I wanted to see where you kept the folder with ways to annoy me," I joke.

The corner of his mouth tilts up. "Ah. You thought I'd leave that out in plain sight? It's extremely confidential, which means you haven't found my secret drawer."

"Not yet, but my quest continues. I'm not a quitter." I move further away from my crime scene.

"You certainly are not." Sweat glistens on his flushed forehead, a bead sliding down his cheek salaciously.

He reaches up and wipes it away with the hem of his damp, gray shirt, revealing a sliver of tan skin. A trail of hair. The outline of defined abs.

Good grief.

My gawking is clearly obvious because he quickly drops the shirt, fabric covering his muscles, and uses the back of his hand to finish wiping away the moisture that's accumulated on his body.

"I'm going to jump in the shower," he says, and I swear his voice sounds deeper than before. "Still feeling okay?"

"Yeah. I think I might take a nap."

"Want me to get you up for dinner later?"

"That sounds perfect." I follow the hallway to his room, leaving the door open as I crawl into the bed.

"I brought some more water." Jack sets a glass down on the bedside table next to my phone. A flash of domesticity jolts through my brain, imagining what it would be like for this to be a nightly occurrence.

With him.

All that's missing is a kiss to my forehead.

I hum in response, eyes relaxing as I rest my head against the fluffy pillows. The bathroom door snicks closed and I freeze at the sound of shoes hitting the floor and clothes following shortly after, understanding what *jumping in the shower* means.

Jack is getting naked. Feet away from me. While I sit idly in his bed like it's no big deal and happens all the time.

Fuck, fuck, fuck.

How many women have been in this same spot, coming down from a high after he ravishes them senseless? How many of them have been on these very sheets, withering away as he lets them finish first, again and again, a constant stream of satisfaction? Ten? Twenty? Thirty?

My toes curl, hesitant to learn the answer. I've spent the last two years not thinking about Jack Lancaster in anything but a strictly professional way, but now all I can focus on is...

Him.

Under the shower, hot water and steam kissing his lithe body as he hums in contentment, droplets rolling down his thighs and hips.

Washing his hair, fingers rubbing against his scalp as wet, bronze curls stick to his neck like vines seeking sunlight.

His head tilting to the side, muscles flexing as he scrubs up his arms and down his sculpted chest, soap suds following along the ridges of his hard abdomen.

His mouth parting in pleasure, forehead resting against the tile, eyes closed, a lazy smile blooming on his face as his hand tightens around his hard di—

Nope.

No. Full stop.

We are not going there.

We *can't* go there.

Being kind and taking care of me is one thing. But *lusting* after my colleague? That cannot happen.

Dirty, indecent visions cloud my still fuzzy brain and I reach for the water he left, attempting to cool myself down. A single glass won't do it, but a whole bucket might.

The shower turns off and I throw the covers over my body, squeezing my eyes shut.

Out of sight, out of mind.

"I know you're awake," Jack says, voice full of humor as I squeak in surprise.

"What? No I'm not! I'm sleeping soundly!" The covers stay firmly over my body to hide the pink tint attacking my skin.

"You're practically shaking like a leaf under there. I'm decent now, don't worry."

"I wanted to give you some privacy."

"How thoughtful of you."

"I didn't want you to feel like I was watching you."

"Mhm. Certainly not."

"I'm also really tired."

"Of course. You looked positively exhausted a minute ago when you practically skipped down the hall."

"I didn't skip!"

"Right. My apologies. Any preference for dinner tonight?"

I slowly peel the cotton sheets away to reveal my head,

looking at him over the top of the duvet. He's fully clothed and wearing a knowing smirk on his face.

Bastard.

"Um. Tacos?" I blurt out the first thing that comes to mind, not expecting him to agree.

I swear his eyes twinkle as he turns on his heel and leaves the room, a trail of quiet chuckles left behind.

"Tacos it is."

TWELVE
JACK

I've survived with Josephine in my house for almost 24 hours. Sure, half the time she's been unconscious, asleep, or faking sleep while hiding under the covers to avoid a conversation with me, leaving little room for us to fall into any old habits.

But still.

We've been in the same space, under the same roof, and both survived. I'd never admit this to her, but I wish some of our old habits would return. Her eye roll earlier gave me the smallest flicker of hope for the first time since I found her in the bar that *she's* still in there. Unharmed. Unhurt. Unscathed. I'm close to begging her to call me a name. To throw an insult my way. I wish she would yell at me, or toss a snarky, biting comment my way.

It would help soothe the ache and anger I'm carrying, which doesn't compare to what she's dealing with. She's repeatedly assured me she's okay like a broken record throughout the afternoon. I'm still not convinced.

The words do nothing to calm my mind. Physically, she's alive and functioning. She's breathing. She's eating. She's talking. I can't read her thoughts, though, and I don't know if she's dealing with any emotional turmoil after what happened to her. I imagine she is, but I'm clueless about how to help, which is all I want to do.

Last night wrecked me. I've never been so terrified and furious. Seeing her in my arms, body limp like noodles, head drooping to the side while I sprinted us to my car and nearly broke my ankle in the process...

I thought she was dead. She *looked* dead.

My hand on the steering wheel shook the entire drive home while the other rested at the base of her neck, thumb on her pulse point, counting her heartbeats again and again and again.

I almost took her to the hospital. In hindsight, I should have. They could have done a better job than me. After frantically talking to Rebecca, Neil's girlfriend who's an ER nurse, and hearing there was no guarantee they'd even let me stay with her, I decided to bring her to my house and keep an eye on her, afraid someone else might hurt her or she'd wake up alone, confused and scared, with no one to sit by her side.

Not fucking happening.

I tucked her in my bed and pulled the covers tightly around her. I've never been a religious man, but last night, I rocked back and forth, knees digging into the rug as I prayed to every deity I've ever learned about to keep her safe. I would have sold my soul to the devil for the rest of my life in exchange for her health and safety. A single, perfectly timed tear fell from my eye, landing on her arm and branding her like a tattoo. I brushed it away before I could think twice, attempting to pull myself together and embarrassed by the display of affection.

Never again will I berate her. Never again will I go out of my way to make her life hell. Never again will an email from her go unanswered or ignored. All were words I whispered into the silent room, no one but the trees outside to listen to my pleas and promises to be better. To try harder. To cut the shit out and treat her with respect. The animosity stops now. No more. I don't want it; not when I was so close to losing her.

It's like a switch has flipped in my brain. A complete 180-degree turn, ending up on the opposite side of the spectrum from where we first started.

I'm not sure if I ever actually *hated* her, or if the annoyance and disdain were masking something far deeper and more permanent. Seeing her last night, in pain, almost gone, was a wake-up call.

I like her.

And not in a teasing, *Jack has a crush, let's rib on him* way. I fully and completely like her. In a relationship way, too. Not a one-night stand way. That's strange to admit, no longer scoffing at the notion of attraction or rolling my eyes and passionately proclaiming I have no feelings toward her. Perhaps I've always known, but last night cemented the awareness in reality.

I almost went back to the bar and killed the two men who hurt her. A phone call from Henry, the lawyer of the group, stopped me in my tracks. He said he would be pissed as hell and charge me triple his usual rate if he had to leave the model tied to his bed behind and bail my ass out of jail. So, I regretfully stayed put, a hatred like nothing I've ever experienced before pumping through my blood.

My head aches from the lack of sleep, and my cheek won't stop throbbing where I got decked and Josephine touched me, her palm a hot iron against my skin. For her, I'd gladly burn.

Three different times last night I nearly dropped my head onto the mattress and fell asleep right there, my hand cradling hers, ink-stained fingers gently stroking over the soft spots of her wrist. It wasn't an intimate gesture. It was an *I'm going out of my fucking mind with worry* gesture.

Yeah, touching her was invigorating. Spellbinding. But this

isn't about me. This is about her and making sure she's okay. I got no physical enjoyment out of seeing her in pain.

God, if I didn't want to sob in relief each time her chest moved with every breath. Rebecca tried calming me down when I talked to her, but worst-case scenario after worst-case scenario ran through my head.

Something shifted between us last night and today. I can tell by the way she's nearly gnawed her lip raw and snuck glances my way, not expecting me to catch her. I pretend to not, refusing to acknowledge the not-so-subtle glimpses. Her mouth keeps opening and closing like she wants to ask a question, but she doesn't follow through, turning her attention back to her phone and leaving me to ponder what the hell is going on inside her head.

I'm slowly going insane.

I'm afraid I've done something wrong. I've racked my brain for every interaction we've had, and nothing's out of place besides the salient way she's invaded my bed and damn brain for hours on end.

Not even a run could distract me.

She's sitting next to me on the couch, holding a plate of tacos with a smile on her face. A sight I never thought I'd see; it's not a mirage. She's actually here. We've conversed lightly throughout the evening. She helped make dinner and we only bickered twice, which might be a record.

The first disagreement came when discussing if we should pre-cheese the taco shells before filling them. She spoke animatedly during her lecture, hands flying in the air, telling me it was a necessity. I finally relented after her demonstration on a broken shell, declining to inform her that she was right and that I'll never make an un-pre-cheesed taco again.

The second came when discussing olives and if they were a required accessory to round out the taco toppings. She wrinkled her nose but didn't protest when I piled an exuberant amount over my finished plate.

Small steps, I suppose.

Now we're watching a rerun episode of *Jeopardy!*. The sun set not too long ago, casting a soft glow throughout the living room. We haven't bothered to turn on any of the lamps, the gigantic television screen on the wall illuminating the surrounding space.

"This is my favorite show," Josephine says, taking a bite of the lone taco she has left. I'm surprised by how much she's eaten, and it calms my nerves to know she's not skipping a meal. As long as she's under my roof, she's not going without food for more than a few hours. Out of the corner of my eye, I watch pieces of ground beef, tomato, cheese, lettuce, and sour cream escape, creating a canvas of colors on her plate.

She's a terribly messy eater.

It's kind of endearing.

"Is it?" I ask, wiping my hands with one of the spare napkins sitting on the coffee table. She's used more than half of them, and I appreciate her willingness to not make a mess on the sectional. "I love it too."

"Mhm. I like that it's competitive and you can learn from it, you know? It used to be one of our things growing up. Every night we'd all watch together. My dad would relax in his recliner, my mom would sit on the couch, and my sisters and I would pile on either side of her. My parents kept a running tally of who got the most questions right."

"What a special memory. Who typically won?"

"I think my dad purposely got answers wrong so my mom could score more points."

"Sounds like true love, if you ask me. Would you ever try out for the show?"

She laughs. "No way. I'm not that smart."

"I think you're plenty smart," I answer, licking the corner of my mouth where a dollop of sour cream has landed. Her eyes follow my tongue before quickly looking away.

"Oh. Um. Thanks?"

"Was that a question?"

"It was an interjection. Maybe?"

"Mmm. Nope. Interjections are set apart from a sentence by things like an exclamation point. Or, if the feeling is not as strong, a comma."

"Did you just quote *Schoolhouse Rock*?"

"I did."

"You nerd!" she exclaims, hitting me with the fluffy decorative pillow sitting on the couch that serves zero purpose. I bought it because Noah insisted the room looks too drab without it. I don't notice much difference.

"Hey!" Taco remains slide dangerously close to the edge of my plate. "No pillow fights with food present!"

"What about if food isn't present?" she asks innocently.

"To be determined. How does remembering songs from my childhood make me a *nerd*?"

"That's not what makes you a nerd. 'I'm Just A Bill' taught me more about the Legislative Branch of our government than my high school history classes did. You said it so matter-of-factly, like you were giving me the literal dictionary definition. Blink twice if you need help, Robot Jack."

All right. Stupid crush aside, I'll begrudgingly admit she's funny. I take a deep breath, turning to look her dead in the eyes. She swallows, and the grip on her plate tightens.

"INTERJECTIONS," I almost shout. She jumps, startled by my increase in volume. "SHOW EXICTEMENT. AND EMOTION." I whip my arm out to the side in dramatic fashion, like an actor on Broadway. "Better?"

She's trying to ward off the laughter.

It's a losing battle and her facade crumbles swiftly as she bursts into a fit of giggles. *That might be my new favorite sound.*

"Holy shit," she says, shaking her head and brushing hair out of her eyes. "Thank you for that stellar performance."

"I'll be here all week. We can discuss conjunctions next. Do you want any more food?" I made plenty, not wanting her to go hungry.

"I'm all set. Three tacos are enough." She pats her stomach, pushing the empty plate onto the coffee table.

"I'm a little disappointed you didn't match your breadstick number."

"I can't use all my party tricks the first time we hang out, Lancaster."

There's teasing behind that statement, and I arch an eyebrow as my heartbeat quickens, wondering where she's going with this conversation.

If she asks me to hang out again, I'll say yes.

How could I not?

Now that I know we can exist in the same hemisphere for longer than sixty minutes and survive, I'd be a foolish man to turn down an invitation from her.

Especially because I think she might like my company.

Maybe.

She's still here.

Yeah, because she was drugged and could barely function 12 hours ago. This isn't by choice.

"You're implying that we'll be hanging out again, I see," I say cautiously, leaving my sentence open-ended.

"Uh, yeah? We have the conference in T-minus four days, buddy. Please don't tell me you forgot."

I deflate.

The conference.

Right.

Nothing else.

"Of course I didn't forget," I scoff. I've only been thinking about it every day for the past two goddamn weeks, torn between elation and sheer anxiety, a panic attack looming over the precipice I'm tiptoeing on. "I wanted to talk to you about that while we're here."

"Sure." Josephine shifts on the couch so she's facing me, legs crisscrossed, athletic shorts bunching up her thighs.

She's a masterpiece in my clothes. The messy bun on her head is slowly sliding out of the hair tie trying to contain her curls, pieces of fiery red flames framing her tired face. The collar of the large shirt dips half an inch off her shoulder, exposing the slightest sliver of pale skin before she shoves it back up, swimming in the expanse of old fabric. We're close to the same stature, but she looks so small wearing my items. I shouldn't let my eyes linger like a lecherous idiot, especially after what she's been through, but I can't help it. She's difficult to look away from.

Heaving a sigh, I move my attention to the cushions of the couch instead of the woman sitting across from me.

"After what happened last night, I want to make sure you're comfortable with me attending. If not, I will gladly back out."

"Why would this weekend change if I wanted you to go?" she asks, frowning deeply. "You weren't the one who hurt me. In fact, you did everything in your power to protect me. Contrary to popular belief, myself included, we're able to be around each other without a world war starting."

"Which is amazing, considering the look of disgust I received when I put ketchup on my eggs earlier and suggested olives as a taco topping."

"Because those are gross, you heathen!"

"Not as gross as wanting cheese in your eggs. Are you *posi-*

tive you're okay with me going? Be honest, Josephine. You won't hurt my feelings."

I hold my breath, waiting for her to use this chance to shun me away. Instead, she smiles kindly, and I swear the room glows even brighter.

"Absolutely. You deserve to be there. Your work is instrumental to the success we've had lately."

"It doesn't compare to what you've implemented. I've been slow to accept the power of social media, but you clearly know what you're doing, and it shows."

"Thanks."

"I also wanted to ask about last night now that more time has passed. Is there anything else I can do?"

"I made an appointment to meet with my therapist Monday after work. I'm pissed off. And thankful, of course. It's just so infuriating women can't go anywhere in this world without being threatened."

"It might not mean much, but you're safe here. I know with the utmost certainty you can protect and defend yourself valiantly, all women can, but if you ever need a helping hand... I'm on standby. Please don't interpret my jumping in last night as thinking you're weak."

The smile morphs into immense gratitude. "Trust me, your willingness to intervene is extremely appreciated. I hope it never happens again. If it does, I know I can count on you."

My chest swells with pride at the sincerity of her words. I nod, clearing my throat to fight against all the emotions threatening to smash into me.

"Do you want to ride together to the airport?" I ask, probably sounding pathetic with the sudden conversation change.

"That would be awesome! I think our flight is at 10. What time do you want to pick me up?"

"How about 7? That gives us enough time to park, get through security, and snag a coffee."

"Perfect. Here, I'll put my address in your phone."

I hand over my device, watching her fingers type away.

I'm so glad she's okay.

"I'll be out front at 7."

"And not a moment later, I'm sure," she jokes, stretching her arms above her head. "I think I'm in a food coma."

"Don't fall asleep. I'm on the couch tonight."

"Uh, no." Josephine frowns, putting her arm on the back cushion and leaning her cheek against it. "I'll stay out here."

I might have spoken too soon.

This will be what sparks the next world war. My nostrils flare at the need to *protect* and *take care*.

"Josephine. You're taking the bed, and this is not up for debate."

I'm sure I sound like a domineering asshole, but I refuse to let her sleep on this awkward-sized, pathetic excuse of a lounging furniture item.

"I don't want to make your girlfriend uncomfortable," she blurts out.

"Girlfriend?" I ask, perplexed. I've never mentioned a woman around her. Where would she get that idea?

"Or boyfriend," she amends, cheeks turning red to match her hair. "I saw the picture in your bedroom. You and the blonde. I didn't mean to snoop, I promise! The picture is right there. It's hard to miss. She's really pretty!"

Fuck.

Me.

I know exactly what photo she's referencing.

I've become so numb and immune to my past, I didn't realize it was still up.

That will be remedied first thing in the morning.

I quell the usual rush of self-loathing that threatens to erupt when thinking about *her*. My fists clench and my spine goes rigid, a near perfect line as my eyes snap shut, flashes of mistakes appearing before me.

Taking a deep breath, I hold the inhale, counting to five before releasing the exhale.

"Are you okay?" Her voice is small and comforting against the roar in my head. Her hand reaches out, landing on my forearm, and I think I forget to breathe altogether.

Her skin. On mine.

Willingly.

Again.

It's beguiling.

Her soft fingers press lightly into my muscles, massaging out the tension of the last 24 hours.

"I-I'm fine," I stammer. "Sorry."

"There's nothing to apologize for. I'm sorry for prying."

"You didn't. I don't have a significant other in my life, and that photo is from another time. Another life. I need to take it down. Thank you for reminding me."

It looks like she wants to ask me a myriad of questions. If she did, I would answer them all. I'd let her see the real asshole I am and the ugly past I keep shielded from everyone.

Always ruining things.

She leans forward, wrapping me into a tight embrace. Her arms settle around my waist, cheek settling into the crook of my neck. This position feels natural. Normal. So fucking perfect, I might explode. I don't remember the last time someone just *held* me, *comforted* me, and the long-forgotten sensation makes my body buzz with satisfaction and fulfillment.

"Can we promise each other something?" she asks, the question muffled and her breath tickling my ear. I nod, unable to find words. I can't bring myself to hug her back, to touch her, so I sit stationary, slowly melting, the roar settling into barely a whisper.

"What?" I rasp discordantly.

"We'll never go back to how things were before. Tomorrow starts fresh. A do-over. A clean slate."

She smells like wildflowers and the first rain after a long drought. I can't say no to her, no matter how hard I try.

"A clean slate," I repeat. "Yeah. Yes."

"Good." She gives my shoulders a parting squeeze and pulls away, untangling us, the buzz going with her. I already want to bring her back in my lap, her head resting against my chest as she falls asleep. A place where I can keep her safe.

A yawn escapes her, eyes fluttering closed.

"Okay. Bedtime. Up, up, up." I stand from the couch, collecting our used paper plates.

"Fine," she grumbles, rising and shuffling away from the couch. "Hey, one more question for you."

"What's that?"

"How did I get into your room last night?"

I freeze.

Lie.

Tell her she walked.

Tell her she was fine on her own two feet and not a stumbling mess who couldn't hold herself up and nearly became concussed on the foyer wall that juts out at the corner.

She wouldn't remember.

I can't, though. I want her to know what I did because it... It meant something to me. And maybe it meant something to her, too. So I settle on the scary truth.

"I carried you."

The answer appeases her, and I'm rewarded with a coy smile as she turns for the hallway. "I was hoping you would say that. I wish I remembered what it was like. To be in your arms. I bet it was wonderful."

She walks away, pausing in the foyer for a few moments. I crane my neck, trying to figure out what she's doing, and notice her staring at the door. Before I can ask if everything is okay, she disappears toward my room, leaving me wishing for a thunderstorm in a meadow instead of the lonely, despairing silence.

THIRTEEN
JO

At precisely 7:00 a.m. on Wednesday morning, I watch a car pull up outside my house. Right on time.

Jack is an exceedingly punctual person. I can look past the ketchup eggs because he's outside exactly when he says he will be. And I appreciate that.

I wipe the Pop-Tart residue off my hands and grab my suitcase, double checking that the lights and appliances are off before walking outside. Keeping my back to the driveway, I lock the door, pushing against the steel to ensure it's properly closed and checking the deadbolt two times. Three times. My eyes bounce back and forth between both locking mechanisms, finally satisfied with my assessment. Hoping to not draw any attention to myself, I turn around and see Jack walking up the path.

"Need help with your bag?" he asks, reaching for my suitcase unasked. He's wearing a plain gray t-shirt and black joggers.

Good lord.

Those pants are obscene.

The sun isn't fully up yet, barely cresting over the horizon as it paints the street in hues of light pink and orange and Jack looks really freaking good this early in the morning, like he's climbed out of a retro Hollister catalog from the early 2000s. I, meanwhile, can still feel the sleep sitting in the corner of my eyes, a far cry from put together.

The bruise on his face has receded in the handful of days since I last saw him, the color fading and giving way back to his natural tan. I slipped out of his house early Sunday, taking an Uber to my car at Mickey's instead of waking him up to chauffeur me around.

"Thanks." I follow him as he rolls my bag down the small brick pathway to a black Toyota that looks like it's been around since the '90s, perfectly parallel parked on the side of the road against the curb.

Ah. He's one of *those* drivers.

I bet he also backs into spots, causing a traffic pile-up as he takes his sweet time reversing in small parking lots.

"I'm sorry. What is this?" I stop short of the vehicle and look at him.

"My car. Why, what's wrong?"

"Are you kidding? Like, you're 100% serious this is what you drive daily? How did I not notice this in your driveway?"

"I repeat, what's wrong?"

"Nothing. I'm... surprised."

"This could be fun. What were you expecting?"

"Honestly? Not a car that belongs in the Oregon Trail computer game from the old Macs we used to use in elementary school and looks like it's about to fall apart if a gust of wind comes through too aggressively. Will I die from dysentery?"

"That is a strangely specific observation." He's trying not to smile.

Dipping his chin, he breaks eye contact, fascinated with the tar of the road as he runs his hand through his hair, neck straining at the effort it requires to not emit any laughter.

"You played the game, right?"

"Of course I did, Josephine. I was partial to the Yukon Trail version, though. I assure you, this is a cholera-free car."

"You strike me as a Jeep or Range Rover type of guy. Or some other gas-guzzling monstrosity."

"Hey!" Jack opens the trunk and places my suitcase inside, sounding offended. "This is a 2009, thank you very much. It's hardly a relic, and certainly not going into a time capsule soon. She has a couple of years left."

"It probably still has a CD player inside, doesn't it?"

"I'm not answering that question."

"Oh my god, it does!"

"Climate change is a very real crisis, Josephine, and I'm doing my part to help the earth. The gas mileage on this baby is economically beneficial to my wallet, and environmentally friendly. I'd call that a win-win."

"Couldn't you help the earth by buying a reusable water bottle? Using a paper straw? Planting a tree? Not by forcing me to ride in some death trap. Are you trying to kill me? I knew that was your plan all along."

"If I was going to hurt you and spend the rest of my life in prison, I'd at least wait until after the conference. I need to enjoy a vacation before embarking on life behind bars. Maybe I'll do it on the way home."

I bite the inside of my cheek to keep from giggling.

"This is a horrible idea."

"I hope you know I would never intentionally put you in harm's way."

"Fine." I open the passenger door, letting myself spill into the small space, surprised the door doesn't fall off the hinges. It does make an ominous squeaking sound. Someone short last occupied the seat; my knees are practically in my face. I adjust the chair back a few inches, letting my legs stretch out.

Jack slides into the driver's side with more grace and poise, turning the key in the ignition. To his credit, the car starts with no sputtering.

I'm shocked.

"Ready?"

"If I remember correctly, you're the one who coerced me into this vehicle."

He barks out a laugh, not bothering to hold back this time as he shifts the car into drive and peels onto the street. "I'll upgrade my ride when you eat six breadsticks in front of me. I'm a man who can compromise."

Airports are a lawless place. Where else in the world can you find one person drinking a coffee, sitting next to a person eating a cheeseburger, beside a person chugging a Bud Light at 9 a.m. on a Wednesday? And none of them are *wrong*.

That's what I think as I pull my suitcase through the crowded terminal to our gate, silently cursing myself for not splurging on the more expensive luggage with four wheels instead of two. My shoulder is already throbbing, a large, over-stuffed tote bag hanging off my arm.

"Josephine." Jack appears as sly and quiet as a cat. He's holding a cardboard tray with two drinks in his hands. Talk about a role reversal.

"That's where you went! Two cups of coffee? You must have been up late last night."

"One is for you. Tea. One cream, one sugar. Did I get that right?" he asks, extending one of the large Styrofoam cups toward me like a peace offering.

"That's right," I say haltingly, taking the drink from him and eyeing it wearily. How in the world did he know exactly how I take my drink?

"I didn't poison it. I thought you might like a caffeine boost if you're feeling as exhausted as I am already."

"Telling me you didn't poison it is exactly what someone who *did* poison it would say." I bring the cup to my mouth and take a sip. The warm liquid revives me instantly. If it is poison, it's a tasty way to go. "Thanks for this."

"My pleasure. We'll probably start boarding soon."

"I can't believe we get to sit in first class! I've never sat up front before."

"Neither have I. It's funny that while we don't have the budget for a new hard drive for my dying computer, expensive seats to Key West are doable."

"I bet the conference is paying for them."

"Perhaps you're right."

"Oh, I like when you say that! Do it again."

"Hush." He gently taps the top of my head with his boarding pass. Of course he printed out a paper copy instead of using an electronic device like the rest of the population our age. "What seat are you in?"

I check my phone. "3C. What about you?"

"3D."

"I hate the aisle." My foot taps nervously on the carpeted floor, the anxiety associated with flying settling in my stomach. "I think I'm going to ask them if they can swap me to a window if it's not too much trouble."

"Why don't you take my seat? I love the aisle."

"Are you sure? It's a long flight."

"I'm positive. It gives me more leg room. You forget I'm taller than you. Besides, it looks like it's going to be a full flight. I doubt they have a ton of space to move us around."

"You're taller by, like, an inch."

"Or two. Occasionally three, when the weather is nice."

"Okay, you're delusional. Three inches? What is it with men not knowing how to measure things? Look, I'll concede the height difference today because I'm more worried about this flight. Flying is not my jam," I admit. "Every time I get on a plane, something traumatic happens. When I was younger, my dad told me my pet rabbit died while we were flying to visit my aunt in Texas. Another time, I found out I didn't get into my top college choice. And, most recently, I flew home from New York after getting my heart broken. Don't get me started on the turbulence. Just giving you a heads up if I start acting weird or fidgety."

"I'm assuming you didn't replace the rabbit?" Jack asks, taking a sip of his coffee. He ditched the lid, and steam rises to his face, kissing his pore-free skin.

"No. The only rabbit I'll ever have in my house now is the sex toy. It gets the job done. Quite well, actually."

He chokes, covering his mouth with his hand, and blushing as his eyes dart to my suitcase. I've flustered him, and it makes me grin. He probably won't survive if I tell him it's in my bag right now.

"Right. Noted," he sputters, voice strained. "You've successfully completed college, correct?"

"Obviously, given it's been six years since I got my master's degree and I'm still paying my student loans. Was it worth it? Can't say for sure."

"I didn't know you have a master's degree."

"There's a lot you don't know about me," I counter. I adjust the falling strap of my tote, pulling it back up my shoulder.

"And no boyfriend, correct? No chance of your heart getting broken. Ergo, this flight shouldn't be too bad."

"Ergo? Are you performing in a Shakespearian play? I didn't know you were logical, Lancaster."

"There's a lot you don't know about *me*," he replies, taking another sip of his drink, not a flicker of disgust on his face from the bitter beverage. "I wasn't aware social media is an avenue someone could pursue a master's degree in. It sounds more like an undergrad program. Not higher-level education. Kind of easy."

I narrow my eyes, that familiar feeling of *not good enough* stirring, threatening to rear its head.

"I got my master's in Global Strategic Communications while also focusing on public relations. Believe it or not, I don't spend all my time scrolling through social media."

A loud tapping coming from the speakers above us interrupts my diatribe. Having to defend my occupation and career path isn't anything new. When I started school, I wasn't sure what route I wanted to take. While my brain isn't in tune with the analytical thinking that surrounds professions relating to math and science, I do have a creative-focused mind. I like looking at a blank canvas, imagining what I could create with the proper resources. After my first Intro to Marketing class, I was hooked. I haven't looked back.

"Folks, we're ready to board our flight to Key West. We're going to start with our first-class cabin."

Taking a deep breath, I roll my suitcase and apprehensively approaching the podium.

"Good morning, Ms. Bowen," the ticket agent says, scanning my boarding pass. "Heading on vacation? Honeymoon?" she asks, her attention traveling from me to Jack.

"Neither, actually. Work."

"Not a terrible place to be stuck for work," she jokes.

Her gaze lingers on Jack a moment too long, eyes roaming

down his body, and I experience the oddest sensation in my chest.

It's unexplainably tight, a burning heat flaring between my breasts as my fingers twitch around the handle of my suitcase in irritation. The moment passes as quickly as it began, and I shake my head as I pull my bag down the jet bridge.

The flight attendant at the boarding door gives me a kind smile as I step onto the aircraft.

"Good morning," she says.

"Hi," I reply, smiling back and pushing my suitcase down the aisle, stopping in the third row, two large leather seats positioned next to each other.

"I'll get your bag," Jack says from behind me, his voice dangerously close to my ear.

"Thanks."

I slide into our row, out of the way. He places his cup of coffee on the small, shared space between the armrests. Lifting my suitcase—with one hand, mind you—he hoists it into the overhead bin with ease. He grabs his suitcase next, repeating the movement, not an ounce of strain on his face. The hem of his shirt rises as he lifts the bags, and I see that trail of golden blonde hair on his stomach leading below the waistband of his pants.

Looking away, I distract myself with the window shade and another sip of tea so I don't ogle him like some debauched idiot. My tongue deserves to be burned for the thoughts that keep popping into my head.

"You can do whatever you'd like with the window shade," he says, plopping into the seat next to me.

"I'm going to leave it up for now." The morning sunlight beams through the plexiglass, warming my skin despite the chilly air on the other side. Our first snow will come any day now, and never have I been more grateful for an escape to paradise.

My phone dings and I pick it up, seeing a message from Abby.

AJ: Have a safe flight! Please don't kill Jack!

JB: I am not a murderous woman!

AJ: Give him a chance!

JB: I'm giving him a chance!
JB: He bought me tea.
JB: And knew how I like it.

AJ: I feel so sorry for you.
AJ: Your poor, tough life.

JB: It's going to be real awkward when we get into an argument.
JB: He probably likes peanuts over almonds or something insane like that.
JB: Maybe the flight will be turbulent and we'll have to ~hold hands~
JB: How's that for a romance novel?

AJ: I've never wanted anything more! ;)

JB: I'm kidding. Don't manifest it.

FOURTEEN
JACK

Josephine giggles at her phone screen, and I shoot her an inquisitive glance.

"Everything okay?"

"Abby thinks she's funny."

"Let me guess. Something about us?"

"How did you know?"

"There's a bet going around the office about how long it will take us to get into an argument."

"How have I not heard about this?!"

"Because I can't have you sabotaging me to win so I decided to keep it to myself. I saw a paper in the kitchen. Half the office is participating."

"There's an actual paper? What are we, MMA fighters people in Vegas are betting on?"

"Carla thinks the first attack will happen shortly before takeoff. Tyler seems to have the most faith in us. His guess is that a Coke will somehow end up in my lap during the drink service. Accidentally, of course," I add.

She grins, and I can't help but smile softly too. Her happiness is infectious.

"He knows me too well. I'm a little offended, however, he thinks I would stoop so low as to ruin your clothes."

"Maybe I'll wait until you fall asleep to draw a mustache on your face."

"Okay, Ross Geller. We could get through the entire flight without arguing. That'll really show them."

"I don't know what they expect us to disagree on. We're going to be 30,000 feet in the air in a metal tube. There's not a lot of room for hostility."

"Room? No. Potential? Yes. Come on, it's us! We could compete in the Olympics with our sarcastic remarks. You insulted my degree in the boarding area ten minutes ago. What did you say? That it was easy? Technically, we've already lost."

I wince, hoping she had forgotten the transgression. "I'm sorry. I don't know many people who have their master's degree and pursued social media work. It's unconventional, but I didn't intend for it to be offensive."

"It's not social media work. It's marketing and advertising. Yeah, there's a component involved with apps and stuff, but that's not what I spend most of my time on. It's a different avenue than other people might go. I still work very hard."

"I know you do."

"How would our coworkers know if a fight happens?"

"Tyler informed me I must submit photographic evidence after we land to prove that no sodas were tossed or food was thrown."

"I wasn't thinking about throwing any food your way, but now I kind of want to. We can livestream the whole thing!"

"Behave, Josephine," I say. "Are you planning to work during the flight?"

"Work? Are you kidding? We're on a paid trip to the Florida Keys! My out of office email is on until Monday. It would do you some good to live a little, Lancaster. Life can go on without a computer in your hand constantly."

"All right, Bowen. You win." I tuck my laptop away, back in my duffle bag, swapping it for a book.

"Yes! Welcome to the side of relaxation! It's great!"

"I'm not sure I've relaxed since 2016."

"I never would have guessed. You're the epitome of chill."

"Your sarcasm is unappreciated."

"Is there a prize with this bet?"

"Yes, unfortunately. $300. The office pooled their money together. Seems drastic, if you ask me."

"$300?!" she squeaks. "I'm not sure if I'm honored or affronted by them betting real money on us. Don't they have anything better to do?"

"One would think they have a business to run, but apparently that's not the case."

A voice comes over the PA system, letting us know the boarding door is closed, and the flight attendants will now show a safety video.

"Let me know if you need anything," I say quietly, opening my book. The pages might be in front of me, but I can't focus on the words, too busy watching Josephine out of the corner of my eye. She's clearly nervous. The engines rev up loudly, vibrating beneath us. She holds both armrests tightly, her knuckles practically turning white.

"Hey." I pull out one of her earphones so she can hear me speak, interrupting her television show. "Squeeze my arm if you need to."

We're already off the ground, the concrete tarmac disappearing from view behind us. The takeoff is smooth—a steady climb into the clouds as we pass over the buildings below.

"I think I'm okay for right now," she exhales.

"You know where I'll be if that changes."

Darlene, the lead flight attendant, serves us a meal halfway through the flight. We both decide on the meatball sub, which, on an airplane, is an absolute mess. Whoever decided it as a meal option has never had to fly next to Josephine.

She has sauce all over her fingers and there aren't enough napkins in the world to save her from the disaster she's created. A small army of tomato-stained papers has taken over the armrests, nudging my elbow out of the way.

Again. Endearing.

"Did you eat *any* of your sandwich? Or is it all over your hands?" I ask, popping a bite of chocolate chip cookie into my mouth.

"Hilarious," she draws out, wiping away the final stain of red. If someone were to pass by, they'd think we've committed a murder and done an abysmal job of cleaning up the crime scene. "I didn't know you ate sweets. You don't look like you'd indulge in cookies."

"What do I look like I indulge in?"

"A single stick of celery. Maybe a tepid cup of water that you swish around in your mouth, then spit out."

I snort.

She makes me want to laugh way too easily.

Maybe that's why I'm not surprised by how quickly our flight passes, conversation gently flowing for the next couple of hours. She pauses her show and I slide my bookmark into place, stopping my reading and turning to face her as we discuss a wide range of topics. Our knees knock together a handful of times, and I notice that after each one, we're slower and slower to move out of each other's bubble.

Josephine told me her favorite movies—*Titanic* and *Love Actually*.

I've shared my favorite cookie flavor—snickerdoodle, but chocolate chip is sufficient enough to fight off the cravings. I think she's still suspicious that I'm lying to her about eating sweets.

"What's the best kind of cereal?" she asks, leaning against the side of the plane, legs pulled up to her chest, chin resting on her knees. Her hair, which started our journey in a bun, flows down her shoulders, hanging halfway down her arms. "Cereal hierarchy time!"

"Do you ask these invasive questions to everyone, or am I the only one lucky enough to be badgered with the randomness of your brain and forced to rank food?"

"I do. I enjoy learning about others! That includes you, too, shockingly."

My chest puffs up at the implication, and I sit straighter in my seat.

"Cinnamon Toast Crunch."

"What?" she exclaims, feet dropping to the floor as she shifts closer. "You're not serious."

"Are you telling me there's something better than my answer?"

"Obviously. Frosted Flakes are the superior choice."

I tut, shaking my head. "You're a smart girl, Josephine. Frosted Flakes have zero flavor."

"That's not true at all! The way they cr—"

She doesn't have time to finish her sentence as the plane jolts, falling from the sky as we enter extremely turbulent air.

Her shoulder nudges into mine, a rough bump, and she lets out a startled yelp. Terror flashes across her eyes before they squeeze shut, her left hand reaching out and unintentionally gripping my forearm while her right holds onto the opposite armrest for dear life.

The aircraft rumbles, shaking the interior of the cabin for several seconds before a crackled voice comes over the intercom. "Uh, hey, folks, this is your captain. Sorry about that, but, uh, we're going through some rough air as you can see. Uhhh, we'll be landing in about thirty minutes, and I expect it to be bumpy for our descent, so, uh, I'm going to ask the flight attendants to clean up the cabin and get ready for arrival so they can sit for their safety. We'll see you on the ground shortly."

"Fuck," she whimpers, head thumping against the back of the seat. She's tense and rigid with fear, shoulders quaking and chest rising and falling rapidly.

"Hey," I whisper, trying to get her attention and distract her from what's causing her panic. Her eyes remain closed, and she's muttering to herself. "Look at me, Josephine."

Slowly, she obeys, turning her head to meet my gaze, and *fuck* if that look and her listening skills don't go straight to my cock. Her eyes are wide, unblinking as she stares at me and bites her bottom lip, teeth dragging across the skin. Her legs part slightly, not even a centimeter, but I notice the shift.

I remove her digging, bruising fingers from my forearm, carefully prying them away.

Her apology is forming, panic and guilt written across her face. I wordlessly slip her hand into mine, palm against palm, cradling her damp hand to my chest.

Holy shit.

A key going into a lock. It's a perfect fit.

Static surges where we're joined, and she lets out a gasp. That damn sound.

Okay.

Okay, this is fine.

Don't freak out.

She's freaking out, and the last thing I need to do is act like a moron.

But...

Touching her like this gives my lungs the oxygen they've so hopelessly been seeking.

I feel awake; like I've risen from a long slumber.

Perfectly. Fucking. Normal.

I'm struggling to think straight.

When I finally have the courage to speak as the airplane stops rattling, my voice is off-kilter. It's not from the bumps.

"I've got you," I say, attempting to convey calmness when really I sound like a croaking frog. "It's okay. I think we're past the worst of it. Can you take a deep breath for me?"

She nods, inhaling deeply, the jitters that trembled her body a few moments ago steadily abating. "Yes."

"Good girl," I encourage her, the praise slipping out unintentionally. "Another."

She squirms in her seat, wiggling her ass against the leather while her fingers curl tightly around mine. A faint splash of color crawls up her neck and her breathing hitches. She listens again and this time something dark and needy exists behind the green windows peering back at me.

That reaction is like kerosene, burning me alive, flames and heat engulfing my every fiber and nerve.

I can't fester on that pull deep in the trenches of my stomach, shifting to my lower spine. The intimate way I want to push her hair out of her face, slide my hand up her leg, and distract her in a way I *know* she'd enjoy. A pulsing desire to learn what else she likes flutters through me, and I have to shove the thoughts away because now she's speaking and upset, and I refuse to be horny on a damn airplane.

"I-I'm so sorry. I didn't mean to make a scene or manhandle you," she stutters, embarrassment soaking her words.

"Shh," I coax her, my thumb absentmindedly stroking her lifelines, up and down, end to end as she relaxes, panic disintegrating. "You didn't. It startled everyone. Is it okay that I'm touching you?"

Consent is important to me, even more so after what she experienced the other night. I know she's hugged me, but I'll never assume it's okay to just touch her without asking.

"Yes," she rasps out.

Using my free hand, I tilt the air conditioning vents toward her. She sighs in relief.

"I don't think the captain liked your answer to the cereal question," I murmur. Up and down. Back and forth. Over her smooth, callous-free palm, finding a pattern she likes.

"I hate you," she replies with no malice.

"I don't think that's true."

"No," she pauses, turning to look at me, sincerity behind the lone word. "I don't think so either."

Giving her a reassuring squeeze, I gesture out the window. "Look. We're about to touch down."

As soon as the wheels are on the ground, she unravels her hand from mine, breaking our connection. It had to end sometime. It's not like we could walk into the conference holding hands like giddy idiots, but I'm uncharacteristically reluctant to part from her.

After a short taxi to the gate, we're piling off the airplane. I grab Josephine's suitcase without thinking, and we walk toward the signs for baggage claim. She's been silent since we landed, and I'm afraid I did something wrong. Overstepped some boundary lines.

She always speaks her mind, though, so if she were truly upset with me, I think she'd give me an earful.

"What's going on in that head of yours?" I ask cautiously as we exit the air-conditioned building, greeted with a blast of heat that feels unnatural this late in the year. I can't believe people *enjoy* living in this climate.

"Huh? Oh. Nothing," she says, putting on a pair of sunglasses.

"You sure?"

"Yeah. I'm being contemplative."

"Are you excited?"

"Hm. Excited is one of the many adjectives I'm feeling right now."

I frown, not understanding her passiveness. "Are you all right?"

"I will be." The smile she plasters on her face is fake and forced. "Can we drop it?"

"Sure," I sigh. "Of course."

FIFTEEN
JO

We climb into the van, sitting far apart from each other.

Jack is frowning at his phone, attention diverted. It gives me time to think about *him*, and not the nightmare waiting for me at the conference.

There's a dull ache stretching through my ribs, and my fingers are tingly, missing the closeness we shared on the plane. I never expected to crave his proximity, but when he took my hand without hesitation or disgust and held it in his, an electric current ripped through me with a white-hot intensity. And when his fingers traced lightly over my palm in the same pattern, a pendulum swinging across my skin, my eyes almost rolled to the back of my head.

He wasn't trying to turn me on; I know that. His touch was driving me wild and felt *right*, leaving me starry-eyed and bewildered like a schoolgirl with a playground crush.

It was the same when I embraced him on the couch the other night, our limbs entangled, wondering what it would be like if I wrapped my legs around his waist and never left. My body hummed in approval, welcoming him with open arms. I let go of his hand when we landed out of fear I would do or say something detrimental to this friendly game we're playing. And out of fear of the small, bubbling attraction that's growing toward Jack.

We'll table that for a later discussion.

The drive from the airport is short, and soon we're pulling up to a large entryway. The valet unloads our bags onto the stone driveway and we're escorted into a massive lobby.

Chandeliers hang from vaulted ceilings that belong in a cathedral. Crystals shine in the sunlight, small rainbows flashing across the marble floor so clean, I can see my awed reflection staring back at me. Floor-to-ceiling windows flank the sides of the lobby, and I've never seen something so opulent and swanky in my life.

"Holy crap," I breathe out, my head pivoting around, trying to observe every inch of the resplendent space. "I know people shit on Florida and want to cut it off from the rest of the states, but I'm sure glad they haven't. This is beautiful."

"Only a step above a Holiday Inn, I'd say," Jack says.

We walk toward the seashell-shaped concierge desk next to a large sign that says TDS on it in bold letters. I notice a familiar figure standing in the queue, laughing with a short woman. My blood chills. I know that body intimately.

"Stop," I hiss, throwing my arm out to prevent Jack from walking any further. Yanking him behind a large column by the hem of his shirt, our shoulders press together so we're standing side by side, suitcases rolling to a stop in front of us.

"What is going on? Is there a reason we're camped out behind a pillar? I didn't want anyone to see us together either bu—"

"Will you shut up?!" I ask, forcibly elbowing his side.

The urgency and painful elbow get him to be quiet.

He cocks his head to the side, questioning my theatrical antics and waiting for me to reveal why I'm acting absurd.

Sighing disconsolately, I pinch the bridge of my nose, admitting defeat.

"You might recall the night we were at the bar. You know, when you overheard me and Abby..."

"Discussing my sex life? I remember it vividly."

"That's the guy Abby mentioned."

"Your ex?" he asks dubiously, eyebrows mingling with the rogue bronze lock of hair that's fallen out of place and into his face thanks to my accosting and manhandling. "You can't be serious."

"Trust me, I wish I wasn't."

"This is the one you wanted to make jealous?"

"Jealous isn't the right word. No part of me misses him. I don't get it. I had his dick in my mouth, then he ghosted me after two years of being together. Who does that shit? A spineless asshole, that's who. He could've at least sent me a text message after all the pain he put me through. Or a carrier pigeon. He told me he *loved* me, and then went radio silent. And people wonder why women believe true love and romance are dead."

"I cannot, for the life of me, fathom how you ended up with a guy like that."

"What is that supposed to mean?" I seethe, crossing my arms over my chest defiantly.

"Don't worry about it."

"No, go on. You said you didn't want to be seen walking in together, so why not keep the insults coming? Do you think I'm hideous? Can you do better than me? Why would someone like *him* ever waste time on someone like *me*?"

Okay, that might have gone a little too far, because his face shifts and he looks revolted.

Jack turns to me and I press my back firmly against the marble column. His hands bracket my head, landing on either side of my cheeks, and I swallow thickly, trying to rid the pressure building in my throat.

His sneakers touch the tips of my sandals. He has flecks of green in his eyes, making them appear almost teal. I never noticed before, but the sunlight streaming through the window makes the new discovery now impossible to miss.

"Never in my tenure at Itrix have I ever spoken about your looks. Since you're basically pleading with me to share, I will."

"*Pleading?* You would know if I was pleading for something," I fire back, charged and electric, the closeness from the plane returning.

"Fucking hell," he curses, chin dropping to his shirt and breaking our eye contact. "When you talk like that, Josephine..."

"Tell me," I breathe out, egging him on, wondering if he felt what happened on the plane too.

"I can't."

"Why not?"

"It would ruin *everything*." He snags on the last word, taking a moment to collect his thoughts. "That guy is so clearly a four."

"You can tell that by the back of his head?"

"Do you want me to be honest?"

"Yeah, I do."

"I can't give you a number that's high enough to convey how beautiful you are, okay?" Jack blurts out, voice raising. I'm glad we're tucked away so no one can hear him. "Ten doesn't seem sufficient. You're off the scale. And I know that sounds cheesy and stupid, but it's the goddamn truth."

"What?" I sputter, gaping at him.

"You can do so much better than a dude like that," he continues, ignoring the information he revealed and moving several feet away. "Especially one who can't text you after having a relationship. Wait. Is this why you wanted a fake boyfriend?"

"Yeah. I know it's stupid."

"I'm assuming you didn't find anyone."

"No, I didn't."

He peers out from behind the column, his brows furrowed. "He's gone."

I sigh in relief, happy to pass the first hurdle of the trip.

"Lovely. Want to get our rooms?"

The check-in process is swift. The front desk offers a printed itinerary of all the social events and presentation line-ups. After bidding Jack a terse and awkward goodbye, I take the elevator to my room, opening the door and grinning at the sight.

I leave my bag in the foyer after locking the door behind me and checking it twice, striding across the carpet and throwing the curtains open to stare at the breathtakingly beautiful beach below. The sand is rich and white, contrasting against the vivid blue water rushing onto the grains, playing a game of tag.

Palm trees rise from the ground, their lush green fronds billowing gracefully in the gentle breeze. Towels, umbrellas, and chairs dot the shoreline, a multitude of bright colors blending together. I turn the knob of the window, pushing it open. The temperature outside is comfortably warm, not a scorching hot. I relax immediately, stress melting away. Difficult coworkers and toxic ex-partners aside, how can anyone be upset here?

I haven't been to the beach in years. My family used to go every summer when I was growing up, the rickety station wagon packed to the brim with coolers, sandwiches, and drinks. Mom would boogie board in the ocean with me while Dad built sand-castles with my younger sisters on the shore. We applied sunscreen every half hour, leaving our skin shiny and oily. I smile at the thought, knowing my mom would have loved to see this view.

I want to relax under an umbrella right now and let the sun's rays hug me as I wiggle my toes in the sand. Exhaustion hits me, and I know a shower and nap are what my body needs after a long day of traveling. The ocean will be there later. We have plenty of time.

Twenty minutes later, I crawl into the comfortable king bed, sighing with happiness. My head sinks into the pillows and I yawn, closing my eyes, thankful for sleep.

My alarm goes off too quickly, and I'm disoriented when I silence the blaring sound. I groan, stretching my arms over my head. The kick-off happy hour starts at 6 p.m. tonight, with tapas and small plates available. It's designed to encourage attendees to mingle with other conference goers and the speakers.

Rifling through my suitcase, I decide on a pair of skinny jeans and a sleeveless top that's cute yet professional. I brush my hair, trying to tame the wild curls, and pull it half up, half down. I rarely wear makeup, often opting for a more natural look—also known as wanting to sleep 30 extra minutes every morning—but I put on some neutral lipstick and a light brush of mascara. Slipping on some white sneakers, I look at my reflection in the full-length mirror.

"You're a strong, independent woman who doesn't need a man. What he says will not phase you. You will be the bigger person. You're happy. Successful. You can do this, Bowen."

The quick pep-talk rejuvenates me. I take the elevator down to the lobby level, following the signs to the area of the hotel roped off for the event. There's a table covered in name tags and I locate mine, pulling the lanyard over my head. I survey the room quickly, not seeing Jack or Greg. Good. I have a moment to breathe before everything inevitably goes to shit.

SIXTEEN

JO

Greg and I officially met at a company event in New York City. We were at an establishment in Brooklyn, the entire room rented out for us. I had been at my job for a few weeks, taking the scary plunge to leave home and familiarity for a new city. Who could say no to New York?

While the people I worked with were nice, I didn't feel like I quite fit in. I was the odd man out. Cliques had been established. Friendships were already formed. When I arrived, no one blinked twice at my entrance, barely offering me a welcoming smile on my first day.

Then, along came Greg.

He smiled at me the night of the company event, our eyes meeting from across the room. I turned around, pathetically looking over my shoulder to find who he was looking for, certain it wasn't *me*. I had seen him in the office a handful of times. He never gave me a second glance when he passed my desk, often with a friend or woman, laughing over some inside joke I wasn't privy to. I was practically invisible.

He grinned as he took in my confusion, slinking toward me with an air of arrogance and swagger that demanded attention. I was drawn to him in some weird way. He was different; mysterious, sexy, and hard to look away from.

A bad boy aura surrounded him. He was the guy your parents warned you about and would bring you home hours after curfew, not taking any responsibility. If only I had listened to my gut when it screamed in protest at that coy, assuming smile. I wasn't the only one who fell victim to his glamour; he didn't just fool me. He fooled our colleagues, too. He probably still does, regarded as the nice and funny guy and not the violent asshole I know him to be.

"Josephine, right?" he asked casually, leaning against the wall next to me, a half-drunk beer bottle in his hand. I had spent much of the night by myself, awkwardly smiling at a handful of people as they passed by and receiving the silent treatment in return. It shocked me he even knew who I was, and it gave me butterflies.

"You can call me Jo," I said quickly, smiling nervously at him.

"Well, Jo, I'm Greg. It's nice to meet you." He was taller than me, well over six feet, and I remember feeling so timid and small, dwarfed by his size and dominating personality.

He introduced me to everyone for the rest of the night, moving an inch closer with each greeting. It's amazing how much my colleagues warmed up to me with *him* by my side. They suddenly saw me, looped around the arm of everyone's favorite coworker. At the end of the event, his large palm gripped my shoulder, and I couldn't stop laughing at the stupid jokes he told. His dark eyes were mesmerizing pools of unknown, evil darkness.

Greg invited me back to his place that first night with a casual invitation for drinks. I politely declined, telling him I didn't want to get involved with someone from work and knowing *drinks* would turn into *sex* and *a thing*. He smiled at the response, saying he admired my dedication to my job, and I must be an outstanding employee. It was easy to tell he would be the guy I'd cast my morals aside for.

Three measly weeks was all it took to fall victim to his bravado, agreeing to join him for dinner one night after work. We went out for Mexican food and had a few margaritas, the flirting and touching intensifying throughout the night.

I sat in his lap on the cab ride home, his hand clenching my parted thigh tightly, mouth on my neck as he trailed down to my chest. It was thrilling, being touched like that, in the back of a car where the driver could see us. When he pulled me inside his apartment and kissed my lips for the first time, I thought I was in heaven.

I fell fast, which was so unlike me. I'm always cautious in relationships, fearful to surrender all of myself too early. In the beginning with Greg, everything was *perfect*. We never argued, and he constantly agreed with my ideas and suggestions for meals or date nights. I should have known it was a trap.

We ate lunch together in the break room, sharing jokes and subtle touches while we laughed over pizza and salad. He'd kiss away the mess on my face and I'd buy an extra bag of his favorite potato chips out of the vending machine to surprise him with an afternoon pick-me-up. He came to my apartment almost nightly, and I visited him the other times. We spent some evenings on the couch in sweatpants watching a movie, then went out for an extravagant dinner on 5th Ave a few nights later.

He left cute notes on my desk at work, dotted with hearts and smiley faces. I cooked dinner for him before giving up and ordering from the delicious Italian restaurant I knew he loved outside my building. We never defined the relationship officially, but it *seemed* serious. I never saw him with other women, and he left a toothbrush and changes of clothes at my apartment, tucked beside my sleep clothes in the dresser.

I was smitten. Greg was courteous. Kind. Funny. Well-liked. Outgoing and *fun*. Whenever I would FaceTime Abby, he'd pop on the screen, waving hello and promising to meet her soon. He seemed like a perfect match for my loud, often spirited personality. We exchanged *I love you's* fairly expeditiously, and it was my first time sharing the eight letters with a significant other and meaning it.

He introduced me to some of our female colleagues. I grew close with them, joining in wine nights and even starting a book club. I finally felt like I belonged. Like I had a home.

And then, after about a year and a half, something changed. Heaven looked like hell. Greg became critical of every facet of my life. He told me I was looking too skinny. Too fat. My skirt was too tight, and he called me a whore. My dresses were too frumpy, not sexy enough, and he called me plain.

He said I laughed too loudly. Too often. I was *too much*. Too difficult.

He constantly snapped that my job wasn't challenging, and I had no reason to be stressed out, since he had actual work to do as a sales director of a multi-million-dollar tech company. Our intimacy became... forced. Out of control. Unenjoyable and unstoppable. Bruises littered my skin in the same spots where his mouth used to roam. I wore turtlenecks and long-sleeves in the middle of summer, preferring the sweat that accumulated on my body over gossiping whispers about how I sustained my injuries.

At first, I brushed it off as him being overworked and tired. He wasn't abusing me and didn't mean it. He *loved* me. My sexual preferences in the bedroom gravitate toward the rougher end of the spectrum. So wasn't he delivering what I wanted? We all make mistakes, and I thought the marks and lashing anger were two of his.

The visits to my apartment became less frequent and he

insisted on hooking up in the break room or supply closet after everyone had left the office for the night instead of the bedrooms we used to share.

The notes ceased, and my texts went unanswered for days at a time. I was feebly trying to cling to whatever scraps we had left, grasping for any shred of our previous life. I should have seen the warning signs, but what I interpreted as infatuation and love clouded my vision, sullying me from the reality happening right in front of my face.

Eventually, Greg told me he needed time to think. He asked for space, so I gave it to him. After two weeks of being ignored in and out of the office by him and my so-called friends, I learned he called me a ladder-climbing whore who would sleep with anyone to get ahead. I applied for the job at Itrix that day, packed my bags, and left the city and its ghosts far behind, never looking back, lasting a measly two and a half years before escaping.

I didn't hear a peep from him after; not that I expected to. I wanted to be furious and angry at him. And I was. But I was more disappointed in myself. I had never been the type of woman who let a man dictate her life, and on the plane ride back home, amongst the tears and a mountain of tissues handed to me by a sweet flight attendant, I vowed to never let a man consume me so wholly again. If I could ever love someone in the future, I'd never give *all* of myself to them. No one deserves that prize. Not when they can so easily turn it around and throw it in my face, laughing on the way out.

When I got home, I realized I needed to talk to someone as an outlet for my grief and pain. To share my hurt so I could let go and try to find my way back to the light. Therapy changed my life and helped me climb out of the pit of despair I snuck into. Talking with a professional has helped me learn and accept that what I endured wasn't my fault.

I did nothing wrong. I was merely the outlet of hate and evil for a cruel, sick person. When I started casually dating again, intimacy was a struggle at first, but in the years that have passed and after several dozen sessions (that I still attend), I've learned to trust men again, accepting not everyone is like Greg. Not everyone is hellbent on ruining my life. There are good people out there, and sometimes it takes sifting through the monsters to find them.

I think the thing that infuriates me the most is that he *won*. He was the one who fucked up, yet I was the one who paid for it, physically and emotionally; the aftermath effects still lingering around even now. Every ounce of me is glad I got out of that toxic, dark place. While I'm not looking forward to seeing him over the next few days, a small part of me is enthralled with showing him how confident and happy I've become.

Ladder-climbing whore, my ass.

This happy hour event is far from fancy. Most people have dressed casually, moving throughout the room instead of sitting, a buzz of energy surrounding me—voices and laughter, introductions of new acquaintances, and greeting of old friends.

I snag a cocktail table off to the side, sipping on an ice water and plopping into a chair. My eyes look around the room, observing the fellow attendees. It's stifling in here, like the air condition isn't working and humidity has infiltrated the overcrowded space. For the first time in my life, I wish Jack was beside me. He's familiar. He wouldn't make me feel alone.

I love people. Just not *this* many people. It's sensory overload. I inhale deeply, breathing in through my nose and out through my mouth, steadying myself.

"Jo?" The voice comes from behind me, sounding like sharp nails on a chalkboard. I recognize it immediately. My body reacts exactly how it did at the end of our time together.

Everything tenses. I flinch. My ears ring and my hands tremble.

Him.

Carefully, I set my cup down, snapping out of the full-body

curse, and turn to confront the demon disguised as my ex. There's Greg, wearing a perplexed look.

"What are you doing here?"

"Greg, it's nice to see you," I say cordially, standing and smoothing out my jeans. A smile, as fake as it is, finds its way to my lips as I look up at him. "I'm attending the conference, obviously."

"How? Why? You aren't here for me, are you?"

His egotistical side wastes no time hiding, choosing to show itself instantly. Memories of other selfish encounters we've had flicker through my mind at rapid speed. Him grinding against me, coming on my leg before getting up to shower, forgetting I'm even there.

Never asking me if I wanted anything to drink when he grabbed a beverage for himself.

Cooking dinner only *he* enjoyed and telling me I can figure out how to eat on my own as he smirked.

Not offering me an extra blanket when I was shivering, freezing from the window to his apartment being left open in the middle of December while I tried to sleep.

Good grief. Why the hell did I stick around so long?

"Don't flatter yourself," I laugh lightly, tossing my hair over my shoulder. "My company got two invitations, and they selected me."

"Your job doesn't deal with technology. Why in the world would you get invited? Speaking of, who do you work for these days? I haven't kept track. You could have been dead for all I know."

"I'm aware." I return to my seat and turn my back to him. It won't end our conversation, but it gives me a fleeting reprieve from his attack.

"Huh." Greg takes the chair opposite me without asking, relaxing back against the wicker. "What a small world. It's been, what, over two years?" The starchy fabric of his khaki pants skims my jeans, and I tuck my feet under the footrest of my chair.

"Hm. Maybe. Haven't kept track." I shrug nonchalantly, volleying his words back to him.

"Come on. You can't forget me that easily," he laughs, leaning forward, infiltrating my personal space. The top of his shirt is open at the collar, and I want to stab his neck with the fork that's near my hand. "Best you've ever had, right? Wonder if that's still true? We always had a lot of fun. Nothing you wouldn't try," he purrs, his palm reaching out to cup my cheek.

I yank out of his grasp, delighting as his hand falls to the table and he winces. "I would like to keep this a professional discussion," I say, my voice shaking. All the confidence I had walking into this room evaporates, particles of cowardly dust left in its wake. "That kind of question is off limits."

"Seeing anyone?" he asks instead, taking a sip of his beer. The trace of a mocking smile sits on his face. "I kind of miss having you pinned under me. We could sneak upstairs."

"I am dating someone," I blurt out. "He's amazing."

"Oh, really? Who?"

He raises an eyebrow, and for a moment I don't think he's bought my lie. He *has* to believe me, otherwise I foresee these next few days being filled with countless questions, attempts to corner me and attack my character.

I freeze, no name coming to mind. My lips open and close repeatedly, desperate to speak but unable to communicate.

Speak, Jo. Any fucking name will do!

"That would be me," Jack says, appearing out of thin air, an angel emerging from the black cloud that surrounds me. I want to sob in relief. *I will never curse this man again.* His warm hand cups my cheek, palm flat against my skin as he gently tilts my head back, our eyes interlocking. "Finally. There you are, sweetheart. I was looking for you everywhere."

"Hi," I whisper, voice cracking.

Sweetheart.

I was looking for you.

His words feel real. So real. Tickling my heart, coiling around the muscle and squeezing tightly in a lover's embrace.

Jack smiles softly, eyes crinkling in the corner. The soothing blue darts to his hand and back to me, a silent question, and my head jerks to convey my approval.

"Sorry it took me so long. The line for the bathroom was out of control. I missed you."

"T-that's okay," I stammer. His palm drops from my cheek as his arm settles over the back of my chair. "I missed you too."

"No, shit! Jack Lancaster! It's nice to actually meet you, man!" Greg reaches over and slaps Jack's shoulder. "Your work is legendary. I can't believe you don't want to give a lecture while you're here."

Holy shit. Do they know each other? Are they *friends?* That's something Jack would have told me before we got to this moment, right? Suddenly, the lover's embrace is ripped away, replaced by betrayal and deceit.

"Public speaking isn't my forte," Jack replies, adjusting his position so our sides nearly collide. "And you are...?"

"Greg," he says, smiling brightly.

"Ah. Can't say I'm familiar with you."

Thank God.

The smugness from Greg's face wavers before another cool smile takes its place. "You two are together? That seems highly unlikely. I would have heard about that through the gossip mill. She's not nearly as hot as—"

"We've been dating for six months," Jack interjects, cutting Greg off mid-sentence.

"Best six months of my life," I respond, leaning back half an inch, trying to bring myself closer to him. The movement makes me feel safer already, like I can nestle myself into his arms, protected from the world and the man in front of me.

"How do you two even know each other? Jack, my man, everyone knows who you are. You're a tech industry god and software development genius. I'm not sure how someone with your caliber of intelligence and work ethic winds up with Jo."

The insult hurts, a slap across my face, and I have to look away. Jack flinches beside me. When he speaks, his tone is dripping with ice and malice, fragments of hate and disdain laced into his next words.

"Not that it's any of your business, but we're colleagues. Josephine is phenomenal at her job. I have the utmost faith and confidence in her professional abilities, and also who she is as a person."

"You think she's amazing at what she does? Dude, she sits on social media all day. Pretty sure my ten-year-old niece can do that shit."

The remnants of Jack's smile fade and his jaw clenches. That thing could cut glass.

"She's helped our sales increase by over 25% in the last few months, thanks to social media traffic. She also designed a new website from scratch that has been extremely successful. I looked at feedback myself, and it's been positive from clients. Just the other day, she secured an advertising partnership with a multi-billion-dollar investor. We're lucky to have her, and I'm lucky to be by her side. There's a reason our company is rising to the top 20 in the country, and yours hasn't cracked the top 100. I doubt it ever will, if they're employing people like you."

Fucking hell.

Did he really say that?

How the heck does he know where Greg works?

Am I about to watch a fight go down like in *West Side Story*? That would be hot.

"Thank you," I mumble, low enough so only Jack can hear. His fingers press into my shoulders gently, tapping twice. My skin flames, scorched by the mark of his touch.

"Hmm." Greg looks down at his phone, temporarily uninterested. "I'm going to meet my girlfriend. Jack, it was nice to meet you, man. Jo, you've looked better. See you later."

Jack moves in front of me, blocking the rest of the room from view. "I despise him," he says, looking furious. His brows are pinched and his mouth curls down. "Absolutely despise him. Why didn't you tell me how horrible he is, Josephine? Are you fucking kidding me? A four was beyond generous. He's the scum of the earth."

"That makes two of us, man," I joke, not wanting to elaborate or answer his question. How would he react to the stories from my past? "Should we play a drinking game? Every time he calls you dude, we take a shot?"

"We'll be drunk within the half hour, and that'll make me want to pulverize him. I don't want to get arrested; Florida's laws are too erratic for me to go to jail. And I'll have to say things like *y'all*."

I hold back a giggle. "I'd love to hear you say y'all regularly. Thank you for jumping in. I-I pathetically froze when he asked who I was dating. I can probably avoid him the rest of the time we're here. You don't have to actually pretend to be my boyfriend."

"I don't mind faking a relationship with you for a few days, Josephine. Especially when it's around someone who hasn't been kind to you. How difficult can it be? It means nothing, and when we get home, it's over. No big deal." There's something dark behind his eyes, and I shiver, nodding in agreement before I can think twice.

"Okay," I whisper. "I'm not sure how we should go about this."

"I'm clueless, as you probably assumed."

"We probably shouldn't talk about pretending to date in a room with someone who now thinks we're together. That seems dumb. Do you want to meet up and figure it out?" The thought of spending time with Jack *not* in a conference room or hotel van sends a jolt up my back.

"Sure. Where?"

"My room?" I flinch at the implication before amending my suggestion. "Anywhere? The beach? The pool? A golf cart that half the state probably uses to drive around?"

"You'd get on a golf cart but have issues with my car?"

"A golf cart tops out at, like, 20 miles per hour!"

"There's not even a door to protect you."

"There's a windshield!"

"With fake glass. We're getting distracted. Your room sounds good. I need to say hello to some people first. Would you like to join me?"

"That's okay. I think I've had enough socialization for one night."

"What room are you in?"

"1246. Up in the second tower."

"Give me 30 minutes and I'll meet you there."

EIGHTEEN
JO

Okay. This is normal.

Perfectly freaking normal.

My former-nemesis-turned-fake-boyfriend slash guy-who-saved-my-life is coming upstairs to talk with me about how we're going to sell this definitely fake, absolutely not real partnership between us to my toxic ex, who's spending the next few days in the same hotel as us.

Wow. I need a flowchart to keep up.

This is going to blow up in our faces epically, isn't it? How can it not?

I pace the floor in my hotel room, unable to sit still. My skin is warm, my muscles are tight, and I'm restless. I hate lying. I'm not *good* at lying; especially when the two of us are going to be under scrutiny from the person I despise most in the world, searching for any slip-up or mistake to call us out and declare himself a victor.

It's hard not to dwell on the comments from Greg. I thought I would handle the interaction better. Jack was nice to jump in, but he shouldn't have had to. It's been years since my last interaction with Greg; why does he still have such a hold on me?

I know I'm not weak. Therapy has taught me that. Deep discussions and positive affirmations aside, I have it embedded in my brain that I'm too much to handle while simultaneously not being good enough.

I'm not sure how this idea is going to work. I know exactly zero things about Jack Lancaster, besides where he works, and how he takes his coffee. Oh, and that when he scowls and his lip turns down to the left, he's irritated. And when it tilts to the right, he's refraining from sharing exactly what's on his mind. He likes to ruffle his hair when he's particularly frustrated about something, and rubs his jaw when he's thinking deeply, contemplating his next move.

Okay, maybe I know more than I think I do. Talk about a fairytale love story. They'll write books about us, I'm sure.

A knock on my door interrupts my woeful lamentations. The familiar mop of bronze hair greets me through the peephole.

"I'm beginning to think you simply enjoy sauntering around in business attire while the rest of us wear casual clothes," I remark, opening the door and leaning against the frame. Jack is still in his dress shirt, tie, and fitted pants. His eyes flick down to my bare legs, then back to my face, barely lingering for a millisecond. I ditched my jeans for shorts when I came back to my room, and now I feel underdressed and overexposed.

"You saw what I wore on the airplane. And to the bar."

"Besides that. I envision you walking around in a tie while you fix yourself breakfast."

"You've also seen what I wear in the house. Did I have a tie on while flipping your pancakes? My ten-year-old Levis are hardly business casual."

"Ten-year-old Levis. Ten-year-old car. I'm sensing a trend here. Come on in, *babe*," I say, emphasizing the term of endearment as I push the door open with my hip and walk inside.

"Your room is bigger than mine," he observes from the small entryway. "And I can already tell your view is better. You get the waves, and I get the screaming children."

"You probably pissed off the hotel gods. They cursed me with turbulent air. You're cursed with crying babies, splashing infants, and their floaties."

The mattress bounces as I plop onto the bed, scooting against the pillows. Jack takes the chair at the desk, sitting rigidly.

"I'm not going to waterboard you. You could try relaxing."

"The good news is we won't be around each other during the day too much," he says, bypassing my statement and pulling out a folded piece of paper from his pocket. He sets it on the desk. "I printed off a list of the lecturers for you."

"Thank you." I reach for the social itinerary on the bedside table, looking at the scheduled events. "Let's see. There's a happy hour tomorrow night, a dinner on Friday, and the formal reception and farewell dinner on Saturday night. Wow, they really want us to talk to each other, don't they?"

"If I had known conferences were this social, I would've stayed home," he grumbles, loosening the tie at his collar, fingers expertly working on the knot. I'm captivated by the way he moves, knuckles grazing against the fabric and exposing more of his long neck. "There have also been rumblings of more enjoyable unofficial gatherings."

Blinking, I look away from the mole that sits on his left windpipe, a few centimeters below his ear. "I like unofficial gatherings!"

"That doesn't surprise me."

We sit in stilted silence, a cicada chirping outside the window finally filling the room with noise. "I guess we should talk about our relationship."

Huh. There's a word I never expected to use in context with *Jack*.

"Are you mad I said something?" he asks.

"Far from mad, actually. Surprised, maybe? Nervous, too."

"Good. I overheard what he was saying, and I couldn't stand idly by and let him speak to you like that. I hated every word. He treats you poorly, Josephine."

"You have no idea," I mumble, bringing my legs to my chest and wrapping my arms around them, my chin dropping to my knees in my favorite comforting position. "He has a tendency to mess with my brain."

"Is it too early to repeat that I really dislike him? If he somehow went missing tonight, I don't think anyone would be upset."

"Please don't make me an accomplice to murder."

Jack scoffs. "I would never."

"How did you know about his company's performance? And how Itrix is doing better than them?"

"You don't think I do research? I asked for his name after check-in, did a quick internet search, and found their website. Then I found a forum talking about how shitty their company has become in the last few years. It wasn't hard to put together."

"Wow. You're Nancy Drew! He knew who you were, and for a minute I thought you two might be... friends."

"Friends? Please. The people close to me are a higher caliber than the atrocity he appears to be. I created a stupid video a while back that went viral in our industry. It wasn't anything too special, but my name is attached to it. He must've done his research as well."

"Nancy Drew *and* a celebrity? I'm a lucky girl!"

"Hush. Back to our relationship and the reason we're meeting up. Is there anything important I should know about you that a non-fake partner would know? Any tattoos? Piercings? Surface-level things that aren't too nitty gritty?"

"Nitty gritty? Are you trying to romance me with sexy words?"

He scratches behind his ear, the tips rapidly pinking. "No. For once, I'm the one asking the questions."

"Do you feel powerful?"

"Strangely, yes."

"Don't get used to it. I have zero tattoos. Needles terrify me, but I want my nipples pierced. You already know about my mom. I have two sisters, Bethany and Amy."

"Who's the oldest?"

"That would be yours truly."

He's quiet for a moment before he gives me a small, reverent smile. "Ah. I get it now. Jo. Beth. Amy. *Little Women*. I love that. Was it intentional?"

"Yeah. It was my mom's favorite book. She used to read it to us when we were younger. We would all crawl into their bed late at night, well past bedtime. Before she..." I clear my throat and sit up, crossing my legs in front of me. "She said when she was pregnant, she could picture exactly what we would be like before we ever entered the world. She was spot on, of course."

I pause, the memories of the past flickering before me.

The picnics we would spontaneously go on, all of us in the car singing "I Want to Break Free" at the top of our lungs while my parents held hands in the front seat, exchanging sweet glances. The way Dad would embrace Mom in the living room, dancing close together with no music, the energy of love and hope coursing through the room despite her recent diagnosis. Some nights I would sit on the bottom step and watch them, mesmerized that even after all those years, they still made each other happy. They made love look easy.

The happy images fade away, replaced with sour memories

of my dad, his head in his hands in the sterile hospital room, tears staining his cheeks as he said goodbye to the love of his life. I was young when she passed but I still understood the finality of the event, and that his heart, and mine, were now broken, an irreplaceable hole stitched out in the middle.

Deep down, I think that's what has made me afraid of relationships; to know that you could love someone so powerfully, and it wouldn't be enough. They can—and will—leave you and this world behind at the drop of a hat. Nothing in life is guaranteed, and not even true love can save you.

"Are you all right?"

Jack's voice pulls me back to the present and I blink, my eyes readjusting to the dim hotel room lighting, wet with the onset of tears. He's leaning forward, elbows on his thighs and wearing a worried look.

"Sorry. Reminiscing." Dipping my head, I stealthily wipe my eyes, disguising my sniff as a cough.

If he senses my emotional turmoil, he doesn't let on, letting me calm down before continuing our conversation. "Tell me more about yourself."

"This sounds like an awkward first date."

That earns me a chuckle. "Trust me, I've had much worse."

"I think there's a compliment somewhere in there. Okay. Let's see. I like to read. I know you do, too."

"What's your favorite genre?"

"Romance, obviously. What about you?"

"Historical fiction, but I also like thrillers."

"This scheme of ours is the premise of, like, 72% of the books I devour."

"What makes up the other 28%? Do I need to download something to my Kindle to catch up?"

"I'm not sure you want to know the answer to that question. Your Kindle might explode."

"Now you have to tell me."

"Maybe when we hit the one-year mark," I joke. "I enjoy weather—hurricanes fascinate me. I eat something sweet every night before bed. Cookies are my favorite, but anything like cake, brownies, or ice cream is fine by me. I doubt you've ever had a piece of cake in your life. Or, if you have, your favorite is probably carrot cake or rhubarb pie."

"You're straight up slandering my character. Chocolate cake is my favorite, thank you very much. And I've eaten frosting out of the can in the middle of the night."

I arch an eyebrow. "You sure like to live dangerously, don't you?"

"You are such a smart-ass."

"You're just now realizing this? It's probably my best attribute."

Jack laughs, his head tilting back as his shoulders shake. "It's better than being a dumbass, I suppose."

"It's the little things."

"Favorite food?"

"Mashed potatoes, obviously. Don't forget our potato hierarchy. And I hate raisins in my trail mix. Can you share something now? It's like I'm talking to a wall."

He sighs heavily, clearly dreading divulging such personal information to me. "Fine. But fair warning, I'm a boring human being."

"That's not true. Your coffee choices are positively *wild*."

Jack's eyes narrow but I see a sparkle there, tangoing with the blue. The corner of his mouth tugs up as he scoots his chair an inch closer to the bed, knees knocking against the mattress. I try not to dwell on the way I hold my breath at his movements, wondering what the boundary is and where he plans to stop. Do I *want* him to stop? How close could he get before I shift away, wanting distance?

I'm not sure I do, to be honest. If he crawled on here, positioned himself right next to me, and laid his head on the pillow six inches away from my face, I wouldn't protest.

It'd probably make me smile.

Crap.

"My parents are still together. I have an older sister who has three kids and is an engineer. My younger brother is getting his master's in Latin and recently got engaged to his partner of six years."

"Middle child syndrome. Everything makes sense now!"

"Absolute freaking smart-ass," he growls.

That... that is an interesting sound.

And I don't hate it.

In fact, I think I'd like to hear *more.*

It's infinitely better than the antagonizing tone he normally takes with me. This one I feel at the pit of my stomach, working its way precariously down my thighs that I subtly try to squeeze together.

"I'm left-handed," Jack continues. "I played sports growing up. In fact, I went to college on a baseball scholarship and still play in a league for fun."

"Princeton, right? I think I've read that in your email signature once or twice."

"Sorry, but the men in this industry—well, every industry, I suppose—treat everything like a pissing contest. It's always a competition to see who can have the longest, most obnoxious email signature."

"Is 'email signature' code for dick length?" I ask, using air quotes and winking at him.

He chuckles lightly. "Unfortunately, you're not too far off."

"Any tattoos?"

"None. But I'm open to the idea. No piercings, either."

"Are you a dog or cat person?"

"Dogs."

"Favorite color? You're not allowed to say blue. Or black! Too cliché."

"So you want me to lie? We're starting off on the wrong foot, Josephine. I guess yellow? Or purple? Aquamarine?"

"All acceptable answers."

"And here I was, afraid of failing."

"It's kind of outrageous I've learned more about you in the last five minutes than I have over the course of the two years we've been colleagues. I had no clue you were left-handed."

"Going forward, ask me whatever you'd like. We should talk about touching boundaries. PDA. How much? How little? What do the romance books say?"

"It's what we're comfortable with. They aren't playbooks, you know. There aren't any CliffNotes out there that tell us what we can and can't do."

"Okay. Let's talk this through and make our own rules. Hand holding. Acceptable?"

"Yeah. As long as you're okay with it."

"I am. Light touches?"

This isn't a dirty, sensual conversation about what I like in bed or how I like to pleasure myself, yet the questions are making me start to fidget.

"Also okay."

Is my voice raspier than before?

"I'm comfortable with both as well. I do have a hard boundary."

"Sex?" I blurt out like a prepubescent teen playing the penis game in middle school.

Jack licks his lips and the room is twenty degrees warmer. "I was going to say kissing on the mouth is off the table. It was fun to hear you say sex, though."

"God, I would never ask you to! I can resist you for three

days, believe it or not. This has a very solid end date; the minute we get on the plane home, we can resume our regularly-scheduled programming and never touch each other again!"

"Tell me how you really feel, Josephine," he says, all the amusement and light and glimmer from a few moments ago disappearing. His brow furrows and he frowns.

Is he mad at *me* for being so agreeable to the no-kissing rule? He's the one who brought it up! It's a struggle to bite back a retort and not snap at him, so instead I change the topic.

"Can I ask you a personal question? I don't mean for it to sound offensive."

"I can't wait to hear this."

"Is there a reason you're so... the way you are?"

"Clarification, please."

"Grumpy. Sullen. Um, angry? Perhaps?"

He pauses before answering, taking his time when he speaks. "I need a drink before I share that story. We'll have to save it for another day."

"Fair enough. Can I ask you another question? Why would you ever agree to help me?"

"Why would I not?" he counters. "It's hardly any sweat off my back. Besides, I told you, I hate that guy. No man should ever let another man talk to a woman that way."

"Are you going to hold it against me? Demand I owe you a favor?"

"What kind of person do you think I am?" The crease between his eyebrows grows exponentially. "You don't owe me, or anyone else, anything. Ever."

"It's an exceedingly thoughtful thing to do with no reward. I'm curious."

"We're starting fresh, right? It'll also be nice not to have Wally, my best friend, constantly badgering me about my dating life. Or lack thereof. You'll meet him tomorrow. He can be intrusive and blunt sometimes. I know he wants the best for me. Having him think I'm happy…" Unspoken words hanging barely out of reach.

"Are you happy?" I ask.

"At this moment? Or in life?"

"Well, I'm sure you aren't too happy right now. I'm forcing you to sit here with me when you could be down with the friends you haven't seen in a few years."

"You aren't forcing me to do anything, Josephine."

Warmth spreads down my body.

The way he says my name.

Josephine.

It used to sound so callous and bitter, pricking my ears. Now it's like he's caressing my skin lovingly, teasing me with feather-light touches as his tone transforms into something savory. I'm suddenly painfully aware of the proximity of our bodies and the intimate nature of our positions. Him in the chair, legs spread open. Me against the pillows, my calf near his thigh. He could be on top of me in one quick lunge. I gulp.

"Thank you for helping me."

"To answer your previous question, it depends on the day. Some days I'm happier than others."

"What's the deciding factor?"

He looks at me, his eyes traveling from my hair to my bare legs. "You," he says simply.

"Me? You once told me that seeing me was abysmal."

"Ah. What does King George say in *Hamilton*? Oceans rise, empires fall?"

"You've seen *Hamilton*?!" I sputter.

"Indeed. Things change, you know. People, too. Sometimes the stubborn ones take a bit more time," he says, rising for the chair. "You've probably learned that I am extremely stubborn. Tuesday is my favorite day of the week. I'm sure you can figure out why. Some of the other attendees are meeting up at the bar, and I said I would stop by. Sorry to cut this short."

"Have fun!"

"Thanks." Jack heads for the door and opens it, pausing in the doorway. "I'm happy to be part of your scheme, Josephine. We're in this together."

He looks over his shoulder at me one more time before closing the door and leaving me to stare at the space he occupied for a long, long time.

NINETEEN
JACK

She's late to breakfast, and tardiness isn't a word in Josephine's repertoire. She's usually punctual, always the first one in our meetings, coffee delivery in hand, and the last to leave, staying to help clean up whatever mess our colleagues leave behind.

This morning, however, she's nowhere to be found.

I frown as I search the breakfast buffet in the ballroom one more time, unable to spot her red hair through the diminishing crowd. I'm not sure what the protocol is in this situation. Do I go to her room to make sure she's okay? Do I leave and pretend I don't notice her obvious absence?

Fuck, did something *happen* to her? Her shitty ex-boyfriend is running around this hotel too, and I swear to God if he as much lays a finger on her...

I rub my temples with my hand, sighing as I stare at the food.

Plate. I'll bring her a plate.

That's something a boyfriend would do, right?

I scoff, feeling severely out of practice of being a significant other. There have been a handful of dates over the past two and a half years. A night at a concert. Dinner at a fancy restaurant that had me counting down the minutes until our bill arrived. A Sunday afternoon movie. A lucky few made it past the first date before going awry after the second or third, a train on a collision course. There have even been a couple of physical flings. A mutual agreement to let out whatever sexual tension we were both experiencing in a safe and mature manner, parting ways in the morning and never speaking again.

The fault for the lack of companionship is mine, and mine alone. Nothing has stuck. No one has quite captured my attention like...

Her.

Ever since I walked into the office and saw her for the first time, no woman has compared. Not even close. It took a while for me to connect the dots, but after the other night, it now makes sense.

We aren't going down that road. I'd be stupid to lose sight of the blatantly obvious fact that *nothing* about this arrangement is real. It's fake. Very fake. A ruse to shove in the face of someone who's treated her poorly in the past and to make Josephine look happy and healthy.

That's it. Nothing more. Nothing less. Feelings and emotions and declarations are *not* in the cards for the next three days. Or ever, really. We'll play this game, then resume our existence as Jack and Jo, colleagues only.

Grabbing the spoon sitting in the pile of eggs, I build a plate for her, putting a little of everything on it and adding in some extra potatoes. Her favorite.

"Hey!" I hear a bright voice greeting me and I have to bite back the smile that instinctively finds its way to my mouth at the cheery sound. Josephine appears next to me, fanning her face.

"There you are. I was worried you were skipping the most important meal of the day."

"Sorry!" she apologizes. "I snoozed my alarm too many times. I probably missed breakfast. For the record, dinner is the most important meal of the day. It's the appetizer for dessert."

"Food," I announce, thrusting the plate I've created toward her like an uncivilized caveman attempting to learn to speak.

Real eloquent, Lancaster.

Her eyes sparkle, rivaling the rarest diamonds, as she grins at the overflowing portions. "This is for me?!"

"Yup. If you want it."

"Thank you! Are you in a rush? Do you have time to sit?"

"I have about 30 minutes until the lecture I want to attend starts. Let me grab another coffee and I'll join you. Do you want tea?"

"That would be great. One cr—"

"One cream, one sugar. I remember. I'll be back."

I take my time at the hot beverage station, willing myself to calm down.

Jesus Christ, it's coffee and tea. I'm not asking her on a fucking date.

She's slept in *my bed* for God's sake, and *this* is sending me spiraling?

I want to pull out my phone and ask the guys for advice on how to handle this. Do I ask her questions? Sit in silence?

Calm. Down.

Taking a deep breath, I fix our drinks, grab a couple of napkins, and walk back toward the table she's taken over. Only a handful of attendees linger in the room, and I sit in the chair next to her, passing over the sweetened beverage.

"My savior."

I busy myself with a long, piping hot sip of my coffee to stop my blushing at the compliment. "What lectures are you going to attend today?" I ask, diverting all attention away from me and the way our knees are almost knocking together under this table.

"I'm not sure. I was going to look over the list you made me. Since you're here, you can help!" Josephine reaches into her bag and pulls out the paper I left on her desk last night.

As she opens it, I slam my hand down, covering the list so she can't open it further, rattling the china. "You don't need to look at that."

"I don't?" she asks curiously, glancing down at my palm. "Why not?"

"Why read it when I can say it?"

Her eyebrow arches as she takes a bite of food, giving up easily. "You're being weird."

"It's embarrassing."

"The list you made me is embarrassing? It's not a game of MASH instead, is it?"

"I don't know what that is."

"Somehow, that doesn't surprise me," she chuckles, tossing her hair over her shoulder. She doesn't pry, waiting patiently for me to speak. There's something in her gaze that makes me want to be honest.

"I... I go overboard on things sometime," I admit, retracting my hand, fingers curling into a fist. *For you*, I want to add, thinking back to the Post-It notes after the night at the bar, but I don't, punctuating the sentence there. "It's unnecessary and over the top, and I'd hate to make you feel like I was doing it to antagonize you. That wasn't the intention."

Her face shifts, and I see the moment she realizes that I'm being honest about my uneasiness. "Oh," she says softly. "I wouldn't think that at all."

"Ah." I nudge the list toward her. "Then go ahead."

"Are you sure?"

Fixing my eyes on the wall, I give her a curt nod. "Positive."

I listen to the rustle of the paper as she unfolds the page and the sharp inhale of breath she takes.

Yeah, I went overboard. Way fucking overboard. In my defense, I had six beers and was still panicking that we were going to be on an island together, and just started writing.

Two hours later, I had highlighted the speakers I thought would interest her the most, putting smiley faces next to my favorites after looking them up online. I summarized the discussions and wrote out keywords in the margins so she could determine if it was a topic she would find beneficial. Knowing she works with social media apps frequently, I added the handles of the all presenters and their companies so she could look them up on her own time if she so desired. It was the first time in six months I'd opened my Instagram app, and I ignored the influx of activity to get the information needed for her.

"Jack."

"Josephine."

"This is incredibly thorough and thought out. Thank you for putting in the time to do this."

"It's nothing."

I feel her hand come to rest on my forearm and I freeze at the touch, the way her fingers press into my skin.

"It's not nothing. It's wonderful."

I turn and stare at her, met with a kind smile in return.

"You're welcome," I get out, synapses firing away rapidly from her touching me so openly. Again. Fuck, it feels amazing.

"So, which of these do you deem worthy enough to grace with your presence?" she teases, dropping me from her hold, and I miss the contact already.

"Dr. Brooks was one of my professors in college. He's great. I'm going to attend his first thing this morning. Before lunch, I'm going to listen to the one about computer coding. After lunch, it's going to be about the future of technology. Broad, I know. I hope we learn about aliens. Last one of the day will be on website design and how to drive more traffic to your site."

She stares at me, blinking rapidly, green eyes puzzled and concerned. "I feel so out of my element here," she mutters, shoving another bite of egg into her mouth. "I knew this was a mistake."

"That's not true at all. Look, here are some I thought you would like." I point to the discussions about social media, the rise of interactive platforms, and their correlation to sales. "You're also more than welcome to join me at any of the aforementioned discussions, though I'll warn you they won't be very fun. Honestly, I'd probably prefer listening to someone talk about InstaSpace and FaceGram."

The feeble joke elicits a giggle from her, and I want to bottle the sound and unleash it as a never-ending soundtrack on my worst, most brutal days. It's a mix of sun rays on a warm summer night—heat in the air and fireflies lighting up the night sky. Pure happiness and contentment with life. Sweet-dipped honey; warm around the edges and caring and gentle in the middle.

It's a sound I've only been fortunate enough to hear in passing over the past two years, filtering through the conference room, twisting and winding down the halls, and in the communal kitchen, following me to my office two floors up and lingering in my ears for hours after, never intended for me but cloaking me in hope and optimism.

I've been lucky recently, earning the privilege of hearing it more and more frequently. Because of me. For me. It's a breathtaking melody that you feel from the top of your head to the tips of your toes, casting a glow, and it makes me want to kiss her passionately, right here, right now, not caring about the repercussions, to show her all the unspoken ways she's changed my life for the better.

"Do you have social media?" Josephine inquires.

"Of course I do. I update my Facebook status once a year."

"That regularly, huh? I figured it'd be less." Her attention turns back to the paper, which now has breakfast potato residue on it, and I take another sip of coffee to hide the smile forming at the sight. "The technology ones sound cool. I think those will be the priority today."

"Do you want my phone number so you can text me if you need anything or if that asshole shows up and irritates you?"

She sighs in relief, nodding quickly before retrieving her phone out of her purse. She hands it to me and I put in my contact information and number.

"I better get going," she says, shoving one more enormous bite of food in her mouth before standing. "I'll see you tonight?"

The question sounds different from the other ones she's asked me. This one is laced with hope.

"Of course. I'll be at the mixer thing."

"Awesome. Have a good day, Jack."

Before I can think twice, she leans forward, one hand resting on my bicep while the other stretches over my back, covering my shoulder blades. Her lips press against my cheek over the day-old stubble I didn't bother to shave; a quick, chaste kiss that stretches for eons but still isn't long enough. Her mouth feels like heaven, awakening deep, wretched feelings in the pit of my stomach.

As she pulls away, hair like a curtain shielding her face from view, a splotch of red on her cheeks reveals itself to me, matching her hair that's somehow still radiant even under the harshness of the artificial lighting. Giving me a grin, she sprints from the room.

I watch her leave, transfixed and flabbergasted by her boldness.

I blink once. Twice. Three times, my smile forming then faltering before it reaches its crescendo.

An act. That's all this is.

Pretend.

A show.

A lie.

For the most fleeting moment, I let myself daydream about what torment and chaos she could inflict on me if this was real.

Disastrous. In the best way.

I'd welcome it with open arms.

I'm unable to move from the chair for several minutes, still processing the feel of her mouth on my skin long after she's gone, leaving nothing but joy in her wake.

TWENTY
JO

The first day of the conference passes in a blur. Jack's notes are beyond helpful, and the lectures and discussions I attend are exactly what I was looking forward to. At no point did I feel inexperienced; in fact, it reaffirmed that I *love* working in marketing and advertising. So far, everyone I've spoken to agrees social media will be the way of the future, driving sales more so than basic, traditional websites or word of mouth. The discussions give me confidence that the work I'm doing is crucial to a successful business.

At lunch, I grab a sandwich, chatting with a lovely woman, Carol, who works in California. We bond instantly over our turkey and cheese as she shares how she's struggling to get some of the older associates at her company onboard with a more digital footprint rather than using phones and cold-calling. She said one of her coworkers still uses a Rolodex, and I promise to email her some tips and tricks I've implemented that have helped Itrix along the way.

By the time I'm getting ready for the mixer later that evening, I'm exhausted, brain overstimulated, and there's still two more days of lectures to attend. I'd love nothing more than to curl up in a beach chair and stare up at the stars as they twinkle in the ocean under the moonlight. I'm quickly learning personal time is nonexistent here. It's full of socialization, note-taking, and networking. I've barely had a second to breathe.

I slip into a light blue sundress and wedges before pulling out my phone to send Jack a message and see where he is.

JB: Did you really save your name in my phone as 'Jack the Great'?

JL: That doesn't sound like something I'd do.

JL: Perhaps you put it in there subconsciously, Josephine.

JB: I'm going to change it to Jack the Ripper.

JL: More fitting, I'd say.
JL: Are you coming down for the happy hour?

JB: Yeah, I should be there in five.

JL: I'll meet you downstairs.

"Hey," I say enthusiastically, walking to meet Jack in the lobby a few minutes later. When he spots me, he stands up straighter, smiling faintly. "How was your day?"

"Long, but good. How about you? How were the talks?"

"Great! Your paper helped so much. I even made a friend!"

"That doesn't surprise me. The asshole of the year is already inside. If he calls me 'man' one more time..." Jack trails off, shoving his hands into his tailored pants pockets, fists clenched.

"An expanded vocabulary wouldn't be the *worst* thing in the world."

"Wow, and that's coming from someone who probably carries around a pocket-sized dictionary. Maybe you can loan it to him, *man*."

"No dictionaries. Only a thesaurus. Come on, there are some people I want you to meet who are infinitely better than the ones we'll do our best to avoid."

He puts his hand on my lower back, guiding me into the ballroom.

Jack is a comforting presence for the rest of the night. He introduces me to people he met earlier today, only leaving my side for a handful of seconds to bring me a fresh water without asking. He saw my glass getting low, excused himself, then returned with a full cup.

And two pieces of fried macaroni that he handed to me with no explanation.

Did I *really* think this man was an asshole?

It's dawning on me how incredibly stupid and naïve I am, and without a doubt the girl people roll their eyes at when she cries about how much the guy hates her.

Yeah, okay.

I think Abby might have been onto something.

Despite not being an overly social person, Jack is at ease, working the room of conference-goers. He's engaging and expressive, and I'm surprised he includes me in all the conversations we take part in. If there's something I don't quite understand, or terminology that sounds unfamiliar, he leans over and gives me a quick translation—quiet, whispered words only I can hear, his breath warm against my ear, leaving goosebumps in its wake.

"Jack!"

We both turn at his name as a tall Black man who looks

around our age approaches us. "There you are!" He pulls Jack into a firm hug, clapping him on the back. When they separate, Jack is grinning, and it's the happiest I've ever seen him.

Shoot.

The dimple has a perfect, beautiful twin.

Double trouble.

"Josephine, this is Walter, my college roommate," he says, beaming.

"Oh, hell. Stop. You always think you're funny when you do that. It's Wally. Walter is my father." Wally shakes his head, turning to me. "And who is *this*?"

"Hi! I'm Jo! He has a habit of calling me by my full name, too."

"My girlfriend," Jack adds, and Wally's eyes widen. I nearly drop my cup in surprise, shocked that we're riding the lying train all the way to best friend town.

"No shit! It's great to meet you, Jo! Is she the one you've mentioned before?" he asks Jack excitedly. His ears turn pink, and a scathing glance gets tossed Wally's way.

"We're colleagues," I say. "I work in marketing and advertising."

"An office romance. A modern-day Jim and Pam. I can't believe you didn't tell me," Wally says. "I mean..." His voice drops to a quiet octave, and I'm practically falling forward to hear him speak. "After all the shit that went down, I'm glad to see you're doing okay. It's hard to trust your text messages when they're sporadic and come once a month."

I try to decipher the cryptic statement. Jack hasn't shared anything traumatic that might have happened to him in the past, but that doesn't make it false. It's also not my place to interrogate him and ask.

"You know I'm a private person. This is still new, and I didn't want to share too much or jinx anything."

"That's for damn sure. I can't even get this man to post on Facebook! Maybe you can do a better job than me, Jo. How else am I supposed to keep up with him?"

"He can be pretty stubborn," I joke, putting my arm around Jack's waist. Our sides press together, my hip resting just above his, the shoes I'm wearing giving me the height advantage tonight.

"She hasn't been successful either," Jack adds, his arm falling easily to my shoulder. I lean into his touch because I *want* to, not because I *have* to.

"Jo, how do you feel about karaoke? I'm asking for research."

"I freaking love it."

Wally turns as he hears his name called from across the room and groans. "Good answer. If you'll excuse me, I have to go mingle with other people I don't like nearly as much as you two. It's really hard to appear interested in someone when it's the fifteenth time you've shared about your job. I'll see you two at dinner tomorrow night? Try to save me a seat!"

Jack nods, his hand reaching out to shake Wally's. "Of course. Send me a text later."

"Jo, it was great to meet you. Thanks for helping to put him back together. I haven't seen him look this good since college."

I tug us out of the center of the room, finding a private corner to hide out in.

"Are you all right?" I ask him.

"Why wouldn't I be?"

"You froze when Wally said he was glad to see you're doing okay. Your voice changed, too."

"Am I that easy to read?"

"No. I think I pay too much attention to you. How else will I end you if I don't know your weaknesses?"

He hesitates, an important disclosure on the tip of his

tongue that gets swallowed down, buried to rest for another time. "I'm not ready to talk about what happened."

"I wasn't expecting you to. You're allowed to have private things you don't share with the world. I wanted to offer the same courtesy you've extended to me and check in to make sure you're okay."

He deflates. "Thank you," he whispers, gratitude seeping through the two syllables.

Another piece of the Jack Lancaster jigsaw puzzle is revealed. I need to figure out its place.

"We didn't have to lie to your best friend, though." A waiter approaches us with a tray of sliders and I grab two, juggling them in my hand. "I feel like a jerk."

"I know it might seem like there are a lot of people here, but the industry is fairly small, and word-of-mouth travels fast. You heard how Greg brought up my... Never mind. Besides, Wally thinking I'm happy is beneficial to everyone. The last thing the everyone here needs is for him to parade me around in search of a girlfriend like I'm a pig at a country fair."

I giggle. "Does he do that often?"

"Only when he drinks. He means well."

"Can I ask you a question?"

"You defeat the purpose by asking beforehand."

"Was there a time when you didn't look good? A time when you weren't happy? I don't need specifics."

Jack studies the wall in front of us before dragging his eyes to meet mine. The vibrant blue is dim and sedated, appearing sad. Contrite. Gutted.

"Yes."

"I'm sorry for whatever happened," I whisper, reaching out for his hand and finding it right away. I give it a squeeze.

"It's not your fault. You, of all people, do not need to apologize."

"That may be the case, but no one deserves to feel pain and agony. Not even you."

"You amaze me sometimes, Josephine. You find the good in every situation. In every person. Even a dark soul like me. How is that possible?"

"Trust me, you're not a dark soul. You're simply searching for the light. There's a big difference."

"What's the difference?"

"You're trying, even if you aren't whole yet. Sometimes, that's what is most important. Sometimes, trying is half the battle."

He stares at me, eyes peering straight into my soul. The look conveys enough on his afflicted face.

Thank you.

I'm healing.

One day, I'll be better.

"I do not deserve you. Not your friendship. Not your kindness and joy. Not your fake feelings as a fake partner. I ruin things, Josephine, and you're too good. Don't let me taint you or dull your shine."

"That's where you're wrong, Lancaster. I'm not positive yet, but I think... I think you might help me shine brighter. And I do the same for you."

"If only you knew," he murmurs. "I'm sorry, but I've reached my quota for social interaction for the evening. Are you going to hang out for a while?"

"Yeah, I'm going to find my new friend Carol and see how the rest of her day went. Want to meet up for breakfast in the morning?"

"I think I'd like that," Jack nods.

I felt bold and powerful when I kissed his cheek earlier in the day, swept up by the thankfulness for his generosity over a piece of paper. This time he's the one kissing me, an unexpected turn of events that I don't hate. Not in the slightest.

Warm lips graze the side of my cheek near my earlobe, three gentle pecks planted in quick succession. His thumb runs across my bottom lip as he pulls away.

"Good night, Josephine," he says roughly.

"Good night," I answer, hand coming to rest where his lips vacated.

This wasn't a good night.

It was perfect.

TWENTY-ONE

"J! How's paradise?"

Four faces grin at me as I FaceTime Henry, Patrick, Neil, and Noah during my lunch break on our second day. I took my sandwich and potato salad up to my room, needing an escape from the constant stream of communication and interaction.

I don't hate people, contrary to what I convey in the office. After endless hours of answering questions, listening intently, practicing my best nonverbal communication skills, jotting down notes, and introducing myself to others, I'm tapped out.

Peace and quiet is what I'm craving.

I need the hum of the air conditioning rattling against the wall and blowing the curtains, not the buzz of voices echoing across a large banquet hall.

I need a secluded space where I can rest my fingers on my forehead, massage my temples, and not have 100 people staring at me, wondering why I'm more content by myself and not in a circle, laughing at a joke someone is telling.

It doesn't help that I didn't sleep a wink last night, too busy mulling over Josephine's words again and again in my head.

"You're not a dark soul."

"You're trying."

I am. I'm trying to be the best person I can be, to help her out in a tough situation. Even if it's for a few days, playing pretend like we're the perfect couple.

A couple that spends the night with each other, limbs intertwined.

A couple that knows each other's phone passcodes and how they like their burgers cooked.

There's magic in being around her. I float when she's nearby.

Everything stills.

The tension at the base of my neck eases, notch by notch, when she smiles at me, bright and wide. My hands uncurl, releasing clenched fists while my fingers relax for the first time in days, wiggling free. The constant brick that sits at the bottom of my stomach, entombed under anxiety and discomfort, cracks, a single fracture that begins to spiderweb out of control.

"Not bad. I haven't had much of a chance to enjoy the paradise part. It's been all lectures and boxed lunches so far. How are you guys doing?"

"Nothing new to report here," Henry says, shrugging.

"How's the girl?" Patrick asks.

I clear my throat. "We're kind of fake dating?"

"I'm going to need some clarification," Noah says. "How is fake dating different from real dating?"

"We're only acting like we're dating. But with no actual feelings or physical benefits. And it'll end when we get on the plane home. Never to be talked about again."

"And how did this come about?"

I groan, scrubbing my hand over my face. "It's my fault. Josephine's ex cornered her and asked if she was dating anyone. She lied and said she was. He asked who, she couldn't speak and I... I inserted myself into the conversation."

I wince, recalling the interaction. It was really an obtrusive thing to do without getting clearance from her beforehand and considering how she felt about the matter. She's tied to me for the rest of our time here. My irritation got the better of me, and my mouth moved without talking to my brain first, some stupid hero-complex kicking in. What if she met someone she wanted to spend time with? Or connected with a fellow attendee, wanting to go somewhere private and get to know each other better? I've blocked her from doing that, all because of my big mouth.

Thinking about her with someone else makes me sick.

"Wait, this could be perfect!" Henry exclaims excitedly, clapping his hands together.

"Please tell me what's perfect about this," I deadpan, tossing the finished carton of food into the recycling bin.

"I understand what Henry's saying," Neil interjects, and I'd be willing to bet he understands *nothing*. "You show her how good of a boyfriend you can be."

"I'm not going to pressure or manipulate her into liking me, no matter how I feel personally."

"You aren't! You're showing her what kind of man you are."

"Trust me, Josephine is well aware of the man I am. It's futile anyway. It's for show, nothing more." I hesitate, not sure if I should include this next part. "She kissed my cheek."

"WHAT?!"

I pull the phone away from my face. Way too loud.

"Dude!"

"Again, everything she does is because people are watching us."

"Was anyone watching when she kissed your cheek? The ex?"

I pause, thinking back to yesterday morning.

The room had cleared out, only a few hotel employees

sticking around to clean up the space as they hurried in and out, not paying us any mind. We were utterly alone at that point.

"No."

"She did it because she wanted to!" Henry exclaims, fist pumping the air. I'm not sure what he's excited about; he's adamantly against relationships, constantly lecturing us about why he never wants to settle down and how casual sex is infinitely better than monogamy.

"Look," I say firmly, needing to shut this down before anyone gets further invested. "I appreciate the insight, but nothing is going to happen with her. When we come home, we'll settle back into our old ways. She'll write an insult on my coffee cup. Kisses on cheeks won't matter."

"Hang on. You mentioned how you personally feel. What do you mean?"

"It's become very obvious that I'm attracted to her. I like her. I didn't jump in to help her in hopes she'd start to like me, either. Truly all I wanted to do was make sure she was okay."

"Shit, man, that's awesome of you."

"I'm not a hero. If anything, I'm selfish."

"We want what's best for you, whatever that is," Patrick says. "If that's acting like a fake boyfriend, we're happy for you. Or if it's something more serious and permanent, we'll support that, too. We love you."

"Yeah, I love you guys too. This is kind of a lot. All the people. Her. The shitbag who keeps harassing her."

"We're a phone call away if you need to vent!" Noah says, and the other three nod reassuringly.

"Don't forget to take time for yourself, too," Henry adds. "Shut your brain down for a few hours and relax."

"Thanks. I appreciate it. I'll text you guys later."

Giving them a wave, I end the call and pinch the bridge of my nose. I still have another five hours of lectures this afternoon.

The more time I spend at this conference, the more I think that the office life isn't for me.

I like my job. I'm good at my job. At times, though, I'm unfulfilled, realizing something is missing. Something barely out of reach, on the top shelf, hidden behind other containers that I can't see. I just can't distinguish what *something* is.

A few more hours, Lancaster. You can do this.

Sighing, I grab my bag and head out for the rest of the day, the feeling of discomfort magnifying every minute she's not by my side.

"Hi."

I look up from my phone and find Josephine gliding toward me, smiling from ear to ear.

"Hey." I slide my phone into my pocket. "How was your day?"

"Good. Exhausting. My stack of business cards is growing. I'll probably need a separate suitcase to transport them home."

"I don't know what to do with them. I know it's the formality of exchanging information, but is anyone going to send me an email after this? Probably not. Do I keep them? Toss them? What happens when I need someone's information but I threw it away six months ago?"

"Exactly! It's such a hassle. Do you want to get dinner? Maybe we can find Wally! I know I'm a few minutes late. Hopefully he grabbed a table."

"I'd love that. It's down the hall."

We walk together to the large room that's set up with four-person tables to encourage mingling.

"I've been thinking about this meal all day," she admits. My stomach grumbles on cue.

"Tell me about it." My eyes dart across the room, searching for an empty spot. I see Wally in the distance and wave. He gives me a thumb down, gesturing to his full table. "I guess we should've gotten here earlier."

"Ugh, that's my fault. I got distracted talking to someone, and I lost tra—"

"Jack! My man!"

Greg's shrill voice pierces through the sea of people, pushing past the minglers to stop in front of us. "Oh, hey, Jo," he adds as an afterthought, barely acknowledging her. "I've been looking for you, J! Come grab dinner with us."

"Sorry, I'm going to have to decline. Josephine and I are a package deal, and we're about to find a table," I reply cooly, my arm snaking around her possessively.

"Liz, my girlfriend, has one already. Everything else is full, so that works out perfectly! The girls can talk about whatever it is they care about, and we can talk shop. Two smart men shooting the shit," he laughs.

My eyes slide to Josephine's, exchanging a look.

There's nowhere else to go.

The other seats are already occupied, and the waitstaff is moving around the room, taking orders and offering beverages.

She gives me a small nod.

"Fine," I say curtly. "Lead the way."

Greg starts for the other side of the room and Josephine follows before I give her arm a gentle tug, preventing her from moving any further.

"Hey," I mutter. "We do not need to sit with them. We can get room service and eat anywhere else. Hell, I'll eat in the bathroom with you."

"Honestly? I kind of want to. Not because of the uncomfortable affair it's going to be—because holy shit—but I want some closure. And, as appealing as eating over a toilet sounds, I'm not really in the mood."

"You don't have feelings for him anymore, do you?"

I shouldn't be asking; it's none of my business. I can't help but wonder about the answer, though, needing to make sure she's not hellbent on using me so she can get with someone else. Josephine doesn't strike me as that kind of girl, and the second the words are out of my mouth, I feel like a bastard for asking.

"For Greg?" she spits out, frowning deeply. "Hell no. Did you think I did?"

"I thought you wanted a fake boyfriend to win him back. Or to make him jealous."

"Jack." Her hand latches onto my wrist, fingers gently stroking the skin there, unknowingly tracing my jagged scar and causing me to suppress a shudder. "I don't have feelings for him. He made my life hell, and I wanted to prove to him I can be happy without him. Trust me, it doesn't make *any* sense that I would even want to be in the same room as him, but this is a big step."

I exhale, nodding as her words sink in, relieved that she doesn't want to run off into the sunset with someone so vile. "Good. That's good. I mean, not *good* good. You deserve so much better than that." I jut my chin across the room, ignoring the beckoning wave coming from the asshat in question. "I'm ready when you are."

"If shit goes south, we'll bail and eat cheeseburgers together in the family bathroom. Ugh, I wish we were sitting with Wally."

"Trust me, the tales he could share about me would be far more enjoyable than this is going to be. Do you mind if I... touch you?"

"Oh. Yes. Please. Er. That's fine," she answers, her voice breathy and light. I slowly place my hand on her lower back.

The shirt she's wearing has a dip, exposing a dizzying amount of bare skin, and two of my fingers rest directly on the uncovered pale expanse. Every outfit I see her in is a new form of torture.

She's so warm. And smooth. Her head tilts to the side, eyes fluttering closed for half a second before snapping open, like she forgot where she was.

"Ready?" I ask huskily.

Josephine has the audacity to lick her lips as she looks at me, the side of her mouth titling up. "Let's go, boyfriend."

Fuck me.

TWENTY-TWO
JO

The only thing I can focus on is Jack's hand. The press of his fingers into my skin, almost enough for me to arch my back. The path he traces from the base of my spine to the swell of my hip, lingering for a moment on my curves, savoring them, before moving on to another unexplored area. My body reacts to his touch; I'm hot. Flustered. Unsteady on my feet and aware of his heated eyes and citrusy smell, his presence overtaking all of my senses.

For half a second, I forget that we're about to sit down and eat dinner with a couple I couldn't care less about.

For half a second, it's *us*.

"Jack! There you are!"

Greg's voice yanks me from our private moment. "This is my girlfriend, Liz. Liz, this is Jack. And Jo."

"Hello." I smile politely as Jack pulls out my chair for me. He gives me the one on the end. An exit, if needed. "Thanks."

"Of course." Jack kisses the top of my head, lips brushing against my curls before squeezing into the chair next to me, long legs folding under the tablecloth. We're against a large window overlooking the sparkling ocean and I smile at the sight, wishing I could wiggle my toes in the sand.

After a few terse moments of silence amongst the four of us, the waitress finally comes over, taking our orders. Greg and Liz split a bottle of red wine, and Jack orders us a bottle of white after privately asking if I'm comfortable drinking.

My heart flutters at his kindness.

"Is it possible to get an extra side of mashed potatoes with my meal?" Jack asks with a smile. The waitress grins back, batting her heavily shadowed eyes at him.

"Of course it is. I'll make sure the chef gives you a generous portion," she says with a wink.

"Those are for you," he whispers in my ear. Warmth blooms in my stomach. "My potato connoisseur."

"Is the flirting included? Or is that a bonus for waitresses only?"

"I'll flirt with you if it'll make you as happy as the mashed potatoes do."

Greg wastes no time in talking Jack's ear off, tossing around words I'm not familiar with. I tune them out, instead focusing on Liz, and quickly learn she doesn't have the faintest idea who I am. Thank god. Now this meal can be only semi-awkward instead of full-on Dinner Party awkward like in *The Office*.

Jack's arm rests on the back of my chair, fingers idly tracing the freckles on my exposed shoulder. I'm not sure he's aware he's doing it, but his attention to detail is making it difficult for me to sit still.

The waitress arrives with our food, distributing the plates around the table with another wink and toothy smile directed at Jack. A feeling of jealousy lands right under his alluring touch, the same sensation I experienced when boarding the airplane.

That's new.

Am I allowed to be jealous?

No. I'm not.

That crosses the line of *helping someone out*. If he wants to go out with the waitress or flirt with her, he's allowed to. What we have is just an act.

I cut my food aggressively, silently stewing, when I notice Jack not touching his plate.

"You're not eating?"

"I'm waiting for you," he answers simply, eyes flicking to my silverware poised halfway over the chicken breast I picked for dinner. "Take your time."

"Thank you," I whisper.

He squeezes my knee in response and offers a small smile, the gesture enough to erase every past negative interaction between us. The past is wiped clean. Easily forgotten.

"How did you two meet?" Liz asks after our table has been cleared of plates. I look at Jack, conveying to him he's in charge of telling this story.

"We work together. What started as friendly conversation turned into flirty banter with little jokes, light touches, and roaming eyes. Probably more on my end than hers, but I saw how she would sneak glances at me when she thought I wasn't paying attention. Sure, most of them were scathing death glares. Sometimes she'd peek at me and have this small smile on her face. Like she knew, deep down, I wasn't terrible. There was a lot of tension, and as content as I was being her friend, I always wanted more.

"It took some convincing until she finally agreed to have dinner with me. We've been together ever since. Would you believe the way to her heart is through Olive Garden breadsticks? I sent her a picnic basket full for our six-month anniversary."

I choke on the sip of water I'm taking, surprised and delighted by the inside joke no one else is privy to. His story flows so easily, as if we've been sharing it with family and friends for years. Even I believe the web of deceit he's weaving, and I'm half of the participants.

"I like to think it's going well. Josephine is a simple woman, and I'm slowly learning everything about her and all the ways to her kind heart."

The sincerity behind his words drowns me, causing me to gasp for air.

"Yeah. I think it's going really well," I say softly, smiling.

He hasn't shaved in a couple of days and stubble lines his handsome face. I want to run my finger across his cheek and feel the prickle against my palm.

"I've always had eyes for her," Jack continues. "One time, before we were even dating, I accidentally caused her to spill her tea in a head-on collision. I had to loan her the spare shirt I keep in my office. When I saw how she looked in it..." He turns, eyes earnest, addressing *me* and no one else. "That day solidified my feelings. It hit me like a fucking wrecking ball. She is the most beautiful, hottest woman I've ever laid my eyes on. It's a hard task, to be both beautiful and hot, yet somehow, she achieves it with ease. I lost my damn mind at the sight of her. I don't tell you that enough, sweetheart. You're so fucking gorgeous."

His warm hand cups my cheek protectively, thumb running over my skin, and my jaw nearly hits the table at his sensual words.

"Oh my gosh, that is *so* sweet and sexy!" Liz gushes, clapping her hands together. "I kind of think we need to leave the table and give you two a minute alone, because, phew!"

I forgot she was here; I forgot anyone was here besides us.

I barely register her voice, still processing what Jack said and how he's still looking at me.

Just me.

How often has he pictured that day when we saw each other in the elevator, long shirt tucked into my skirt and his eyes raking over my body? How often have *I* looked at *him* subconsciously, unaware of what I was doing? In meetings. Out front of our office building before our gazes met and eyes narrowed. Over my shoulder in the hallway, wondering if I'll hear his footsteps approaching. At the bar, his shoulders relaxed and a grin sitting on his face, looking like the most handsome man in the universe surrounded by friends. On his couch eating tacos, tongue darting out to clear up the rogue sour cream that fell out of the shell. His face against my palm, eyes closing as I studied his bruise.

Small, nearly indiscernible moments I didn't realize were leading to something *more*.

"What about you two?" Jack asks. His finger keeps drawing on me, boldly dipping lower, down the side of my arm parallel to my breast, like he's writing his name on my skin to mark me as his own and no one else's. It's doing things to me, and I can feel moisture pooling between my thighs.

It's been months since I've experienced a physical reaction like this, and he's not intentionally trying to rile me up.

At least, I don't think he is.

Suddenly all I can think about is where else he could touch me if he wanted to. My neck. My thighs. My...

Stop it, Jo.

He doesn't want to.

If he did, he would've acted on it already. He's had plenty of opportunities.

This is a specially designed show for the audience across

from us. And damn if Jack shouldn't win an Oscar for his believable performance.

"We met on a dating app," Liz says brightly. I blink, focusing back on the conversation and not the intimate trail Jack is leaving. "It's been three great years. Well, almost three years. Wow, our anniversary is next week, baby."

Three years.

The words screech in my ears, tires spinning out on a rain-soaked road as I do the mental calculations in my head.

"I'm sorry. Did you say three years?"

"Yes! I swear it was yesterday when we met. Time flies when you're in love." She stares up at Greg with the most lovesick face I've ever seen. "Have you two said that yet? He told me after only two months!"

It hits me at once. The infidelity. The reason *our* relationship flipped so quickly, and the overlapping timelines. Not only did he put me through hell, but he did it while sleeping with someone else before coming home and putting his hands on me.

My body shakes as I pull the napkin from my lap and place it on the table.

"If you'll excuse me," I say, exuding a calm I didn't think was possible with the rage forming inside me. Without another word or polite apology, I stand, leaving the dining room as fast as my legs will take me, not looking back. Racing through the lobby, I dodge suitcases and guests before landing outside on the sand, gulping down fresh, salty air.

Gathering myself and catching my breath, I walk down the rickety wooden boardwalk, straight for the ocean. I want to dive in and swim far away. I settle for slipping off my shoes and wading into the refreshing water; the salt kisses my calves and simmers the anger with the crest of every wave.

I sense him before I hear or see him. Eyes watching me, a cautious, careful step as he approaches from behind.

"Josephine," Jack says. He's stopped a few feet away, and I peer at him over my shoulder. He looks absolutely ridiculous out here in his dressy outfit, trekking over the sand in his shoes. His head cocks to the side and he juts his chin down the desolate beach, void of any other humans or lights. "Want to take a walk?"

"A walk? Now?"

"Is there somewhere else you need to be?"

I think for a moment and realize that walking with him sounds like the best thing in the world. "Okay," I relent, and he smiles faintly, letting me lead the way and not trying to make small talk.

The sun has disappeared, playing hide and seek with the rising moon, the sea appearing like ink to our right. The cool night air is a break from the humid heat that surrounded us earlier. We walk in a companionable silence, clumpy sand sticking to my damp feet. The only noises accompanying us are the crash of the surf and the sway of the palm trees in the gentle breeze.

Have you ever felt like you were being suffocated by everything around you?

"Yes," comes Jack's voice. I didn't know I asked out loud. "All the time."

"I'm glad I'm not alone."

"You didn't know he cheated on you," he says simply. I turn, observing the frown on his lips and the hands shoved into his pockets.

"No. I didn't. Hearing that still hurts, which I hate. It still resonates with me, even after all these years. It shouldn't."

"You're allowed to be upset. What happened to you was shitty. He's an asshole, but you still cared about him at one time. Hurt is hurt, no matter how much time passes."

The wind billows around us, my hair blowing into my face,

red flying everywhere. I brush it away, releasing a breath. "I think it's good that I heard that, because now I know everything. And I can finally let go of the last little piece of my past."

Jack doesn't answer me as he lowers himself into the sand. I mirror him a few feet away, lying back. The grains are cool, helping to ease the tension that's lodged its way between my shoulder blades.

"I think it's time I tell you a story."

"What kind of story?"

"I was engaged to someone. We were college sweethearts. We met our first day on campus and became inseparable. Friendship quickly shifted into love."

"Oh?" I push myself up on my elbow to have a better view of him, wondering where this is going. He doesn't meet my gaze, shifting nearer to get away from a pile of washed-up seaweed. Is he going to tell me someone passed away? An old love who broke his heart by leaving earth? Is that pain something we have in common?

"We dated for eight years, and before our ninth anniversary, I finally proposed. It's what I was supposed to do. My parents were pressuring me. My friends were pressuring me. *She* was pressuring me. We bought a house. Got a dog. I bought a ring. That's the sequence of events we're told to abide by, right? Everything was perfect.

"Some of the couples we knew had been struggling in their relationships. For us, it was easy. Simple. I never dreamed of myself with another woman, and she was incredible. We always joked that nothing could break us up. Then, I started working later and later. I was at a startup before joining Itrix. The hours were long, the pay was meager. I believed in the company, though, so I put in a lot of time."

I observe him, the way his shoulders droop the longer he talks. His expression hardens; gone is the faint dimple, replaced with the firm line of his clenched, serious jaw. I realize that is the longest he's gone while talking to me consistently, and I'm afraid to hear how this story ends.

"Time spent at work became time away from home. We were planning a wedding, too. A week before we were supposed to walk down the aisle, Claire—that's her name, and the one from the photo in my room—told me she had feelings for someone else. My best friend."

It knocks the air out of my chest and my mouth drops open at his raw admission. "Jack..."

His smile doesn't reach his eyes. "I was home less frequently. She started talking to him with no malicious intent. They hung out because I wasn't around to spend time with them. One thing led to another." He sighs, tousling his hair. "She told me she loved me, but loved him more. Maybe it would have been different if I tried harder, she said. Maybe, if I put in more effort, she wouldn't have fallen in love with him. Maybe I could have worked harder. I wish she had cheated on me. That would've given me a reason to hate her. It was my fault, though. I stopped being present. I stopped listening."

"That's why you said you ruined things," I say gently. He nods once, rubbing his lips together as he stares at the ocean. "It's not your fault. It takes two people to have a relationship."

"It only takes one to screw it up. I moved away after the breakup. It gives me enough distance without having to worry if she's going to be in the milk aisle at the grocery store when I go in."

"Sometimes the appeal of a new life helps mask the pain of your current one."

"The day with the spilled coffee. I told you I got an email. It was their wedding invitation."

"What?" I squawk, flabbergasted. "They invited you? I can see why you were distracted."

"Mhm. Included in the save the date was a personal message. It said they know it might be hard for me to attend, and they understand if I don't come. They can forget the past if I can, too."

"Holy shit. That's bold as hell. Are you going to go?"

"Probably not. It's at the same venue we picked out. God, that makes me sound jealous. I'm not. That part of my life is over. No point revisiting it."

"Are you sure you won't regret that decision?"

"Yup. I can assure you I'll be fine. Do you have any regrets?" he asks.

I ponder the question for a moment. "I don't think so. There are some aspects of my life I wish I could change or do again. But do I regret anything? No. As cliché as it sounds, I truly think everything happens for a reason. Even the shitty parts. It's like we have to wade through the mud, puddles, and persistent rain to find the rainbows, you know?"

"What if we don't have an umbrella?"

"You find someone who will share."

Jack hums. "I used to regret working so much. Maybe that would have saved my relationship. If we couldn't last ten years, though, it never would have lasted eighty. I loved her very much; there's no denying that. The more I dwell on it and run through the mistakes over and over in my head and at therapy, the more I've accepted there must be someone out there I'm destined to love more. Someone who will make the pain and suffering worth it. The only regret I have in life has nothing to do with her, ironically."

"I hope you find her one day. That someone to share an umbrella with."

"I do, too. I think about what you asked me before. Why am I the way that I am? That's the verbose way of telling you that after all the shit went down, I changed. I became closed off.

Moody. Depressed, if I'm being honest. Using that term was daunting and intimidating, but it's the truth, and I shouldn't be ashamed of it. Days were very dark and gloomy for a long, long time, and for a while, I never thought I'd see the sun again.

"Wally's right. There's a time in my life where I looked and felt much worse than this. It's taken me a while to get to this point, and I still have a ways to go. Some days are harder than others, and I know I struggle to connect emotionally. You deserve an explanation. It doesn't excuse my moods, behavior, or any of the unkind things I've said or done to you when I've been in a funk. I'm working on it. Therapy helps a lot. It reminds me I'm not alone."

I want to reach over, pull him into my arms, and hug him close, holding him while he finds his sunshine, wherever and whoever that might be. He's been through hell and back. Suddenly, words I've hurled at him come crashing into me, and I think I'm going to be sick.

TWENTY-THREE

JO

"You know, you could at least pretend like you tried, Jack."

"This isn't good enough."

"I feel bad for whoever he goes home to each night."

"Shit," I whisper. "The things I've said to you. I-I've been so mean."

"Stop," he says firmly. "Don't you dare. I was just as cruel to you, calling your job stupid and unneeded. You didn't know."

"No, I didn't, but... I hope I didn't make things worse."

"Trust me, you haven't. I told you, Josephine. You are good. So very good."

"I'm still incredibly sorry. You never know what someone's going through, and I've been a bitch to you." I reach out, grasping his arm. "Thank you for sharing that with me."

"Was Greg your last relationship?"

"Yeah. We worked together in New York and got involved when we shouldn't have. I was lonely, and he was hot. A lethal combination. I've had little success with dating since. I've done the friends with benefits route. Hookups. Some casual things. Nothing has ever really stuck. I think it's me. How much longer can I say why I'm single?" I shrug, kicking the sand with my foot. "My sister is getting married soon, and everyone keeps asking me when it's my turn. To be honest, I'm not sure I even want to get married. And if I do, it'll be at the courthouse without an audience."

"You don't?"

"To me, it's pointless, which sounds cynical. It's so much money spent on a day that isn't guaranteed to last forever. I don't judge others if that's what they want as an end goal for a relationship. If marriage is their jam, good for them! I love going to weddings and celebrating love!

"So many girls plan their big day at a young age. They know exactly what dress they want to wear, and which bouquet would match. I've never envisioned that for myself. Society places these unrealistic stigmas around women and marriage, ostracizing us because we want to deviate from tradition. I hate it. We still deserve a happily ever after like everyone else. It may look a little different, but happiness comes in all shapes and sizes."

I've had this opinion for as long as I can remember, always afraid to voice it out of fear of being perceived as "trendy" or "not like the other girls." Before Mom passed away, I tearfully shared with her I was scared I would never find someone who had the same mindset as me. I would have to settle and compromise my hopes and desires for theirs. She stroked my hair and told me that no person was worth settling for, and to hold out for the one who loved and accepted me for *me*, lack of wedding plans and all. Love doesn't pick the pretty parts to like about someone; it's all-encompassing.

"That's an incredibly refreshing way to look at things. I got down on one knee because I was supposed to, not because I wanted to. I wanted to spend the rest of my life with her, but I felt forced into doing so. I didn't need the wedding or the ring or the huge celebration. I just needed her."

"Trust me, I get it. I don't want kids either, and apparently that's not politically correct to share with people. An unmarried, child-free woman? I'm probably going to be burned at the stake. People make me feel guilty about that decision all the time, and it fucking sucks."

"Hang on. You don't want children?" Jack sounds startled.

"I don't. Is that a problem?"

I'm assuming a defensive stance right off the bat, knowing how this conversation goes with a man who thinks he can change my mind. I've had it before. They often paint me an idyllic picture of not having to work and spending all day lounging around the house, cooking a family dinner when he returns from work and tucking two little ones into bed after a bath and reading time. I don't want that life. I applaud the women who *do,* but it's not me.

"No. Not at all." He rubs the back of his neck and looks up at the sky pensively. "I don't want children either. It's tough to convey that without sounding like an asshole. And it's even tougher to convey that to women. Why don't you want them, if you don't mind me asking?"

"I adore kids. When I was younger, I always wanted, like, four of my own. When my mom passed, I saw how much responsibility went into being a parent. I'm not saying I don't want to be responsible, but it's more that I'm selfish, I guess. For most of my childhood, I played the role of *Mom,* watching over my sisters after she left, losing out on my childhood to help make sure theirs was worthwhile. It took a lot out of me, and it's not something I want to do again."

I grew up quickly, teenage years replaced with adulthood. I dedicated my free time to driving my two sisters around to dance class and debate team, folding the laundry and helping my dad make lunches while he worked full-time to put dinner on the table. I would never dream of *not* helping, and I have no resentment or bitterness associated with the role I filled. It helped me bond with my sisters in a way other siblings don't. It came at the price of an unfortunate loss, but the three of us grew closer in the face of tragedy. In that tragedy, my desire to have no children of my own magnified, reaffirmed every day.

Bethany, my middle sister, has two kids of her own who I love dearly and spoil rotten. I frequently volunteer to babysit for her so she and her husband can enjoy a much-needed, kid-free night. They go back to their home at the end of the day, no longer under my care. That's plenty for me. I haven't felt this honest and vulnerable with someone in a long time. It's effortless to share these truths with Jack, despite the barriers of our past.

"Thank you, again, for jumping in and helping me. There's no way I would've been able to face that shitshow by myself. I'm sorry I left the table so abruptly. It was rude."

"We may not get along all the time, Josephine, but there are far worse people out there to fake date. I told them you weren't feeling well, and that we were going to turn in early."

I laugh, reaching over and giving him a playful shove. Sand falls in his sky-blue shirt, catching in the crevice of his rolled sleeves. "I'm a catch, thank you very much."

Jack halts my shoving, taking my hand in his. "Yes. You are."

This differs from on the plane. This is intentional. Electricity zips through my veins. Want and desire pull at my stomach, and the fuzzy outline of *deeper* cautiously approaches us.

"Is this okay?" he asks, and I nod. "Who knew all it would take for us to be cordial was a trip to an island where we nearly suffocate from the humidity?"

"You're not too bad, Lancaster. We've had some disagreements, but I'm thinking that maybe we could be friends."

"Friends," he repeats, somewhat mournfully, giving my hand a squeeze before letting go.

"For the record, you're a catch too," I blurt out.

He is, I'm learning.

Thoughtful and detail-oriented.

Kind and loyal.

Fierce and determined.

He catches onto things I like and things I don't like quickly, making mental notes.

He's learned that his fingers on my skin cause me to stutter and his elusive smiles make *me* smile.

It's a shame I spent two years thinking of him as anything less than magnificent.

"Your face looks much better." I scoot closer to examine his battle wound for a few nights ago. He doesn't pull away. "May I?"

When he nods, I bring my hand to his cheek, resting it on his skin.

We *still* haven't acknowledged the night. The faint mark is a constant reminder of what he did.

"Much better," he rasps, eyes closing, a grain of sand stuck to his beautiful eyelash. I wish I could wipe away the hurt he's experienced. I wish I could convey how thankful I am for everything he's done for me. To tell him he's a good man, no matter what other people say. It's scary when you want to be raw and honest with someone, unsure of how they'll react.

"Jack," I start, my voice barely above a whisper. My fingers run over his stubble, down his cheek, my palm resting on the side of his neck, thumb on his pulse point. His eyes snap open, and I hesitate, afraid I've gone too far. "Sorry. I wanted to touch you."

"Keep going," he pleads, jerking his head, provoking me. "Wherever you want."

We're so close.

I think back to our disagreement in my office, his ruinous

eyes on my mouth. They're looking at me again, studying me, and I practically melt.

I need to lean forward.

I'd do it this time.

That's what this is, right?

I want to kiss him.

I need to feel his lips on mine.

His hand moves to my arm and I swallow as his lips hover a hair's breadth above mine. He knows it's happening, too.

"I think I want to ki—"

My phone rings in my pocket, cutting through the quiet air. We jump apart, Jack tumbling in the sand while I end up on my side.

"Shit, I'm sorry. It's Abby trying to FaceTime me."

"Take it," he says kindly.

"Are you sure?"

Please say no.

Say you want me to throw it into the water and put your hands back on me.

Touch me like I'm yours and make me see the stars.

"Of course."

"Hey, Abs!" I greet her, trying to look composed.

"Jo! Where the heck are you? I can barely see you!"

"Sorry, Jack and I took a walk on the beach."

"Hi, Jack!"

"Hello, Abby," Jack replies, and I turn the phone so he can wave to her. "How are you?"

"I'm awesome! How are you two?" I hear the amusement in her voice. "A walk on the beach sure sounds romantic. And without chaperones, too!"

"It's because I found out that Greg cheated on me and we abandoned dinner."

"What the fuck? I hate him," Abby hisses.

"Agreed," Jack adds.

"I knew I liked you," Abby says.

"That was not fun to hear. I think we're about to head back to the hotel. Everything okay?"

"Everything's great. Just wanted to check in since you've decided to ignore my texts. The news is saying we're probably going to get snow in the next few days. You know how that goes; it always ends up being nothing."

"Ugh. Snow?! Being down here has made me forget that winter exists! I'll send you a text tomorrow, is that all right?"

"Sounds good. Have fun! Bye, Jack!"

Abby disappears from my screen, and I click it closed, shoving it back in my pocket.

"Sorry."

"Why are you apologizing?" Jack asks.

"I feel like she interrupted something."

He hums noncommittally, extracting his own phone. "Wally invited us to karaoke back at the hotel."

"Hell yeah! I'm down!"

"I don't do social outings, so you might have to take this solo."

"You, Jack Lancaster, don't do social outings? I had no IDEA! If only I had learned that before you refused to come to *any* of our events at work!"

"Hilarious," he says flatly. His lip twitching betrays his attempt at boredom.

"You go to Mickey's!"

"Yes, with a few friends for a relaxing night. Not to be forced to sing 'Man, I Feel Like A Woman' or anything of the sort."

"You think Shania is my go-to song? I'm a little insulted. No offense to her. It's a catchy tune. When I hear, 'let's go, girls,' I do, in fact, want to go somewhere. Still, it's not my karaoke jam. Too predictable."

"Enlighten me. What's your pick?"

"Queen or David Bowie, obviously. If I had to pick one, it would be 'Bohemian Rhapsody.'"

"Obviously."

"Come on, Jack! It'll be fun! And after tonight, I think we both need some fun! Pleaseeee? Don't make me beg!"

"Maybe I'd like that."

My mouth parts. He meets my gaze, eyes dark.

Hooooly fuck.

That was flirting.

That had to be flirting, right?

I didn't know those four words strung together would make me want to moan in pleasure, but here we are. Would I get on my knees and plead for him to sing into a microphone? Or something much, much dirtier?

After hearing how his voice shifted, abso-fucking-lutely. I'd probably crawl to him and enjoy doing it.

"There's a good possibility that the douchebag of the year will be there," Jack continues, glazing over what he said and missing my sexual breakdown. I nod, no coherent words tumbling around in my brain. "You have nothing to say?"

"I'm still processing the part where you said you'd enjoy me begging. It was a joke, right?"

He smirks, rising from the sand like a god from the ashes. "I seem to recall you relishing in discussions centering on my sex life, Josephine. I'll let you decide for yourself."

He extends his hand to me and I grasp it, my palm shaking as he guides me to my feet.

"Shall we?"

I nod again, following him back to the hotel, his hand still intertwined with mine.

Pull it together, Jo.

"Thanks for telling me about your past." He needs to hear this. "I think you're a wonderful man, and I'm sorry that happened to you. You deserve someone who would fight for you. Even on the dark days."

Jack squeezes my hand. "Thanks. I don't think she's very far away."

Maybe it's the trick of the night sky, moon beams reflecting off the rocking water. Maybe it's the bottle of wine we split at dinner, alcohol warming my blood, or the honest conversation we shared, laying our weapons down and coming clean about our pasts.

Right now, my feet buried in the sand and a bird soaring above, I realize Jack's unlike anything I've ever seen before. He looks carefree with a youthful glow. Dimples return to his face despite the harshness of what he told me. Eyes twinkling like the stars, a supernova of blue and beauty. An attractiveness that makes me swallow hard, wanting *more*.

This is the terrible, wretched moment I realize I'm a goner.

TWENTY-FOUR
JACK

"There's the happy couple!" Wally bellows as we enter the large bar space where karaoke is being held. There's a round of applause and my cheeks heat at the unwanted attention. I've blushed more in the last few days than my entire life. Josephine, however, soaks it up like a celebrity, giggling and waving to the crowd.

I scan the room like a private investigator, eyes narrowing as I spot Greg on a barstool.

"He's here," I murmur, lips brushing across Josephine's temple. Greg must have heard our entrance, because he scowls, arms crossing over his chest. He really is an ugly motherfucker. Knowing he got to *touch* her makes my skin crawl.

"Good," she replies. "We can tell him my food poisoning magically cured itself. It's amazing what not being around bullshit does."

I snort. "Do you want a drink?"

"Yes, please!" She sounds giddy. We consumed an entire bottle of wine at dinner, and, observing her now, I notice a flushed neck and glassy eyes.

I'm not letting anyone hold her drink except me. I snag two beers from the bartender and we move over to Wally.

"Sorry we weren't able to sit together at dinner," he says, shaking my hand and giving Josephine a peck on her cheek.

"I hear you have lots of stories to share about Jack. I need to know them all."

"You certainly do not," I interject.

"You look like you're about to have a root canal," Josephine says, taking the drink from my hand. "It wouldn't kill you to live a little."

"I'm not singing."

"That's what you think," she laughs, patting my arm. "I'm going to mingle until karaoke starts. Don't be a stranger! It's perfectly okay to socialize with people. Who knows, maybe you'll make a friend or two. We don't bite."

She winks, tossing her hair over her shoulder and sauntering away, hips swaying in the jeans that hug her curves in a way that makes my imagination run wild. The hem of her tank top rides up as she leans forward to give a woman a hug, exposing a small sliver of pale skin.

Greg's eyes follow her, and I'd like to bash his face in.

"You okay?" Wally asks, and I nod curtly.

"Fine," I grumble, taking a sip of my drink. "That dude used to date Josephine. And I don't think he was very nice to her. Now he's staring at her and salivating."

Wally follows my focus. "Does he know you two are dating?"

"Yeah. And he has a girlfriend." Another swig of my alcohol.

"The worst kind of guy. Men like that ruin it for the rest of us."

"I told Josephine about Claire."

"Oh, shit. What did she say?"

"She feels bad for me. I don't know why. I'm the one who messed up."

"Will you cut that shit out? Are you going to think like that for the rest of your life?"

"No. Maybe. I don't know. It makes me scared about starting a new relationship."

"You mean with Jo?"

"Sure."

"I'm confused."

I scrub my hand over my cheeks. "We aren't actually dating."

"Huh?"

"We're not a couple. We're acting like a couple around dipshit over there."

"You're joking."

"Nope," I say, popping the p.

"But you like her."

"I—"

"Drop the bullshit, Jack."

"Yeah. I like her."

"And she likes you."

"Debatable."

"She looks at you like you hung the moon."

"She looks at everyone that way." I steal another glance at her across the room, seeing her deep in conversation with a man and a woman, head nodding along to whatever they're discussing. "She doesn't know how I feel."

"Why not?"

"Did you miss the part where I said I'm the one who messed up last time? Why would I ever put another woman through that? Especially *her.*"

Wally sighs, putting his hand on my shoulder. "You're going to therapy, right?"

"Yeah," I say gruffly. I'm not ashamed that I go. Not at all. I'm always hesitant to announce it to the world, afraid of the reaction of others and wishing it was more accepted. It's been the most healthy and helpful thing to get me through the last few years.

"Good. You haven't tried to...?"

"No. Not in almost three years. Not since..."

"Ah. You're in deep."

"Doesn't matter."

"I hate that you don't think you're allowed to be happy."

"I'm getting there. Slowly. It's an uphill battle. And very, very steep."

"You should open your eyes. That woman likes you. Maybe she doesn't realize it. Maybe you don't, either. I think happiness has been right in front of you this whole time."

"Hey!" Josephine reappears, interrupting our talk. "You guys haven't moved."

"I'm going to get another drink. I'll be back," Wally says, giving me a look.

"Did you meet some people?"

"Yeah! Everyone is so nice!" She puts her empty bottle on the table to our right. I'm sitting on a barstool, and she stands in front of me between my parted legs. "Sing with me!"

"Are you drunk?" I ask worriedly, reaching out to steady her as she sways on her feet.

"I'm not drunk. I'm pleasantly hydrated. There's a big difference." She grins.

"Pleasantly hydrated, huh? That's a new one," I chuckle, relaxing.

"Please, Jack," she whispers, eyelashes fluttering up, and my hand tenses around her. "I'd beg for you."

Oh, fuck.

Fuck.

This woman is going to kill me. My name on her lips. The *please.*

I didn't answer her question earlier.

Yes, I absolutely would like to watch her beg. She wouldn't have to try very hard. I'd give her anything she asks.

Glancing at the ceiling, I count to ten, trying to regain any functionality of my rapidly scrambling brain.

"Fine." I push off the stool, our toes touching. "I'll sing with you. On one condition: I pick the song."

"This has made the entire trip worth it!" she squeals, clapping her hands together. "What are we going to sing?"

"It's a surprise. Let's go, girl," I smirk, stepping past her to head for the stage in the center of the room. I stop at the DJ booth, speaking to the guy about my request before reaching the small set of stairs lifting to the stage. I offer Josephine my hand, guiding her onto the platform.

"I don't want to make a fool of myself by not knowing the song," she whispers.

Grabbing the two microphones, I hand one off to her, our fingers grazing in the exchange. "Do you trust me?"

"Yes."

The affirmation delights me.

"You picked Queen?!" she shrieks.

"I'm hoping you can carry us because I have nothing to contribute and will absolutely bring us down."

Josephine grins, shifting so our shoulders are touching. It feels magnificent.

Thankfully, "Bohemian Rhapsody" is one of my favorite songs, and I have the lyrics memorized. The entire crowd does too, and we give the audience five roaring minutes of perfect pitch and theatrics.

I play the air guitar. Josephine jumps around the stage, so energetic and full of life people are going wild. When the bridge comes, we look at each other and start head banging with such ferocity, I think I'm going to tumble off the stage.

By the time we finish, I'm smiling wide and Josephine's cheeks are bright pink. We exit to thunderous applause. The atmosphere in the bar is electric, the air sticky with excitement and humidity.

When we're safely on the ground, I pick her up in my arms, swinging her around as she laughs hysterically.

"That was incredible! You were incredible! Who knew you had such good pipes, Lancaster?" she squeals, and I gently set her down.

"What can I say? You bring out the fun side of me," I answer, smiling back at her.

The happiness doesn't last, though, as Greg appears next to us.

"Quite the performance, you two." He smirks, sipping a beer.

It's taking a lot of restraint to not reach over and slice his throat with the glass. I've never been a violent person. I've never even been in a fight. In fact, I'm a big advocate for using words and not fists. Right now, however, I'm close to injuring this guy beyond belief. Anything to wipe the stupid look off his face.

"Where'd Liz run off to after dinner, Greg?" Josephine asks. "Did you leave her in the room so you could come down here and bang someone else? I know how much you love cheating on your significant other."

My arm falls over her shoulders like it's the most natural thing in the world, and I give her an encouraging squeeze. I love when she gets feisty.

"When your significant other is good enough, you don't have to cheat. It's a shame you'll never learn what that's like," Greg retaliates.

"Josephine and I were about to head out for the night," I jump in. "So if you'll excuse us."

He scoffs. "You really expect me to believe this thing between the two of you is legitimate? There's zero chemistry happening here. Jack, you could do so much better."

Yeah. I really want to kill this guy.

"Believe what you want," I say through clenched teeth. "My woman is going to fall asleep tonight happy and satisfied after I fuck her into oblivion, knowing her boyfriend doesn't have a micropenis. I doubt Liz can say the same about you. Now kindly, fuck off."

I tug Josephine away from the conversation, and she bursts out laughing.

"Micropenis?!"

"I'm sure I could have come up with something more articulate, but I didn't feel like instigating more shit."

"You took the high road. Even if the high road means telling someone they have a micropenis. I'm putting that on your cup next week."

The first reminder that our time together will be coming to a close sooner rather than later.

"Your unwavering support in my lackluster insults is what's keeping this relationship afloat, Josephine. Want me to walk you to your room?"

"Where you'll fuck me into oblivion?" she asks, her voice sounding sexier than before. "I'm on the other side of the hotel from you, so I can manage by myself. Thank you for tonight. For talking with me. For singing with me. For opening up. And for being an all-around wonderful man."

She envelops her arms around my waist, face buried in my shirt.

I try. I try really fucking hard, but I can't help but stroke her hair, brushing through the red locks. As I embrace her, I smell lilacs and vanilla. Scents that remind me of happiness and joy and goodness in the world. I want to inhale deeper, but I refrain. For now, I'll enjoy this brief interlude before pulling away and letting her go, missing her each second she's gone.

"The pleasure was all mine," I murmur, my thumb sliding to the nape of her neck, applying the slightest amount of pressure. She melts further into me, chest grazing against mine, and I swear I can feel her nipples harden through her shirt.

"Jack? Can I ask you a question?"

"Anything."

She peels herself off my body. "Do you think we have chemistry?"

I study her, wondering how she wants me to play this.

"No. I don't think we have chemistry."

Her face crumples. The light in her eyes fades and her back hunches. "Yeah, me neither." She jabs the up button for the elevator repeatedly, and I reach out, my hand covering hers.

"I think we have so much more than chemistry. But not yet. Not like this. Not because of him," I whisper.

She studies me, gnawing on her lip before she nods. "Okay," she answers, breathless. "Not like this."

I bring her hand to my mouth, lips trailing over her knuckles. She shudders in response.

"Good night, sweetheart."

"Good night."

She steps into the elevator. The steel doors close, shuttering her from view, exactly like the first day we met.

Her question makes me feel hopeful. Inquisitive. Daring to take a step closer to the deep end with her. I can't shake the feeling that we're heading down the same path as before.

Destruction.

TWENTY-FIVE

JO

I'm packing my suitcase after our last day at the conference when a knock on my hotel room door causes me to pause, shoving my unused bathing suit into the side of my bag. What a scam. Four days in the Keys and I didn't get to experience the ocean water more than a quick dip of my toes last night. The waves were taunting me during the wrap-up discussion this afternoon, ebbing and flowing on the other side of the window like they were beckoning me to throw my papers in the air, yell *"screw it,"* and run outside. I stayed in my seat and tried not to glare at the colorful umbrellas fluttering in the breeze while listening to the ways technology is going to shape our future. For someone with a more creative-driven brain, it was almost a snooze-fest, even if it is my area of expertise.

"Oh, hey," I say, opening the door to see Jack. He's wearing khaki shorts and my eyes wander to his long legs.

Toned.

Defined calf muscles.

Tan like the rest of his body.

I snap my gaze up quickly.

"See something you like?" he asks curiously, a smile ghosting his lips.

"Yes. No. Maybe. What's up?" I lean against the door frame, trying not to fall over, surprised by the sight of him. I thought we parted ways until the airport tomorrow morning after the last reception of the conference earlier this evening.

"People have requested our presence on the beach. And by people, I mean Wally. Food was mentioned, as well as a bonfire. Cornhole, too. I was told to bring my better half, and, knowing you like food and to make a mess while you eat, I figured you'd be interested in joining."

"A bonfire? That's spontaneous of you! Who all will be there?"

"If you're asking about the dickbag of the year, I'm not sure, to be honest. He strikes me as the kind of guy who would show up even if he wasn't invited."

"That's fine. We leave tomorrow, and then I won't have to see him ever again." I grab my phone and room key sitting on the perch by the door. "Lead the way, Lancaster."

We find our way to the beach where a raging fire burns bright, the fading sun drenching the sand in orange and pink. There's a buffet table set up off to the side. Wally waves at us from around the flames and I hurry over to him as Jack heads for a cooler in the sand.

"There's my favorite couple!" he exclaims.

"Hey, Wally," I say, grinning as I give him a hug and take the empty chair next to him. "How's it going?"

"Better, now that you two are here. If this prick doesn't stop bragging about all his so-called accomplishments, I might scream," he grumbles, and I follow his finger to find Greg laughing and sitting awfully close to a blonde woman who is *not* Liz.

Old habits die hard, I guess.

"The only reason I'm glad we're leaving tomorrow is to get away from him."

"Jack told me you two dated. I find it hard to believe, but I guess we all have a mistake in our past."

"You have no idea. Hopefully your mistake isn't as horrible as the one over there."

"The opposite, actually. My mistake is the one that got away. Is my boy treating you right?"

"Jack? He's great! I'm so lucky!"

I'm a complete asshole for lying to someone so close to Jack, but we're hours away from leaving and I can hold it together a little while longer.

"I know you two are faking it."

"What?!"

Wally grins. "Yeah. He told me last night."

"That little jerk," I mumble. "I'm so sorry. For the record, I've felt horrible this whole time."

"Psh. Don't. It's funny that you two think it's fake."

"It is..." I say slowly.

"Mhm. I worry about him. I know you know what happened, so you can understand why. It's obvious you bring out the good in him."

"How can you tell? You've seen us interact for, like, twenty minutes!"

"Trust me, I know these things. I know he can be a bit..."

"Menacing? Brooding? Grumpy? Irritated?"

"All perfect adjectives. And all correct. He's different around you."

"How so?"

"I can see his facade trying to crack. I wish he would let it."

I look over the fire and notice Jack waving me over to the buffet table. "Maybe I need to take a sledgehammer to it myself and see if that works. I'll be right back."

"Greg is here," Jack mumbles when I join him by the food.

"I saw," I reply, reaching for a plate and piling it high with pulled pork, tater tots, and a piece of cornbread. I ate the provided dinner only an hour ago and I'm already starving again. "Why didn't you let me know you told Wally this is fake?" I hiss as we make our way back to the bonfire.

"I knew you felt bad about it, and I wanted to be honest, too."

"A little heads up would've been n—"

I freeze, staring at the lone chair that's unoccupied.

"I'll stand," we blurt out in unison.

"You will do no such thing," he argues, neither one of us budging from where we've stopped in the sand, a few yards away from everyone else.

"I can assure you I know how to eat standing up. Take the chair."

"And not offer it to my girlfriend? Absolutely not."

"I'd offer for us to share, but my ass is way too big to fit on that piece of wood only halfway."

"I like your ass," he mumbles before his eyes widen in horror. "Shit, please pretend you didn't hear that and I didn't just objectify your body like a sleazeball."

I grin at him slyly. "I'm afraid I heard it loud and clear, Lancaster."

His face is bright red, and he's fumbling for words. "I was going to offer a different kind of sharing, but I'm not sure if that's wise after my comment."

"What was your suggestion?"

Greg's staring at us, rubbing his jaw, and I'm seconds away from panicking.

Jack puts his hand on my elbow, gently spinning me to face him. He pulls me close, my paper plate pushing against his chest. The piece of cornbread almost falls into the sand as he rests his forehead against mine.

"What's your idea?" I repeat, desperately hoping it's what I'm thinking.

"We have two options, Josephine. You can sit in my lap and we can continue this fake dating dance as we ride off into the sunset, one last hoorah before heading home. Or, we can turn around and get the hell out of here."

My cheeks burn. That is exactly what I was thinking, too.

"I don't want to make you uncomfortable," I whisper.

"I'm merely a pawn at your disposal to help in any way I can."

"Fine. Yes. Let's share."

Jack walks to the chair and scoots so his spine meets the back of the chair. I eye his thighs and take a deep breath, drifting toward him, turning around and perching on the edge of his knees.

Wally regales us with tales of a drunken sophomore Jack, who snuck into the prestigious Princeton library and moved the location placards to random places. He turned biographies into law reviews and peer-edited papers into chemistry books. My sides hurt from laughing so much and Jack, despite his huffing and puffing at being the center of attention, has a smile on his face.

Carol, who I learn is a mom of two, breaks out a handle of vodka and everyone cheers.

"Doing okay?" Jack asks while everyone is distracted, too busy pouring themselves a shot to pay any mind to our hushed conversation. Wally takes a gulp straight from the bottle, bypassing a cup altogether.

I nod, my curls brushing against his cheek. "I am. Are you?"

"Never better. You don't look comfortable."

"My back is hurting."

"That's because you're sitting at a bizarre angle like you'd rather be in the sand than in my lap."

"Do you have a solution for that? Are you a chiropractor?"

He pauses, clearing his throat. "Lean back against me."

"Right. Okay. Well. Sure. Easy enough."

I stand, flipping off Wally after he gives me a sly smile. Taking a deep breath, I face away from Jack and lower myself onto his legs. The world has stopped moving as I shift, my shoulder blades pressing into his chest.

"Better?" His voice is coarse as he puts his chin on my shoulder.

"Much," I squeak out, my ass shifting on his thigh. His hand comes up my side, resting on my waist.

"Two taps on my hand if you're uncomfortable at any point. Got it, Josephine?"

"Got it."

"Good girl."

The word of praise singes me. I think he used it on purpose. I'm glad he did.

This is past enemy level.

This is past cordial colleague level.

This is past two people trying to move forward as friends level.

This is slide back a few inches and I could sink onto his dick level.

And hell, that turns me on more than I care to admit.

"So, Wally, you didn't bring a special someone with you?" I ask brightly, trying to ignore the way I can feel *everything Jack* against me.

His chest muscles and how they flex, the thin material of his shirt barely protecting me from the onslaught of his masculinity and defined, solid features.

His breathing leaving goosebumps on the curve of my neck,

trailing down to my collarbone and disappearing across my breasts.

How his fingers press subtly into my hip like he's playing the piano, gently drumming, thumb to pinkie and back again.

My body craves his, trying to morph and contort into his space so we're one and not two.

"Nah, I'm not lucky enough like Romeo behind you to find someone permanent yet. One day soon, hopefully."

"Something like this is worth the wait," Jack agrees, and I feel him brush my hair to one side of my shoulder.

Oh, god.

I shudder to think what it would be like if we were alone.

And not pretending.

My nipples are hardening under my tank top.

My thighs press together, squeezing tightly.

I must start squirming because Jack pushes into my hip with more force, stilling my movements.

"If you don't stop moving, Josephine, we're going to have serious problems," he murmurs.

"What kind of problems?"

"Problems that will make it very difficult for me to stand up without the entire world seeing the effect you have on me."

"You're my boyfriend. It wouldn't be totally unreasonable."

"I'm your boyfriend for one more day."

"Not even," I whisper.

"Jack, my man, up for a game of cornhole?" Greg interjects, interrupting what feels like our final goodbye.

People around the fire look at us, eagerly waiting for an answer.

"Are you going to fight for my honor?"

"Do you want me to fight for your honor?"

"Beanbags aren't nearly as hot as swords, but it would be entertaining to watch."

"Sure, I'll play," he announces. "Under one condition."

"What's that?" Greg replies, arching his eyebrow.

"If I win, you stop talking to Josephine. Period. No snide comments. No side conversations. You'll pretend like she doesn't exist."

A chorus of *ooohs* comes from the circle and my mouth drops open.

Greg's lip curls in disgust.

"I'll agree to your terms. But if I win, you and I go get a beer and we can compare notes about all the things she likes in bed."

Jack growls behind me, already rising from the chair. "Game on."

TWENTY-SIX

"You really don't have to do this," I plead to Jack as he stretches
—actually stretches—arms crossing over each other. "You proved
your point. Everyone knows Greg's an asshole. We can leave it
at that, and you can bow out gracefully."

"Sorry, Bowen. It's time to fight to the death. Public humili-
ation isn't what I usually gravitate toward, but I think this
particular situation warrants bringing out the big guns." He
kisses my forehead and I sigh, stepping out of the way and
joining Wally on the sideline of the designated game area.

Thirty people surround the two boards, the group seeming
to multiply as they form a half circle, ample space between the
two pieces of wood in the center of the action.

"This is stupid," I mutter. "Why must everything be a
pissing contest for men?"

"Agreed. It's also entertaining and the most fun part of the
whole conference. Learning about data entry has *nothing* on the
smackdown about to occur. I have to give Jack credit; if anyone
said a line like that to my girlfriend, his face would be two feet
deep in the sand right now," Wally says.

"Fake girlfriend," I amend.

"Tomato, tomato."

"He wouldn't be out here at all, ready to avenge my enemy, if I wasn't a complete idiot and could confront my demons head on instead of using a proxy. I'm sure he'd prefer to be in his hotel room reading a book."

"That does sound like him," Wally agrees, chuckling. "He's talked about you for a while now, you know."

"Pardon?"

"When I asked him about work when he first started at Itrix, he constantly grumbled about the infuriating woman in the office destined to ruin his life. Slowly, he changed his tune. The adjectives changed. 'Irritating' became 'intelligent.' 'Annoying' became 'kind.' It frustrated him that no matter what he said or did, you never gave up on him."

For the first time, I allow myself to wonder if maybe Jack isn't pretending at all. There have been too many interactions over the last two years to categorize every minute detail, but I noticed the subtle shifts in his behavior. His shoulders relax when I approach him outside the office building on Tuesday mornings. When he spots me, his phone always goes into his pocket, and I have his full, undivided attention. Like I'm the only one in the world.

The half smiles he hides when he picks up his drink, trying not to look too eager to discover what name I've given him that day.

The time he knocked his shoulder into the investor who wouldn't stop talking my ear off in the hallway at work, even as I kept scooting away, so uncomfortable I almost ducked into a broom closet to hide.

The Post-It notes.

The saved coffee cups.

The kisses on my cheeks and hands.

Things that, in the moment, I didn't pick up on.

Watching our time together play back, I can't believe I've been so blind. A fog lifts, and I can see clearly.

Finally.

He likes me.

And I think I like him, too.

"Did he ever share what changed?"

"Nah. Not specifically. He realized he's allowed to be happy, even if it's a difficult task. And that there's someone out there who isn't afraid of him, even the not-so-pretty parts, no matter how hard he tries to push them away. At the end of the day, isn't that what we're all searching for? Someone who welcomes us with open arms, exactly as we are?"

"There's got to be a better way to convey that than a stupid game involving Greg."

"I'll have you know, Jack, I've played a lot of cornhole," Greg says boastfully from his side. He tosses the first bag, and it slides into the hole easily. A grumble goes through the crowd. "A lot of my friends have rooftop patios in the city. You should come hang out sometime."

"Pretentious asshole," Wally mutters under his breath and I nod in agreement.

"Is that so?" Jack picks up his own beanbag, weighing it in his hands for a minute. Looking over his shoulder, he finds me in the crowd and tosses me a grin before launching the bag. His also lands straight in the hole, and everyone around us erupts in cheers.

It's pretty evident the spectators are on Team Jack.

Greg's swagger falters slightly. His grin drops, but his aim doesn't. His second bag sails right into the intended target. "Looks like we have a good match here, my friend. I'll get my notes ready."

"I probably should have told you I played baseball in

college," Jack retorts, his second bag landing in the same spot. "Starting pitcher."

"Pitcher?!" I ask Wally, elbowing him. "Are you kidding me?!"

Greg's third bag drops in the hole and a ball of nerves forms in my stomach.

"Oh, yeah, he was unstoppable," Wally laughs, unfazed by the game as Jack's third toss copies Greg's.

Three in a row for each of them.

A tie game.

"Took Princeton to the championship his freshman year."

Greg's final toss lands in the sand, inches away from the board, and he grits his teeth in annoyance.

"Did they win?" I ask nervously.

"10-0. Jack pitched a perfect game."

I watch as he tosses the final bag and it soars across the sand in slow motion, landing with a thunk through the hole.

Shrieking, I run to him, wrapping my arms around his neck. "That was incredible!"

"Don't kiss me," he says quickly, the excitement of the winning moment dissipating immediately, leaving behind a sour residue. "Please, Josephine. Not here."

"I-I wasn't," I stammer, my grip around him relaxing as I fall back onto my feet.

"Good."

The words shouldn't sting but they do. I swallow hard, pulling away from him and wanting to disappear. Wally wasn't right at all. Jack wants nothing to do with me.

"Great game."

"Anything for my girl," he says, loud enough for Greg and the others to hear.

"I'm going to head up. I need to finish packing."

"I'll go with you."

"That's okay," I say firmly, turning my back on him as I walk over to Wally to say goodbye. "I'll manage."

"Don't tell me you're leaving," he groans. "You're my favorite person here."

"I'm sorry. It was so great to meet you, and I hope I can see you again one day."

Wally pulls me into a hug and I giggle. "You and Jack should come visit Alabama. I know it sounds like a boring place, but I promise we have some fun things there."

"I'd love that," I say. My throat constricts knowing it'll never happen.

"If Jack gives you problems, let me know and I'll take care of him."

"Thanks, Wally."

I give Carol a quick hug as well. We exchanged personal information earlier and I'm excited to send her an email when I get home to set up a call on strategies. I don't bother giving Greg a second glance, and as I trudge back to the hotel in the sand, I hear someone following me.

"Josephine? Can you slow down?" Jack's voice echoes.

"You didn't have to walk with me," I answer as he falls in step next to me. We enter the hotel, the cold air making me shiver.

"Of course I didn't. I wanted to." He nudges my shoulder gently. "Are you all right? I hope I didn't overstep a boundary when I made that wager with Greg."

"I'm fine," I say poignantly as we file into the elevator. "I don't care about the wager. I'm glad you won."

"Then what else is going on?"

"Nothing. It's not important."

I'm certainly not going to tell him what's been pounding through my head. The genuine feelings that have developed and stir inside me, slowly awakening and the stupid crush that's emerged from our time together. I'm also not going to turn his refusal to kiss me into a big deal. He said at the beginning of this fiasco that was a hard boundary for him. Why am I shocked he'd still adhered to that ask? It's not part of our game, and I'm being selfish for wanting him to throw everything aside to cater to my cravings.

When we leave here tomorrow, everything stops. One kiss wouldn't change that, and it's for the best that we don't complicate things before we head home. We're a plane ride away from returning to reality. So what if I'm imagining what his lips feel like? If he'd sink his teeth into my bottom lip and tug when he pulls away, and what a swipe of his tongue tastes like? It doesn't mean anything. When we exit this carefully constructed bubble of ours and fall back into sync with our normal lives, the need and curiosity of experiencing Jack in salacious, intimate ways will fade away.

Right?

"You're thinking very hard over there."

"Sorry. I have a lot on my mind."

"Anything I could help with?"

"No. You've done more than enough." I reach into my pocket and pull out my room key, fumbling the card against the digital lock. It clicks, and I shove the door open. "Thanks for everything."

He runs his hand through his hair. The evening ocean breeze made it messy, and I'm going to miss how it looks down here on the island. "You don't need to thank me for anything, Josephine. I had a lot of fun as your fake partner. If you ever need my services again, I'd be honored."

"Cool. Have a good night, Jack."

He reaches forward, tucking a curl behind my ear before his finger runs down my neck. A soft smile sits on his face, dimple appearing. He stares at me like he's committing me to memory, as if he'll never see me again. I watch his eyes travel from my forehead to my chin, expression turning from content and happy to regretful. In a way, I guess this is the last time we'll see each other this way. The second this door closes, that'll be it. We'll no longer be Jack and Jo the couple.

"You too, Josephine." Learning forward, he gently presses his lips to my cheek, so delicately it doesn't feel like he's there at all. "I'll see you in the morning. Sweet dreams."

I watch him walk away, his head hanging low and hands shoved in his pockets, body becoming more rigid with each step. I wait, wondering if he'll look over his shoulder. Hoping. He turns the corner without another glance, and I sigh, sliding into my room and closing the barrier to Jack and our time together on the island. It's time to go home.

TWENTY-SEVEN
JACK

"I can't believe I have to sit through another flight with you," Josephine says as we pull our luggage through the small airport. Security was a breeze, and we're at our gate with plenty of time to spare.

I'm in a foul mood this morning, unable to contain the scowl residing on my mouth the moment I woke up from a stilted, disjointed sleep. Since I said goodbye to Josephine last night, I've been disappointed. Irritated. Bummed.

I didn't want to walk away from her door. I should have asked her to sit under the stars again, listening as she talked about everything and nothing and anything in between. Let her toss sand my way and nudge my shoulder with hers. Instead, I forced myself to leave, each step harder to take than the last. My eyes stayed trained on the carpeted hallway and it took everything in my being to not turn around. She was standing in her doorway, waiting to see what I would do. Holding onto a small thread of hope that I'd come back to her. Her door didn't snick closed until I turned the corner, disappearing from view.

"Such hardships in life," I reply. "The plane isn't here yet."

"Maybe it's delayed? There are some seats over there."

We make our way to a row of unoccupied chairs, sitting side by side. I pull out my laptop for the first time in four days, powering it on.

"Vacation is over, huh?" she observes, kicking her feet up on her suitcase and pulling a book from her purse.

"I'm terrified to see how many emails I have." I click on my inbox, watching the number grow. "Fuck, there's 300 of them."

"300?! That's absurd. Who in the world do you talk to? I know people think you're important, but you're not *that* special."

"You're right. I'm not special. I imagine some are from the conference." I scan the screen, fingers typing away methodically.

"I love hearing you admit when I'm right. Forget whispering sweet nothings in my ear."

"Hush. How's your book? What genre?"

"Far more interesting than those emails. It's a romance novel."

"Tell me more. Believe it or not, the emails are exceedingly dull. I already have a headache."

The pressure in my forehead is building. I spent last night tossing and turning, too busy thinking about the hurt look on Josephine's face when I told her not to kiss me after I won that stupid game.

She took it offensively, and I don't blame her. I just... I didn't want the first time we kissed to be in front of a whole crowd, an audience watching our every move. I wanted to do it right and savor the moment.

Now that we're heading home, I don't think a first kiss will ever happen.

It's my own damn fault.

"Maybe you're getting old and need glasses," she jokes and I throw a glare her way. "It's a spicy scene, so unless you want me to read borderline porn to you in the public airport, I'll pass. Romance novels are so cliché with sex, but we keep buying them."

"Oh? Cliché how?" I ask, my curiosity piqued. I turn my body to face her, our knees resting against each other. Her face reddens. She wasn't expecting me to ask for clarification, but I'm glad I did.

She checks to see if anyone is nearby. When she talks, she keeps her voice low, and I lean forward to hear her.

"For starters, everyone lets out all these breaths they didn't know they were holding. How do you not know if you're breathing?"

"Maybe they're so enraptured by the sight in front of them, they physically couldn't breathe."

"Don't get all romantic on me, Lancaster. When in your life has that ever happened?"

"Once." *The first day I met you.*

"Interesting. Care to elaborate?"

"I certainly do not."

"Shocking. Next, both characters always come at the same time. You're telling me that a couple is so in tune with each other, they can come on command from a single word, together? It's unrealistic. Seventy-five percent of women don't orgasm from intercourse alone."

I raise my eyebrow. "Seventy-five percent? Are you sure? That's quite high."

"Positive. I read an article about it recently. I'd love to see more books incorporate other aspects of a sexual relationship, you know? Toys. Foreplay."

I cannot believe I'm having this conversation with Josephine in the middle of an airport before noon. She's tossing around words so casually.

Orgasm.

Intercourse.

Sexual relationship.

Words that I would rather have whispered in my ear, hotel sheets pooled around us, her on top of me as she comes apart, hands clutching my shoulders for balance while she takes what she needs. I want to be her undoing.

"You know how I feel about that subject," I say evenly, checking out the window to see if our plane has arrived yet. I can't sit here much longer if she's going to keep talking about foreplay.

The worst part is I *want* her to keep speaking. I want to hear what other dirty, filthy things she'll say. I want to ask if she brought her sex toy with her on the trip, and if she's used it any of these nights.

I'm going to need a dozen cold showers when I get home.

"Yeah. I do. Lastly, I hate when authors skip the good stuff. I spend 250 pages reading about sexual tension. Sensing the chemistry between two characters. Screaming at them to kiss. When it comes to the final product, I want to see results. I want details!"

"Wow."

"Sorry. I'm sure I sound like a smut-obsessed charlatan."

"Far from it, actually. I can't say I've read any romance books, but you make valid points. You should write your own."

"Uh, no thanks. Writing is way too difficult. I'll stick to reading."

A loud voice full of static comes over the speakers.

"Thank fuck," I mumble, closing my computer and shoving it in my bag.

"Ladies and gentleman, we received word that our flight is going to be canceled today. Due to a heavy snowstorm in the Northeast, the plane is unable to take off in New York to fly here and fly you all back to Massachusetts."

Canceled? What does that mean? Are other airlines flying out today? Surely someone has a flight somewhere off this island.

"We're booking hotel rooms for you all, as it appears unlikely you'll be getting out of here in the next few days. We apologize for the inconvenience. When you hear your name called, please approach the podium. It's going to take us a few minutes to get things set up, so we kindly ask you to stay in your seats until we call your name. I promise we will get to you."

"I gave Jensen a heads-up," Josephine says.

"Good idea."

"Bowen? Josephine Bowen and Jack Lancaster? Can you approach the podium please?"

I sigh in relief, gathering my belongings and walking to the counter, Josephine in tow behind me.

"Hi," she says, smiling at the agent behind the desk. "I'm Josephine Bowen."

"And I'm Jack Lancaster."

"Can I check your IDs?"

I reach into my pocket for my wallet and she pulls hers out of her purse. We hand them over and the woman clicks on the mouse a few times before smiling up at us.

"Great. Thank you. We have you booked at the Hilton. A king room for four nights."

"Tha—hang on. Two rooms, correct? And four nights? We could drive back faster than that!" Josephine speaks first, and I catch up to what she's saying.

A king bed.

One room.

For the two of us.

Of fucking course.

"No, just the one," the agent says, her smile wavering.

"We aren't together," I interject.

"Oh, I'm so sorry. You're on the same reservation, the seats were purchased with the same credit card, and you were sitting next to each other." Her eyes frantically look at the computer in front of her. "I-I don't have anything else available. All the area hotels are full for the weekend. It's a miracle we got as many rooms as we did. Perhaps when you arrive at the hotel they can figure something out for you," she concludes nervously.

"Thank you so much," I say tightly, taking the stack of papers off the counter.

I turn and walk away, as fast as my legs can take me.

"Can you slow down?"

"It's fine, Josephine. You can take this one. I'll find something online."

"Flights are canceling left and right. We're on a small island full of tourists, and I highly doubt anything is available. Why else would they put us together?"

I step off to the side of the concourse, pulling up hotel websites.

Nothing.

Lovely.

Being alone with her means being forced to confront these feelings I've been experiencing so heavily the last few days.

The way she looks so beautiful in the moonlight, the night sky casting a soft glow over her features.

How we almost kissed on the beach, her hand on my cheek, both of us leaning toward each other like magnets, inches away from finally capturing her lips with my own.

How, when she touches me, my body responds so eagerly and excitedly. My emotions simmer. My blood hums. Breathing is easier. Her unknowing touch is fucking magic, working me up without even realizing it. If she *tried*, I'd be a puddle on the floor.

She makes me feel alive. More than I have in my entire life.

Her laugh gives me air. Her smile jolts my brain. Her hands, delicate and soft, coax me awake with the slightest graze against my skin.

Spending multiple days in a single, tiny hotel room with her... Fuck, I'm already warm.

Yeah, several cold showers are in my future.

"I'll see if they have a last-minute cancellation when we get there. Maybe there's a supply closet or something," I mumble as we walk toward the airport exit.

"Hey. We get extra days on a beautiful island. Will we have to share a room? Most likely. I won't let that bother me, though. We made it through four days unscathed. We can handle a few more. You don't snore, do you?" she asks, yanking her bag off the escalator forcefully as the wheel gets caught.

"I've never been told that I do."

"Great. We'll see what the sleeping arrangements look like and go get a milkshake. The good news is we're off the hook for the whole dating thing. We're free to do whatever we want. We can live separate lives."

"You might be the only person I know who would pick a milkshake over a piña colada. There's the hotel van."

"Hey, folks," the driver says, waving at us. "Are you arriving or did your flight cancel?"

"Canceled, unfortunately," Josephine says, climbing into the van. Rolling our suitcases to the driver, I pull out my wallet, handing him a ten-dollar bill in appreciation for helping with our bags. I follow behind her, settling on the bench seat and leaving the middle open.

"What flavor milkshake are we talking about?" I ask, and she giggles. "That might be the deciding factor on if I'll be accompanying you to the beach or pretending like I don't know you exist based on your horrible taste in ice cream."

"Cookies and cream, obviously. If we have to pick from basic flavors, swirl is superior. Do I pass the test?"

"With flying colors," I say, giving her a genuine smile. She grins right back. My heart swells three sizes.

"Here comes the last party we're waiting on," the driver announces. I hear voices behind us and the slam of the trunk.

"Jack! My man! And Jo! What a surprise!"

Greg's voice rings through the vehicle and I suck in a sharp breath.

I like to think I'm an okay human. Sure, I'm not exceedingly friendly, but I'm not rude, either. I hold the door open for people and let someone with fewer items go in front of me at the grocery store. I try not to talk badly about others, and I brush my teeth and floss twice a day, which I know is infinitely better than most of the population.

Right now, however, it feels like the universe is really out to get me.

"Greg."

Josephine doesn't acknowledge his presence, but her entire persona changes as he and Liz clamber into the van. She curls in on herself, knees to her chest, becoming small, like she's trying to hide from the world.

I don't know the entire history of their relationship, and frankly, I don't care to. Learning what he's said and done to her will not only fuel me with a deeper rage and fury than I'm already experiencing, but it'll entice me to punch him in the face and have zero regrets.

I'm unbuckling my seatbelt and scooting across the scratchy fabric, settling by her side before I can think twice.

"Hey." My arm drapes over the seat, and my shoulder smushes into hers in what I hope is a comforting gesture.

"Hi," she says back. I can hear the hurt and pain in the single word. She keeps her eyes trained ahead.

"Can I put my arm around you?"

She hesitates for a second, and I don't push it. I'm about to move back to my side of the seat when she nods. Slowly, carefully, I let my arm drop around her shoulders, tucking her into my side. I angle my body so *he* can't see her. Can't speak to her.

"Thank you."

"There's nothing to thank me for, Josephine."

"This means we'll have to keep pre—"

"Shh," I say, my right hand tilting her head up to get a better view of her face. Her eyes, normally full of light and happiness, look cautious and guarded. "I don't care. Fuck it. All I care about is you and making sure you're okay."

"A freak snowstorm and we both end up back at the same hotel? Crazy, huh," Greg scoffs from behind us.

The word sets her off. Her head jerks away and her grip tightens around her legs.

"Crazy," she repeats. I try to keep my features schooled as I stare straight ahead, my jaw flexing.

The driver saves us, starting his spiel about the hotel. "We'll get you all checked in. It's all-inclusive and dinner is in the main restaurant downstairs. We also have a couple of casual dining options if that's more your scene, and an exquisite five-star restaurant, too. We have a slew of activities at your disposal. Swimming. Snorkeling. Parasailing. You can go out on a boat in the afternoon. We also have our own private beach, as well as two pools, one with a water slide."

"I love water slides," Josephine says.

"I don't think they're designed for a thirty-one-year-old, Jo," Greg laughs, voice dripping with sarcasm. I'm going to put him through the roof of this car.

"That's not true!" the driver interjects, playing referee. "Everyone goes on them!"

He pulls us into a massive complex, larger than where we

spent the last few days. I open the door to the van and climb out, holding out my hand for her. She takes it, stepping onto the pavement. I swipe my thumb across her wrist and her eyes drop to where we're joined. Moving her palm into mine, I grab our suitcases with my spare hand and we walk to the lobby, not offering the asshole behind us another minute of our time.

"Can I help you?"

The young man behind the counter smiles at us. I step to the side to let Josephine run the show.

"Hi! We had a canceled flight, and the airline booked us here. Last names are Bowen and Lancaster."

"We're so excited to have you with us. Unfortunately, we are booked up for the next few days. All I have available is one of the presidential suites due to an inbound cancelation. Will that be okay?"

"Uh, that should be fine," she answers, and I nod in agreement.

Presidential implies lots of space.

Space that can be used to stay away from her.

"We have you down for four nights. I can't believe how bad the weather is where you live! The news is saying it's the earliest snowfall on record, up and down the entire east coast! Now you get to stay longer," he adds brightly, handing us two room keys. "My name is Marcos if you need any more help."

"Thank you," we say in unison, heading for the elevator and riding in silence. I can't bring myself to say anything to her, dread pulsing through my veins. We follow the signs on the wall to our room. There are fewer rooms up here, only four in total. When Josephine opens the door, I can't help but drop my mouth open in surprise.

"Holy shit," I whisper, awestruck as I step into the suite. I've never seen something so grand and lavish before. The space is massive, a hallway sprawling every which way and leading to multiple doors and separate rooms. If it's as big as I think, we'll be able to cohabitate amiably without any issues.

The foyer guides us to the main common area. It's a full-sized living room complete with three couches, two on either side and a longer one in the middle, all facing a wide-screen television sitting on a high, glass table. White curtains flutter in the breeze, running from the floor to the ceiling, promising large windows.

To the left is the kitchen, which has a refrigerator, stove, and oven, as well as an island in the middle with four barstools. The floor is marble—clean and cool. To the right is another hallway leading to the rest of the space.

"I can sleep on the couch," Jack says right away, nodding at the three pieces of furniture and putting his duffle bag down, marking his spot. "It looks plenty big."

"Maybe there are two beds in the bedroom." I'm certain there's going to be only one. I know how this goes.

Walking down the hall, my suspicions are confirmed. A single bed sits before us. Sure, it's a massive California king that could easily fit three people, but it's still one damn bed. The headboard is a rich brown, similar to the one back at Jack's house. Fifteen pillows litter the mattress, a combination of sleep and decorative.

"Okay," I start slowly, trying to choose my words carefully because this is a hell of an idea I'm about to lob his way. "I propose we share the bed and put a barrier between us so you don't have to worry about me rolling on you or taking all the covers. I've been known to do that in the past."

"That's not what I'm worried about," he replies, rubbing his jaw roughly.

"The couches look fancy and comfortable, and they probably are for a couple of hours. For the whole night, though? Forget it. Your legs definitely won't fit on there. My legs won't fit on there, and you're taller than me."

"Did you admit that I'm taller than you? I've been waiting for this day."

"You know you're taller than me, loser. It's scientifically proven, and I've said so before. The last thing I want to hear is you complaining about a crick in your neck when I'm trying to enjoy paradise. Would it be fun to tell you I was right? It always is. We don't have to make this weird. No one is around. We're nothing more than two people who happen to be sleeping on the same mattress at the same time but not... together. No spooning or cuddling is required. I relieve you of your boyfriend duties."

Jack stares at the bed for a moment before heaving the world's loudest sigh. I think the walls quake at the ferocity of his exhale. "Fine. We can share."

"Hooray!" I exclaim. I have zero ulterior motives for spending the night inches apart from him. It's not like I'm going to reach over and touch him, no matter how confused my brain might be. Jack drops his duffle bag on the floor and moves his suitcase against the wall before leaving abruptly, an irritated look on his face.

"I'm going to the beach," I announce down the hall, closing the door to the room so I can change. I take off my plane outfit, exchanging it for a one-piece suit and jean shorts I leave unbuttoned. I slide on my sandals, tie my hair back away from my face, and grab my sunglasses.

Jack is sitting on the couch in the living room when I approach him.

"Do you want to come?"

His eyes jerk up like I startled him, moving from my shoulders to my chest, down my stomach and to my legs. His mouth opens, then closes, not bothering to be subtle with his assessment.

"Fuck," he mutters, barely audible. I'm not sure I even heard it. "No. I'm going to stay here."

"Okay. If you change your mind, I'll be down there. Text me! You're welcome to join!" I head for the door, slinging my purse over my shoulder.

"Josephine?"

"Hm?" I look over my shoulder. Jack is intently studying the floor. The plush rug is fascinating, apparently. More so than my presence.

"You look really pretty."

"Thank you," I say softly, evacuating the room as quickly as I can.

I pass the day under an umbrella on the beach, a book in my hand and a heavy coat of sunscreen covering my sensitive skin. It's already coloring from the unrelenting rays, not used to this kind of weather so late in the year. Back home we're in sweaters and boots by now. And, apparently, snow gear. The faint red covering my shoulders finally provides evidence that I've spent time outside while I was away.

As the sun sets, orange and pink lighting up the sky while it dips below the waves, I make my way to one of the quick service restaurants in the hotel for a burger and fries, famished after filling up on Vitamin D.

I pull out my phone before ordering to text Jack and ask if he wants me to grab him some food. That's the cordial thing to do, right? If we're going to be sleeping six inches apart, the least I can do is offer to get him dinner first.

JB: Paging Jack the Ripper.

JL: You're impossible.
JL: Hello, Josephine.

JB: Hiya! I'm not sure if you have plans or if you've eaten already.
JB: I'm going to order a burger and fries.
JB: Want me to bring you some?

Three dots appear then disappear on the screen, again and again. I'm about to click my phone closed and forget I asked when an answer finally comes.

JL: Sure, if it's not too much trouble.
JL: Burger and fries sounds great.

JB: More information, please.
JB: How would you like it cooked?
JB: Any toppings?
JB: Medium fry or large fry?
JB: Don't answer that, I'm getting two larges.
JB: #WhenInRome

JL: Wow.
JL: Medium well.
JL: Lettuce, tomato, onion.
JL: Large fry, always.
JL: #DoTheyEatFriesInItaly?

JB: Cool! I'll grab them and be back soon.
JB: Dessert?

JL: Don't tempt me with a good time.

JB: I can feel the enthusiasm oozing through the phone.

JL: Smart-ass.
JL: See you soon.

Twenty minutes later, I put my keycard against the door, pushing it open with my hip.

"Honey, I'm home!" I call out, making sure to project my already loud voice so Jack can hear me come in. The last thing I want to do is catch him off guard.

He appears from the hallway wearing gray sweatpants. Gray. Freaking. Sweatpants.

Looking like every dream book boyfriend.

I can literally see the outline of his dick through those things.

A plain white shirt stretches across his chest, and his hair is damp, the small ringlets of bronze clinging to his forehead and neck.

This is going to be an impossibly long night and it's a wonder I don't drop the food I'm carrying right onto the tile floor.

"Hey," he says, offering me a smile and taking the bags from my hands, oblivious to my sexual meltdown. "How was your day?"

I follow him into the kitchen where he sets all the items on the island. I kick my sandals off along the way, keeping my eyes focused only on his shoulders and above. Nothing lower.

"Good! I finished my book!"

"I sure hope you got the details you were looking for."

"Every scandalous one," I grin, jumping onto a barstool. "I sat by the ocean for most of the afternoon. It was so nice to be outside. There's something calming about the sound of waves. Didn't get sunburned either, just sun-kissed, so all in all a successful day! How was yours?"

"After all those emails, I'm never going on vacation again."

He opens the cabinets until he finds the one with plates, bringing them to the counter.

"That sucks. Hey, are you okay? You were a little tense earlier. I know you're stressing about the hotel, and I'm sorry for joking about our living situation and making light of it. I wanted to make sure I didn't upset you, and if I did, I'm sorry."

"I didn't feel like going out. I'm tired from all the socialization these past few days. The introverted side of me was perfectly content sitting in silence. Want a beer? I grabbed some from the convenience store in the lobby."

"Of course I do. You can't eat a burger without beer."

He slides a cold bottle toward me as I open the paper bags. I pull my burger and fries out before handing his food to him.

We eat in silence, kitty-corner from each other, and I can't shake the feeling that something is wrong. His shoulders are tense, up by his ears, and he purposely avoids my gaze, getting up off his stool whenever I'm about to speak to search for random things: ketchup, napkins, a fork.

"Do you have plans tonight?" I ask, breaking the silence as I wipe the last remaining blob of ketchup off my fingers.

"Plans?"

"Yeah. I didn't know if you were going to go down to the bar or something. Or run away. If you need some space, I completely understand."

He crumbles the empty food bag and walks to the trash can. "No bar for me. I'm fine. I'm trying to work through some things."

"So we should get drunk, eat the dessert I brought up, and watch trashy television?" I laugh, attempting to throw my bag of food away from my seat. I miss, wide left, and Jack scoops it up, putting it in the bin.

"That depends. What kind of dessert did you bring?"

"It's a surprise."

"Are you okay with drinking?"

"You make me feel safe."

He pauses, his face shifting and jaw relaxing as he blinks at me. "That's a very kind thing to hear, Josephine."

"Well. It's true. You saved my life. Don't try to say otherwise," I add quickly, cutting off the protest I can already see forming.

"Thank you. That means a lot. Want me to grab some different beverages?"

"Sure. Maybe margaritas? Meet you on the couch in thirty minutes?"

He walks to the door before turning back to look at me. "It's a date," he says before leaving the room.

I raise my eyebrows in surprise, a grin splitting across my face as I hurry down the hall to the bathroom.

The shower is ridiculous. There's a bench inside and I could live here if I wanted to. It has three shower heads, two on either end and a large one above, taking over the entire ceiling. The water is the perfect temperature; scalding hot and enough to make my skin burn.

Reluctantly, I turn the water off with my pruny fingers, wrapping a thick towel around my body. My wet curls cling to my back, dripping down my spine, freshly washed and conditioned. I crack the door to the bedroom open to make sure it's empty and rummage through my suitcase for my pajamas.

I wish I had something nicer than old boxer shorts and an oversized T-shirt to wear; I look like a fraternity dude in college tailgating at a fall football game. Maybe it's time to invest in a cute nightgown or something more *adult* and *sexy*. I'm well aware nothing intimate is going to happen tonight. I just don't want to look like a slob next to the hunk of a man out there.

Twisting my hair up into a high bun on the top of my head, I pull on high socks to keep my feet warm. Habitual sock sleeper here. The sounds from the television echo through the suite as I make my way down the hall.

"Hey," I say from the entry to the formal living room. Jack is on the sofa, a beer in one hand and remote in the other. He's relaxing against the cushion, his legs parted, looking like a god waiting for an offering. "I hope casual attire is appropriate for our date."

Jack's eyes roam down my body, chugging half his beer before speaking.

"I got margarita mix."

"Wow. How many people are you inviting over?" I ask, walking into the kitchen and gawking at the supplies on the counter. "You already made the margaritas, too? How long was I in the shower? Do you want one?" I pour myself a generous portion into one of the tall glasses.

"If you could bring me another beer, that would be great."

I head back to the living room, both drinks in hand. "Can you grab a coaster for these? This table costs more than I make in a month, and I don't want to piss anyone off."

He snags two coasters, putting them on the wooden coffee table in the center of the room. Taking a seat on the opposite side of the couch, I sip my drink.

Jack tosses the remote onto the cushion between us. "See if you can find anything good. I've had no success."

I scroll through the channels, nothing interesting jumping out at me. We settle on a game show where the contestants have to do an obstacle course. The more I drink, the funnier it becomes. After almost an hour of quiet, I decide to break it.

"Can I ask you a question?" Turning to him, I bring my legs against my chest. His arms drape over the back of the couch, hands almost reaching mine. I try to ignore the way those damn pants cling to his thighs. It's nearly impossible.

"You like asking questions."

"I like getting to know people. Besides, this is my only chance. Once we go home, you'll resume your no-smiling pact and welcome back your grumpy persona with open arms. Vacation Jack? Who is that?"

"I'm not *that* grumpy, am I?"

"I don't know. You didn't eat any birthday cake last year. I'm not sure what to believe."

He chuckles. "Fine. I'll concede that I tend to be a bit of a grump at times."

"Is software development your dream job? If you could do anything in life, what would it be?"

"That's not what I was expecting. Here I was, thinking you were going to coerce me into playing Truth or Dare to get all kinds of dirt."

"Dammit. Maybe next time."

"Hang on. Before we start having a heart to heart, I think I need some dessert."

"I almost forgot!"

I hurry to the kitchen, grabbing the last paper bag and bringing it back to the coffee table. Turning it upside down, a heap of treats falls out. Candy bars. Cookies. Gummy worms.

"A few days together and you're taking after me, Josephine. This is quite the stash."

"I didn't know what you liked, so I got one of everything."

"I'll say." He reaches for the Oreos, opening the package

and offering me the first cookie. I smile, nodding my thanks and taking two. "You'll think my answer is silly."

I rest my chin on the top of my knees and smile encouragingly. "Try me."

He's quiet for a minute as he pulls the Oreo apart and eats one side. "I've always loved teaching. When I was in college, I would host tutoring sessions. I was happiest when I got to watch someone figure out the *aha* moment when they were struggling to comprehend a topic. My dream job is to be a professor. Or mentoring others about software development, engineering, and coding. Maybe in high school where classes like that aren't usually offered. We need more people in the field, especially women, and it would be cool to encourage others to pursue jobs they might not have thought about before. I know it wouldn't pay as much as working for a large corporation, but it would be more rewarding."

"I thought you didn't like public speaking?"

"I despise it. Having that kind of attention on me is unnerving. It would be different in a classroom environment. More beneficial, more rewards. I wouldn't be lecturing to people while they pretend to not fall asleep in the last row. I would share and listen and help people learn. What kind of job could be better than that?" he asks wistfully.

"You should teach," I say firmly. "What you described sounds incredible. And exactly the kind of mentality a teacher and leader should have."

"I've thought about it. More so in the last few months, to be honest. I'm afraid it might be too late now."

"It's never too late to go after your dreams." Jack snorts and I roll my eyes. "Okay, yes, I realize how corny that sounds. You're good at what you do. I know that firsthand from all the work you did to put the new website together. People at the conference were practically begging you for an autograph, lining up to pick your brain and ask you questions.

"Life is short. Take it from me. You think you have all this time. Time to spend with loved ones. Time to be in a mediocre job because you're not ready to take a leap and try something new. Time to not share feelings with others because you're afraid of the repercussions. The people that think time is infinite have never lost someone they love. Someone they care about. Someone they'd give anything in the world to have one more minute with."

I take a steadying breath before continuing. "In reality, life is too short to not do what you love. Too short to not give someone a hug or kiss when you've been thinking about it for years. You have to do what you love, Jack, and forget about the rest."

"I'm not sure I've ever been truly happy."

"Just because you've never experienced euphoric happiness doesn't mean you don't deserve it. It doesn't matter if your smiles are rare or if you smile every day. You should go after what you want, because we all deserve to smile at least a little bit. We should find joy every day."

"That might be the most beautiful thing I've ever heard," he says honestly. "You have an incredible way with words."

I blush shyly. "I do not. As your friend, I'm obligated to tell you that people will absolutely fall asleep during your classroom discussions. You could try adding some inflection to your voice. It can be exceedingly dull and monotone at times."

Jack launches a pillow at me and I duck out of the way as it tumbles over the arm of the couch.

"Noted," he chuckles. "I'll work on it."

"Next question!" I announce, clapping my hands together. "Why do you call me Josephine? Even the teller at the bank calls me Jo."

His face falls. "Does it bother you?"

"Not anymore. I always thought you did it to annoy me. Why not call me Jo?"

He thinks for a minute, setting his beer on the coaster. "In the beginning, I'll admit I used it as ammo against you. I liked that it got a reaction out of you. I also like Josephine. It's a beautiful name. Over time it evolved into something I kind of cherished getting to say. You correct everyone immediately when they use your full name. You don't correct me. I don't know. It makes me feel special. That's stupid," he grumbles.

"It's not stupid at all. I used to cringe when I heard it, to be honest. Even though we have our insults, Josephine is something only the two of us share. A secret common ground no one else knows about."

"Do you want me to stop?"

"No. I don't think I do."

"Good," he nods. "Can I ask you a question now?"

"Of course. It's only fair. A question for a question."

"In that case, I get two. Do you know how beautiful you look tonight?" he asks with the utmost sincerity.

"What?" I laugh, holding up my foot near his face. "You mean with these knee-high socks that have tacos on them and my boxers from 2007 with a hole in the ass? I'm bringing sexy back, that's for damn sure."

"I'm not kidding."

He reaches out, taking my foot in his hands. His eyes skate up my leg, stopping at the hem of my shorts.

"I meant what I said the other day. You in my shirt was devastating. Catastrophic. The things you did to me," he murmurs, pressing his thumb into my heel and rubbing in small circles. I practically moan. "But this?"

He lets out a shaky breath, bringing his fingers over the cotton of my sock, slowly up my calf, stopping right before reaching my bare skin. My toes curl at the teasing, taunting motion as his hand moves back down my leg then up again one more time, climbing higher than before, fingertips brushing my upper thigh. I want him to keep going until he reaches the part of me I so badly want him to touch.

"This is my favorite look of yours," he whispers. "Relaxed. Natural. So fucking beautiful." His eyes are heated, blazing with the ferocity of the sun at high noon on a summer day.

Jack gently lowers my foot back onto the couch, his hand slow to leave. Color overtakes his neck as he clears his throat, looking away, hands busying themselves with a loose piece of thread hanging off the cushions.

"That was inappropriate. I'm sorry."

"No," I blurt out. "I liked it." My voice quivers as I speak. Not from nerves. From desire.

"I'm going to call it a night. I want to get up early and run."

"I'm going to turn in too. Do you care if I join you?"

"Not at all."

"Cool. I'm going to brush my teeth really quick."

The sun didn't burn me, but it did suck up my energy. Coupled with the stress from the airport, seeing Greg again, a heavy meal, margaritas, sexual tension and desire sharp enough to cut glass, I'm depleted. And horny.

I slip into the bathroom, washing my face and brushing my teeth rapidly, not wanting to make Jack wait for too long. When I reenter the bedroom, he's assessing the bed like it's an overflowing landfill.

"All yours!"

"I'll be out in a few."

He scoots past me, leaving a wide berth. While he's gone, I take the chance to place three large pillows in the middle of the bed, establishing a boundary. The border is clearly defined.

I take the side near the window, hoping Jack won't have any

objections to getting murdered first if someone breaks into the room. It will give me time to sneak out to the balcony.

"I figured you'd be okay sleeping closest to the door?" I ask as he emerges, fluffing the pillows on my side and turning to face him.

"Whatever you're most comfortable with."

He's shirtless, nothing covering his beautiful form.

His shoulders are broad but not wide, helping him stand tall and proud. Abs traverse down the toned expanse of his golden chest. Fine bronze hair travels from pectoral muscles to the waistband of his pajama bottoms, disappearing from view. A defined V is chiseled on his lower stomach, sharp lines a clear definition of the effort he puts into maintaining his body.

I think I've stopped breathing at the sight of him, unable to stop staring. It's absurd, really, that a man this attractive hides under suits and jackets. And yes, I shouldn't be objectifying his physique. I truly cannot help it, spurred on as he stands there, long fingers teasing and trailing down the length of his breathtaking figure.

"Holy shit."

"Sorry," he winces, folding his arms over himself quickly. "I'm not used to sleeping with a shirt. I don't normally have company. I promise that wasn't intentional."

"It's fine." I wave my hand, feigning nonchalance, but *holy fuck*. I'm never going to get the image of his lithe body out of my mind. "I put those pillows up in the middle."

"You didn't have to do that." The bed sags under his weight.

We don't speak, our backs turned to each other as a stillness settles throughout the room. I squeeze my eyes shut as tightly as possible, trying to rid my head of the dirty visions of Jack. Shoulders that I could squeeze my legs against while I sit on his face. Hands that could cup my ass as he flips us over, crawling up my body.

Hell. I wish the pillows weren't there. I wish his arms were around me. He carried me through his house the night after the bar incident, and I'd give anything to experience it again.

"Are you still awake?"

"Barely," he replies through a yawn.

"You didn't ask your second question."

He doesn't answer, and I think he's fallen asleep. When he finally decides to speak, I can barely hear him.

"Do you want me to kiss you?"

"W-what?"

"Do you want me to kiss you?"

"I... uh... Yes?"

"You don't sound too sure."

"Is this a trick question?"

"No. It's a life is short question."

"Yes. Yes, I want you to kiss me." My voice shakes with the truth.

"Noted. Good night, Josephine," he says, voice already thick with sleep.

"Good night, Jack," I whisper back, unsure if I said something incredibly stupid or incredibly brave.

THIRTY
JO

The room is quiet.

Too quiet.

And I can't sleep.

At home, I have a very fixed nightly routine that I never deviate from. A routine which includes checking the front door to ensure it's locked. No matter where I am—my house, a friend's house or a hotel—the process is the same. Except for tonight. This evening threw me off, and now I'm never going to fall asleep.

It's deeper than a haphazard glance as I walk to my bedroom, barely paying any attention while I stride past the door. It's a rigid process; one that I keep hidden away from everyone but those closest to me. I made the mistake once before to let someone witness this side of me and the jarring words, merciless teasing, and biting insults still follow me.

The anxiety disorder stems from my childhood, as early as I can remember, and accompanied me to my adult years, the compulsion to make sure everything is properly secured, closed, and latched a constant ringing in my ears.

I'm not embarrassed. It's more the idea that people don't

understand the severity of my mental turmoil when jokes get tossed my way. They don't understand what the big deal is; it's *just a lock*. What's the worst that can happen?

I suppress an audible groan, doing my best to not disturb the sleeping human next to me and willing myself not to cry out in frustration. The longer he stays asleep, the fewer questions he'll ask.

Questions are bad.

Questions mean sharing.

The minutes crawl by as I stare at the ceiling, hands folded over my stomach as I tap my fingers, unsure of what to do. It's still dark outside which tells me it's the middle of the night. If it were early morning, I'd forgo sleep altogether, but I have several hours left until it's a reasonable time to rise.

The smart, logical thing would be to slip out of bed, check the door, then attempt to sleep. But I can't move, afraid of the sounds I'll make in the eerily quiet room.

Way. Too. Quiet.

Skipping the locks isn't even the worst part. It's the suffocating and debilitating stillness.

Quiet makes my mind race, and I can feel the dreaded sprint beginning to happen. Violent, terrifying thoughts hit like lightning, nearly paralyzing me. One second I'm focused on the ocean outside our window, and the next I'm grasping the sheets as tightly as possible, afraid someone is going to break into the room and murder us.

I sit up quickly, scenarios spiraling out of control in my head like they frequently do. When these ideas start, they come on suddenly and are impossible to stop, giving me no opportunity of escape to handle them privately.

Throwing my legs over the side of the bed, I attempt to stand. My feet push into the carpet but don't move. I've become immobile as the hyperventilating starts, a staggered, labored breath escaping my mouth involuntarily.

"Hey." The deep, sleepy timbre of Jack's voice slices through the night. He's crawling across the mattress and settling beside me before I can think twice. "What's going on?"

I let out another gasp, chest tight and hands shaking as I try to stomp down on the familiar anxiety creeping up my body from my toes to my neck, wedging between my breasts like a lethal dagger straight to the heart.

"What can I do to help?" he asks, gathering my hair from the base of my neck where it's starting to plaster itself and moving the curls to the side, cooling my skin. A cup of water ends up in my grasp, and he guides it to my mouth. I swallow it in three gulps, closing my eyes as mortification replaces panic.

"I'm so sorry."

"There she is," he murmurs, taking the empty glass and setting it aside. His right hand stays at the back of my neck, rubbing in small circles. "Talk to me."

"I'm fine. I'm sorry. Sometimes I..." I gnaw on my lip, unsure of how to voice this side of me.

"Tell me," he gently coaxes, fingers pressing into the nape of my neck, relieving the building pressure. "Tell me so I can help fix it."

"You'll think I'm crazy," I mumble. I despise that word. It's been tossed around in my life too frequently. Its connotation is harsh and wounding.

"Doubtful."

"I don't sleep very well," I admit, wringing my hands together. "I can't sleep in silence. I need noise around me, otherwise I begin to panic. My thoughts get out of control, thinking about worst-case scenarios. Someone breaking into my house. Murder. Dying. Death is my biggest fear, and when there's nothing around me but quiet, I fixate on these things. Like, how when we die, that's it. There's no more. For as long as the world spins, when we're gone... We're never coming back. I can't fathom the idea, and even talking about it right now is freaking me out."

"Oh," he whispers. "You could have told me. I'm so sorry, I was right next to you and had no idea."

"Most people don't get it. They try to talk me down from the ledge like it's no big deal. Once it starts, it's impossible for me to calm down. I ride it out. It may take minutes. Or an hour."

"Have you talked to a professional about this?" he asks, keeping his voice low. His touch dips, tracing my vertebrae. "I don't mean that offensively, and I know you go to therapy. Is this part of your discussions?"

"No. We discuss other things not relating to my sleep habits. I've been reluctant to share, because I'm not sure anyone will ever get me to accept this fear, you know?"

"I understand. Your fears are valid."

"This could have all been avoided."

"How so?"

"I have to check the locks on all the doors before going to bed. I didn't do that tonight, so I've been lying here, knowing I should get up to check but not wanting to move and disturb you."

"I want you to disturb me, Josephine, if it means you're sleeping soundly through the night and not tossing and turning, holding onto these fears without anyone to help you."

"I didn't realize it until you were already asleep. There was a whole conversation in my head about if I checked them."

"Do you have to physically see that it's locked? Or is a photo sufficient?"

"I need to see for myself."

Jack nods, his touch dropping from my back as he shifts off the bed to stand. "I'll go with you."

"What? You don't need to do that. I'm so sorry I woke you up. I'll be quick. You can go ba—"

"I don't need to do anything. I want to," he says firmly, ending the argument. He holds his hand out to me and I take it, climbing off the mattress.

We're facing each other, the back of my thighs hitting the edge of the bed. I've forgotten he's bare above his waist, and my eyes dart down to where we're almost touching, hardly any separation between our chests.

"Would you like to stare a little longer, or go check the door and then fall asleep?" he jokes.

"Sorry. You're distracting."

He chuckles, the grip on my hand unwavering as we walk down the hall.

"So are you."

Even though the suite isn't too large, it feels like we're crossing a desert in the middle of summer. The distance stretches for miles.

As we approach the foyer, he turns on his phone flashlight. I move closer to the door, noting that it's indeed locked with the extra deadbolt in place. My hand pushes against the sturdy wood, satisfied with how it looks. I walk two feet away before turning to check again. And then I repeat the action two more times, my nose inches away from the locking mechanism.

When I'm finally content, I sigh. "Thank you," I breathe out, shoulders sagging in relief.

"Of course," he replies casually. "We have one last stop to make. Come on." Collecting my hand again, he wanders down the hall before stopping in front of a closet. "I saw this when I was scoping out the room earlier. You know, making sure there wasn't a passageway to Narnia or anywhere cool." Opening the door, he pulls out a small fan. "Will this work for sound?"

My eyes fill with tears, and I wipe them away quickly. "That's perfect. Thank you."

"Hey, why the tears? Tell me what else I can do."

"You're being so nice. Too nice."

"It can happen on occasion. I noticed you the night at my house, glancing at the door. I almost asked then, but I'm glad I didn't. It wasn't my place to assume or interrupt."

I choke out a laugh, shaking my head. "Do you want me to move to the couch? I don't want to keep you up."

"You're not sleeping on the couch. Let's try the fan out, and if it doesn't work, we'll come up with another solution."

Closing the bedroom door behind us, Jack plugs the fan in off to the side, whooshing air filling the room.

"Perfect," I say, heading for the bed.

"Can I move these pillows? In case you need anything else?" he asks hesitantly, gesturing to the barrier.

"Sure." I climb under the covers as Jack tosses them to the side. "I promise I'll let you sleep in peace."

"Kick me if you need me."

My eyes finally feel heavy as I burrow myself in the covers.

"Josephine?"

"Hm?"

"Did someone in the past call you crazy because of these things? These parts of you?"

The words sound regretful on his tongue, and I don't think he enjoyed saying them.

"Yes."

I try to force the memories away, said by another man staying somewhere in this same hotel.

"How many times do you need to check the damn door, Jo?"

"Yes, it's locked."

"You know you're crazy, right? Can't you be fucking normal for once?"

"I could kill him. I'm sorry anyone's ever, at any point, made you feel less than absolutely wonderful. Including myself. Because that's what you are. Perfect in every way."

"Thank you," is all I can reply, emotionally drained and doing my best to prevent a fresh wave of tears from falling.

Wonderful.

Perfect.

He's not irritated or disgusted. I haven't shared these quirks with anyone in the last two years, nervous about a reaction. And, before that, only one relationship ever got deep enough to expose them.

I almost jump out of my skin when fingers reach out tentatively, pinky looping around mine and bringing my hand to his chest. Jack stays silent, his breathing slow and controlled, like he's already asleep and never awoke in the first place.

Our fingers stay wrapped around each other, pressed to his heart. I'm safer than I've ever been in my entire life. I sleep through the night.

The world is still dark and cool when I escape the room to go on a run.

When I woke up, far too early, Josephine was halfway in my arms, her head dangerously close to my shoulder while my hand gripped her palm to my body like she was an IV keeping me alive.

Needless to say, I carefully extracted myself from the sheets, resisted the urge to jerk off, told my hard dick to fuck off, and went on an eight-mile run, pounding the pavement to clear my convoluted head.

What she revealed last night took a lot of courage. I've always known her to be fierce and strong, but sharing a raw, honest part of herself so openly isn't easy. The fact that she's comfortable disclosing her fears, nightmares, and demons with *me* fills me with honor and wonderment.

I get no response when I knock lightly on the closed bedroom door after finishing my sweat session, silence greeting me on the other side. Turning the knob and opening the door gently, she's exactly where I left her an hour ago, hair discombobulated and tangled, face buried in a pillow, the smallest drop of drool hanging from her mouth.

My smile comes naturally at the sight, admiring how beautiful she is even while dozing in a peaceful slumber. She must sense my presence because after a few seconds, she turns over onto her back, noticing me in the doorway.

"Hi," I say softly, approaching the bed and kneeling on the carpet next to her. The last thing I want is for her to think I tried to run away from her honesty last night.

"Hey," she answers, voice scratchy, and I make a mental note to put a fresh, full glass of water on her side of the bed this evening. "What time is it?"

"Still early. I went for a jog. Saw the sunrise."

"I bet that was pretty."

"Mm. This view isn't bad either."

"Of course you run on vacation," she grumbles through a lazy smile, eyes half closed and lounging on the pillows. Her arms fold behind her head, raising the hem of her shirt up several inches, displaying smooth, unblemished skin.

"Should I invite you next time?"

"Absolutely not. I've always said that I refuse to end up in a family that runs 5ks on national holidays."

"Today might be Arbor Day," I joke, and her smile grows.

She's so fucking beautiful. Whoever gets to wake up next to her for their rest of their life is a lucky asshole.

"Did you eat breakfast?"

"Nope. Do you want to go together?"

"I'd like that," she says, pushing up on her elbows.

It'd be so easy to crawl on top of her, capture her mouth with mine, and wake her up with my fingers and tongue while I coax her to come on my hand.

Surprisingly, breakfast doesn't sound nearly as enticing as her.

"What are you thinking about?"

"Wildly inappropriate things."

"Anything I can help with?"

"Nope." I stand up and shuffle to my suitcase, thankful to turn my back on her so she can't see the growing tent in my shorts. "Do you mind if I shower first?"

"Go ahead. It gives me time to take care of some things."

"What kind of things?" I ask over my shoulder, pulling out my bathing suit.

"Wouldn't you like to know?" she answers, and I spin to see a wicked grin on her face. Her mischievous eyes dart to the front of my pants. "Looks like the same thing *you* need to take care of."

My mouth opens as she climbs off the bed, still wearing those damn socks I never found attractive. Until now. I want to peel them back with my teeth.

Is she... Is she going to get off in the same room as me?

I'm going to have a heart attack at the ripe old age of thirty-two, visions of her fingers disappearing under her stupidly short sleep shorts projecting in my brain like a goddamn movie theater screen. I bite my tongue so hard I think I draw blood.

"You cause all sorts of problems," I rasp as she slinks toward me.

"Enjoy your shower, Jack," she whispers seductively in my ear. "I know I will." She pats my shoulder and leaves the bedroom.

Fisting my bathing suit in my hand with a death grip, I slam the bathroom door closed and turn the shower as cold as it will go.

I'm not ashamed to admit I got off thinking about her. I know what she's doing. She's trying to seduce me. Or, at the very least, get me to pay a lot of fucking attention to her. It's working. Way too easily. Last night she told me she wants me to kiss her, putting everything out in the open. I want to kiss her too, dammit. But I want to approach this correctly and not screw anything up.

After getting dressed and still feeling unfulfilled, I walk to the living room and collapse on the couch, pulling out my phone to text my friends.

> **JL: We have a situation.**
> **JL: Please tell me someone is awake.**

HD: Team No Sleep over here.
PW: Reporting for duty.
NR: It's too fucking early.
HD: Don't even bother waiting for Neil.
HD: Late game last night.

> **JL: I literally cannot believe I'm typing this.**
> **JL: And I'm a big advocate of not sharing personal business.**
> **JL: But. I need help.**
> **JL: Josephine implied that she was going to get off.**
> **JL: While I was in the shower.**
> **JL: Feet away from her.**

PW: Am I allowed to say that's hot?

> **JL: No.**
> **JL: Yes.**

JL: Just this one time.

PW: That's fucking HOT.
PW: You're losing your mind, aren't you?

JL: My teeth will be stumps by the end of this trip.

HD: You should have offered to give her a hand.
HD: Get it? Hehehe

JL: Jesus Christ.
JL: Haven't even kissed yet and you want me to...
What?
JL: Put my hand down her pants?
JL: Absolutely not.
JL: Boundaries, Dawson.

HD: The evidence is overwhelming, dude.
HD: SHE PROBABLY WANTED YOU TO WALK
OUT WHILE SHE WAS DOING IT.

JL: Fuck me.

PW: She's waiting for you to make a move.
HD: And if you don't hurry up and do something...
NR: You might miss your chance.

JL: I hate when you finish each other's sentences.
JL: You're right. Okay.

HD: Jerked off in the shower, didn't ya?

JL: **None of your business.**
JL: **... Yes. I did.**

HD: Good man.
**PW: Jack, the universe is begging you to get off
your ass.**
**PW: Your flight was canceled. You're in the same
hotel room.**
PW: WITH ONE BED.
PW: And the girl of your dreams.
HD: What's the worst that happens?
HD: She says she isn't into you?
HD: Wouldn't you rather try?
NR: Instead of spending your life wondering?

JL: **Fine. Okay.**
JL: **I'll do something.**
JL: **I'm not sure WHAT.**

HD: Good luck!
PW: Let us know if you need any help!

JL: **I know how to get a woman off.**
JL: **But thanks.**
JL: **You all are the best.**

"Ready for breakfast?"

I look up, nearly dropping my phone in surprise. Josephine's in front of me wearing a blue sundress and a satisfied look on her face. I see bathing suit straps peeking out from under her clothes.

"How was your shower?" I ask.

"Hm. Could've been better."

"Is that so? You sure look happy."

"It's amazing what a few fingers can do."

My nostrils flare. "I know what you're doing."

"I'm not doing anything," she says innocently, adjusting the oversized beach bag she's carrying.

"Maybe if you can be patient like a good girl, you'll get whatever it is you want," I say huskily, and her pupils dilate.

Bingo. Game on.

She thinks I don't know how to get under *her* skin? She's incredibly easy to read when you pay attention.

"Time for food," I add brightly, patting her shoulder in the most platonic way possible and heading for the door. It takes a second for her to follow, and I smile smugly as she nearly trips walking into the elevator.

"Before we eat, can we stop by the front desk? I want to see if there are any activities we can do," she says, filing in behind me and moving far away.

"Sure. Anything in particular you're looking for?"

"I think a boat would be fun. Maybe parasailing?"

"I'm afraid of heights, so I'll pass on being suspended in the air."

As we approach the concierge desk, Marcos beams at us.

"My stranded friends! How was your first night?"

"Perfect! The room is spectacular! Are there really people who turn their nose up at something that nice?!"

"You'd be surprised." He hides his eye roll well, perfected from being in a customer service job. I could never work with people in this capacity; I'd be fired within minutes. "What can I help you two with?"

"Is there a list of things to do around the resort? I think we'll probably hang out today, but maybe a boat? Snorkeling?"

"Of course!" He claps his hands together excitedly, reaching for a laminated pamphlet and laying it out on the limestone counter. "We have a boat that holds about fifteen people. It goes to a smaller, uninhabited island. They provide lunch, and it's a beautiful place to hang out for a bit. That's my top recommendation. We also have some scuba diving excursions, too, if you're feeling adventurous."

"No scuba diving," I say quickly, and Josephine nods in agreement. "The boat sounds awesome. Can you put us down for two spots tomorrow?"

"Perfect. I have you and your wife down for the noon departure!"

"We're not married," Josephine laughs.

"Boyfriend?" he tries and my lips twitch.

"Colleagues," I correct him.

"We were at a conference that my asshole ex was also attending. We've been pretending to date for the last few days," she adds, and Marcos nods in understanding.

"Ah. I see. Well, in any case, I also want to give you this." He slides a smaller piece of paper toward us. "I made reservations, complimentary of course, at the exclusive restaurant upstairs for tomorrow night. Fine dining. Cocktail attire required. The food is to die for. Six forty-five p.m.!"

"That's very generous of you," I say, taking the piece of paper. "We aren't special or anything."

"Perhaps not. I think you two will find it to be exactly what you need." He winks, as if I'm supposed to understand the implication behind the statement when I'm utterly clueless. "The boat will pick you up at the end of the boardwalk, to the left. You can't miss it. I work the afternoon shift the day after tomorrow, so you'll have to let me know how everything goes. Have fun!"

"Aren't we fancy?" Josephine giggles. "Are you okay spending the whole day together?"

"It'll be tough, but I think I'll survive. Come on, let's get some food."

We snag a table at the restaurant where complimentary breakfast is being served by the window. Josephine's eyes light up as she looks outside, smiling at the ocean. Small, unassuming things make her happy, I've learned; they illuminate her face like a Christmas tree.

Like when she found out I knew her tea order.

A breeze coming through the trees, no regard for the way it tangles in her hair, little pieces of red flying around manically.

Multiple candy bars for dessert so she doesn't have to pick one.

Watching *her* happiness brings me plenty of joy.

"What are you going to do today?" I ask.

"Sit on the beach again. It was so relaxing! I could live down here. Do you want to join? I promise it's not boring!"

"I'd love to."

Breakfast is delicious, complete with fresh fruit, flaky croissants, and crispy bacon. When Josephine runs to the bathroom, I make sure extra breakfast potatoes end up on our table before she returns. She beams when she spots the treat.

"Do you need to go back to the room?" she asks, sliding her sunglasses on her face as we walk through the lobby.

"Nope. I'm already wearing my swimsuit. Should we grab some snacks and water?"

"I'm always on team snacks."

Stopping in the small convenience store, we stock up on an excessive amount of food. We argue briefly over which is better, Goldfish or Cheez-Its, before ditching both, settling on Combos instead.

Soon our feet are in the sand and I'm kicking off my flip-flops.

"What a beautiful day," she exclaims, her arms raising to the side as she spins around, making an offering to the sky. "Want to snag those two chairs?"

The two reclined loungers are under a massive umbrella and I set my towel and book on the left one. "I'm not a huge fan of the sun," I confess. "I'll probably spend the majority of the time in the shade, so don't let me hold back your fun."

"Me too! I can't believe this is your first time outside during the day our whole time here!"

"That's why conferences at nice places are a joke. You think you have all this free time until you're sitting in the presentation room, staring out the window, wishing you were out here instead of in there. It's too distracting."

I tug the hem of my shirt off over my head and drop it into the sand next to my chair.

"Dammit," she mutters.

"What?"

"Nothing." She busies herself with her beach bag, pulling out items left and right.

"Could I borrow some sunscreen? Maybe I can do you, and you can do me?"

"Pardon?" she chokes out, whipping around to stare at me.

I grin slyly, appreciating that I caught her off guard. "I spray your back. You spray mine."

"Right. Yeah. Obviously." She takes off her sundress and tosses it onto the chair, hands resting on her hips. "It's not spray. I hope that's okay."

"That's fine," I rasp out, my voice hoarse.

The sun isn't frying my brain; the sight of Josephine's blue one-piece bathing suit is. It has a dip that stretches down toward her stomach, revealing a tasteful amount of cleavage. It hugs her hips perfectly, and a tiny piece of her ass is exposed from the cut on the side. The color makes her skin seem fairer and hair more vibrant.

I abruptly turn my back, unable to look any longer without giving the impression that I'm gawking at her.

"It's probably going to be cold," she says as her lotion-coated hand lands on my neck. I hiss in response, and she giggles, spreading the sunscreen across my shoulders and down my back. "Sorry."

"No, you aren't."

"Nope. Not one bit."

I fidget under her exploratory touch. She's going slower than necessary, taking her time to cover every inch of my skin. Goosebumps form under the trail she draws; shoulder to shoulder, down my back, up again. My muscles relax and my head lolls to the side. I have to bite my lip to keep from moaning. When her hand drops to the waistband of my swim trunks, I almost erupt as her fingers dip right under the material before tapping my hip twice.

"Done!" she announces.

"Thanks." I face her and twirl my finger. "Spin."

She moves immediately, feet spinning and kicking up sand as she presents her back to me.

Such a good fucking listener.

I feel emboldened from her stunt earlier, shifting closer than necessary to her as I lather my hands with the lotion. Moving her hair away from her neck, she sighs, her head tilting back so it hits my chest. She gasps when she recognizes how close I am.

I take my time as well, studying her shoulders as I work in the sun protection. Listening to the changes in her breathing. Noticing how her back arches as I rub the base of her neck, fingers pressing into the tendons there. How her ass backs up, flush against my front, grazing over my dick.

"You are a deviant," I say when I finish, not pulling away.

"How so?" she asks, her feet bracketed by mine.

"Getting off while I'm in the shower and telling me about it," I whisper, my lips above her ear, aware of how close the other beachgoers are. "Wearing this suit that leaves too much to my imagination while looking like a fucking goddess." She's practically panting now. "Being such a good girl who listens so well."

She spins around to face me. "What are you going to do about it?" Her question is breathy, and I don't miss the way she squeezes her thighs together. I slowly grin as I take her chin in my hands.

"Nothing yet. Soon."

I kiss her forehead and release her, trying not to laugh as she grumbles under her breath and throws herself into the chair.

It takes everything in me to not take her upstairs right now and give her anything she asks. I need to make sure she really wants this.

One more day.

I can wait one more day.

The nice dinner tomorrow will be the perfect opportunity to tell her everything that's racing through my chaotic brain. I'll lay it all out there and see what part she takes.

All I want is her.

Josephine splashes in the ocean, a megawatt grin on her face, hair stuck to her cheeks. Water slides down her arms and hips, landing on her thighs. The setting sun's rays make her hair look like a fiery explosion, leaving nothing but a beautiful disaster in its wake.

"Hi," she says brightly as she climbs out of the salt water, plopping next to me in the sand, not a care in the world that the grainy substance is clinging to every part of her wet body like a second skin. "You don't want to go in?"

"Nah. The view is plenty good from here," I answer, and she smiles.

"Today was a good day."

"One of the best I've had in a while."

It's true. We spent the hours under the umbrella, Josephine reading some of her reverse harem romance book aloud to me. That's what the other 28% of her literature material is; pure fucking filth. She couldn't go two days without sharing. It's hot.

I dozed for a little bit, waking up to her sneaking a photo of me on her phone. I retaliated, capturing one of her while she built a sandcastle in front of our chairs. Being with her on the island, sand caked on my thighs, dried salt on my arms, makes me realize I've been drifting like a ghost these last two years, half-alive and going through the motions of existing, because life hasn't felt like this when she's not around.

Rejuvenated would be a good word to use. Refreshed, also.

The things that normally cause me pause or anxiety are nonexistent, far away in another world. Another life. Not this one.

It wasn't like this for the near-decade I spent with someone else. Not even close.

"What should we do for dinner?" she asks, wringing her damp hair out. The beach has started to clear out, people shuffling back to their hotels for a shower and food.

"Hm. Pizza? I'm not used to eating out so much. I normally cook all my meals at home. Let's stay out here for a few more minutes, though. I'm enjoying the scenery."

"Is there anything you *can't* do?"

"Fold a fitted sheet. Can't do that to save my life."

"I don't think anyone knows how to do that," she laughs.

A pleasant silence falls between us, neither in a rush to speak. A seagull flies overhead before dropping for the ocean, wings spread wide. The sun slowly disappears over the horizon. "What makes you happy?" Josephine asks, breaking the quiet. Her toes dig into the sand and wiggle around. "What's the thing that lights up your world? Fuels your fire. Makes you want to get out of bed every morning."

She turns, her chin resting on her knees as she gives me an encouraging smile, hair spilling down her back like a waterfall.

"What makes *you* happy?" I ask in return, not ready to tackle such a deep question.

She hums, looking back at the water. "A lot of things. When I wake up before my alarm and realize I have another hour to sleep. Fall mornings when you need a light jacket to stay warm, a crispness in the air. Abby. My family. Dogs. I love dogs. What makes me happiest right now is knowing one day, life is going to be better than this."

"What do you mean?"

"Things are okay now. Great, even. I'm not complaining. But it's not the end. One day I'll have a better job that invigorates me and motivates me to keep working hard. I'll have a partner who treats me like an equal. You remember our conversation the other night? About not wanting to get married or have kids?"

"Of course."

How could I forget? We share similar values and life goals. Goals I didn't think I'd ever find in a woman. Yet somehow, I have. She's sitting next to me.

"Sometimes I feel like I'm lagging behind everyone else. They're moving quickly down some path I'm not taking, leaving me alone. I want something. Someone," she clarifies. "In what capacity, I'm not sure. I've realized lately I'm so fucking lonely. Having a partner doesn't define a person, of course, and they would never become my sole provider of joy. It's just... I want... I want to be loved. Properly, this time. Wholly and fully. And each day that passes where I'm not, I think my happiness diminishes. The little things help. I'm not *unhappy* or sad, and I recognize that what I have is good and enough. I'm just saying it would be really nice to experience life with someone by my side, because some days I'm afraid it'll never happen."

"I'm lonely too," I admit, unsurprised by how easily the admission comes. "I have been, for a long, long time, I think. Longer than I care to admit. It's a fear of mine that I won't find someone who sees eye-to-eye with me on things. Who understands my character and what I've been through. Why I'm hesitant to act a certain way. For me, even all the happiness and brightness in the world can't replace the nagging sensation of feeling utterly alone."

"We can be alone together," she offers through a sigh, and I swear my heart breaks in two. "Two confused people who aren't sure what they want. We don't have to suffer by ourselves; that sounds miserable."

"I... I'd like that. You make me happy, you know," I say quietly, unsure if she hears me. "Very, very happy."

It's the truth I've slowly come to discover over the last few weeks. She thaws my heart and hugs my beaten, battered soul with her gentle, kind words. Embraces my mood swings and grumpy, angry disposition. I've always known she was special, but being here with her solidifies the fact that she's heaven-sent.

"You make me happy too, Jack."

Then she scoots four inches to her right, her arm knocking into mine as her head falls to my shoulders and nestles into the crook of my neck like she belongs.

It's perfect.

Soon.

That damn word haunted me all night. It haunted me this morning when I woke up, my calf thrown over his hip and his hand on my thigh, just below the hem of my boxers. It haunted me while we ate breakfast and Jack licked icing from a cinnamon roll off the corner of his lip while talking to me, not batting an eye at the way I stared at his tongue.

"Should I be playing 'I'm on a Boat?'" Jack asks as we walk down the boardwalk, following the directions Marcos laid out for us.

"That's so cheesy. Not allowed! We're not going to be *those* tourists."

There's a small group of people waiting in the sand, a large boat anchored a few feet offshore. Jack helps me onto the vessel, holding my elbow as I climb the metal stairs before joining me onboard. There are only ten of us, giving everyone ample space to relax comfortably on our ride to the island.

"This is beautiful!" I shout over the roar of the motor. "I've never been on a boat like this!"

"Me neither," he responds. We're sitting close, thighs

pressing against each other as we sway over the waves at the back of the vessel. My hair keeps blowing in Jack's face, the wind whipping through it like a sheet of paper. I apologize each time. He simply smiles, tucks a curl behind my ear, then looks back at the clear water, not fazed by the suffocation attempt.

"Dolphins," he observes, and I jump on my knees, looking over the rail and searching.

"Where?"

He stands, shifting behind me, his chest pressing into my back as he gently turns my head and lifts my arm, pointing at a shadow.

"There. You see?" he whispers and I nod, his hand still grasping mine.

The mammals rise out of the water, jumping alongside our wake, and I grin, watching their game of hide-and-seek unfold.

"That's so cool."

We pull up to the small island forty-five minutes later, sandy shores greeting us as the captain drops the anchor.

"Folks, lunch is provided. You have about two hours until we head back. I'm staying with the boat, so if you need anything, I'll be here. Watch your step on the way off, it can be slippery."

Jack climbs out first, again offering his hand to me while I descend the stairs. My foot slips on the wet metal, not heeding the captain's warning, and I almost face-plant into the salty water.

Jack catches me, holding me upright as I regain my footing and trudge to the sand. We pick up the provided lunch and snag a pair of chairs off on the side, hidden away from the main part of the island, palm fronds blocking us from view.

"What's your favorite kind of sandwich?" I ask, sitting criss-crossed on the lounge chair.

He bites into the BLT he picked for lunch, wiping mustard off his mouth with an increasingly wrinkled napkin. It's nice to see him not entirely put together, making a disaster of his meal like me. A mere mortal after all.

"That's a great question. Probably a Philly cheesesteak."

"Oooh, good choice! With or without mushrooms?"

"Without. I hate the consistency of them."

"Yes!" I agree excitedly, a piece of tomato flying off my bread and landing in the sand. A bird makes its way to the scrap, enjoying the unexpected treat. "Crap. I'm probably not supposed to feed the birds. It'll mess up their ecosystem."

"They probably heard you were coming and assembled a group, knowing how messy you are when you eat."

"It's one of my best qualities, thank you very much."

"Your turn to answer. Question for a question. Favorite sandwich?"

"Does a burger count? Or tacos?"

"A taco is *not* a sandwich," he says emphatically. "Please don't tell me you consider hotdogs a sandwich, too."

"I mean, per the definition, it's not far off!"

"Wow," he exhales, shaking his head in disbelief. "I'm appalled. And here I was thinking I was getting to know you."

I giggle, throwing a napkin at him. "Leave my answer alone!"

"Fine. You can have all the burger sandwiches you want, Josephine."

"There probably won't be burgers at dinner tonight. I'm glad I listened to Abby and brought a nice dress. Cocktail attire. That's, like, what you live in."

He chuckles. I've gotten used to hearing the sound, but it still catches me off guard. It's warm and deep, a big hug by the fire on a cold winter day. "Yup. Full gala attire is required, or I'm not going."

"Nerd!"

"Do you want to go in the ocean?"

"And swim less than thirty minutes after eating? We're living dangerously today."

"Risk-taker is my middle name," he answers, standing up from the chaise lounge. "I'll throw the trash away for us."

"I'll meet you in the water over there." I gesture to a small beach beyond the secluded area. Jack nods, gathering our garbage and heading for the receptacles a short walk away.

I quickly discard my cover-up and scurry into the warm water, wading out to below my chest and dunking my head under the surf to cool off my shoulders.

"You move fast," he calls out. Salty droplets cling to his chest and waist, finding refuge in the dips and crevices of his muscles.

"Maybe you move slow," I answer. "I wish we had pool floats."

He doggy paddles toward me, his arms pushing and pulling the water as he approaches. "Speaking of pool floats, tomorrow we're going down the water slide. I seem to recall someone getting very excited when they heard about it."

I blush, splashing a handful of water in his face. "We don't have to."

"Of course we do. The driver spoke so highly of it, even I'm intrigued."

"I'll go. Only if you scream like a little kid while you go down it."

"Done."

"You agreed pretty easily."

"An easy compromise to see you happy. It wasn't included in your list yesterday, but I'll do it."

I stare at him, lowering my feet onto the sand beneath me. "I am happy," I say truthfully. I can't imagine being anywhere else right now, or with anyone else.

"Good. I know you're hesitant to do something you enjoy

because someone made a snide comment about it. Why wouldn't I agree? If it means seeing a smile on your face, I'm in. The world's a little brighter when you smile."

A wave hits my back, shifting me closer to Jack as I stumble, losing my balance on the slight decline of a sandbar under our feet. "You've surprised me these last few days."

"How so?"

His hand rests on my side as another small wave barrels toward us. It gently rises us out of the water like buoys then back in. Jack tugs me to him, and my legs wrap around his waist, clinging to him like a koala in a tree.

"I'm glad this is a trip we got to do together. I enjoy spending time with you and learning about you. It's hard to remember what we were like before arriving here."

He cups my cheek, palm slick against my skin. "I've enjoyed spending time with you, too."

"I'm sorry for the other day," I whisper, my eyes locking on his.

"What happened the other day?"

"When we almost... I almost..."

"Words, Josephine." His other hand leaves my side, threading into my soaked hair and massaging my scalp. Words are hard to come by, I'm finding.

"How we almost kissed. On the beach and after the game. I'm sorry for making a move like that on you. I crossed a line. It just felt right."

"Why are you apologizing?"

A stronger wave crashes into us and I let out a squeal as my fingers dig into his biceps to stay above water. A whistle gets blown and I turn my head, watching the captain of the boat wave a flag.

"I basically cornered you and forced you into the situation."

"Forced me?" Jack asks huskily, giving my hair a small but

noticeable tug. I gasp. His blue eyes look entirely different now, a shade I've never seen before. "You should know, Josephine, that if I want something, I make it happen. I get what I want."

"O-oh."

"Forgive me for not wanting the first time I kiss you to be on a public beach while you FaceTime your best friend, or in front of an ex-boyfriend after I kicked his ass in a stupid game. In the ocean surrounded by other people, where anyone can hear the sounds you make. I want to learn every moan, every breath, every little gasp of yours. I'm going to take my time and torture you slowly, relentlessly, until you're begging me like I've dreamed about to touch you in ways *you've* dreamed about. You've tortured my brain, heart, and body, month after month, every goddamn day. And now we have to get back to that boat before we're pulled out to sea, and I never have the chance to show you exactly how I feel about you. To show you what I thought about yesterday in the shower, when you were two feet away, fingering yourself while you thought of me, too."

I'm being electrocuted, my body sparking and igniting from his promising words. Another wave knocks my back and Jack hauls me into his arms, trekking us back to the shoreline. I'm shaking as he holds me, so aroused I can barely think straight.

His gaze stays trained ahead, grip under my legs, dangerously close to my ass. When we finally make it back to the sand, he sets me down.

"Don't you dare apologize," I say firmly, my hand pressing the center of his chest, already prepared for the onslaught of apologies and grimaces. "We're getting back on that boat, we're going to dinner, then we're going to finish this conversation. I'll be damned if you're going to say those things to me and not follow through. You want to hear me gasp? Or scream? You know I want you. And you want me, too. Come and get it, Lancaster. It's all yours. Only yours." I turn away and stomp back to our chairs, slipping my cover-up back on over my wet suit and shoving our things into my bag.

"Sorry, folks, it looks like the seas are getting rougher," the captain apologizes as we pile onto the boat. "I want to get everyone back safely."

I take a seat at the rear of the boat again, watching Jack drift up to the front, looking over the stern at the horizon. As we go over the waves toward the hotel, his chin pivots, eyes searching the passengers until he finds me. When he does, he smiles, whole face lighting up.

He's so beautiful I almost forget to breathe.

Over the past few months, I've learned that Jack has a few different types of smiles in his arsenal.

The first is the polite one, used when he thinks he *has* to smile. It's not quite fake or forced. His lips tip upward slightly. It's courteous, and the most frequent in his rotation, often used when agreeing with coworkers or thanking someone for their help.

The next is when he's interested in a topic or person. His head tilts to the side, and he smiles softly. It's not quite a full-on grin, but his dimples show—at least one, sometimes both. A rarer display than his polite smile, but still glorious.

The last one is the most unexpected; the one where he thinks no one is paying attention to him. Which is silly, because how could you not? His eyes crinkle in the corners and his shoulders relax. You can see all of his perfectly aligned teeth. Sometimes, his nose scrunches too.

That's the one I'm lucky enough to witness right now. The wind whips through his hair, the drying locks the same color as the sunlight beaming down on us. Water from the waves sprays around us, cold against our sun-soaked skin. My heart thumps erratically at the sight. It's as if nothing could hurt him, and his past is nonexistent.

My favorite smile, and no matter what happens tonight, tomorrow, or when we go home, I will forever have it committed to memory. A recollection of a happier time, when nothing else mattered except us.

This. This is what they're talking about. Beauty so captivating it ensnares you and dilutes your brain, unable to comprehend anything but the person in front of you. The person who's been there all along.

THIRTY-THREE

JO

We're silent on the walk back to the suite, staying far apart from each other and not touching. I'm waiting for him to take back his words. To apologize profusely and say he's made a mistake. To run away.

"You can shower first," I say as we enter the room, anticipating pushback or a change of plans. "It's going to take you less time."

Jack doesn't respond, moving into the bathroom. I sigh, rifling through my suitcase for the green dress Abby forced me to bring and a pair of nude wedges.

"All yours." He emerges a few moments later in a t-shirt and athletic shorts, hair damp and smelling clean.

"Not exactly cocktail attire, my friend."

"I can get dressed out here so you can get started. Think you'll be good to go in an hour?"

"Easily."

I slip into the bathroom and jump under the shower, washing and conditioning my hair vigorously, releasing the salt and sand that accumulated during our day on the boat. After I finish, I wrap a fluffy towel around myself as I blow-dry my wet curls, making sure they're totally dry before I start straightening them, deciding to mix it up tonight.

Slipping on a black thong, I shimmy the slinky dress over my head, liking how I look in this outfit. It's forest green, with thin straps and a low scoop back. The material is lightweight and moves with me. It hangs above my knee, a small slit going up the side and landing mid-thigh. Not too risqué, but the perfect balance between sexy and classy for an evening in a swanky restaurant with a hot man.

The dress clings to my figure in all the right places and my breasts look soft and perky, nipples almost visible without a bra. I'm not shy about my curves, and I love that I'm getting a chance to showcase them in an outfit that's outside my usual wardrobe.

"Five-minute warning."

I open the door to the bedroom and smile. "I'm ready!"

Jack is leaning against the wall, staring at his phone before his eyes flick up to me. "Jesus Christ," he whispers, his phone falling to the carpet, bouncing away. He doesn't bother to pick it up.

"What? Is it too much? I thought it might be a tad revealing. Shit, I think I have another dress. It's not as nice, but it might work."

"No."

The single word causes me to stop in my tracks. He stalks toward me slowly, gaze never leaving my face.

"What?"

"You look..." He trails off, biting his lip, clearly struggling to find words.

"You're really freaking me out here," I whisper, my hand going nervously to my hair. I twist a piece around my finger before his palm reaches out, covering mine, stopping the motion.

Jack pulls me flush against him, two bodies becoming one.

"You will be the fucking death of me, Josephine," he

exhales, his touch moving to my shoulder, warm and inviting. "And what a happy death it will be. You look positively exquisite."

"Thank you," I whisper shyly, accepting the compliment and praise.

"Fucking hell." Moving two steps back, Jack looks me up and down, sweeping over every inch of my body. He spends an extra amount of time on my hips and chest. "Can you turn around?"

I blush, secretly delighted by how easily he's falling apart. I spin slowly, obeying his command. I know I'm putting on a show, and he curses. Looking at him over my shoulder, it's obvious he's struggling to behave and keep his hands to himself.

"You look really nice, too," I say, completing my turn and almost salivating at the sight.

He does. He's wearing a white shirt with a black jacket and dark-washed jeans. A green tie hangs from his neck that perfectly matches my dress. Silver buttons on the sleeves of his jacket glitter in the light. His hair looks relaxed, almost falling in his face, slightly lightened from our time in the sun.

"I don't think you know what you do to me," he admits quietly, afraid to share the answer.

"Show me."

Jack hesitates for a fraction of a second, barely short enough for me to blink, before he shifts in front of me again, taking my hand in his.

"May I?" he asks hoarsely, and I nod, hypnotized by his movements. Tentatively, he brings my hand to the front of his jeans where the denim is strained and tight. My fingers spread wide, covering the outline of his hard cock. "I'm five seconds away from dropping to my knees and worshiping you like the goddess you are."

"You won't get much objection from me." I trail my touch

along the zipper of his pants, and he hisses. "I'd be lying if I said you haven't been driving me wild these past few days. When you touched my socks the other night, I almost exploded. You should have kept going."

"It took every ounce of my rapidly diminishing control to not."

"What were you thinking about the other morning? When you went on your run and came back into the room?"

"How I could climb on top of you. Peel your socks back with my teeth. Have you come on my fingers as I whispered dirty, filthy things while you rode my hand."

"I would have liked that," I whimper.

"It wasn't the time. Though, maybe I should have just gone with it, because I'm overthinking everything right now."

Jack pulls my palm away from his jeans, kissing each one of my fingers. His lips feel like fire, and I want to strike a match and burn alive.

"Let's make a vow to work on our communication," I offer.

"Fair enough. I'll start. After dinner, I'd very much like to come back here and continue this," he says. "It's going to be difficult to keep my hands to myself."

"Maybe you shouldn't," I suggest, and he curses again, teeth nipping my sensitive fingertips.

"Keep that up and we'll never make it downstairs," he warns me.

"Where do you want to touch me first?" I lean forward, taking his hand in mine. "Here?" I bring his palm to my breast, gliding down my chest. He growls, capturing my nipple in his finger thorough the fabric. "Or here?" I run his hand up my thigh, over my dress.

"There," he says gruffly. "Definitely there."

"Maybe here?" I move his hand to my ass, letting him gather both my cheeks and squeeze roughly.

"You don't know all the depraved things I want to do your ass." He smacks me gently, and I let out a moan. "You'd like that, wouldn't you?"

"Yes," I whimper.

"I can't wait to learn what else you like, Josephine. Now, be a good girl and stop making those sexy sounds before we skip dinner altogether and you complain about being hungry in thirty minutes. You need your energy for what I'm going to do to you."

"Fine," I grumble, swatting his hand away playfully. "You better follow through on that promise."

He chuckles. "This isn't the end. It's a pause. Trust me, you're what I want."

The restaurant we're dining in tonight sits at the top of the hotel, offering panoramic views of the ocean and setting sun, a soft, orange glow filtering through the room. Floor-to-ceiling windows cover the entire wall, so clean it's hard to discern if there's any barrier stopping you from toppling onto the sand below. As we approach the podium, an aroma of world-class dining fills the air, a combination of spices, cooked meats, and sweet desserts.

"Hi! We have a reservation at 6:45," I say to the hostess who's beaming at us.

"You must be Josephine and Jack. Follow me."

We're led through the winding room to a secluded table, a white tablecloth covering the wood. A small candle sits in the middle. Jack holds out my chair for me as I sit down, scooting me closer as I get settled.

"Thank you." I smile at him, and he smiles back, a beautiful sight brighter than any island sunrise or sunset.

"Are we drinking tonight?" he asks, opening his menu.

"I think we should." I lick my lips and push the strap of my dress up. His eyes follow my hands, temporarily distracted by my answer, before nodding once.

"Wine?"

"Perfect."

When the waiter arrives, Jack lets me order first. We both pick the fish of the day, and when he requests a side of mashed potatoes for the table without any prompting, happiness bubbles inside my chest.

"There's a place back home that does mashed potato pizza," I say, taking a bite of salad. While not my typical food choice, this plate looks like a work of art; vibrant greens of the lettuce and red of the tomatoes jump out like paint on a canvas. "I can't tell you how badly I want to go and try it."

"How does that work? I need more information."

"Simple. You cook the mashed potatoes, put them on the dough, then bake like normal! Tada! Mashed potato pizza!"

"What about the sauce? And the toppings?"

"Okay, I don't have all the answers about semantics! It's similar to nachos, I think."

"I'd like to see this for myself. I'm both fascinated and confused."

"We could go together," I blurt out without thinking about what I'm implying. "As friends, I mean. Or whatever."

"I think I could be persuaded."

"I won't be wearing this dress, though," I taunt him, placing my elbows on the table and leaning forward with my chin in the palm of my hand. My cleavage is visible, and I know he can see the top of my breasts.

Jack's silverware drops, metal clattering against china. "Josephine. You could show up in a literal garbage bag and I'd still think you were the most beautiful person in the room."

I take a sip of wine to steady my nerves and stifle the desire pooling in my belly. "Thank you."

Our conversation flows surprisingly well, exchanging stories about our families. Friends. Our favorite desserts. The way a rainy day makes for the perfect excuse to stay on the couch and read, curled up under a blanket with a good book. Naturally, the conversation eventually drifts to work, a topic we have in common.

"I've been thinking about doing freelance work," I say, unsure what compels me to share the idea.

"What is that, exactly?" He spoons a generous portion of mashed potatoes on my plate.

"Essentially, I'd have my own business, and other companies could hire my services. It hit me at the conference how much I enjoy talking with others about strategies to implement to be successful. It's fun to talk out ideas and learn what works and what doesn't."

"That sounds interesting. Is that something you think you'd like to do long term?"

"I love the structure and rigidity of an office job and the social interactions that come with it. There's only so much I can do in one place, you know? We launched the website a few weeks ago, and it's perfect. It seems like that might be it, as far as what I can do at Itrix. I go back and forth over what would make me happy professionally, and I'm beginning to think that might be somewhere else. I'd still be doing the job I know and love, just in a different environment."

An emotion akin to disappointment flashes across Jack's face fleetingly before it's gone, faster than a blink of the eye. He sits forward in his chair, giving me his undivided attention. I realize, as we approach the end of our meal, he hasn't looked at his phone once. Hasn't pulled it out of his pocket or excused himself to answer a text message or call. His sole focus has been *me*.

That's sexy as hell.

"You're very talented. Lots of people shared that with me once they found out we're colleagues. At one point, I think they wanted to talk to me more about your work than my own, which is fine by me. You have an eye for things, Josephine. You see what others don't, while seeing *people*, too. Your work ethic is unmatched, and you're very good at what you do. I see no reason why you wouldn't be successful on your own."

"Wow. That was unexpected," I admit, dabbing my mouth with the fancy napkin in my lap. There were zero spills over the course of our meal tonight, and now the untarnished fabric gives my jitters something to focus on rather than the heavy compliment and how it's laced with appreciation and drenched in kindness.

Jack reaches over, joining my free hand with his, thumb rubbing over my knuckles.

"I'm so sorry that I ever made it seem like I don't think you're good at your job, or that I didn't care about your work. In the beginning, I know I said some harsh, derogatory things about your profession, and I wish I could take them back. You're truly so instrumental to Itrix's success, and you deserve to hear that every day. What did you tell me the other night? Do what brings you joy? Freelance work sounds, to me, like something that might be very lucrative. You're excited about it, too. Your eyes lit up."

"Did they?"

"Mhm. You're pretty all the time, but you're even prettier when you're happy. This clearly makes you happy. As a pseudo-friend and fake boyfriend, I promise to support you in all your endeavors. I say go for it, Josephine."

"The same goes for you. If you want to teach, I'll cheer you on."

He kisses my palm then motions to the makeshift dance

floor that's been set up in the middle of the room. "Do you want to dance?"

"I'm not very good. I can't guarantee I won't step on your toes."

"A gamble I'm willing to accept."

"What if we table the dancing for next time and head back to the room?" I offer instead, nervous at the proposition.

"Is that what you want?"

"More than anything."

We keep eye contact for four seconds, maybe five, before Jack nods and throws three twenty dollar bills down on the table for a tip. A freaking generous tip. Standing, he offers me his hand. I intertwine our fingers as we silently ride in the elevator, arriving on our floor. My hand is shaking too much to open the door, and he takes the keycard from me and pushes the wood ajar.

I walk to the other side of the living room as he locks the door. I feel nervous, unsure of what comes next. Now that it's the two of us alone, for real, I don't know how to proceed.

Jack moves toward me with a stealthy grace, and I stand my ground, unafraid of him.

"Hi," he says.

"Hi," I repeat. He pulls me against him, muscles warm and firm.

Our gazes meet again, and something unspoken passes between us with that look. Jack's eyes turn into molten pools of devotion, as if he would bow at my mercy, willing to do whatever I want. Shivering, I realize how easily I could throw this man off his axis.

Before, I would think about how I could use this to my advantage. How I could get him to grovel and take whatever I wanted in return. Before doesn't exist, though. It's only Here and Now and After. It's only him. Nothing else matters.

My hand rests on his face, thumb stroking under his eye and down the cheek that is bruise-free, exploring the lines, shapes, and textures of his wickedly handsome features.

"Josephine," he whispers, my name sounding like a beautiful plea. "Please."

The word, the sincere *ask* punctures and wounds me, knocking me into a frantic, different world. I'm ready to fall and experience him everywhere. My head bobs up and down, a wild movement conveying my answer.

"What do you want?" he asks breathlessly, and I swallow. "Tell me, and it's yours. You have to know by now I'd find a way to give you anything you ask."

I do.

This is it. Whatever I say, whatever route I decide, he'll honor my decision. His fingers run through my hair, freeing the knots that have developed from the humidity, the question waiting patiently for me to answer when I'm ready.

My hand drops to his chest, and I can feel his heart beating under the buttoned shirt, a quickened staccato pace, anticipating what's going to come next.

"You."

It's a leap, and I decide to jump. A single word of truth that I know will forever change the trajectory of Us. I'm not ashamed to admit I want him more than I've ever wanted anyone in my life. Not just physically; yes, I yearn for his hands to cover the planes of my body, learning the curves and dips along with the places that make me squirm. But I also want him again in the morning, and the next day after. I want to learn everything about him; I want him to consume me.

I'm drunk on him, yet he's somehow the antidote and the cure.

His eyes flare possessively, absorbing the single word. "I thought you'd never, ever ask. I'm yours. I think I always have been. Since the moment I first met you. You've wrecked me in unimaginable ways."

The smile I'm rewarded with lights up the whole room, an explosion of warmth, honesty, and steadiness.

"W-what?" I ask shakily, not comprehending. "What about the salt in my tea? The emails? Ignoring me? Every other fight?"

Jack rests his forehead against mine. "The second I walked into that meeting and saw *you*, I was done for. You had such a fierceness about you. So beautiful and strong standing there, hands on your hips, rage in your eyes. I was so flustered. I didn't know what to do, so, naturally, like most men, I acted like an asshole."

"None of the animosity was real?"

"Don't get me wrong. You drive me up a wall sometimes," he growls, smooth hands rubbing up and down my arms. "I never drank coffee before you joined Itrix. After you started coming to our Tuesday meetings, I saw it as another chance to talk to you for a handful of seconds, even if all you did was hand me a stupid paper cup. Now every time I take a sip of black coffee, all I think about is you."

"All this time... All these years. I thought you hated me. Despised me. Looked down on me."

His face crumples, remorse etched deep into his penitent eyes and disappointed frown. "You plague my thoughts, Josephine. Day after day. You haunt my dreams, an inescapable cycle. And you brighten my darkest, most sorrowful nightmares, lighting up my gloomy world like a million lanterns. Hate you? I could never, ever hate you. I've never felt something so strongly before in my life, and it's confusing as hell. Frustrating. Exhausting. But god, so fucking worth it."

"You... I..."

I gape at him, inundated with understanding on behalf of his admission of the life-altering words.

That's why he was so distraught after the night at the bar, frantically keeping notes and refusing to sleep, keeping a watchful eye on me his only purpose.

That's why he agreed to sing karaoke with me, performing the song I love most without a real argument or gripe, beaming like a lunatic.

That's why he woke up when I was having a panic attack, soothing me and calming me down, no matter how much it disturbed his sleep cycle.

I noticed an obvious attraction between us this last week. A pull like a magnet. The sparks whenever he touches me. But this? This...

I've felt it, too. For a long time. Gradually building and ending here. Right now. This isn't a small crush. It's something much, much larger.

"I'm sorry," he whispers, kissing my forehead, hands cupping my cheeks. I can hear the genuine apology in his declaration. "I'm sorry that I interrupted you. I'm sorry for being closed off and cold." A kiss to my cheek. "If I could go back to that first day, I'd show up twenty minutes early, tea in hand and a smile on my face, just for you. You know that's why I always made sure I was the first one to every meeting, right? So I could have an extra second, two if I was lucky, with you."

I smile weakly, tears threatening to overshadow the elation and joy of this pivotal, romantic moment. "I forgive you. How could I not? Now kiss me, please, because I can't go another minute without your lips on mine."

He obliges, warm, hesitant lips covering my own before I can blink. With one touch, one press of his mouth, I'm ignited.

I'm not sure how I survived before; I'm suffocating and he's keeping me alive. The swipe of his tongue is my lifeline. The gentle bite of his teeth is my oxygen supply. My hand moves to his hair, clutching the bronze waves with every ounce of my being, afraid to let go and so desperate to hold on.

A beat passes and we pull apart, heavy breathing syncing in unison. This is my chance to escape. To leave and not look back. He's giving me an out, an opportunity before he wrecks my entire world. I stare him down, the answer written plainly on my face.

No games. Just us.

And I want to be destroyed.

I grab Jack's tie, wrapping it around my wrist and yank him back to me, my lips crashing into his, teeth against teeth, tongue against tongue. The kiss reverberates through my body, his mouth knowing exactly where to go, as if he's known the way all along, patiently waiting for permission.

It's frantic and rushed and frenzied, like we both know it could end any second. Years of bottled-up emotions and wants are finally spilling over. He's soft yet diligent, and it's like we belong together. Like we're made for each other.

A perfect match.

His hand wraps into my hair, giving it a tug, while the other snakes around my waist. Our legs hit the couch and we collapse onto the cushions, a flurry of discombobulated limbs momentarily distracting our quest.

"Fuck," he growls, the curse sounding sensual. "Goddamn pillows." He throws the one between us onto the floor, into the unknown. I don't miss it.

"Hang on. Sit back," I instruct, and he complies, listening without a complaint, legs stretching out before him at a ninety-degree angle. Fumbling with the buckle of my wedges, his hand covers mine, stopping my undress.

"Keep them on," he says roughly, fresh heat overtaking my body. "I've always loved when you're taller than me."

Well, I'm not going to argue with *that*.

Nodding, I shift on the couch and straddle him, legs landing on either side of his hips, hovering inches above the noticeable bulge he's sporting.

"Is this okay?"

"Fucking perfect," he mutters, kissing me again. He tastes like cheesecake and wine and lust, a sinful poison I greedily swallow down, greeting my demise with open arms. His hand rests on my hip, fingers gently tracing the curves of my body, the fabric a brick barrier to my bare skin. I need to get out of this dress immediately.

"Ow," I exclaim, wincing at the sudden pain in my leg.

"What's wrong?" he asks hurriedly, pulling back to examine me, eyes sweeping over my body and concern on his face. For half a second, I wonder how I could have ever despised this man, regretting every callous and rude thing I've ever spoken about him.

He's never hated me.

Not for a damn second.

"My knees hurt. I'm not as flexible as I used to be. I hope that's not a dealbreaker."

"You can relax. Sit on my lap."

With painstaking slowness, I lower myself onto him, gasping at the hardness that greets me, pressing right against the center of my dampening underwear. I'm instantly dizzy with desire.

"Shit," Jack groans, his head hitting the back of the cushions. His throat bobs as he gathers himself before speaking again. "I can't tell you how badly I wanted to spin you around the other night at the bonfire and sink you onto my dick."

"You should've," I whisper, moving forward an inch, then back an inch, his length running along the seams of the black thong I want to rip away to feel him entirely.

Holy shit.

He is massive.

His fingers trace up my arms, stopping at the straps of my dress. He looks at me, eyes ablaze, and I nod, giving him permission. He can take it all.

"Say the word, Josephine, and I'll give you everything you want." His lips graze my ear while his thumb rubs my shoulder in small circles. "I need to hear it, sweetheart."

"Yes. God, yes."

He guides one strap down, so unhurriedly I might explode, my left breast exposed, pebbled nipple on display.

"You're perfect."

Jack takes me in his mouth and I throw my head back, a loud moan escaping from my lips. He slips the other side of my dress away and it slides to my waist. His hand dances over to my right breast, feather-light touches peppering the sensitive skin.

"So beautiful," he murmurs, and I grip his shoulder. "And already so ready. I can't wait to see what else is under this dress. How wet am I going to find you?"

Soaked.

"More," I beg, hand tightening on his shirt collar. I'm close to stretching out the fabric, but I need to feel his skin on mine to know this is *real*.

His mouth kisses the right side of my body, licking the underside of the neglected breast before sucking on my nipple. I wasn't aware I had a thing for nipple play, but *goddamn*, the sensation is incredible.

"Could you come from this?"

His words vibrate against me as teeth gently bite my skin, climbing me higher and higher up the rungs of pleasure. He knows the answer, but I'm going to tell him regardless.

"Easily."

His hand finds its way back into my hair, twisting and giving another pull, harder than before. I let out a guttural sound, lungs burning and body shaking.

"Do you remember what I told you in the bar?"

"How could I not?" I pant, the memory forever engraved in my memory.

"That wasn't a fucking line. Move against me. Now."

His arms wrap around my bare back, hands resting on my shoulder blades. I obey, closing my eyes and letting the friction beneath me dictate my thoughts and movements. It feels *good*. But it's not enough.

Frustrated, I release a huff of annoyance.

"What's wrong?" Jack asks, nipping at my collarbone.

"I need more. Can we go to the bedroom?"

There's no going back once we cross this line. We're past the point of no return, and walking down the hall together, continuing what we've started and going even further, will only make the boundary hazier, adding fuel to the fire of confusion and *where do we go from here?*

I don't care.

"Is that what you want?"

"Yes."

"Then fuck yes we can go to the bedroom," he agrees as he slides the straps of my dress back up, covering me up as he plants another kiss on my lips.

THIRTY-FIVE
JACK

I cannot believe I'm kissing her. It's a fever dream; something I never expected to experience in a million years. I've died and gone to heaven. As I free her from my hold, she grabs my shirt, tugging me closer, reluctant to let me go even though she's the one who asked to move this to the bedroom.

I've thought about this moment before. It's a fantasy that's only grown clearer and clearer the more time I spend with her. I wondered how she would sound and taste and smell. Would she be loud? Quiet? Does she like to be on top? Now that it's happening, I'm totally enraptured by everything *Josephine*.

Her lips are so soft, littering my cheek and neck with a trail of love bites I'm in no hurry to hide. Her hands can't stop touching me, moving from my pectoral muscles to my abs, up my biceps and around my neck. She's drawing a roadmap of places I hope she'd like to explore. She has an open invitation.

I kiss her again, gentler than before. Because I fucking can. This time, it's less hurried. More questioning. Reverent. Sweet and savory with the slightest hint of spice and flavor. A lesson in what makes Josephine Bowen go absolutely fucking wild.

I quickly learn what she likes; it's hard not to when she

reveals her preferences in such salacious, sexy ways. Thighs clenching and breath catching when I discover a new item to add to the list I'm compiling in my head. Mouth parting and back arching with every other kiss.

She enjoys her hair being pulled. Rough tugs that tilt her head up, neck bared to me. She also likes when my fingertips dig into the skin above her hips, applying the right amount of pressure that borders on painful.

She *really* likes my tongue running down the column of her neck, gasping sounds emitted from those beautiful lips as I lightly bite and nip the open highway to her breasts, my fingers pinching her nipples and twisting half a degree. But she wants more, more, *more*, and I'm going to fucking give it to her.

A coy, sexy smile stretches across her face as she extends her hand toward me, rising off the couch and walking down the hall, dress slinking from side to side with every swish of her sinful hips. The piece of fabric is a tease; it hugs her body in the best way but doesn't reveal enough. I follow her, afraid that if I let her out of my sight for longer than a millisecond, I'll wake up and she'll be gone, a figment of my imagination that never existed.

When we get to the bedroom, she looks over her shoulder while I close the door. Half expecting her to pause out of fear or regret, I'm paralyzed, transfixed, and hypnotized by her commanding and confident actions as she stands before me, hand on her hip popped out to the side, teeth sinking into her lower lip.

I expected her to be sure of herself, but she's bordering on sex-goddess territory and so completely out of my league. She knows what she wants, and she's not going to stop until she gets it.

"Should I take this off?" she asks curiously, and I nod hard enough to give myself a concussion. Her hands toy with those damn straps, fingers dipping under the slinky material and leisurely inching the thin piece of clothing away from her shoulders, giving me a private strip tease that's she's eager to draw out. The thin fingers linger on her chest, tracing across her clavicle and running down to her breasts, trying to draw my attention away from her face.

I resist the urge to dip my gaze, take in her body as she steps out of the dress completely, and lose every shred of control. I stay composed, my sole focus those luminous green eyes. A streak of colors go flying out of sight and I'm no longer breathing.

In my head, it's never, ever gotten this far. The second I soak in her naked, sultry body, it's going to be game over from here on out. Lines and boundaries are shattered at this point. We can't go back and I don't fucking want to.

With trembling fingers, more nervous than I have ever been in my entire life, I unbutton my shirt and slide it off, unknotting my tie and tossing it away with it. Kicking off my shoes, I yank my socks off, undo my belt and pants button, shoving them over my knees and stepping out of the denim. I'm left standing in only my briefs.

"Can I look at you?" I ask hoarsely, about to drop to the scratchy carpet floor and beg. The rug burn would be worth it.

"Yeah," she answers.

My eyes finally feast on the sight before me, gaze dipping to study every inch of her bare body.

She's...

God.

Fuck.

Shit.

I'm a ruined man.

I pictured this going a million and one different ways. In some, she throws a shoe at my head as she storms away, disgusted by my advances. In others, she laughs, thinking I'm joking about wanting to take her clothes off. None of the visions prepared me for the sight I'm staring at, and it's nearly impossible to articulate the right words to convey the beauty, sexiness, and sensual power of the woman before me.

With the strappy shoes still on, she's taller than me. I might ask her to leave them on forever because she appears like a queen, waiting for her kingdom to bow before her majestic presence. Her chest puffs out and her skin is colored crimson, glowing in the soft lamplight surrounding us. Moving away from her neck, I study her breasts.

They're the perfect size, the left ever so slightly larger than the right. I can't wait to pinch those rosy nipples again, hard and pointed without even a hand on them.

From her chest I sweep down to her stomach. There's no loose skin there, but it's not totally flat. Small love handles accentuate a trim waist, giving way to rounded hips that I want to use to steady myself while I fuck her from behind. Between her legs sits a patch of hair, and she shifts apprehensively when she realizes what part of her I'm so intimately studying, wedged feet crossing over another, trying to block the view.

"I-I'm sorry about this." She gestures to the hair, crimson fading to a deeper red. "I didn't expect to... I normally..."

"Like I give a fuck," I hiss, wrapping my arms around her and leading us toward the bed. "It doesn't change how your pussy is going to taste, right?"

"N-no," she stammers, letting out a giggle as her hamstrings connect with the mattress, toppling onto the sheets and bringing me down with her in the collapse. I keep my weight above her body, holding myself up, my left hand near her hip while my right lands adjacent to her head. She lets out a small sigh, reaching up to brush a piece of hair out of my face, giving me an even more unobstructed view of nirvana.

"Hi," she whispers. It's so perfectly *her*, the last ounce of pressure to make sure this goes according to plan evaporates. "Hey." I dip to kiss her forehead. "You're so beautiful. So unbelievably sexy. Hot. Stunning. Cute."

"Cute, huh? Careful, keep using that kind of dirty talk and I'll be putty in your hands." Her sharp nails dig into my taut back muscles as my eyelashes flutter closed. Oh. Yeah. I think I'd like to have her claw marks on my body permanently. A constant reminder *who* has been digging into my skin, holding on for dear life while I fuck her senseless.

"You're sexy too, you know. Your body, Jack... It's unreal."

"It's the celery and tepid water, you know."

"I knew it."

Placing a hand on her shoulder, my thumb gently caresses her skin like I would a fine silk or rare, exquisite jewel. My touch moves upwards, the pad of my thumb swiping over her lips as her tongue tries to chase me down. Finally, my fingers run down the slope of her neck, stopping between her breasts before bending forward and quickly biting her nipple. That earns me my first moan in our undressed state.

My eyes wander again, still unbelieving that she's *here*. Under me. Naked. "What's this from?" I trace the faint scar that sits near her hipbone, wanting to learn about every mark and blemish that covers her body.

"I fell off my scooter when I was younger," she answers, hips thrusting to meet my touch as I move away entirely. The whine she lets out makes me smile. "Straight onto a piece of concrete."

"What's the rush? I want to savor every goddamn minute."

"Please, Jack. If you don't kiss me, I might die."

I climb back up her body, lips hovering above hers. "Say my name again. And I want to hear it when I make you come."

"Jack," she repeats, and I swallow her words down with a searing kiss, hand running up her thigh.

My name tumbling from her mouth, a breathless word, catapults me into a kaleidoscope of sexual energy. Holy crap, I need to hear that on repeat for the rest of my life.

Collecting my last bit of wavering sanity, I offer up a silent prayer, hoping I don't lose my mind as I slide my finger over her slick entrance. It's a light graze, not a full-on attack, but she's already reacting. I'm met with so much moisture, so much *desire* I have to restrain myself from bucking my hips into the mattress and coming in four seconds.

Not part of the plan, Lancaster.

"You're so fucking wet," I say, mesmerized. "This is all for me?"

Josephine nods before abruptly covering her face. The air deflates from the room.

"Hey, what's wrong?"

"In the past I've been told..." She quiets, hesitant to divulge the sensitive information.

A flare of protectiveness washes through me. "Told what?" I gently coax her. I'm not going to *force* her to have a conversation, but I want to make sure we're on the same page.

"I'm too much. Too messy. Too responsive. Too loud. In bed. And in life."

"Oh, sweetheart. There's no such thing." I move down her body, positioning my head between her parted, quivering legs. I kiss her left thigh, then her right, nudging her wider. Her feet raise, landing on my shoulders for support, and I grin. "Too messy? Too loud? I want everyone in this hotel to know whose mouth makes you fall apart. Don't hold back, Josephine. I want it all."

I place my lips over her, licking her pussy with the utmost precision, tongue tracing along her slit. She lets out a long groan, back rising off the mattress. My right arm drapes over her stomach to stop her movements, keeping her firmly in place and wanting to indulge in every delicious drop she'll give me.

Christ.

She tastes like heaven.

An iniquitous, wicked flavor I hope seeps into my veins and bloodstream.

"Open up. I'm greedy and I want more."

That earns me another groan as she adheres to my ask, spreading herself wide, and hell, I wish I had a photo of what we look like from above. I don't know where to focus; on her drenched pussy within my reach or the whimper escaping her mouth, hands fisting the sheets with a death-like grip.

I finally give her what she wants. My tongue enters her, parts her, as my thumb circles her clit twice, trying to find the rhythm she likes. Once I do, I'm going to use it to unravel her until she's coming on my mouth from now until eternity.

She's panting as I pull my lips away, eager to see how much she can take. Carefully, gently, I slide my pointer finger inside her, past both knuckles, hissing at the tightness that welcomes me as I curl the digit.

"Fuck," I hiss, not bothering to hold back the expletive. "You're so fucking tight."

Her pussy swallows my finger down, pulling it from view and devouring it. I watch in awe as Josephine's movements become frantic and erratic, desperately searching for a much-needed release.

"More," she whines, feet sliding off my shoulders and onto the sheets, joining her hands. She's fucking my finger, I realize, hips thrusting, out of control movements and horny beyond belief.

"How much more?"

"All of it. Please."

She's not getting *all of it* yet. I take a deep breath before I add a second finger, my moan mingling with hers as I stretch her wider, captivated by the way she moves her body.

She's going to destroy me when I slide my cock inside her.

I let my head drop back between her thighs, circling her clit again, an alternating dance between a thrust of my fingers and flick of my tongue, the cadence she craves already figured out. What can I say? I'm a quick learner, and I'm here to please.

She's close. Her legs are quaking, her whimpers have subsided, shifting to a staccato pant, and a bead of sweat slides onto my hand from her stomach, creeping up my forearm.

I have zero knowledge on how she feels about dirty talk. What I do know is she likes to be praised. Right now, I want to make her see the fucking stars.

"Good girl," I say, kissing her thigh and exchanging my tongue for fingers one final time, ready to tip her over the edge. "Such a good fucking girl for me."

That works.

Soon she's exploding, convulsing and shaking as she chants my name rhythmically, over and over again, a choked sob lodged in her throat.

Not even the finest dessert or nicest wine in the world can compare to her divine taste. I bring her down from her high slowly, gently lapping up the mess she's created and rubbing her clit in soft, leisure circles, drawing her pleasure out as long as I can.

She lets out another sob and I'm off her in a second, cradling her in my arms and pulling her close to my chest as I stroke her hair.

"Hi," she whispers, voice cracking. Keeping my eyes on her, I bring my fingers to her mouth, tracing the outline of her lips with the aftereffects from *her,* wanting to test just how dirty she is and learn her limits. I want to see how well we're going to mesh. I think I already know, and that's why my dick is physically *aching*, almost ripping my briefs in two with how hard it is.

Her mouth opens without question, tongue darting up the length of my fingers and accepting them, deeper and deeper toward the back of her throat. It's my turn to groan, processing how she doesn't flinch or gag, instead trying to take more at the same time, her drool sliding down my hand as she cleans up every last drop.

She's fucking filthy. And perfect for me.

When she's happy with her tidy up, I cup her chin, bringing her lips to mine in a searing kiss. She melts into me, ass wiggling against my thighs, a content sigh escaping her and sneaking into my mouth.

"Hi back," I answer, my chin resting on her shoulder, noticing the water glinting in her eyes. "Doing okay?"

"I'm fucking wonderful," she sighs again. I dry the rogue tears that escaped to her cheeks, dabbing them away with the disheveled bedsheet that's become wrinkled and twisted.

"I didn't hurt you, did I?"

"Hurt me? You sent me to the fucking moon, Lancaster. The tears are a side effect of the incredible journey."

"Now you're stroking my ego," I murmur, kissing her neck and ignoring my still hard cock. It's not the time.

"Do you want me to..." Josephine shifts off my legs slightly, gesturing to my briefs.

It takes a lot to shake my head. I do it anyway. "Do I want you to? Hell yeah, I do. Am I going to let you? Not tonight. You're exhausted."

"I'm not," she retorts, pouting her lips before a yawn slips through.

"She says as she falls asleep sitting up." I shuffle her off my lap and stand up.

"Where are you going?" she asks quickly, her hand reaching

out to snake around mine, anchoring us together. Is she afraid I'm going to leave her alone? Has someone done that to her in the past?

Best not to think about violence right now. Kind of a mood killer.

"I'm going to wash my hands, get comfortable, and bring you back some water. I'm not running away, Josephine, and if you think I'm stopping after one orgasm from you, you're sorely mistaken. I'm just getting started."

I hate that I have to leave for even the four minutes I'm gone, and I rush through my checklist, exchanging my briefs for pajama bottoms, tucking my throbbing dick in the waistband.

When I stride back into the room, her eyes light up. She's lounging against the pillows on her side, still naked, long legs stretched out like a model.

"Have I told you that you're sexy?" I ask.

"It's been about ten minutes. I think I need to hear it again."

"Sexy woman." Placing the cup of water on her side of the bed, I crouch to kiss her.

"Welcome back." She yawns again, rubbing her eyes with the heels of her palms. "Are you sure you don't want to have sex?"

I can't help but laugh. "The first time I fuck you won't be when you're half asleep, my friend. I want you to be loud. Wild. With me, like you were when you came on my lips a few minutes ago. As much as I want to feel how tight you are around my cock while you ride me, I can survive the night, believe it or not."

"That was really hot," she whispers. "Give me all the dirty talk, please."

"I probably should've asked beforehand, but I noticed you like to be praised."

"Yeah. I do."

"That's good to know. For research purposes."

"Oh, is that what we're calling it?"

"Mhm. Strictly for scientific data collection only."

"Well, we better add some more controls and variables to our experiment, then. To determine if it will yield any different results."

"Maybe we should document them, too," I add, testing the waters.

Her eyebrow arches, catching the implication, and her mouth raises in agreement. "With photos."

"Perhaps a video, too."

"It'd be in the name of science, after all."

"Precisely. We want to be thorough."

She hums, dipping her head and unable to hide the smile sitting on her swollen, ravished mouth. "I'm going to check the door, Professor Lancaster."

I whistle. Yeah, definitely a fan of that nickname. "Do you want me to do it?" She said *she* needs to be the one to confirm everything is locked, but I want to offer nonetheless.

"Thank you, but no. I'm so comfortable, I don't want to get up—Hey! What are you doing?!"

I scoop her into my arms effortlessly, walking down the hallway.

"We're going to check together."

"You don't have to do that," she whispers.

"I say this in the nicest way. You're a smart girl, Josephine. When will you learn I don't do things because I have to? I do them because I want to. And that includes checking the locks with you."

I keep her tucked against me while her arms wrap around my neck, head nestled in my chest. When we arrive at the suite door, I move close enough for her to check whatever she needs. I don't speak. I don't tap my foot. I stay still, not wanting to distract her. It takes her a few minutes, but I'm perfectly content having her in my arms, no matter what the reason.

"Thank you," she sighs, kissing below my ear and discovering a new place I didn't know I liked to be touched. I shudder at the contact, turning us back toward the bedroom before stopping abruptly in front of the massive mirror hanging in the living room.

"Look at you," I breathe out, and she pulls her head away from my body, feasting on our reflection.

Her hair is a mess. Her cheeks are still pink, showing the aftershocks from the ecstasy she enjoyed.

Meanwhile, my dick is as erect as a motherfucker, not bothering to hide how turned on I am through the plaid pants hanging on my hips.

"Do you like what you see?" she asks, her own hand running down her neck, across her upper chest before pinching a nipple.

"Fuck yes I do," I growl, watching her shift to the other side, squeezing that nipple even harder. My eyes want to roll to the back of my head at the thought of her pleasuring herself. In front of me. "You're a goddamn vision."

One of her legs drops from my grasp, dangling limply at her side, pussy on full display and magnified in the glass. Fresh moisture stains her thighs.

"Look what you do to me, Jack. I'm ready to go again."

"If you don't close your legs, I'm going to take a picture and make it my lock screen on my phone so I can stare at your pretty pussy all day and night."

"As if you'll get any objection from me. I think we need to revisit this mirror tomorrow, perhaps."

"I think that's a good idea. I'd love to watch you while I fuck you from behind. I've always been an ass man, and yours is nothing short of divine, Josephine."

She chuckles, closing her legs back up and stopping the

heart attack I'm about to suffer from. "An ass man, huh? I'll keep that in mind. Come on, if you're not going to let me jerk you off, we need to go to sleep."

I deposit her on the carpet so she can get ready for bed. While she's gone, I turn on the fan, making sure it's on the loudest setting.

"Is it okay if we cuddle?" she asks as she climbs onto the mattress, turning the lamp on the bedside table off.

"Get over here, Bowen." I open my arms and she scoots over, shoulder blades pressing into my chest. I wrap my arms around her waist, letting out a content sigh. "I missed you while you were gone."

"It was three minutes." She yawns, patting my hand and intertwining our legs, her calf slinging over mine. "But I missed you too."

"What a terrifying thought. Sleep now, Josephine. I'll see you in the morning."

I press a final kiss to the base of her neck, welcoming sleep and dreams of her.

THIRTY-SIX
JO

Light slowly begins to trickle into the warming room. I roll over on the mattress, my arms reaching out and finding Jack's side empty.

God, I hope he doesn't regret last night and bolted in terror this morning, afraid of the repercussions. Or how I'd react.

I certainly don't regret anything.

I haven't come like that... ever. It was intense, a white-hot, searing euphoria. The things he said. The promises he offered up. The way he knows how to move his fingers and curve in just the right way. The tickle of his tongue.

I think he might kill me.

Here lies Jo Bowen. Dead from an earth-shattering orgasm.

What a way to go.

And then he carried me in his arms, marched to the door of the suite, and patiently waited for me to run through my check of the locks, not uttering a single complaint. How is this man real?

I smooth my hand over the cold sheets, never expecting I'd wake up in the morning wondering where Jack Lancaster is.

There's a first time for everything.

Pulling the covers up to my chin, I snuggle into the abyss, closing my eyes when I hear the door to the suite open.

Sucking in a silent breath, I wait, wondering who's going to make the first move. Footsteps approach the room, drawing nearer, before a soft voice begins speaking to me.

"Good morning," Jack says. "If you want to pretend to be asleep and act like last night never occurred, we can. Or, if I'm allowed to kiss you again, now would be a great time to wake up."

My eyes fly open, already grinning.

"Good morning," I reply, my words breathy and light, flustered by his acceptance of acknowledging our tryst twelve hours ago.

"Hey." He kneels on the floor beside me. "How'd you sleep?"

"Really well. Did you run?"

"I did. No national holidays today. Strictly a form of torture."

"I'm beginning to think you're a masochist."

"That might be the nicest thing you've ever said to me, Bowen," he chuckles, his hand reaching out to lightly shift the hair out of my eyes. His fingers are soft, and I lean into his touch, humming contently as he rubs my temple.

"You sure about that? I think I called you a cactus once."

"You certainly know the way to my heart," he agrees, inching closer to the bed.

My grin stretches wider, nearly cracking the lips that are dried out from too many hours spent out in the sun. This banter with him is natural. He seems lighter. Excited. An entirely different character from our first acts of knowing each other. He underwent a wardrobe change at intermission. I *knew* there was another Jack hiding under that rough facade.

"You're so..."

"Different?" he finishes for me, and I nod.

"Yeah. It's almost scary."

"I can understand why you'd feel that way. You've only seen one side of me, and glimpses of a second. Trust me, I'm experiencing whiplash myself."

"What changed?"

He blows out a breath. "You."

My brows furrow, confused by the answer. "I've always been me."

"I'm well aware of your you-ness. What I mean is you've kind of... nudged your way into my life unexpectedly. Before I could attempt to understand what the hell everything meant, you were on my mind. Sometimes I wanted to scream at you about your pen color choices and font preferences, and other times I wanted to hug you tight and keep you safe from the evils of the world. But now you're here. Like, here here, in front of me. Sleeping next to me. Waking up in my arms. Without this conference, I never would have confronted my feelings. I would have been content to shove them away, into a deep corner of my brain, and never revisit them. We're here together somehow, and that means I get to touch you and talk to you and watch you smile. *Make* you smile. I dunno. There's something about you, Josephine, that positively rattles me. It's incredibly unnerving in the best way."

"So, what you're saying is I'm kind of like an unexpected paradise, huh?"

"Bold assumption, and perhaps not too far off."

"I like this side best. You're not allowed to go back to before, all cold shoulders and scowls. I forbid it."

"I can't promise there won't be moments like that. You make me happy, yes, but there's also a lot of stuff that makes me unhappy and sad."

"You know I don't mean you can't be you, right? The

sadness and unhappiness are okay. I don't expect *everything* about you to change after one night together. Like, I imagine you'll still ruin your perfectly good eggs with ketchup this morning."

"Have I told you this morning you're a smart-ass?"

"No, but it's right up there with when you call me a good girl under Things I Enjoy Hearing."

"We're starting early, aren't we?" he growls.

"About that kiss."

"Yeah?"

"Any day now would be great, thanks."

He tips his head back, laughing. "So demanding."

"You should laugh more often. It's a beautiful sound."

"For you, I'll try. Now, kindly shut up so I can fulfill your needs. Please," he adds, and I reach my hand out to grab the collar of his sweat-soaked shirt and pull him toward me, uncaring of the smell of exercise that greets me.

The kiss this morning is lazy. Sweet and savory. His mouth parts for my tongue. My teeth lightly bite his lips, earning me another growl that zips through my entire body.

My fingers find their way to his hair, threading through the damp waves and lightly tugging on the strands.

"Josephine," he mutters, removing his mouth from mine.

"Jack," I answer, tugging again and he almost falls backwards on his ass. Oh, he *likes* that. Noted.

"If you keep distracting me, we're never leaving the room."

"What if I don't want to leave the room?"

"Your stomach growled two seconds ago."

"We can order room service."

"You want to go down the waterslide."

"I also want to slide on your dick."

He bursts out laughing, removing my hand from his hair and kissing my palm.

"I'm never letting you meet my friend Henry after that crass comment. I shudder to think what the world would be like if you two came in contact with each other."

"Does Henry know about me?"

"Would it bother you if he did?"

"Nope. Abby knows all about you. Or, I guess she thinks she does. Times have changed. My ear drums are going to erupt when I inform her about this new development."

"Then yes, he's aware of you. My three other friends are, too. And, in the interest of full disclosure, they might be aware I jerked off in the shower the other morning after learning you were out here doing the same."

I giggle. "I'm not sorry for that."

"I didn't imagine you would be." Kissing my forehead, he stands up. "I'm going to shower, then we're going down that damn water slide if it's the last thing I do while I flip off Greg's room."

"*Then* can I slide on your dick?"

"I told you already, Josephine, you can have whatever you want. Let's have a fun day, then you can slide wherever you want."

The water slide is one of the most fun things I've done, highlighted by Jack's genuine yelp at the drop near the end as he plummets into the pool. When he emerges from the water, he's grinning stupidly, both dimples visible and eyes creased in the corners.

After exhausting our slide time, we spend the rest of the day alternating between relaxing in the lazy river on inner tubes and reading under a large umbrella on the beach. Every few minutes he drags his eyes away from his book, tosses me a smile, then resumes his reading.

I wish I could say we gallivant around like a couple who got together for the first time last night.

But we don't.

He doesn't touch me, adamantly refusing my proposition to go down the waterslide together. He doesn't kiss me—not a single peck on the cheek. Sure, we converse easily and laugh lightly, yet we indulge in no physical affection. My skin is *buzzing* being near him, itching for his hands.

I'm thoroughly mystified by his behavior while we eat dinner. Maybe he's not into PDA. I'm not either. Having someone try to shove their tongue down my throat while I'm eating a meal sounds unappealing. He's being less... boyfriend-y *now*, though, than when we were pretending.

I hold up my glass of water after our table has been cleared of food, gesturing for him to do the same.

"What are we toasting?" he asks curiously, grasping his drink.

I think for a minute.

"To new beginnings. And a fresh start."

It's a vague, open-ended remark, with plenty of room for interpretation.

"A fresh start," he repeats. "I like that."

Our glasses clink and we sip. I watch him swallow and his Adam's apple bobs. Fucking hell, he's hot. Carnal. Hedonistic. Commanding and intimidating in a sexy way. Watching him drink is turning me on. Looking away, my ankles cross under the table as I shift in my seat.

"Are you all right over there?"

"Fine."

"You can tell me, you know."

"I'm trying to figure out why you barely acknowledged me

this afternoon. It makes me think we're gravitating toward how things were before we came here," I confess, twisting the paper napkin in my lap, giving my hands a distraction.

"What? We talked a lot today. I had fun, and I thought you did too."

"Today was perfect. I don't mean the communication. For once, we're doing that right. I'm talking about the physical part. If that's how you want to play this, then fine. But can you at least tell me so I can start to forget last night happened?"

He winces, sitting back in his seat. "I'm going to be honest with you. I didn't think I could control myself today if I touched you. Whenever I saw that damn bikini out of the corner of my eye, I got turned on. You wanted me to go down the waterslide with you? So I could have your amazing ass against my cock? The ass I want to kiss and spank and fuck? It would have been game over. I had to say no."

Holy shit, I'm going to leave a mess on this seat.

"I'm *always* looking at you. And now when I see you, I want to do so many things to you. For you. With you. I want to fuck you six ways to Sunday, but I also want to cradle you in my arms while you drift off to sleep. I realize that's not an excuse to neglect your needs, and for that, I apologize, but I'm trying to behave. You make that very difficult."

"I-I didn't know."

"Do I want to kiss you right now? Yeah, I do," he continues, his words a beautiful assault on my ears. "Do I want to hold your hand across this table, letting everyone around us know that we're here together? For real? Yup. Do I want to put my palm on your leg, under your dress, and see how I can make you squirm in the middle of a restaurant? Absolutely, and that's never been a kink of mine before.

"I also want to spend time with you sitting on the beach, hearing you giggle at your book when you think I'm not paying attention. For the record, I heard every chuckle of yours today. Each one warmed my heart a little more. I want to watch you scan the dinner menu, biting the side of your lip while you tap your cheek, trying to decide what you want to eat, even though we both know you're going to wind up with some form of potato accompanying your meal. I'm enjoying learning all these things about you because I'm finally allowed to. If I had acted on my physical needs today, that wouldn't have happened."

This cannot be the same man who once answered my request about a website change via email with a single: *No*.

This cannot be the same man who grunts when I ask him a question.

The man before me writes poems and sonnets. Love letters in cursive by candlelight before stuffing the envelope full, page after page of declarations, and mailing them to someone he cares about.

Me. I'm the one that brought on this change. I'm the one who handed him the quill and jar of ink, patted his shoulder, and opened his world to new colors.

"I was struggling today, too. I wanted to cuddle in your arms while we both read our books and I've never been interested in affection like that. I wanted to do something that made you smile or laugh. I wanted to know you were enjoying spending time with me. I'm glad you don't regret last night."

"Regret? Far from it. If anything, I'm hoping I didn't say too much in the last five minutes that prevents you from wanting to go back to the room with me."

"You didn't," I say quickly, reaching over to give his hand a squeeze. "We're working on communicating, remember? Thank you for sharing."

"You ready to head up?"

"Yeah. I think I am."

The trek back to the room is never-ending. The elevator

moves too slowly and is crowded with people. The hallway stretches too long, the finish line nowhere in sight. When I finally open the door to the suite, my entire body is trembling.

Jack makes his way to the kitchen to put away our leftovers, and I drift toward the living room, looking out the large window at the ocean below. His arms wrap around my waist, kissing my neck through my hair, and I smile.

"Everything okay?"

"Everything's perfect."

I spin around, facing him, and when our gazes meet, I see wildness behind the normally docile eyes. They're wide. Hungry. Consuming.

"Can I?" I ask, and the small dip of his chin answers my question. I unbutton his shirt, pushing it off his body. Eagerly, I let my hand roam from his shoulders down to his stomach, across the expansive planes of his toned abdominal muscles, goosebumps erupting under my investigative trail. A forest of fine, thin hair tickles my fingers as I dip lower, toying with the waist of his pants.

"Josephine," he says, voice rough and stilted, struggling to speak. "If you don't stop, I'm not going to be able to control myself."

"What if I don't want you to control yourself?" My palm slides inside the denim of his jeans, thumbs hooking on his briefs. He inhales sharply, the warm air hitting my cheeks. "What if I want you to take me?" I continue, dipping lower and lower and lower, cresting over the top of his cock. "Claim me as yours? Do anything you want to me?"

He lets out a guttural groan, gripping my waist like a lifeline. "If that's what you want, all you have to do is ask. I'm entirely at your mercy. Whatever you want is yours."

His lips are centimeters away from mine as his eyes sweep across my face, searching for any sign of refusal or hesitancy.

"Please," I whisper, knowing the power the word has over him, arching my back so my chest presses against his. I've never craved anything—anyone—like I crave him. The word is his undoing, and before I can form a coherent thought or decide all the ways this could end in flames, or catastrophe, or pure and utter destruction, he lifts me into his arms, hands cupping my ass, lips on my neck. "I need you."

"Say it again," he demands breathlessly, half full of possessiveness, half full of wonder. He moves us until my back hits the window behind me and I hiss at the contact, the chill of the glass subduing the burn of my skin from his torrid touch. My nipples peak at the temperature shift. "Say you need me again."

His teeth lightly graze the side of my neck, over my pulse point, and I let out a choked sound of awe and pleasure at the hands of the feral man before me.

"I need you, Jack." This time, it's not a kind ask. It's a desperate plea. My hands cup his cheeks as his eyes bare into my soul. "Make me yours."

His mouth finally crashes into mine, a mix of sloppy, heady, frantic kisses full of teeth and tongue. I open, welcoming him, begging him.

"Fuck." His fingers dig into my love handles while my calves wrap around the small of his back. "I've waited so long to hear you say that. To hear you ask that." I tip my hips forward, canting closer to him, grazing along his hard length. "If you keep doing that, though, I'm going to take you for the first time in front of the entire fucking world."

"You think I'd care that the world watched while you were inside me for the first time?"

Jack growls, pulling me off the window and heading for the bedroom. "Let me amend my statement," he clarifies, nipping my earlobe as I squirm in his grasp. "The second time, sure, we can have an audience if that's what you want. I'll fuck you on the beach in broad daylight and risk public indecency. But right now, it's you and me. No one else." He deposits me on the mattress near the pillows, sitting back on his calves.

"Hi," I say, and he shakes his head, adjusting his pants. From here, I can see the outline of his cock, the denim doing nothing to mask the hardness. The attraction. The need for me.

"I'm turning into one of Pavlov's dogs. You say that damn word and I instantly get hard."

"We can remedy that, you know." I reach out, wiggling my fingers in an inviting gesture.

"Scoot back on the pillows."

I'm caught off guard by his demand, but I comply, maneuvering until I'm flush against the headboard.

"Good girl," he says, silky smooth. I fidget, toes already curling.

I've always loved to be praised. An old boyfriend said it once in my early 20's, and I haven't looked back. It's not a tidbit of information I normally share with a partner in the beginning. It's not for everyone, and I can get off just fine without it. Somehow, Jack has picked up on what makes me want to lose control.

"Anything else?"

"Dress off, please."

"With pleasure." I slide the straps off my shoulders and down my hips, tossing the garment away.

"There's my girl," he murmurs, the endearment sweet and syrupy amidst the charged energy of the room. "Everything off, now."

I nod and unhook my bra, throwing it and my underwear out of the way. "This would be a lot more fun if you were touching me," I whine, fists grasping the sheets.

"Josephine. I don't want to just touch you. Let me also be the one to take care of you."

I bite my lip. This is a moment in life that I could spend time planning out the hypotheticals. The what-ifs. Instead, I breathe out, "Yes." A loaded answer and one that I'm happy to give.

"Okay. Okay." He nods, scratching behind his ear, huffing like he didn't think this through. "If there's anything. *Anything*," he emphasizes, shuffling on his knees, "you don't like, I implore you to tell me. Promise?"

"Promise," I agree, nodding chaotically.

"In that case, touch yourself. Show me what you do to get off. What you did the other morning. I want to watch."

Taking a deep breath, I bring a shaky hand off the sheets, settling it on my thigh, fingers inching upwards. I take my time, teasing myself like I do at home, tentative touches to start and get my body warmed. My thumb circles my clit once, eyes never leaving his.

I'm powerful. Bold. Ready to run a marathon or conquer an entire city. Adrenaline courses through me. As I slide my finger inside myself, Jack shifts closer to my body, watching my every move with a rapturous gaze. Observing how deep I get. The rotations I use. How I alternate between finger and thumb, thrusting and rubbing.

"Can you do something for me?" I whisper, my words catching between gasps as I work myself, trying to reach the edge I so desperately want to tumble over.

"You already know the answer."

"C-can you call me Jo? I've always wondered what it would sound like coming from you."

His fidgeting stops, gaze making its way to my face. I interpret his silence negatively, assuming I've done something wrong.

"Sorry, that was stupid," I mumble, moving my hands to the sheets, ignoring the throbbing forming low in my stomach, ready to hide.

The spell breaks, and Jack crawls, actually *crawls*, toward me on all fours, positioning himself between my legs while leaning forward.

"Jo," he whispers, kissing my forehead reverently. "Jo." A kiss on my cheek. "Jo." A kiss on my breasts, both sides, his body draping over mine. "Jo. Jo. Jo. Jo. Jo," he repeats, over and over, mouth trailing down my skin, worshiping and praising every inch he can reach.

Something cracks within me when I hear him say my name like a prayer to a goddess, a fissure forming within my chest. He's looking at me with an expression I've never seen before, eyes bright and almost misty, and the sight is enchanting.

"I like how that sounds. A lot. I'm yours, Jo. Any and every way you want me."

It might be the most romantically poetic thing I've ever heard, and I'm ten seconds away from throwing caution to the wind and never leaving this island, staying here forever with him by my side, a sanctuary of bliss and ecstasy.

"I want you inside me. I want you to fuck me, Jack," I say, voice almost unrecognizable.

He peels off his shirt and I reach forward and trace his muscles, fingers running over every hard ridge. He's the perfect combination of lean and firm without being overwhelmingly bulky and huge. My fingernails skirt down his flesh and he tips forward, head dropping to his collarbone. Reaching for the button on his jeans, I look up at him through my eyelashes.

"May I?"

Jack nods weakly. I unfasten the button, slowly lowering the zipper. His briefs do little to conceal his hardness, and I tug the waistband of his jeans, indicating what I want. He moves off the bed, standing on the carpet and pulling the jeans and briefs from his long legs in one quick swoop.

I almost combust right there.

I'm kicking myself for not exploring him last night like I wanted to.

He's big. *So big.* I've never been a fan of dicks. Sure, I like the purpose they serve and the job they accomplish, but I never want to *look* and admire them. Now, though, I can't stop staring, watching as he gives himself a tug with his own hand, grip tight. He's long, the perfect girth, and a faint vein runs up his length. He could be a Renaissance statue sculpted out of the finest marble.

Blowing out a breath, my cheeks warm. "I... I know this is so cliché to say, but you might not... fit. There's no way."

"You know me, Jo. I've always liked a challenge."

Jo.

Jack climbs back on the bed to me, arms encircling my waist, our naked bodies finally connecting. He's warm; so warm. Gently lowering me to the sheets, he puts his hands on either side of my head, holding himself over me as if he were doing a push-up. His cock grazes my thigh and I shiver at the contact. His eyes roam down my figure again, up close and intimately.

"You're stunning," he whispers, before slipping two fingers in me, finally giving me what I crave. I gasp at the unexpected intrusion, the stretch deliriously good. "What do you want?"

Grabbing his neck, I pull him to me, letting our lips crash together. He opens his mouth, his tongue swiping over mine. "I told you what I want."

"Come on my fingers first, Jo. Then I'll fuck you any way your heart desires." His thumb circles my clit three times. "Take your time. I could do this all night."

My mind goes blank at his eagerness to satisfy me, never having experienced someone pay so much attention to my body and needs.

"Don't stop," I pant. His hand shifts, gripping my thighs as he throws my calves over his shoulders and slides down the mattress, exchanging his fingers for tongue, swirling once, twice, three, four times before I fall apart, my eyes snapping closed.

I let out a loud moan, the quick orgasm tearing through me without warning. His mouth slows but never stops, drinking in everything I give.

"Fuck," I gasp, a bead of sweat sliding down my forehead. I open my eyes, blinking back to reality. Jack plants twin kisses to both of my thighs, bringing his hand to his erection. He rubs up and down the length slowly, my eyes following his motions.

"Doing okay?" he asks.

"Mm. There aren't strong enough adjectives to describe what I experienced. I'm going to refrain out of fear it'll go to your head. That might be a record for the fastest I've ever finished. What the hell?"

"You don't want me to get cocky?"

"I want you on your back, Lancaster."

He grins, pressing a quick kiss to my lips. "I think I like you calling the shots, Bowen."

He rests on the pillows, one arm tucked under his head, lounging lazily. Moving so I'm parallel with his hips, I kiss his hip bone and flat stomach. My hand moves down his thigh and back up teasingly.

"Do we have condoms?" I ask, realizing we should have discussed this beforehand.

"I might have been a bit overzealous and went to the gift store after my run this morning to grab a pack."

"So you're a planner, huh?"

"More like hopelessly optimistic," he amends. "We don't have t—Oh, fuck," he groans as I interrupt his train of thought, taking his cock in my mouth. Enough talking. "Fucking hell."

Jack's hand gently loops in my hair. He doesn't push or guide me, keeping his palm still while massaging my scalp with his thumb.

My head bobs up and down, cheeks hollowing out, trying to take as much of him as I can. I feel him growing in my mouth, nearing the back of my throat. I can't fit him all the way in. Not yet. But I do my damnedest. My teeth lightly graze his shaft, lips sliding up and back, all the way to his base.

He makes an indistinguishable sound, a cross between a moan and a curse. "J-Josephine. Jo. You need to stop. I don't... I want..." I pull off of him, his head popping out of my mouth, understanding.

I lick away the trail of saliva that's gathered on the corner of my mouth, Jack watching me with heated eyes.

"Dirty girl."

"See something you like?"

"I do, but I think I'm going to like seeing you with a mouthful of my come even more. Check the drawer over there."

Fuck, this man can talk dirty.

I grab a condom from the box, ripping the foil off with my teeth before sliding it onto his still hard cock.

"May I?" I ask, straddling his hips, knees on either side. He nods in response. I lower myself onto him cautiously, taking only the tip first, his thick head breaching me. We hiss in unison, the sensation already almost too much.

"Damn," he gasps, struggling for air, clutching my hips.

I breathe past the small wiggle of pain, letting my legs relax, spreading wider before sinking down slowly, taking him inch by inch. I stretch around him, accommodating his size, getting used to being *filled* like this again. And fuck, does he fill me. He's hitting a spot my fingers and toys can't reach. A spot I've needed touched for so long.

"Is this okay?" I ask, my hair spilling over his face. "I want you to feel good like you've done for me."

"Shh," he murmurs, one hand running up my back and holding the nape of my neck with the slightest bit of pressure. "It's perfect. You're perfect. Your pussy is so fucking tight, Jo. How did I ever survive before this?"

I raise myself off of him slightly before pushing back down, farther this time. After a few more tries, he's fully buried in me. His thumb rubs over my clit, surprising me, and I moan.

His other hand moves to my ass, squeezing it tightly, fingers bruising my cheeks and letting me control the pace. I can tell he's restraining himself, reeling in the wildness he wants to unleash.

I roll my hips, and Jack's fingers push into my skin even harder.

"Jack," I whisper in his ear.

He leans forward, putting my nipple in his mouth and sucking on it before answering. "Yeah, baby?"

"You're holding back."

"I'm trying to behave and not lose my goddamn mind."

"Lose your mind with me, then. I want that."

He pulls back, peering up at me. "Yeah?"

I nod. "Yeah."

Before I can think twice, Jack flips us, trading our places while never sliding out of me. My back hits the sheets and he throws my leg over his shoulder, looking down at me. I nod and he kisses my calf before thrusting.

The angle helps him get deeper, an excitement like I've never experienced racing up my spine. This is Jack losing his mind. Moving without abandon. Fingers pinching my nipples, teasing my clit, pulling my hair, threading through the curls and yanking. Hard. Sweat forming on his brow, mouth parted, grunts and groans blending with my own as my hands reach for his shoulders to sturdy myself. To anchor myself to him, the only thing keeping me from soaring to the sky. Eyes closing, already knowing the way of my body, hips meeting mine again and again. Rough. Sweet. Wicked. Thoughtful. Kissing my palm, lifting my other leg, both calves bracketing his head, my hamstrings pressing into my chest.

"I'm... I'm going to..." I pant after only a handful of minutes.

"Please," Jack practically begs, and I fall apart, eyes squeezing closed, chest heaving, legs shaking and unable to stay open as the orgasm launches me into the sky, pleasure sending me flying.

I've never come twice in a row that quickly, and never during sex. Before I have a moment to breathe, Jack shifts us again so I'm in his lap, feet wrapping around his lower back.

"Ride me, Jo."

I nod, doing my best to find a rhythm in my exhausted state, working his cock up and down. Unintentionally, I clench around him, earning a a loud and long groan.

"That's my girl. Make me come in that tight, sweet pussy of yours. You want my cock so bad, don't you?"

I nod again, determined. My hands make their way to his hair, threading through the waves, tugging in the way I know he likes. My fingers crawl down his neck, to his back, nails digging into his skin again, leaving red marks down the path of his spine. I raise then lower my hips, rolling, twisting, moving in every way I can find.

His breathing changes. Normally so controlled and even, it's releasing in huffs now as his forehead rests against my collarbone, tongue teasing my nipples.

"Jo," he warns, and I know he's close. His movements start to slow, his thighs flex, his hands start to tremble.

"Yeah, baby?" I toss back to him, raising up, all the way to the tip of his cock, before slamming back down. The mattress bounces under us as I ride him, bringing him closer and closer to oblivion.

It takes another minute, maybe two, before he lets out another long moan, his movements halting, my name a whisper on his lips. I milk him all the way through, until I feel him release a breath, his arms falling to my waist, hugging me close to his chest.

"Shit," he pants. His hair is matted to his face, wet and damp, sticking to his forehead. "That was something else. You are something else."

"I think that's a compliment."

"Smart-ass. You sent me to space and back." Jack withdraws out of me and I grimace, the emptiness settling in. "I'll be right back."

I nod, watching as he climbs off the bed and walks toward the bathroom, his sculpted ass illuminated by the moon from the open curtains. So much for not putting on a show.

I lie down, knowing I'm going to get up in a few short minutes. The bed sags, and Jack scoots behind me. He draws me to his chest, and I sigh, nestling my cheek against his bare skin. "That was incredible. Best sex of my life. It's like we had months of foreplay."

"Is that what that was? And here I was thinking we got into petty fights for the hell of it."

"I've always thought you were hot."

"Liar."

"I'm serious! I remember the first thing I thought about you was your eyes. They're beautiful."

"You were able to see them while you shut the elevator door in my face?"

I pinch his hip and he laughs. "Shut up. What was the first thing you noticed about me?"

"Hm. Your smile. You were smiling when I walked into the conference room. It was the prettiest thing I had ever seen. But, the more guy answer is your hips. They're incredible."

"To think this all started because you jumped in and pretended to be my boyfriend."

"It started before that, I think. At least on my end," he admits.

"Maybe it's been that way since the beginning for both of us. I need to go check the locks. You don't have to come with me. I'll be right back."

"Does it bother you if I come?"

"No."

"Then let's go." He lifts me with ease, rising off the bed. I smile, my hand resting on his pectoral muscle while we traverse down the hall, stopping in front of the suite door.

"Thank you. I have a lot of other quirks, you know."

Jack squats down a smidge so I can see the deadbolt is in place. I push against the wood, eyes scanning the top lock then bottom a handful of times before giving him a nod.

"I know you do. I've learned some. You double check anything important. Locks. Papers. Computers. You tap your pen against your cheek three times before you highlight something. You can't have any rogue hairs on your clothes. You crack your knuckles, right hand first, then left. I'm sure there are more, and I can't wait to learn about the others."

The blood drains from my face. "Is it that obvious?" I ask, mortified. "You must think I'm a freak. There are so many flaws. I... I'm obsessive about certain things. Clearly."

"Flaws? You think those are *flaws*, Jo?" he scoffs, peering down at me. "I swear to God if someone called them flaws before..." His jaw flexes before continuing. "These things are part of you. Parts that make you special and unique and wonderful. They aren't mistakes or blemishes. They're beautiful, just like you. If you need to check the computer is off four times before leaving a room, that's no bother to me. That stuff doesn't make me want to run away. It makes me want to pull you closer to make sure you're real, because my God, I've been waiting for someone like you for a very, very long time. Thank you for sharing this part of yourself with me." His lips meet my forehead in the gentlest kiss.

My lip quivers at his raw words and I hold back a sob. I want to smother him for being so accepting and understanding of things I've always been reluctant to show anyone else. Things I've kept buried deep, deep inside me, swearing to never let anyone get too close long enough to learn these things about me. No one has ever taken the time to see me. *All* of me.

"Thank *you*."

It doesn't seem like enough. It doesn't convey how much the soliloquy means to me. The way it calms my fears and quiets my self-doubts; the deprecating thoughts that arise whenever I think about how I may have to hide facets of my life.

He isn't running. He's staying right here.

"Maybe one day I can get you to try ketchup on your eggs," he adds, lightening the mood.

I wrinkle my nose. "Sorry, Lancaster. It's going to take more than your hot body and moody personality to get me to ruin breakfast food."

"What a bummer," he murmurs, breath warm on my cheek. "I can be very convincing."

"Thank you for being so understanding."

"You never have to thank me, sweetheart. It's an honor."

He stops us in front of the mirror again, both still naked from our rendezvous from a few minutes prior.

"Jack?" I whisper in his ear.

"Hm?"

"Do you want to watch while you bend me over the couch and fuck me?" I kiss his neck, my tongue running down the length of his throat. He hisses, fumbling me in his arms but never letting me go.

"You need to warn me before you say such filthy things with that gorgeous mouth of yours," he growls, capturing my lips with his, the kiss rough. "I want that. More than I can express."

"What are you waiting for? I'm right here. Willing." I'm prodding him, I know. Now that I've had Jack inside me, I need *more* of him. He's like an addiction. One small dose isn't enough to quell the desire and scratch the itch.

My body craves his hands, his lips, his touch. He drops me now, carefully and intentionally depositing me on the floor, and yanks me to the couch located in front of the floor-to-ceiling mirror. It's a gentle tug, enough to let me know I can break free if I desire. His urgency makes me grin. Bending over the arm of the couch, I rest my chest on the cushions and lift my ass in the air, on full display. He exhales loudly, and I grind my thighs into the fabric, shifting onto my tiptoes.

"I'm committing this to memory. You in my shirt, on my desk, is the ultimate fantasy. We'll make that happen, but I'm not going to say no to *this*."

His voice is low, and he doesn't touch me. I'm self-conscious, just for a moment, but it's short-lived when the caress of his already hard cock against my leg jolts away any lingering self-doubt.

"There is something about you, Jo, that makes me want to fuck you on every surface of this hotel room. Of any goddamn room."

"So do it." I wiggle my ass, and I'm rewarded with his palm smacking my skin. I moan at the sting, waiting for his fingers, my pussy unabashedly craving them. His lips trail from my shoulder blades to the small of my back before coming to rest on the back of my thigh.

"Spread your legs," he orders, and I do, stepping my feet apart. "You listen so well. Would you do anything I ask?"

"Yes," I whisper.

"I know you would."

My skin heats from the praise as he dips to kiss my spine, lips soft against my sweaty skin.

"Jack," I whisper. The couch pillows are resting close to my abdomen, rubbing against me, mere inches away from where I need his touch the most. *God, am I going to get off against this couch?* If he doesn't do something soon, I may have to.

I hear the rip of a wrapper and I vaguely wonder if he brought a condom with him for this sole purpose. Where was he even hiding it? There's no warning before he lines his cock up against my entrance, sliding into me all at once, fully seated. I moan, legs parting wider while my chin drops to my chest. I feel a tug on my hair and my neck tilts back.

"If you're going to demand that I bend you over the couch, Josephine, you're going to watch your pussy take every inch of my cock," Jack says, and my head whips to the right, staring at our reflection. "Eyes up the entire fucking time."

It's the hottest thing I've ever seen. Ever heard. His hair is wild and his lips are parted, eyes locked on mine in the glass. His leg muscles are straining as his hands grip my sides. He slams my hips into his hard, and I groan.

"That's it," he mutters encouragingly. "I can't reach you like this, Jo. Can you touch yourself? Use the couch."

He sounds feral, out of control, and I nod frantically, my shaky hand coming to rest on my already swollen clit.

"I can't... I'm not... It's too much," I sob, my eyes squeezing shut. Jack's hand pushes my back, my chest dropping completely flush against the cushions so he can get deeper.

"Do I need to stop?" he asks, and I shake my head.

"No, no, please no." I grind into the fabric, letting out the loudest moan of my life as I hit the perfect spot, alternating between moving up and down on the arm of the couch and back and forth on Jack's cock.

"How much longer, Jo? How much longer until you come on my cock? I want to feel it." He pushes into me with force, my body shakes, convulsing at the tidal wave of sensations and pleasure.

"C-close," I stammer, the pressure building up my legs, on a collision course. His fingers coasts down my sweaty back, slowing as they approach my backside and land between my ass cheeks. I nod, a single jerk of my head, gasping as his wet pinky gently circles the only part of me he hasn't explored yet, slowly pushing in, barely to his first knuckle. The surprise sends me spiraling over the edge. I cry out Jack's name as I come, my body spasming with satisfaction. Relief. Joy. Tears slide down my face and my breathing is ragged, trying to gulp down any air I can find.

"I've got you," he whispers, kissing my neck. "I promise. Can you stay up for another minute?"

I nod mutely, my eyelashes fluttering open, enough to watch him in the mirror. He pulls his body away from mine, standing tall. Jack's mesmerizing when he lets go. Our hips meet again and again, the sounds of where we're joined filling the room, slick thrusts echoing on the walls around us. I feel no shame, only arousal, watching him *use me* to finish, whatever tempo and ferocity he wants. He lets out a groan, and a few seconds later, a small smile sits on his lips before he stills, movement ceasing.

"Are you okay?" he pants after a moment of silence, pulling out of me.

"More than okay," I rasp, throat dry and scratchy. I slowly peel myself off the couch, my limbs confused on how to function.

"Are you sure?" Jack turns my shoulders so we're facing each other. He looks me up and down and I smile at him reassuringly, putting my hand on his chest.

"I promise. You weren't too rough. I loved that. I didn't know checking the locks could be so fun."

"It looks like we made a mess," he chuckles, and I spin to see a wet spot on the arm of the couch, left behind courtesy of me and the third orgasm that tore through me. "I never thought I'd be jealous of a sectional, but here we are. God, baby, look how much you came," he says in wonder. "If I haven't reiterated it enough in the last hour, you're perfect."

I kiss him, lips taking his. "If they send us a housekeeping bill, I'm making you pay it. It's your fault."

"Don't think I didn't realize what sent you over the edge, Bowen. You're hot as hell."

Blushing, I tug him back to the bedroom. "Don't think I didn't realize what you'd like to try, Lancaster. The answer is yes, by the way. Shower then bed?"

"That sounds incredible. As much as I'd like to have round three, I don't have it in me. I'm getting old, you know."

After a scalding hot shower, we're in bed, the fan running off to the side. Jack's chest presses into my back as his arm drapes over my breasts. His hand comes to rest on my neck, keeping me close, like he's afraid I'll bolt from the room if I escape his grip.

I don't want to escape. I want to stay here in his hold. Our own private paradise. His thumb presses into my windpipe ever so slightly, making me want to do *so* many things I don't have the energy for. Like scoot my hips back and delight in the way I know he'd moan.

"Jo," he mumbles, voice thick with sleep, seconds away from succumbing to unconsciousness.

"Yeah?" I ask, gently biting my lip to suppress the grin.

Jo.

How long have I wanted to hear my name like that come from him? How long did I wish he would drop the formalities and treat me like something precious?

"I'm glad we came to the conference together."

"Me, too," I admit, shifting in his arms to face him. His eyes are closed, but his hand drops to my waist instinctively, tracing my hip bone with a gentle touch.

"You might be my favorite person in the world."

"You're half asleep. You won't remember saying that in the morning."

"I remember everything, Jo. Especially when I've known it for a long, long time. Sleep now, sweetheart. You're safe."

The words are like a spell, settling over me and slipping me into a trance. For the first time since I can remember, my eyes close, no feeling of panic or anxiety present, and I'm at peace as I drift off to sleep.

THIRTY-EIGHT
JACK

"You look contemplative over there," I say to Jo, my fingers grasping hers as we walk through the small Key West airport. It's unbelievably hot in here, the gentle ocean breeze nonexistent in this cramped building. "The only time I see you this deep in thought is when you're devising an insult or sarcastic retort that's usually lobbed my way."

We spent our last day together on the island yesterday relaxing in the room in bathrobes, eating pancakes, and sitting on the balcony. The airline let us know we were booked on a late morning flight back to the Northeast, and while I'm looking forward to the weather back home, I'm reluctant to accept that we'll have to return to reality.

Being here changed me. It forced me to relax. Not rush through life. Stop, take a step back, and appreciate the small things; like how Jo with syrup on her fingers is a sight that makes me happy. And horny. Especially when she poured some of the sticky, sugary topping down her chest and I peeled her robe away and licked it off, my tongue happily cleaning up the mess she created.

It's like we've been in a bubble, and I'm afraid to admit I'm unsure how to proceed when we land back at home. Each night I've fallen asleep knowing a conversation needs to be had with Jo about what happens next. How we proceed from here. Instead of opening my mouth like a mature adult who has been hooking up with his former-enemy-current-orgasm-provider, I pull her closer, remaining silent and hoping we can leave the old us behind.

Returning to reality means returning to our roles and routine. A routine that we'll have to figure out how to navigate together. If that's something she even wants.

"I'm tired," she assures me, giving my hand a gentle squeeze. "Someone kept me up way too late last night."

Yeah. I did. Using all the tools in my arsenal. My fingers. My mouth. My dick.

"Funny. I didn't hear you complaining."

"And you won't. Ever."

"I'm going to grab a coffee, because *someone* decided to wake me this morning before the sun was up with an out-of-this-world blowjob, and I'm exhausted. Do you want tea?"

"Yes, please!" she says excitedly, kissing my cheek. I give her ass a light tap before heading to the small kiosk off to the side. I join the line while I pull out my phone, realizing I haven't texted my friends in two days.

JL: Test. Test.
JL: Is this thing on?

PW: Oh, there he fucking is.
HD: About time you graced us with your presence!
NR: HE LIVES!
NL: J! What up!

JL: Sorry. I'm alive. Heading home today.
JL: I've been... distracted.

HD: Does that mean what I *think* it means?!

JL: I'm not giving you any details.
JL: But. Yeah. Josephine has priority over you guys.
JL: I'm not sorry, either.

PW: YES!!!!!!!!!!!!
NR: Thank GOD!
NL: Finally!!

JL: Yea, yea. I know.
JL: She's fucking incredible.

HD: ;)

JL: I meant as a person, weirdo.

HD: Ok. But was it as good as you thought it
would be?
HD: All the tension. All the buildup.

JL: ... better.
JL: And that's all you get.

PW: Look at our boy. All grown up and happy.
NR: Let us know where to send the wedding gifts.
NL: And a baby registry.

I frown reading the last two messages, rubbing my chest. That is jumping the gun excessively. This isn't that serious. Not yet. We're just hanging out. Or maybe something more but certainly not *wedding gift* level. Fuck, I don't ever want another wedding gift in my life.

HD: Shut up, you're going to scare him.

> **JL: Nah. I'm good.**
> **JL: See you guys this week?**

PW: If you can leave your girl long enough, yeah!

> **JL: Shut up. Talk to you guys soon.**

I slide my phone back in my pocket, almost reaching the front of the line, when a hand clamps on my arm. I expect to see Jo behind me.

"Jack! My man! What a small world!"

My spine straightens at the sound of Greg's voice and I mumble an expletive under my breath.

"Hey," I say gruffly, not bothering to give him my full attention.

"You guys have fun the last few days?"

I turn around, peering over his shoulder and seeing Jo sitting in a row of plastic chairs, biting her lip and smiling at her phone. I can see the blush on her cheeks from here.

We took a lot of photos together; one she snuck of me sleeping, my butt on full display. I retaliated, taking a photo of her in the morning sun, stretched out on her back, naked from the waist up, sheets pooled around her hips with her hands above her head. I woke her up shortly after, whispering in her ear to not move her arms while I fingered her until she was a withering mess. My personal favorite photo is one we snapped yesterday morning, her in my lap, robe sliding off her shoulder, my eyes on her while she kisses my cheek, the biggest grin on her face.

"Yeah. A great fucking few days," I answer, bringing my attention back to the asshole in front of me, only because I'm going to get hard if I don't.

He snorts. "She's fun, isn't she?"

My fingers curl around themselves. "I don't have to try and be nice now that people aren't around. I'd be careful what you say, and I warned you not to talk about her again."

He sighs wistfully. "Does she still make the same sounds? Little breathy moans? Those were always my favorite. One of the only good things about her."

"I swear to God," I growl, taking a step toward him.

"Oh, no, she liked it rough, too. When she said stop, it was the biggest turn on. When she tried to tell me she didn't want something, I could tell she did. She was *wet*, man, even when she tried to shove me off of her."

I swallow the bile that's rising in my throat, and I push him against a wall.

"I'd pick your next words very carefully."

"She hasn't told you." He grins.

"Told me what?" I ask, hating myself for wanting to know.

"The bruises I'd leave behind made her skin look good. Finally gave it some color."

"Bruises?"

"You know, when she would mouth off a little too much. Or wouldn't suck my dick when I asked her to. Kept things interesting. The ones around her throat were my favorite. Those she actually liked. Begged for it, too."

My vision goes fuzzy, anger and rage simmering to my fingertips. I fist his shirt, shoving him against the cement, not caring that he winces when his head hits a little too hard. "I'm going to fucking kill you," I whisper. "I will rip you apart, limb by limb, and feed you to the fucking alligators. I will destroy your career. I will make sure you never work in this industry again. I will burn every bridge you think you have. You won't have a job. Or friends. I'm going to fucking destroy you."

"Jack."

I hear *her* angelic voice, the single word dulling the roar in my head. Calming my blood.

"Jack," she says, firmer this time, hand landing on my hip. "Let him go. People are watching. Please."

I don't want to let him go. I want to beat his face to a bloody pulp.

"Never talk to her again. Don't look at her. Don't touch her. Don't think about her. If I ever get word that you've reached out and tried to weasel your way back into her life, I will end you with my bare fucking hands and enjoy doing it."

Greg looks as white as a ghost, and as badly as I want to punch him in the gut, I drop him from my hold, storming away to a secluded corner in the airport.

"Jack," she whispers, following behind me.

I hesitantly reach out to her, taking her hand in mine. My thumb rubs over the pulse point of her wrist, a sorrowful smile on my face.

"Sweetheart," I exhale, blinking rapidly. My eyes are wet; from rage, from anger, from sadness. I'm not sure. "He... He... Did he..." I choke on my words, unable to continue. Her arms wrap around my waist, burying her face in my shirt. "He hit you. He hurt you."

"Yes. He did. Three times."

"Three times too many. I hate him so much. He was *gleeful* I didn't know and excited to tell me. As if I'd agree with what he did. You don't deserve to be treated like that. No woman does.

I'm sorry. I'm so sorry. I didn't mean to go off. I'm not like him. I've never been so angry in my life, and I wanted to hurt him like he hurt you."

"Shh. I know. I know." She reaches up, thumb wiping away the dampness from my cheeks. "The only person who knows what happened is my therapist."

"Abby?"

"No. I'm too embarrassed. I always justified it because we were in a relationship. I like things rough, so where was the line? I like my hair being pulled, how different is that from him back-handing me across the face when I told him his dinner choices sucked?" I draw in a sharp breath, trying not to picture my strong, fierce Jo shielding herself, all alone, no one to protect her. "Now I know it wasn't okay. It's never okay. I just... How could it be abuse if we were in love?"

She's crying now, her shoulders shaking, tears staining my shirt. I rub her back in small circles.

"I feel horrified that I... I hit your ass. *I* pulled your hair. *I* fucked you rough."

"Stop. I've worked through my intimacy issues extensively. It's still something we discuss. I don't allow him to have a hold over me like that anymore. *He* doesn't control my life anymore. I do, and I trust you, Jack. You'll never hurt me. You're the first person... the first person I've let do that since. The first person I've been myself around."

"You're the strongest person I know."

"Thank you for sticking up for me."

"I want to be the one to take care of you," I murmur. "If that means killing your wretched ex-boyfriend, then so be it. Promise you'll always be honest with me. If there's something—anything —that brings up bad memories or rubs you the wrong way, you'll let me know. Immediately."

"I promise. The same goes for you. I know you weren't physically abused, but verbal abuse can be equally damaging. I know you hold yourself to unachievable standards because of someone in your past."

I wince, hating how the word *abuse* sounds coming from her. It's the truth, though. My ex never called me nasty names or brought down my appearance. Never hit me or pushed me down a flight of stairs. But she did like to point out my flaws. What I was doing wrong. How I wasn't trying hard enough or what I could do to be better. Nit-picking comments and jabs that weren't constructive and have stuck with me long after the relationship ended.

"I promise," I agree, hugging her tight.

This woman. She's fucking incredible. I would go to the ends of the world for her to protect her from any evils she might experience. I never thought we'd have a conversation this heavy in the middle of an airport, people bustling past us, unaware of the inner baggage we're carrying.

"Do we have to get on the plane?" she sighs, prying herself away.

"Sadly, I think we do. Unless you're partial to sweating nine months of the year."

"Ugh. You're right. That sounds horrible."

"Hey. I hope you know I wasn't trying to be your knight in shining armor. You can take care of yourself. I reacted without thinking."

"I know." Jo squeezes my hand, grabbing her suitcase. "But I'm glad I have you to defend my honor. In cornhole. In line for coffee, your teeth bared like a wild animal."

"Come on, sweetheart. Let's go home."

THIRTY-NINE
JACK

In the two weeks we've been home, Jo and I have fallen into a routine. It's easy. Fun. She'll come here. I'll go there. Other nights we bypass seeing each other all together, opting to hang out with our friends or spend time alone. When we are together, we have fun. We watch television on the couch. We wake each other up in the middle of the night because we can't keep our hands to ourselves. We laugh over bowls of ice cream, her mismatched socks in my lap and my hand on her thigh.

It feels... good.

Weirdly good.

Good enough where I keep looking over my shoulder, waiting for the other shoe to drop, destroying everything like dynamite.

We've kept our time spent together a secret. No one at the office has picked up on us seeing each other, and I'm inclined to keep it that way. I'm not embarrassed by her. Far from it. Jo's a freaking grand prize I'd love to show off to the world, proudly boasting that *I* get to stand by her side.

I'm slightly afraid of what comes after people find out.

They'll ask us where we see this going and what the future holds.

Questions I don't have the answer to, because it's been only a handful of days with Jo, and I'm clueless about the next steps. It's selfish of me to think we can stay hidden away forever, just the two of us, but I'm enjoying it for as long as I can.

In the back of my mind, under the happiness and delight, however, there's a small niggle of doubt. Of unsureness and unease. Of confusion and hesitancy. Fun with someone is one thing. But translating those passing feelings to a long-term, committed, lasting relationship is an entirely different feat.

We can't keep it easy and casual forever. At some point, a conversation needs to happen. We're in our thirties; people our age don't just mess around for years on end without establishing a definitive answer to: *"So, what is this?"*

And, as much as I enjoy spending time with her, the idea of taking a giant leap of faith onto a stepping stone and the foundation of real partnership is really fucking scary. Mainly because she's been through a lot and deserves the world. Can I be the one to give it to her?

Tonight is going to be the night I suck it up and ask her to be my girlfriend for real. We can figure it out together along the way, one step at a time. At least, I hope we can.

The door to my house opens, breaking me from my conflicting thoughts, and I hear footsteps approaching the kitchen.

"Hey," I say, turning to smile at her, being met with a grimace in return. I can read her like a book, knowing something isn't right. "What's wrong?"

"Nothing," she mutters, dropping a bag of groceries on the counter. She was hell-bent on making me mashed potatoes tonight, telling me that sour cream is the secret ingredient to making sure they taste delicious. I'm not sold on the idea, but I'm willing to give it a go for her.

"Doesn't look like nothing. What's up?" Holding out my hand to her, she sighs, sliding her palm into mine and resting her head on my chest.

"Permission to have a serious conversation?"

I stroke her long hair, nervous to hear what she has to share. No one ever starts off good news by asking to have a serious talk. Serious implies something bad. Shit, what did I do? Or, better yet, what didn't I do? Have I been so absorbed in spending time with her I haven't bothered to ask where she sees herself in the future? If there even is a future together? "Sure," I say cautiously.

"I got an email today for a job interview."

"What? That's awesome!" And not at all what I was expecting. This is a good thing.

"In Denver."

The air deflates from the room. "Denver... Colorado?" I clarify, confused by the location.

"Yeah," she huffs, rubbing her forehead.

"Whoa, okay. That's far away. I didn't know you were applying to other jobs."

The last time we talked about careers, back on the island over dinner, she expressed excitement about freelancing. She positively lit up when she spoke about it, and I assumed she might look into how to pursue *that* avenue. Not a job in Colorado.

Fuck. Was I supposed to be asking about the next steps in her career? Am I holding her back, tethering her to a town and job she might not even like?

Okay. Serious conversation time. I can do this. We can do this.

"I wasn't. I sent in my application months ago, did a phone

interview soon after, but haven't heard anything since. I forgot about it, to be honest, until this afternoon. It's for a top-five tech company who wants to revamp their marketing department. The salary is lucrative, and the office sounds like Itrix but bigger. Good environment. High employee morale. They want me to meet the team and the bosses."

"Wow, Jo. That's incredible! It sounds like it's not so much an interview but more of a final meet-and-greet before formally offering you a position," I say, a sudden dark cloud of dread settling in the room, blocking out the sunshine she brings.

"I don't know what to do," she admits, looking at me for solace and guidance.

"What do you mean? You should go. Obviously."

"What? What about us?"

I inhale, staring at the wall over her shoulder.

Us.

Such a small word carries such significant importance. A question I don't have an answer to. Not in the ten seconds after being presented with this giant, monstrous announcement. How can I think about an us thousands of miles away when I'm just now gaining the courage to ask her to be my girlfriend *here*? In the same zip code.

"I-I like you, you know," Jo continues.

We've tiptoed around expressing our feelings too strongly since we've been home. There's no doubt in my mind she cares about me, but hearing her say it makes it all too real. All too serious and permanent and important.

I like her too. A lot. Probably more than one should after a few short weeks together. She has to know that, right?

Have we flown past the point of slow and casual already without realizing it, careening toward *forever* and *always* in the blink of an eye? Did I miss the glaringly obvious signs?

Fuck. Imagining her not in my life makes my chest hurt. I

rub across my shirt, unable to breathe. In every vision of us together, I never pictured an ending. Or, at the very least, not a *sad* ending. But here we are, teetering close to a schism that will end in our demise.

There's so many words I want to say. So much I want to talk with her about. I want to beg and plead and ask her not to go, to stay here with me. But I can't. I could *never.*

I pick my next words carefully, speaking logically, and not with my heart.

"I don't think it would make sense to keep seeing each other if you're somewhere else. Halfway across the country somewhere else."

"I don't even have the job yet!"

"Jo," I say kindly. "People like you always get the job. You're exceptional at what you do. You're nice. Kind. Friendly and approachable. They'd be stupid to pass on you."

"Okay, let's say I get it and accept the offer. Long distance wouldn't interest you?"

I pause, thinking about my past. Would I try harder with her? Would I make myself more available? Or would it last for two or three months before we reach our wit's end, fizzling out without so much as a conversation?

"We're two very different people. We've always known that. Relationships take work. And making it work when we're not around each other is even harder."

"Jack."

"Maybe," I start, the cracked words difficult to release from the lodge in my throat. Shit, I'm about to lose it. Why are there tears in my eyes? "Maybe this can be a clean break, you know? We don't have to leave on bad terms. It's just... over. Or paused. For the time being."

"You're saying that about something that isn't a sure thing!"

"Do you *want* to go to Colorado? Did you get excited when you saw the email?"

"I..." She fumbles for words, moving out of my grasp and leaning against the counter, huffing out an irritated breath. "Yeah, I got excited. At the very least, I'm intrigued and want to fly out to see what it's like."

"There's your answer, sweetheart. If you get the job offer, which you will, you should go. You *have* to go."

"Why aren't you more upset by this? Or, I don't know, committed to figuring out how to make us work in the small chance I get the job?"

"What do you want me to say, Jo? Don't go? Stay for me? I would never ask you to do that. You know that."

"Have the past few weeks meant so little to you you'd just let me leave? You wouldn't fight for me?"

"I'm sorry, but I'm not going to fight you on your dreams, baby. You have to make this decision for you and you alone. We had a great time together. This might be a good chance to spend some time apart and see what we really want, you know? If you really want to go to a new job, I want that for you, too. You shouldn't give up an opportunity for me. A couple good fucks in the sun doesn't mean anything permanent. Who knows if it'll last? We got caught up in the moment on the island. Now we're back to reality and can't ignore these other important parts of our lives, like careers and the future. I'm so proud of you, sweetheart. I'd be resentful toward myself if you didn't accept a job on my behalf, just so you can stay close to me."

She reels back, face horrified at my crass words.

"Quick fucks, huh? That's all it was when you held me close and whispered in my ear?"

I wince. Volleyed back to me, the words feel like a slap across the face. A slap I rightfully deserve. "I didn't mean that. I'm sorry. There's a lot going on here."

"What do you mean, Jack? All I hear are excuses."

"Go to the interview, Jo. After you get back we can talk. Some space would probably do us some good. We've been caught up in our own little bubble, forgetting the real world exists outside. Maybe after a few weeks or months, we can try to figure something out."

"All those nights when you..." Her lip quivers, only once, before she bites down, the sadness evaporating.

I scratch the inside of my wrist, remembering the memories there. How I haven't had a similar thought in the years I've known her, an angel who pulls me back to the light, saving my life day after day. An angel I have to let go so she can spread her wings and see where she wants to land.

"I'm sorry," I finally say, hoping she hears the truth in the statement. "It's not forever."

"Then why does it feel like it is?" She wipes her hands on her jeans and grabs her purse, heading for the door, potato plans forgotten. "If anyone was ever going to break my heart again, I'm glad it was you, Jack," she whispers. She doesn't cry. Doesn't yell.

She simply takes one final, disapproving look at me and sighs, slipping out of my house, and maybe my life, for good. It's so different from how we first interacted; then it was a chaotic burst of energy full of mirth and agitation mingled with curiosity and interest. Doors closing and raised voices in a conference room. Heated emails and grumblings. Now it's solemn. Regretful. Betrayed.

I can't bring myself to move. I stare at the closed door for minutes, maybe hours after. When my feet decided to work, I find my way to bed. I don't remember sleeping. I don't remember the sun setting then rising, pulling the covers over my head, blocking out the world from view.

She's the only thing I think about.

The curve of her smile. The shape of her waist. The way her hand slots into mine, a perfect match.

The curl of her hair and the sound of her laugh. The sparkle in her eyes and the kindness in her voice.

The tilt of her head when she's thinking hard.

The taste of her lips, rivaling delectable candy and expensive wine.

The fairness of her skin.

The sleepy breaths in the early morning.

The fingers in my hair, nails scratching down my back.

Her.

All parts I'll have to forget. Parts I'll have to let go of, tossing into the wind and never looking at again while she'll find someone somewhere else, and makes them happier than they've ever been.

I don't know how much time passes. I don't remember eating or drinking or using the bathroom. I float through my house in a haze. Under a trance. Unaware of what's happening outside. My bed becomes a cave I don't retreat from, reveling in the quiet and dark that I've created. That I deserve. When I hear footsteps in my house, I'm not even alarmed.

"Jack."

Henry's standing in the doorway to my room, a worried expression on his face.

"Hey," I grumble, voice raspy. When was the last time I talked?

"What happened?"

"I happened."

"Guys, he's in here."

Three other voices filter down the hall, light laughter

bouncing off the walls. I pull my comforter up around my body, sitting up.

"Oh, shit," Patrick curses, stopping in the doorframe.

"What's wrong?" Noah asks, peeking over his shoulder, trying to look at me.

"Move over, dingdongs," Neil huffs. "I have the food."

"What are you all doing here?"

"You didn't show up last night," Henry supplies, moving to sit on the edge of my bed. "We were worried."

"What day is it?"

"Thursday."

"Fuck," I mumble. Three days. I haven't moved in three days. "I messed up. I let Jo walk away. I didn't fight for her. Didn't even offer a suggestion on how to make things work. I just gave up."

"What happened?" Patrick asks, taking a spot on the floor. "Last we heard you two were happy as clams."

"She got a job interview in Denver. She suggested long distance, but I know that would never work. So I pushed her away. Basically ushered her out the door. I told her all the wrong things."

All four of them wince and I feel horrible. Disgusted. Angry with myself.

"You need to eat," Noah says, handing me a paper plate with a slice of pizza on it. "Don't bother arguing. I'll force feed you if don't."

I sigh, relenting, accepting the food and taking a small bite.

"Start from the beginning," Neil encourages.

"She applied for the job a few months ago. Did an interview, not thinking anything of it. She hadn't heard a peep since, until she got an email the other day asking her to fly out to interview in person. It sounds like a done deal, to be honest."

"And how do you factor into this equation?"

"I don't anymore. I told her to go, she asked about us, and I said it wouldn't make sense to continue down this road. Everyone knows long distance doesn't work. She'll text me when I'm trying to go to bed, and I'll answer her before heading to work, turning my phone off for eight hours. Sleepless nights will turn into sleepless days, holding onto resentment and disappointment in the other thanks to a lack of communication. It's not worth it. We didn't break up, but it feels like we did. It's inevitable."

"You sound very sure about that," Henry interjects.

"Well, given my ex-fiancé fell in love with someone else while I was still living with her, it doesn't bode well for future relationships 2,000 miles apart, does it? Why fucking bother?"

"Dude, that wasn't about you. That was her," Patrick says, trying to be helpful. It doesn't work.

"I would never ask her to stay. Not when she's being presented with an incredible opportunity."

"Would you chase after her?" Noah asks.

"I don't... I don't know. I have a life here now. A job. You guys. She wouldn't ask me to come with her, either."

"What would make you happy? Right this second?" Henry asks.

"Her. Always her. But I'm not sure I can offer her the happiness she needs or deserves. Not from here. And I'm not sure I could offer it from there, either."

"So, that's it?" Patrick asks, and he sounds sad.

"That's it," I repeat.

"NO," Henry says firmly, standing. "Absolutely not. I'm not buying this bullshit."

"What bullshit?"

"You. This. I know what you're doing. You're pushing her away like a fucking idiot because of something that happened in the past. Yeah, it sucks that you were left. Yeah, it sucks your heart was broken. But guess what, buddy? You have the chance to finally be fucking happy. And you turn it *down*? Why? Because you don't want to get on a goddamn airplane once a month to visit the girl of your dreams? Or give up a weekend so you can spend time with her? Are you fucking kidding me?"

I blink at him, perplexed by his outburst. Henry never gets riled up, and he's almost yelling.

"Look, I'm sorry. You're not an idiot. But Jesus Christ, it seems to me like there's such an easy answer to this problem. A new job isn't reason for a breakup. Why wouldn't you try out long distance?"

"Because it NEVER works," I throw back, standing as well.

"Never tell me the odds."

"Okay, Han fucking Solo, what do you propose?"

"I propose you get your head out of your ass, realize you have a good thing in your life, and see what happens."

"So I can break her heart in six months? A year?"

"Or, you know, just *don't* break up. That's an option too."

"Says the guy who's never been in a relationship," I scoff. "You wouldn't know how to do jack shit when it comes to making someone happy because all you do is fuck a woman then leave. Forget feelings. Forget caring about someone. You think it's *easy*, don't you?"

"Says the guy who's letting another woman walk out of his life because he's too much of a coward to try. The common factor in these scenarios is *you*."

"Whoa. Boys. Stop," Noah says, intervening and stepping between us. "That's enough with the personal jabs. Uncalled for on both accounts. Apologize."

"Sorry," I mumble sheepishly, rubbing the back of my neck. "I didn't mean it. I'm mad."

"I'm sorry, too. I didn't mean it either," Henry sighs. "I'm mad for you. You're finally happy and I'd hate to see you give that up."

"She deserves better," I supply for the umpteenth time.

"May I offer an idea?" Patrick asks timidly.

"Might as well before Henry starts spouting off more motivational *Star Wars* quotes."

"Before she leaves, I think you need to be honest with her about how you feel. Not that you like her. Hopefully she knows that. I'm talking about how much she means to you and what you see down the road. Do you want to spend your life with her? Would you seriously be okay if you never saw her again? She deserves to have everything presented to her before making a decision. The job isn't set in stone yet. That includes you speaking like an adult, having a real conversation, and opening up."

"Finally, someone in this group with half a brain," Noah mutters.

"Rude. I have a brain," Neil interjects and we all snort.

"Sure. Yeah. Of course you do. Patrick, that is an excellent idea."

"Leave it to the high school principal to outsmart the lawyer," Patrick responds smugly. "No PhDs needed."

"You realize I don't have a PhD, right?" Henry throws back.

"HEY!" Noah says again. "Stop your dick measuring contest. Jack. What do you think about the suggestion?"

"I guess I can be honest with her. I wasn't exactly kind, so I doubt she'll even listen to me."

"Oh, no. What did you say?"

"I... I said that we had a couple good fucks in the sun."

"Jesus, man," Patrick mumbles. "It's like you're *trying* to push her away."

"I wish I could take it back. That was so cruel. I think maybe I am trying to push her away. To make it easier."

"It's not going to be easier. Do you want to lay it all out there for her?"

"Holy fuck, what if she leaves for good?" I ask, beginning to panic, realizing what's at stake. The severity of the situation, the effect of what I've done begins to sink in. "And that's the last thing I said to her? Not that I think she's amazing and funny and spectacular. But that what we had was a quick fuck when it was actually deep and meaningful and the best connection I've ever had. I want more. I want it all."

"Whoa, slow down, J, it's all right. We'll figure this out. I know you want to jump into action, but maybe you need to take a few days to think this over, yeah?" Noah says and I nod.

"Why don't we reconvene on Monday? Take the next few days and the weekend to clear your brain and decide what it is you truly want," Henry declares and I nod. "You have to be sure. You can't start to grovel at her feet with some half-assed apology if you don't fucking mean it."

"Monday. Okay. I can wait until Monday. And I'm going to need to do a lot more than grovel."

FORTY
JO

I haven't seen Jack in a week.

A really long, agonizing week. He made the smart decision to end things between us, though.

Not end.

Pause.

Which means delay the ending.

I've read enough romance novels to know that long distance rarely works. Usually someone gets bored or frustrated, irritated that communication decreases. The relationship becomes strained. Exhausting. It begins to take more work before eventually one party has the balls to end things once and for all.

I've always known that people, no matter what they promise or how they feel about you, almost always leave. Whether it be by death, moving onto a different partner, or simply recognizing a lack of attraction anymore, they disappear. It was only a matter of time before Jack followed suit. He's right; we're different people who built a fantasy world in our head while on the island; no obligations, days full of laughter, and the chance to hide from the rest of the world.

Being back at home shows that a relationship takes work.

And when one side isn't committed to making things work, well, what's the point?

We've gallantly avoided each other in the office, drifting like ships in the night, never steering too close. I don't go to the kitchen and I get to work 15 minutes early every day, slipping in through the side entrance to avoid any possible confrontation. For all I know, he might not even be in the building.

I skipped the weekly meeting yesterday, purposely scheduling a call with an investor at 9 a.m. to give me an excuse not to show my face. I don't care if it's childish or petty. It's for the best.

Despite the lingering sadness and disappointment that I've carried with me the last seven days, the interview has me excited. I've been corresponding with the company's H.R. personnel who have been nothing short of helpful and accommodating. My flight is later this evening, and I brought my suitcase with me to the office so I can take a ride share straight from here. It's barely past noon, though, and I have six more hours until I'm free for the day.

I'm tweaking my resume, making sure I've included enough power words, when my thesaurus search for synonyms associated with *dedicated* is interrupted by a knock on my door. For half a second, I freeze, wondering if Jack is on the other side.

"Come in," I say, clearing my throat and doing my best to sound put together. When the door opens, I'm met with a handsome man beaming at me.

"Who the hell are you?" I ask in surprise, and he quirks an intrigued eyebrow at my question, seemingly caught off guard that I don't know who, exactly, he is.

"That might be the fastest anyone's ever rejected my charm before. I'm impressed. Jack will be happy to know it doesn't work on you. One of only two people in the world."

"The famed Henry," I say, realization dawning on me.

He beams. "Josephine. Sorry. Jo. I know we've recently graduated to friendlier names. May I?" he asks, gesturing to the empty chair across from my desk.

"Uh, sure?"

Henry chuckles, closing the door behind him and sitting comfortably, his foot crossing over his knee.

"You are... I wasn't expecting... huh."

His beam grows. "Someone so handsome? Good looking? Oozing sex appeal?"

"I can see why Jack didn't want us to meet," I smile. "I've heard a few things about you."

"And I, you." He glances at the suitcase sitting near the wall. "What time is your flight? Congratulations, by the way!"

"You know about that?"

"Yup."

"What else do you know?"

"Not as much as you might assume, I promise. Jack's a private guy."

"My flight is at 9. What in the world are you doing here?"

"He didn't send me, don't worry. I'm here on my own accord."

"Okay..."

"I wanted to stop by and say thank you."

I blink. "For what?"

Henry sighs, running his hand through his hair. "For helping Jack. This isn't an attempt at a guilt trip, or to make you feel bad about your decision to interview at another job. If anything, I'm mad at Jack for being a fucking idiot."

"I'm not following."

"The first time I met him was at a recreational baseball game. I play in a league, and we had a new guy sitting on the end of the bench, a scowl on his face, arms crossed over his chest. He looked miserable. So, I went up and talked to him. Quickly learned *why* he was miserable, and rightfully so.

"We became friends. He had been working at Itrix for a few weeks, and I distinctly remember a Tuesday evening he stumbled into the restaurant where our group was meeting for dinner. He collapsed into the booth, spent thirty minutes talking about this woman who closed the elevator doors in his face, had a whole presentation on social media apps and websites, and was his new coworker. When he finished complaining, he chugged a beer and informed us that this was the worst day of his life. When I asked *why*, he told me he blew any chance with the woman already way out of his league, and he vowed to continue to be an asshole."

"That was..."

"Two years ago, yeah. Since then, I've learned all sorts of things about you. Love the names on the cups, by the way. And I, too, think black coffee is disgusting."

"Does this story have a point?"

"Ever since that Tuesday night, Jack's been different. Before he was in a constant state of anger. Sadness. And then, one night, he started smiling more. He would laugh at our jokes. He opened up to us. For a long time, I couldn't figure out why. What changed? Why now? And then I realized whenever he said your name, he'd light up. It wasn't anything super noticeable like a Christmas tree or anything that absurd, and if you didn't know him, you might have missed it. But I could tell. His eyes got brighter. His smiles got wider. He sat up straighter when he recanted the meetings he had to sit in with you. He slept better. He was nicer to be around. It hit me that *you* brought on that change. Without even realizing it.

"You brought him out of the dark, slowly but surely. And I know he didn't fight for you. He let you go. But I wanted to say thank you, from the bottom of my heart, for saving my friend. It's not my place to share the rest."

His monologue punches me in the gut. "I-I knew he liked me, but those are really strong words. I don't know what to say."

Henry chuckles. "You don't have to say anything. You needed to know." He stands from the chair and tosses me another grin.

"Thank you for telling me. I... I don't know what I'm going to do yet job-wise, but can you take care of him? He's a good guy."

He puts his hand over his heart. "I promise. You seem really cool, Jo."

"Jack told me he was nervous for us to ever meet. It's a shame we'll never be friends."

"Ah," he says, heading for the door. "Never say never, sweetheart." Tossing a wink my way, he leaves the room with a wave, and it's hard to hold back the tears.

―――

"What time is your flight?" Abby asks over FaceTime, carrying her phone with her through her house. Leaning back in my chair, I stretch my shoulders.

"Nine. I'm leaving here in about an hour."

"Have you seen you-know-who at all?"

"Nope. I skipped our meeting yesterday," I sigh, putting my chin in my hand.

"Are you doing okay? I know you're tough but this sucks."

"I'm fine. I'm aware I can't put my life on hold for someone who doesn't want me in return."

"And you're *certain* that's his decision?"

"Uh, I mean, the conversation we had in his kitchen felt

pretty real to me. It's so frustrating. For half a second I got carried away and thought..."

I've never been good with discussing my emotions; yeah, I experience them, but when it comes to sharing with others, I tend to run for the hills, afraid to be too honest or too open.

"Thought what?" Abby asks, coaxing me gently. She waits patiently as I take the time to collect myself.

"That he might care for me, too. I know he liked me. And I can't deny I have feelings for him, too. I do."

"I'm proud of you for admitting that and acknowledging those feelings instead of trying to suppress them. When you two were talking, did you ever ask him how *he* felt?"

"Why would I? Did I skip the part where he told me it wouldn't work? Or that it meant *nothing* to him?"

"You know I'm always on your side. And as someone who's in your corner, I think you're making a big mistake by not talking to him."

"Are you s—"

"Hang on. Let me finish. Yes, what he did was shitty. If I ever see him again, I might curse the day he was born. But maybe he has a reason for acting so flaky and wishy-washy. Maybe he's equally as scared about this as you are. You said his ex-fiancé messed him up pretty bad.

"I'm willing to bet he has a hard time letting someone in, just like you do, too. It's obvious he likes you and cares about you. Can you imagine for a minute getting left by the person you thought you were going to marry? The person who's been a constant in your life for so long? If Raul did that to me, I wouldn't be right for years. I might not ever trust a man again. I'm not justifying his actions by any means. He's probably freaking out and pushing you away so he doesn't have to acknowledge he's a total dick, when in reality he's in love with you."

I gape at her, lost for words.

Fuck.

I've only considered how I might see everything that's happening. I never stopped for a moment to wonder if he's overwhelmed. Caught between his feelings for me while simultaneously being terrified of messing up another relationship.

"I'm an idiot," I grumble. "I walked out of his house without even trying to talk to him."

"You are not an idiot," she says firmly. "You're someone who's been through a lot. Don't you think you finally deserve to be loved?"

"I think for so long I convinced myself I was fine being by myself, especially after Greg. And I am. But being cared for like that? To feel wanted and desired? That was special. I can see myself being in love with him one day. Would that be enough? LC never went to Paris and Rachel got off the plane. I don't want to live with any regrets. I don't want to resent him for taking something away from me if I were to stick around. What if I'm supposed to be in Denver? Or somewhere else? I have no fucking clue what I want to do with my life. Is he okay with waiting around while I figure that out?"

"Oh, Jo," Abby sighs. "Rachel got off the plane to be with the love of her life. LC never went to Paris but is still wildly successful without an internship in Europe. That stunt was totally staged, by the way. You'll never, ever be the girl who gives her life up for a man. There will always be great jobs out there for you, whether it's this one in Denver or somewhere else. Love isn't always going to be pretty. A lot of days are really freaking hard. I know that firsthand. But it makes it easier when you have someone next you to get through those days together. It's so worth it. Don't you want to try?"

"I think the question is, does he? We're not exactly on good terms after he called the nights we spent together 'fucks.'"

"There's only one way to find out. If he makes it obvious he truly feels *nothing*, you can move on with your life, and I'll help you. You have an out—potentially a new job. If he cares about you too—and I think he does—it's worth the risk. You'll hate yourself for never trying."

"You make way too much sense sometimes," I groan, shaking my head.

"That's what I'm here for. I know I'm the love of your life, Jo. It's time I'm replaced."

"You're right." Checking the time on my watch, I jump up from my desk. "Shit. My ride will be here in 10 minutes."

"Go. Let me know when you're on the plane!"

"I will. I love you, Abs. Thanks for the pep talk."

"Have a great flight! I'm proud of you!"

Ending the call, I grab my suitcase and purse, making sure my computer is powered down. I'm about to walk out my door when I hear another knock and footsteps scurrying away.

"What the hell?" I mumble, turning the knob, searching for the ding-dong-ditchers. Spotting no one, I look down and see a trail of white substance on the ground.

The color stretches to the elevator, a straight line from my office to the metal doors. Slowly, I follow the path, looking over my shoulder and seeing the floor empty. When I arrive at the elevator, there's a number six drawn out with an arrow. I press the up button hesitantly, filing into the empty elevator and hitting the button for the sixth floor, tapping my foot on the tile and wondering if I'm about to embark on a wild goose chase. I have five minutes before I need to head downstairs to the car, but curiosity is getting the best of me.

When the doors open, the trail resumes, winding down the hallway and disappearing from view. It's quiet up here, almost all the overhead lights have been extinguished, and I can barely see the way to go. The white beacon leads me to a door, stopping at the crevice where a band of light escapes.

Jack's office.

My heart beats rapidly in my chest. I almost turn around

and storm away, but something compels me to stay put and bang on the wood with my fist before I can think twice.

"Come in."

I push the barrier open to reveal Jack sitting on his desk.

"Josephine," he says, standing.

"What the hell is going on? I have a flight," I answer angrily. A whole week without talking and now he wants to play a game, minutes before I need to get on an airplane?

"I know you do. I just wanted to say hi. Can I have five minutes?"

I think back to Henry earlier in my office, telling me that I *saved* Jack. Sighing, I nod. "Fine. Five minutes. Hi."

My gaze flicks to the crotch of his jeans then back to his face. His lips tug upward in the corner as he watches my assessment. "Believe it or not, Bowen, at the age of 32, I can suppress an erection from you greeting me."

I snort. "What's with the sugar? Or is it cocaine?"

"You think I'd smuggle drugs into the office to get your attention?"

"I'm not sure I know you at all anymore," I fire back, and his lip turns down into a frown, the small uptick vanishing.

"I went out with someone last night," he says, and I freeze.

"Like a date? Why would you ever think to tell me that?"

"Well, she's a lesbian and not remotely interested in me, so, define date?"

"A lesbian," I repeat slowly, and his mouth quirks again.

"Indeed. One of my best friends from college was in town for a work thing. She, Wally, and I used to be inseparable. Anyway, she's a therapist. Not *my* therapist. But a therapist, nonetheless. She took one look at me and told me I looked like utter shit."

"You do look like shit," I mumble, and his shoulders relax, notching down two degrees away from his ears.

"I told her everything that's been going on the last few months with us. Our original meeting and poor working relationship. That night at the bar, and the snowball effect it had. The path of friend-like behavior we started cautiously tiptoeing down. I shared how we went on this trip and we ended up fake dating. Things happened and feelings started getting involved before I was a total fucking idiot. How I think..." Jack sucks in a breath, closing his eyes. "How I think I'm slowly falling in love with you, more and more every day, but I don't think I'm good enough for you. I don't think I'll *ever* be good enough for you. Or deserving of your love in return, if that's even a possibility. We were there for three hours. I talked for about two hours and 59 minutes until my throat was hoarse and food was cold. Raquel—that's her name—called me an idiot. After talking with her, and my friends, I realized something.

"I couldn't let you leave without telling you explicitly how I feel. I need you to know, and I don't expect it to stop you. God, I'd never dream of asking you to stay because of me, but I couldn't leave it unsaid."

"You said it would never work."

"And it might not. I'm a realist, not an optimist. Despite the odds, I want to try, if you'll let me. If that means long distance, that means long distance. I can fly to you. You can stay with me here for a long weekend. If it means eventually moving to Denver, then so be it."

"You'd do that? You'd fly back and forth across the country, once a month, to see me for a few hours? You'd sacrifice time with your friends, give up PTO hours, and relinquish sleep on the redeye flight home so you're back in time for work on Monday? Would that honestly make you happy?"

"Ah," he smiles sadly, offering me his hand. I take it, moving closer. "That's the thing. *You* make me happy, Jo. An hour with you is better than a hundred without."

"What if I didn't go?"

Jack frowns. "Why wouldn't you go?"

"We've talked about if I do go. What if I didn't? What if I stayed?"

He hasn't shaved in some amount of time, a full-on beard covering his cheeks and he runs his hand over his jaw, contemplating.

"Well. First and foremost, I'd spend every minute of every day apologizing for letting you walk away. For not fighting for you like I should have. Why didn't I chase you out the door and beg you to give me a chance to figure this out together?"

The room is coated in seriousness, an air of heaviness settling between us. In the quiet, I let out an unexpected giggle. The giggle begins to shift into a laugh. Once I start, I can't stop, and soon I'm clutching my sides, bordering on maniacal hysteria.

"Why in the world are you laughing?" Jack asks, blinking at me.

"Oh, God, I'm sorry. I'm not laughing at you, I swear. Abby told me this would happen, and I vehemently denied it because, well, let's be honest. You're you and I'm me and it's so fucking cliché. We work together, we hate each other, and suddenly we develop this connection when we go on a single trip? But here I am, looking at you, and even though I'm so freaking angry with you... It's also so obvious that I'm falling in love with you, too," I get out, cackling again.

"And, I want to make sure I understand this correctly, that's funny?"

Jack, bless him, has the most neutral expression on his face, unfazed by my outburst.

"It's hysterical."

"You love me," he says slowly, backtracking to my previous admission, and I nod, a huge grin splitting across my face, before quickly shaking my head.

"Wait. No. I don't. I said I'm falling in love with you. Don't rush me, Lancaster."

"I would never dream of such a thing," he answers, lips breaking into a real smile, wide and bright, mirroring mine. "God, Jo. You are... It's hard to describe, really."

"You should try. It might take off some of the amount of shit you're in."

"You're loud in the best way. You let your voice be heard and you stand up for others. You're so passionate about all these moments in life. You're smart, yet so eager to learn." His fingers reach out, rubbing against my scalp. I mewl under his touch, anger melting away.

"And?"

He chuckles. "You're selfless. You make me think differently about work. Life. Relationships. Joy. Happiness. The world. You're beautiful, but the lone word doesn't even cover it. There aren't enough adjectives to describe your mind and body."

"You could get out your thesaurus and find some other words?" I offer, and he pinches my arm.

"Smart-ass. I've never met anyone quite like you before. What a lucky man I am, to even possibly get the chance to make you happy every single day."

Staring at him, the words sink through me, pounding in my ears like a drum. I'm rendered speechless, and when I open my mouth to attempt to speak, he holds up his hand.

"That's five minutes, sweetheart," he says softly, tucking a curl behind my ear. "You need to catch your flight."

I shake my head violently. "No."

"No?" he parrots back, staring at me with a hopeful look.

"No. Keep talking. What else?"

"The rest might be ad-libbed because every version of this

I've run through in my mind ends with you walking out that door and not looking back."

"I'm here. I'm not walking out."

"Okay. Okay." He swallows then scratches behind his ear. "I'm not an easy man to love. I'm stubborn and hardheaded. I close off easily, and I'm far from perfect. You make me want to be a better man. You make me want to try. I'm working on it. Therapy is helping—I go twice a week, by the way. Have I told you that?"

"No," I whisper. "You haven't."

"Yup. Tuesdays and Thursdays."

"What if one day I'm not enough?" I ask softly.

"Not enough? Not possible. You're everything, Jo."

My eyes well with tears and I bat them away. "You... You let me walk away. How can I know that won't happen again?"

"You don't," Jack answers honestly. "Do you remember the night on the beach, when we talked about regrets? I lied when I said I only had one. Now I have two. The first is walking in late to that meeting. The second is when I let you walk out of my house.

"A part of me was... is... so afraid to cross the line past *like* with you, because, well, I can't imagine not having you in my life. I know I'm going to screw this up, and I thought that if I maybe pushed you far enough away, it would be somehow easier to let you go."

He scratches the inside of his wrist. "How did you get the scar?" I ask.

"I was in a horrible place after my ex left. I contemplated not existing anymore. Even tried it." He holds up his arm and I reach out, fingers tracing over the jagged lines. Bringing his hand to my lips, I kiss it, ten times, a hundred times, tears staining the mark as I do my best to relieve him of the pain.

"I'm so glad you're here."

"Me too. I thought I would never find love again, and that was only the surface of the depths of my problems. I hated myself. I blamed myself. I became mean. Bitter. I hated seeing other people's happiness, especially couples. Why did they get to be happy, but I didn't? I drank a lot and didn't eat right. I went through the motions of life, not really seeing the point."

"And then?" I ask quietly, his hand still clasped in mine.

He finally smiles. "And then I walked into a meeting late and royally pissed off this beautiful woman. That was the chasm that woke me up. Tuesday became my favorite day of the week because I got to see you for longer than five seconds. It was like you were placed here to remind me there's so much good left in the world.

"When I'm with you, nothing else exists. Everything stills. Everything quiets, and you're there, a smile on your face, ready to guide me back to the light. I don't know what it means, but when I look at you, I... I feel like I finally belong. The monsters inside quiet. And it's only you."

A sob escapes me, unfiltered and raw, desperate and anguished. "I'm so mad at you."

"I'm furious with myself too, Jo. I'm sorry. I'm so sorry. We can fight and yell, but please let me be the one to hold you, sweetheart. Let me be the one to kiss you and wipe away your tears. Let me apologize when I mess up. And I'm going to mess up a lot, trust me. I'm scared and terrified. More than I've been in my entire life. Let me fight against the evils of the world with you, by your side, day in and day out. I want to try with you. Only you. For as long as you'll have me."

"Yes. Yes. Yes," I whisper. "I'm scared, too. You aren't allowed to leave me again."

"Never. Never again."

"You kept the cups." The kernel of knowledge I've been holding onto for weeks finally slips out. "Why?"

He smiles. "I knew you found those. Sneaky."

"You realize they were in plain sight, right?"

"You realize I didn't plan for you to be in my house, right? I couldn't throw them away. It's pathetic that a single word or phrase could make my day, but that's what happened. I smiled when I looked at them and thought of you when I got back to my office after our meetings. Which was a fuckton of times, for the record."

"A fuckton, huh? That's a lot. You're so good, Jack. I'm here. You're here. I want you for your flaws and your stubbornness and your ketchup eggs. For the way you smile at me when you think I'm not looking. For the good days, and even more on the bad days. I want you for the way you challenge me and push me. I want you. Just you."

There's no cocky bravado or elation that he's won some sort of game or contest. Instead, his eyes flutter closed and he sighs. "Yes, Jo," he breathes out. "Anything. All that I have, and all that I am, is yours. In any capacity. Take me. Take all of it."

"What do we do now?" I ask, mentally preparing a checklist I have to accomplish. "I need to cancel my flight. Send them an email and let them know I'm not coming and declining any future offers."

"Is that what you want? Are you *sure?* Don't do this for me, Jo. This needs to be for you. If Denver is where you see yourself, you have to get on that plane. We can figure out weekend visits. We could meet halfway. I don't want you to have any regrets, no matter how we feel about each other."

"I'm sure. I'm positive. I want to do freelance marketing and advertising. Who knows if it's going to work or if I'll fail massively, but I want to take the risk and try. I like helping others, and I want to stay here. With you."

"Thank God," he whispers, exhaling heavily. "Can I hug you?" Jack steps cautiously toward me. "Because this distance between us is too much."

"Please," I let out a rattled sound, voice catching on another sob.

His arms engulf me, pulling me flush against him. Coffee

and citrus. Warm and familiar. Caring and thoughtful. Love and tenderness. All nestled right here.

"I'm here. I'm here. I'm not letting you go," he murmurs over and over into my hair. "You're perfect. You were made for me."

"I'm here too," I answer. "And I'm not letting you go, either."

"Can I kiss you?"

"Jack. The answer to that question will always be a resounding yes."

"Even when you're mad at me?"

"We're going to have a very big fight about this tomorrow. Huge. Like, you might be sleeping on the couch for an extended period of time."

"I deserve every minute of exile to the too-small sectional. But now?"

I grab the collar of his shirt and yank him toward me. "Now you better kiss me like you freaking mean it."

His lips crash on mine and I melt into him, arms wrapping around his neck, the centimeters between us still far too much distance. His hands run down my back, landing on my ass and squeezing. Mine find their way to his hair, pulling the waves, and he groans.

"Get on the desk," he growls, shoving folders to the floor with such ferocity, some of them bounce off the neighboring wall. I want to giggle at the clutter he's created, the mess of papers and array of colored pens scattered on the floor. Instead, I turn my gaze back to him, relishing in the way his eyes are full of lust and desire, apologies and remorse. There's no time for laughter. Not when I need his hands on my body to know this is real, we're here together and neither one of us is leaving.

I comply, hoisting myself onto the edge of the wood, legs dangling and swinging. Jack stands in front of me, studying me, not offering any insight as to what's going through his head. If it's anything like mine, it's a maelstrom of emotions and a flurry of feelings. Nerves. Hesitations. Regrets. *Sorrys* and *I forgive yous.*

My hand reaches out, resting on his chest. His heart beats under my fingers, the thump quickening the longer I touch him like a metronome.

"What else do you want me to do?" I ask, running my finger down his shirt, stopping near his hip. He takes a deep breath and his eyes flick up as he mutters mindless musings to the ceiling above.

I think the most disarming thing about being with Jack is the power I wield. He easily turns me into putty, withering and groaning beneath him. But every time I speak to him, look at him, *touch* him... He acts as if he's in the presence of a goddess, ready to submit to whatever will I demand. As if I'm the only person in the entire universe who can give him life but also cause his demise with the snap of my fingers.

He nudges my knees apart. My calves embrace him, feet resting on his lower back as I draw him to me.

"Hi," he says, his voice rough around the edges in a way that makes my heart melt and my thighs clench. His nose brushes mine. "Do you know how many freckles you have on your face?"

"What?" I blink down at him, delighting in the way I'm slightly taller than him for the moment.

"Your freckles. You have 15." His thumb gently glides over my cheek. "I counted the first morning we woke up together. Before we ever..." He trails off sheepishly. "Every single one is beautiful. I like learning and noticing the big things about you. Your laugh. Your smiles. Your hair. The small, less obvious finds, however, are my favorite. The discrete, hidden ones. Like the socks you sleep in. How your voice sounds in the morning. What side of the bed you prefer. It makes me feel like maybe I'm the only one who will ever know that part of you."

I lean forward, mouth skating over his, teeth sinking into his bottom lip gently in the way I know drives him wild. "You are the only one who knows these parts of me. And no one else ever will."

His restraint soars out the window with my declaration and forgiveness, lips crashing over mine as a fresh wave of devotion overtakes me. I gasp at the intensity. At the way I've missed him. *All* of him. The good and the bad; what is being with a partner if you don't welcome all sides of them? It's easy to care for someone on joyous, sunny days. What about darker, stormier ones?

I part my lips as his tongue slides against mine, my hands shifting to the base of his neck, clutching the ends of his hair to keep myself steady and from free-falling off the top of a skyscraper.

"Lie down," he instructs, mouth never leaving mine. I scoot on the desk, letting my back rest flat on the wood. He steps away, out of reach, his hand running up my thigh, a tantalizing phantom shadow. "Can I take off your jeans?"

I nod, a lump forming in my throat at his care and consideration, the boundaries he respects, even after being together before. Numerous times. "Yes," I answer hoarsely.

His fingers make quick work of the button and zipper, guiding the material down my legs. The cool air causes goosebumps to explode on my bare skin, and I instinctively bring my feet up, letting them rest on the surface, bared open to him.

"This is a beautiful fucking sight," Jack exhales, his voice strained. "You. On my desk. Ready for me. I told you this was a fantasy of mine." His head dips as he lightly presses a kiss to my left thigh before replicating it on the right, a mirror image. My legs open wider, inviting him in, craving more of his salacious touch. "What if someone walked in?"

"I wouldn't care," I whisper, speaking the truth. The ceiling could collapse on us right this second, and only *he* would have my attention.

"There's my girl. I've missed you so much."

"I missed you too."

He runs his hand over my lower stomach, my belly burning under the roadmap he's drawing. I whine at the taunt while Jack chuckles.

"Would you hate me if I said I also missed this?" he asks. His fingers slip inside my underwear, toying with the lace and moving the fabric aside.

"No," I breathe out, back arching off the wood. "If I don't have your fingers inside me in four seconds I swear to—Ah," I moan wantonly, my wish granted as Jack's thumb grazes over my clit, synapses already firing rapidly. The sound echoes through his office, and when he gently pushes one finger fully inside me, I lose control, not caring if the entire staff is outside the door listening.

"Don't worry," he murmurs, somehow reading my unspoken thoughts. "No one else is here. I'll never let anyone else hear the delectable sounds you make, Jo. They're for my ears only."

"Yes," I hiss, his possessiveness making the moment sexier. His hand is back on my stomach and I think I'm going to kill him. "Jack," I groan, pushing up on my elbows to stare down at him. "Please."

"Since you asked so nicely," he replies, shoving my legs apart as his head lowers. "And because I'm fucking starving, Jo. Only you can keep me alive." Then the mop of curls disappears and he *feasts*, devouring me and making me feel more alive than I have in my entire life, adrenaline and need coursing through my body stronger than oxygen and blood.

It takes everything in me to not combust immediately. To not erupt in pleasure and ecstasy from the sensation between my legs and also the mounting pressure in my heart.

My toes curl and my hands reach out to grip the desk like my life depends on it, knuckles turning white. It feels like years have passed since he last touched me, and I'm not sure how I survived during our time apart. I can barely remember my own name, but I'm sure of one thing: I'm never letting this man go ever again.

"Jack," I pant, every care and qualm about how I look and sound dissipating. I get no answer, and the only sign he heard my plea is another finger sliding deep inside me as his tongue works my clit in tandem, a feverish feeling creeping its way up from my toes, a steady incline, desperate to be released.

"That's my good girl," he purrs, pausing his attack. "Can you take three? Is that how many fingers it'll take for you to come on my desk?"

"Yes. Anything," I cry out, reach out and grabbing his hair, forcing him back on his mission. His chuckle vibrates against the ball of nerves he vacated a minute before, nearly tipping me over the edge.

"Breathe, sweetheart," is the only warning I get before he adds a third finger inside, the stretch just shy of painful and blindingly close to nirvana. If this is heaven, I never want to return to earth. "Absolutely divine."

When his tongue returns to my clit, I lose it, catapulting into the sun, a wave of heat inundating me. My legs snap closed, squeezing his head in place, my fingers clawing at the desk. Gently, lovingly, he brings me down with lazy licks and slow thrusts, letting me ride the high until my ragged breathing subsides and my eyes squint open, staring at the light above.

"Hi," I croak out, reaching out, fumbling, searching for Jack.

"Right here," he answers, rubbing the inside of my thighs in small circles until I release his head from my death grip with shaky, unsteady movements.

"Sorry."

"No apologies needed." I blink and he's by my shoulders, caressing my cheek. "You're exquisite," he whispers.

"You're just now noticing this?" I joke feebly, forcing myself to sit up.

"I've always known," he amends, large, warm hands running up and down my arms. "Doing okay?"

"Yeah."

"Good." He presses a kiss to my cheek before dancing over to my mouth. I savor the taste of myself, tongue tracing the outline of his lips, claiming every inch of the wet, thoroughly satisfied orgasm he brought on. "Mm. Hi."

"I remember a conversation about desk banging being one of your fantasies."

"It very much is. Now I want to take you home so we can finish this properly."

"I also remember you telling me if I wanted an audience, I could have one," I pout, jutting my head toward the glass. He hasn't bothered to close the blinds, and with the setting sun, we stick out like sore thumbs to the tenants in the neighboring buildings. "Here you are making me wait."

Maneuvering my shoulders, Jack spins me on the desk so I'm facing the windows, his lips dropping to whisper in my ear. His hand dips inside my shirt and bra, squeezing my nipple. I let out a moan.

"You put on a show for everyone looking outside right now. You think they missed the way your head was thrown back? Your hands nearly ripping apart my shirt and leaving scratch marks on the wood? The only thing they *didn't* see was your delicious pussy. Open your legs and show them, Jo. I'm sure you're still wet. We can talk about my fantasies all you want, but I can't wait to learn each one of yours."

I swallow thickly, realizing it's darker outside than I first thought and the lights in his office are nearly blinding. Jack's fingers move to the other side of my chest, paying attention to the neglected nipple, twisting and squeezing.

"I have a very imaginative mind," I whisper, my head tilting back to rest on Jack's shoulder. "The books I read help."

"If by imaginative you mean hot as hell, then yeah, I agree," he answers, lips kissing down my neck. "What part turns you on the most? Knowing someone's watching? Knowing it's wrong? Knowing other people might want to touch you but I'll kill them if they try?"

"All of the above," I admit, cheeks warm from speaking so brazenly. "It's not something I have to do. I promise. We don't need to join a sex club. I've just always had these ideas that I want to try and I've been... shamed in the past because of them. Been called a slut or dirty. I know it's too much, but I want to be totally honest and open with you."

Jack hums, pressing a final kiss to my cheek. "I would never, ever think that. My dick has been hard for the last twenty minutes, Jo, and I'm glad you feel comfortable enough with me to share what you enjoy in the bedroom. Whatever wild, innovative things you want to try, I'm down. Always."

"Let's go home," I say, squeezing his hand. "Only if you promise we can come back to this desk soon."

"How does tomorrow work for you?" he jokes, picking my jeans up off the floor. "Did I not even take your underwear off?"

"I seem to remember you saying you were *starving*. Who has time for undergarments when there's a life-or-death situation at stake?"

"Smart-ass," he mumbles. "Lie back. Let me put these on you. You can give the guy in the office over there a taste of what he's missing out on."

I grin, letting my back hit the wood again.

"Open up more, baby. You want him to see you, don't you?" Jack asks, maneuvering one foot into my jeans.

I whimper, fingers drumming on my thighs, a fresh restless wave ebbing inside me. "I could come just from this."

"Fucking hell," he mumbles, slipping my other foot in the denim. "I'm torn on making you sit here like this until you're shaking or zipping you up right this second so we can go home and bang in a bed. And then shower. And then sleep. And then fight."

"You better decide quickly."

"Here's what we're going to do. You're going to stay there like a good girl while I clean up the mess I've made on the floor. When I'm done, we'll go home, eat, and then I'll take care of you. Again. Deal?"

My blood hums at the idea and my legs drop open, the urge to please him strong. "I thought you were full of shit at the bar that night. When you said you always let the woman finish first."

Jack quirks an eyebrow while reaching for a rogue folder and tucking the papers away. "And? Opinions on the topic now?"

"I hate when you're right," I grumble without malice, turning my attention out the window, breath catching when I see a man in the building next to ours staring at me, nose pressed against the glass. "Jack. Someone's looking."

"Of course they are." He drops his pens back in the cup on his desk beside my elbow. "Do you think he can tell how soaked you are from there?"

"You don't care that he can see?"

He turns off his computer, following my gaze out the window. "Do I care that he can see that I just ate you out and now you're listening so well, sitting on my desk, wet and ready for another round? Nope. Look how turned on you are right now." His hands dip back inside my underwear. "This is what you want. And I'll always encourage you to do something you want. Besides, he can look for as long as he'd like, but he doesn't get to taste or hear or touch. Give him ten more seconds to stare, and then we're leaving."

The seconds pass too fast as Jack feathers my neck with kisses and filthy words, my eyes closing, and I begin to pant again, the needed sensation swirling just out of reach, nearly arriving.

"We need to get out of here before I jump you," I murmur, fastening my pants and trying to collect myself, tugged away from the orgasm I was approaching. The man from the window is still watching us and Jack has the audacity to wave as we walk to the door, laughing and turning out the lights.

"Don't expect me to be mad about that offer. C'mon, let's go."

I sidestep the pile of sugar outside his office, frowning at the mess. "Who's going to clean this up? I hope you're not going to make the night-shift crew take care of it."

"Absolutely not. My friends will be here soon to handle it. Henry tipped the cleaners generously in advance, asking if they could borrow some vacuums. I kind of wish we could stay and watch; I'm not sure he's ever operated a household appliance before in his life."

I giggle. "You're not going to help?"

"They told me I was exempt. Somehow spending the night with the woman of my dreams circumvents having to assist with the plan they came up with."

"Your friends sound pretty cool."

"They're great." Jack presses the down button, hugging me tightly. "I'm going to make you wait here, though. I want to try closing the doors in your face for once."

"Hey!" I exclaim, swatting his arm. "For that, you're getting decaf tomorrow."

FORTY-THREE
JACK

I can't stop looking at her. The whole elevator ride to the garage, I keep glancing out of the corner of my eyes, afraid that if I blink, she'll disappear and never return. But she's here, a sedated smile on her face, breathing the same air, standing beside me and not running away.

"Your place or mine?" she asks, swinging our joined hands. Was I really going to let this woman walk away without admitting how much she means to me? I've never thought of myself as a coward, but fucking hell, I would have been the world's biggest idiot.

"Your call. Though, you've seen my house already. You have an unfair advantage."

"Let's go to mine," she says excitedly. "Do you walk to work?"

"No, I drive."

"Hang on. You drive to work every day?"

"Uh, yes, I do." I hold the passenger side door to my car open so she can climb in.

"And the elevator goes up to the sixth floor?"

"Yes," I answer, knowing precisely where this interrogation

is headed and the information I'll have to give her after protecting it for two years.

"Let me get this straight. Every day you drive to work. But on Tuesdays, you get off at the lobby level to meet me?"

I groan, tossing her suitcase in my trunk and slipping behind the steering wheel. "No. This elevator doesn't go to the lobby level, only the second floor and up. I would walk back onto the sidewalk from here and meet you out front."

"Oh my god," she laughs, her head hitting the back of her seat.

"Yeah, I know, it's pathetic. Laugh away. I enjoyed those three minutes of bantering I got to do with you, for the record. Even if it meant I had to go through the rainbow shades of dislike your eyes don't bother to hide."

"It's not pathetic at all. We're just so, so stupid."

On our drive, I smile every time our joined hands flash under the streetlights, illuminated on the center console. When I park the car in her driveway, I'm jittery.

"Are you okay with me coming inside?"

"No, I certainly don't want the man I'm seeing to come into my house." She rolls her eyes, climbing out of the car and closing the door behind her. "If you could hurry up, please, that would be great. I'm hungry."

I scoff at her demanding tone, retrieving her luggage before following her up the steps. "Is that code for you're hoping I make us dinner?"

"I was thinking a shower then pizza. Thoughts?"

"I can get behind that. Which comes first?"

"You, hopefully," she jokes, grinning at me over her shoulder as she opens the door.

"Touché, Bowen."

After a shared scalding hot shower and devouring an entire pizza, Jo leads me to her bedroom.

"Oh!" she exclaims. "Could you do me a favor? Can you grab me a cup of water?"

"Sure. Anything else?"

"Nope. I'll see you in a few." Flashing me a smile, she disappears behind a door. I pour two glasses of water in the kitchen before padding back down the hall.

"Jo?" I call, standing in the doorway, the room empty.

The door to the bathroom opens and she saunters out wearing...

Oh, fuck.

My shirt that I leant her weeks ago and she still hasn't returned.

Only my shirt.

The material barely covers the top of her fair thighs as she leans against the doorframe, ankles crossing over each other, hair spilling over her shoulders like crimson rain.

"Hi," she says, voice sultry and seductive.

Yeah, I lied. My body doesn't even try to hide the way it gets turned on by the word. This woman is going to destroy me. I won't make it past 40.

"Hey," I croak out, and her face splits into a grin.

"Someone mentioned I look devastating in your shirt. Is that still true?"

She slowly spins around, the hem of the button-up not doing anything to hide the swell of her ass and the curve of her hips. I nod feebly, rendered speechless and knowing no words could properly convey how incredible she looks right now.

"Interesting," she observes, approaching me and taking one of the cups from my hand. While she sips it, her eyes close, two drops escaping and landing on the corner of her mouth. She lets out a breathy moan when she finishes drinking, tongue sneaking out and discarding the mess she's made.

"I slept in this, you know."

"Did you?" Now all I can think about is her tangled in sheets, the top half of the shirt undone while she touches herself.

"Yeah."

Dropping to her knees, she blinks up at me through pretty eyelashes. Her hands fiddle with the button of my pants. "May I?" she asks, fingers twitching at the zipper.

"God, yeah," I answer hurriedly, as if that will convey how much I want her.

She leans forward, pulling the zipper down with her teeth and tugging the denim away from my body. I step out of the pants and briefs, nearly falling over as her nails sink into my thighs. When her tongue licks all the way up my shaft, base to tip, my eyes roll to the back of my skull. Her soft hand follows the route, gripping me with the perfect amount of pressure and beginning to stroke.

Jo's very good at an array of things in life, but she's exceptional at giving head. She takes me into her mouth, every goddamn inch, blinking up at me with innocent eyes while her nose is smushed against my crotch like she doesn't know she's my kryptonite. Tears fill her eyes, and when her teeth lightly graze my length, tongue swirling over my leaking tip, I wrap my hand in her hair and pull.

"Get on the bed," I rasp. "Now."

She pops me out of her mouth, not bothering to wipe the spit away. Walking to the mattress, she sits on the edge and watches me pull off my jacket, tie, and shirt, casting them aside.

"You irritate me sometimes," she starts, leaning back on her palms. From this angle, I can see she's *definitely* not wearing anything under the shirt. Sensing my gaze, she smirks, parting her legs so I get the perfect view of her pussy. She's already wet, glistening in the dim lighting. Maybe she's still wet from when I got her off in my office, half the city watching. My dick twitches at the thought.

"Is that so? Are you going to tell me how, exactly, I irritate you?"

"Do you want the long version or short version?"

"Hm. Short will suffice." I sink to my knees before her, lifting the hem of the shirt up, exposing the lower half of her stomach. Pressing a kiss to her hipbone, I wait for her to speak.

"The time you told me to turn my computer off then back on without bothering to troubleshoot the problem."

"My job description doesn't include I.T. assistance," I murmur, kissing the inside of her thigh. "What else?"

"The time you made me spill my tea."

"Hm. You came around the corner very fast."

"How you drink black coffee."

"I promise I'm not a serial killer." I slide my finger inside her, not bothering to warm her up. She's still stretched from a few minutes ago, and fuck, I don't care how crass it is to want to fill her up. Jo gasps, her feet dropping to the floor.

"I have a confession to make," she blurts out, and I still, letting my thumb brush over her clit as I peer up at her. She jolts, mouth parting.

"And what is that?" I brush over her again, rewarded with another moan. "Josephine."

"I purposely gave you decaf coffee that Tuesday you thought it tasted bad."

I grin and pull out of her pussy, moving up the mattress in a flash.

"You little minx! I knew it!"

"I'm sorry! I felt bad and didn't want them to waste timing making a new one! There was a girl training that day, and I hate confrontation. I didn't do it intentionally!"

"But you did lie. What am I going to do with you, you deviant, sexy woman?" I ask, lips hovering above hers.

"Maybe you should punish me," she purrs, arching her back to help our mouths meet. "So I can learn my lesson."

It's my turn to groan now, and I take her hands in mine, pinning her arms above her head. "Where have you been all my life?"

"Waiting very patiently for you. Also, I'm on birth control. I know you know that, but I'm also clean. I got tested before we went on our trip and haven't been with anyone since. If you're so inclined, next time you fuck me, you can come wherever you want."

"Fuck," I curse. "Is that what you want, Jo? To be punished and fucked raw so you can feel me finish inside you?"

"Please," she begs emphatically.

"Don't move your arms," I warn, climbing off the bed and searching for my tie. Pulling it free, I look at her, waiting for her approval. When she nods, I slip the material around her wrists, tying them together. "Is this okay?"

Jo pulls on the fabric, testing it out and offering me another nod. "Anything you will ever do with me is okay," she pants, palms gripping the top of her headboard for support. "I trust you. I know you'll never hurt me."

I press a tender kiss to her cheek before crawling away from her, positioning myself in my favorite spot: between her thighs. I want to bite the pale skin, sink my teeth into her, and leave *good* marks on her body. Marks to replace and cover the old wounds and hurt. Marks brought on by her pleasure, not someone else's hand.

"Never. You're in control, always. If you drop your arms, however, I will spank you."

"What if I want that?"

"I told you; you're in control. If you want to be spanked, you know what to do."

Ending our conversation, my mouth finds her pussy again, parting her, opening her, sliding in with ease. I've always enjoyed going down on women, but with Jo, it's a different experience.

She's so reactive. Every swipe of my tongue, her toes curl. Every thrust of my finger, she moans. Every roll over her clit, she gasps, hands fumbling above her head, sliding down the wall.

I've discovered the rhythm she likes, alternating between all three until she's a withering mess, my shirt shoved up under her breasts, hair a bright beacon against the stark-white pillowcase. Four laps of my tongue, followed by five slides of three fingers, stretching her wider and wider as she whines and pants my name. Six rubs of her clit grant me the most enthusiastic response, and before I can repeat the cycle again, I taste her explode, coating my tongue in the sweetest dessert.

I bring her down gently, greedily, delighting in the incoherent words and labored breathing spilling from her mouth. When she finally sounds like she's returned to normal, I pop my head up, being met with a languid smile and closed eyes.

"Could you live in my shirt forever, please?" I murmur, hands skating up her stomach to her chest, pinching both nipples.

"If you insist," she replies. "How would you like me?"

"End of the bed, I think. Feet on the floor."

"With pleasure."

We shift positions, Jo on her toes, legs still quaking, ass in the air and hands bound, me positioned behind her. She turns, chin on her shoulder to look at me, and I run a finger down her spine. Feeling bold and fueled by her words a few moments ago,

I smack her ass, just hard enough to feel good, and she gasps, rocking forward.

"Jack," she pants, and I'll never tire of hearing my name come from her.

"Hm?"

"I need you."

Dropping a quick kiss to her shoulder blade, I line myself up with her entrance, deliberately pressing into her inch by inch until I'm fully seated inside. I give her five seconds to adjust before I grab her hips, pushing away before bringing her back down on my dick, flush against each other.

Jo meets my movements, working with me, and I groan at the sight of watching her from behind; ass bouncing, hair knotted and wild, color creeping up her neck.

"That's it," I murmur encouragingly, thrusting into her again, fingers digging into her sides. "Can you take more, Jo?"

She gives me a chaotic nod, the permission I need to fully lose control and immerse myself in *her*. I slam her hips toward me, feeling her clench, and I gently push on her lower back as her chest falls completely onto the mattress. Reaching around, my right thumb finds her clit, circling her at the same time my left hand spanks her ass again, twice in rapid succession, harder than before.

"Jack," she moans again.

"You're so fucking tight," I hiss. "How is that possible when I fucked you last week?"

"Tight for you," she pants. "Only you."

"You're goddamn right."

I pull out, hearing a whimper before I flip her so her back lands on the sheet. I throw her knee over my shoulder, pinning her arms back over her head. Kissing the side of her leg, Jo gives me a nod and I push back inside, greeted with drenched walls and a deeper angle. Lacing our fingers together, I give her hand a squeeze, reveling in the tempo change of her breathing.

"I-I'm going to..."

"Please," I say, using every ounce of self-restraint to not follow after her until she's done, the tightening around my dick almost too much as she covers me with the best fucking prize.

"Jack, I want you to come in me," she whispers, cupping my cheek.

I groan, the words having an immediate effect, only managing three more thrusts before I still, my movements subsiding.

"You, Josephine, have quite the way with words," I exhale after a few moments, wiping beads of sweat from my forehead and trying to gather myself. "C'mere, let me undo the tie."

"What if I want to keep it like this forever?" she pouts, and I chuckle.

"Next time." I release her wrists and kiss over the pulse points. "Are you all right?"

"Wonderful."

Pulling out of her, I wince, using my tie to clean up my mess. Fuck it.

"It scares me how good this feels," Jo says.

"A good scared, I hope?"

"The best kind of scared," she whispers, and I swallow, throat feeling lodged with happiness and relief, joy and contentment. I want to commit every inch of her body to memory. I want to ingrain it on my skin and imprint it on my brain, never forgetting the feel of her fingernails digging into my shoulders and the color of her hair in the early morning sunshine.

"I... I hope you know this isn't a casual thing for me. My recent behavior might negate that thought, but it's true. I've tried to date over the last two years, but nothing's ever stuck."

"Why?" she asks, propped up on her elbow, half the buttons undone on my shirt, legs curled under her.

I have the sudden urge to cry, hit with a wave of beauty and peace.

"In a weird, higher being kind of way, I think I was waiting for you. Or, more aptly, I was waiting to figure my shit out. You're it for me, Jo."

My eyes fill with tears and I wipe them away. "You're it for me, too."

"I'm serious. If you wake up tomorrow and want to move to Missoula, Montana, I'll be there next to you. If you decide you want to take up botany or become a lawyer, I'll support you however I can. I'll learn how to garden."

"When did everything shift for you? Besides seeing me for the first time. What was the moment that pushed you out of your comfort zone, and you realized how much you cared about me?"

Jack sighs, taking my hands in his. "The night you stayed at my house. I had never experienced such an unsettling moment in my life, and when I carried you in my arms, I vowed I would never, ever be mean to you again. My brain got rewired, I think, when it realized I could've lost you. That was reaffirmed on the airplane when I held your hand during the turbulence. I didn't want to let go."

I nod in agreement. "I felt that, too. It was like an electric current."

"Exactly. I thought I was losing my mind. Our whole time

on the island also showed me I wasn't imagining the tug toward you. And that you were experiencing it, too."

"And here we are."

After a shower and a thorough check of the locks, I'm cradled in Jack's arms, darkness surrounding us as we lie in my bed.

"Tell me about your mom," he says softly, fingers combing through my hair. "I'd love to hear about her, if you're willing to share."

I smile sleepily, turning to face him. "She was wonderful. I don't remember a lot of my childhood, but I remember her always being present. At soccer games. On Halloween when we went trick-or-treating. She helped me make a tamagotchi costume one year."

"Please tell me you have pictures."

"Of course. I'll show you. Even when she was sick, she didn't slow down. She was vivacious and carefree. Kind to others and always lending a helping hand. I like to think I take after her. If she's looking down, she'd be proud of me."

Jack kisses my temple, lips soft against my skin. "I know for a fact she's proud of you. She sounds incredible. She sounds like you."

"I think the most important thing about her was that she loved everyone she encountered so fiercely. She taught me that we should make every day count; even the bad ones. Because a bad day down here is still *living*. And isn't that a beautiful gift?"

"You amaze me," he murmurs, cupping my cheek and tilting my chin. "Thank you for sharing her with me."

"She would have liked you. Her and my dad didn't have a lot of similarities. She liked being loud, he prefers to be quiet. She liked being centerstage, while he's content hiding off-camera. But they worked, you know? They challenged each other. She would be happy that I found someone whose views and goals in life align so similarly to mine. I was always afraid I'd have to compromise myself to fit the mold carved out and designed by another half who wouldn't want *all* of me. Just the nice parts. You haven't made a mold. You give me the materials to craft my own shapes. And for that, I thank you." I sniff, the tears escaping and falling free, staining my cheeks.

"I'd never ask you to change anything about yourself."

"No one's called me perfect before. I'm far from it, actually."

"That's where you're wrong," Jack says, thumbs wiping the damp drops away. "You're perfect for *me*. You're perfect to *me*. You're the best person in the world to me. You've had people in your past who haven't been the most encouraging or supporting. They've hurt you, taken your trust and shattered it into shards. And I don't doubt after the last couple of days it might be hard to trust me again, too. But I want you to know, Jo, I'm going to spend every day making sure you know how perfect I think you are. Fuck what anyone else thinks."

I never knew if my heart could be repaired after my mom passed. After what I went through with Greg and the pain associated with re-learning who I am. After the countless mediocre, passionless dates I went on in the two years since, frustrated by the lack of connection and conversation. In the time I've known Jack, however, I think it was slowly patching itself up. Each encounter was another stitch. Each coffee cup I handed over was another Band-Aid. Each email and text message exchange was resuscitating me, bit by bit, piece by piece, until I was healed enough to see what's been in front of me all along.

A man. A flawed man. This man. A man with baggage, a heartbreaking past, and the fear of not being good enough. A man who waits for me to finish cutting my food and orders extra of the dishes I like. A man who holds my hand while I confront my demons, rubbing my back and whispering kind, empowering words in my ear. A man who fights for me, stands up for me, but also backs down when I'm ready to tackle a problem on my own. A man who keeps the coffee cups I deliver, prickly facade cracking with every witty, funny insult I toss his way. A man who has started to smile more, scowl less, and open up.

I'm far from perfect, no matter what he says. He's far from perfect. But somehow we found each other, two broken souls searching for the one who lights up our lives. The one who sees the flaws, the dark clouds, the stormy weather and walks into it headfirst, an umbrella in hand and rain boots on our feet, ready to jump into the puddles and search for rainbows. The other half who brings us joy; with a handful of headaches and eye rolls along the way, too.

When I used to think about the future, I never expected to find someone so genuine in their attraction to me. That fuzzy, distorted vision I had about a partner has grown clearer every day, sharpening into the man lying next to me, bronze waves scattered across his forehead, tan hands holding mine, and tired, iridescent blue eyes looking at me like I hung the stars in the night sky myself.

Lucky.

That's what I am.

Lucky to find a person like him.

This is the start down the path of love, I think.

No, I don't think.

I *know*.

I'm not going to rush it this go-round. I'm going to take my time, walking patiently. Haltingly. Holding Jack's hand, savoring in the little moments and seeing where the road takes us. If and when the big, scary, life-altering words happen, so be it.

For right now I'm content to lie in his arms, drift off to sleep, and wake up tomorrow beside the person I've slowly come to adore.

"Thank you," I say, kissing his bare chest, above his heart. The heart that belongs to me. I'm going to do everything in my power to protect it with my life.

"For what?"

"Being you. Existing."

"Are we still going to fight tomorrow?"

"Oh yeah. Definitely."

"Good. I'm not sure how to go through life *not* fighting with you."

"Why did you always leave the room when I came in?"

Jack groans. "It's embarrassing. And stupid."

"Now you *have* to tell me," I grin. "Please?"

"I was always afraid I would start spilling my guts out to you. Remember when I told you the shades of your eyes? Yeah, that's exactly why I avoided putting myself in that situation. I didn't want to seem like some creepy, obsessed stalker."

"You aren't obsessed with me? I'm a little offended. I read a stalker romance book once and didn't hate the idea."

"Hush. Being around you meant more opportunity to say something stupid. A chance to tell you I looked forward to the coffee cups late in the afternoon, long after the drink got cold. An opportunity to spill that I enjoy when you're taller than me and marvel at how perfect you are."

"Imagine if I held the elevator doors for you."

"I'm not sure we'd be down this same course if you did, to be honest. I would have thanked you, you would have nodded, we'd be pleasant to each other, and that would be it. I like this pull we have. This give and take. The back and forth."

"I do, too. But this, right here, is my favorite game of ours," I observe, pressing my lips to my cheek.

"Me, too. At least this time we're both winners."

"Oh! I just remembered! I met Henry!"

"You did? When?"

"He came by my office earlier today. Whoa, how was that only a few hours ago? So much has happened."

He chuckles, his arms sliding to my waist. I'm still wearing his shirt; I never want to take it off. "I never thought I'd be naked in bed with you talking about my friend. What do you think?"

"He seems like a good guy. Funny, too. And apparently his charm doesn't work on me. I'm one of two people. I'm flattered, honestly."

He snorts. "That never happens, so I'm sure he was caught off guard and slightly pissed off."

"Who's the other person? Is it you?"

"I, unfortunately, am affected by his presence more than I care to admit. An absolute bastard. He's nice and good-looking. Funny. Outspoken about social issues. Successful. The ladies *flock* to him. The only other human immune is a woman he works with. It infuriates him to no end."

"Sounds familiar," I remark, poking his rib.

"She doesn't purposely give him the wrong drinks, however. Just never gives him the time of day, no matter how hard he tries."

"Hm. Sounds like there could be something there. Are you ever going to let me live down the drink debacle?"

"Nope. I certainly am not."

"Fine. I promise to serve you only caffeinated black coffee from here on out, with an extra shot of bitterness."

"Every day?"

"Every day."

"For a very, very, long time?"

"You'll be sick of me soon, Lancaster. And, no. You know what? You can get your own damn coffee."

He laughs, lighting up the room, brighter than any lamp or

stream of sunlight. "How about we compromise? I'll bring you tea. A little role reversal."

"They say the way to keep a relationship fresh is by mixing things up."

"Smart-ass," he says, kissing me deeply, passionately. "It's you and me, Jo, from here on out. A dynamic duo."

"I know," I whisper, closing my eyes and settling into his embrace. "And what a team we'll make."

FORTY-FIVE
JACK
NINE MONTHS LATER

I'm late.

So very, very late.

My adoring, non-violent, peaceful girlfriend might actually murder me and I'm not sure she'd bat an eye after very specifically informing me the exact time I was supposed to arrive.

Needless to say, I'm fifteen minutes behind schedule. My chances of survival aren't looking good.

I frantically throw my keys at the valet runner, a kid who barely looks old enough to drive, and narrowly miss hitting his head. Three massive grocery bags dangle from my fingers, the circulation slowly being cut off with each step forward. I refuse to make two trips. That's basically asking for a death sentence.

The two bouquets of flowers I meticulously picked out are tucked under my arm, and I'm praying they don't fall to the ground and leave a trail of nearly disintegrated petals behind. Using my shoulder to nudge the sweat from the unrelenting late summer sun already speckling my forehead out of the way, I walk at a clipped pace into the building.

The doors to the hospital lobby slide open as I approach, cool air from the waiting room reviving me from the heat stroke

I'm about to succumb to. My eyes immediately spot Jo chatting with two nurses at the check-in station, and I smile to myself. That woman is a beacon to me; I could pick her out in an over-crowded football stadium in a heartbeat.

Ignoring my blatant tardiness, I take a second to observe her. My body relaxes at the sight of her; the red, flowing hair tossed carelessly over one of her freckled shoulders, frizzy from the outside humidity. Dark jeans that hug her delectable, sexy curves in all the right places. A tank top that reveals the tiniest sliver of pale skin as she talks animatedly with her hands. The way her head bobs up and down in agreement with whatever the other women are saying, a cheery laugh echoing through the room.

She must sense my presence because she stops mid-conver-sation and turns to me, bright green eyes meeting mine. A grin breaks out on her face as she waves goodbye to the nurses and strides toward me.

"You're late," she says. Her words lack any bite or malice, and the still-present smile tells me she's not angry. I sigh in relief.

"I know. I'm sorry. There was a crisis in the chip aisle and I didn't know what kind to get: nacho cheese or regular. Google wasn't much help about what's allowed, so I got both. And then some."

"I missed you," she sighs, arms wrapping tightly around my waist and head nestling into my neck.

I don't care that I'm sticky from the twenty second walk from my car or that we're in a public place, surrounded by dozens of individuals who are watching us intently. Having her here against me, touching me, is my favorite place in the entire world. I'm convinced she could make even hell enjoyable. Kissing the top of her head, I'm grateful for the rare difference in our height as she slouches further into me, her pliant body loosening as she sighs again.

"I missed you too," I admit. I have, and I saw her a handful of hours ago.

Before Jo, I used to think couples were full of shit when they murmured sappy, heartfelt musings to each other like the one that just came from my mouth. Old Jack would have rolled his eyes, shuddering at the intimate declaration, and proclaimed that *nothing is forever*. New Jack's lips tip up, the corners of my mouth pulling and stretching to a content grin like every other time Jo is around me. My past relationships and flings were never like this.

I physically ache when she's away from me; a part of my heart fractures when she's gone. I'm less happy. Incomplete. More on edge. As an introvert and severely individualist human, I stopped trying to understand the effect she has on me long ago, not bothering to decipher why I long her for when we're separated. It sounds poetic and romantic and so fucking cliché, but it's the truth.

"Ms. Bowen?" The nurse Jo was chatting with a few moments ago interrupts our moment. "You two can go on up. Room 318."

"Thank you!" Jo squeals, taking one of the bags from my left hand and shifting it to her own. She beams at me as her fingers thread through mine.

That smile. It unravels me every goddamn time without fail, the air in my lungs leaving my body in a single *woosh* with a simple upward curve of her mouth. It's disarming and deadly; the perfect mixture of sexy, coy, and sweet. I'm like putty when she looks at me; long eyelashes and beautiful eyes shining with joy and optimism. Her infectious kindness keeps me afloat, preventing me from sinking to the bottom, and the brightness she radiates guides me on the bad days.

We pile into the elevator with some nurses, doctors, and various family members here to see loved ones. After a short ride, the doors open on the third floor and we follow the signs to room 318.

"Why am I nervous?" she asks. "Is that a normal emotion?"

"Because this is a big, important moment," I answer, squeezing her hand reassuringly. "Life-changing, obviously. Think of all the sleepless nights on the horizon. Nerves are totally acceptable."

"Okay, good. Did you get all the things I asked for?"

"And then some, sweetheart. Come on, let's go."

"You're excited," she observes, smiling at me again.

"Of course I'm excited! It's also extremely warm in this hallway, so the faster we get inside, the better. God, I hope there's a fan in there."

Jo giggles, giving a gentle knock on the door. "So you're selfish. That's the real motive for hustling me."

"It's been ten months, Josephine. Surely you have me figured out by now."

"Come in," an excited voice says from the other side of the wood.

"Ready?" I ask. Jo nods, bouncing on her feet as I turn the knob, letting her lead the way into the small and, thank the heavens, frigid room.

"Hi, guys!" Abby says, grinning at us. There's a small bundle in her arms, swaddled in a multitude of blankets.

"Hi," Jo whispers, walking to her. "How are you feeling?"

"Labor is a bitch," she announces, and Raul pushes some damp hair off her forehead.

"She's a warrior," he adds.

"That doesn't surprise me at all," I say, moving into the small space. "I've always known Abby is a badass."

"Do you want to see him?" she asks, sitting up on the bed and adjusting her position.

"Him!" Jo squeaks, looking down at the small baby. "He's beautiful. You guys created a tiny human."

"We did," Abby sniffs, dabbing her eyes. "Dammit, I said I wouldn't cry again."

"What's his name?" Jo asks, and I see the jovial couple exchange a look.

"Joseph," Raul says matter-of-factly.

"J-Joseph?" Jo repeats, and I know the waterworks are coming. "Oh, Abby, you didn't."

"I did. You've been there for me through it all. You're the strongest person I know. Loving. Resilient. Kind. Why wouldn't I want to name my son after you?"

"You bitch," Jo chokes out.

"Do you want to hold him?"

"Are you sure? Have you two had enough time with him?"

"I was in labor for 32 hours. A few minutes away is fine. Plus, my boobs already hurt from the feeding. Come here."

I take control of all the bags of groceries, setting them at the foot of the bed and out of the way. After some careful maneuvering and colorful cursing, Abby hands Jo her namesake. I stand next to her, shoulder pressing into hers while I stare at the little one in her arms.

"Hi, baby Joe," she says quietly.

"Congratulations, you two. He's perfect." I give Abby a peck on the cheek. "The food is all for you. I didn't know what to get, so there's one of almost everything. Literally. Also, these flowers are for you, too." I hand her the bouquet of tulips.

"I knew you were a keeper, Jack Lancaster," Abby laughs, accepting the flowers and opening one of the bags, withdrawing a pile of chips and cookies. "Shit! You got the good stuff. Never let him go, Jo."

"I don't plan on it."

"Are you two sure you don't want one of these?" Raul asks. "There's still time to change your mind. You'd be great parents."

We've had several exhaustive talks about children, marriage, and our future in the last few months. We always arrive at the same mutual conclusion: Even though we love kids very dearly, we're still adamant about being child-free. Between our siblings, and now Abby and Raul, we have plenty of nieces and nephews to spoil. It's a relief to have finally found someone who agrees so whole-heartedly with me without compromising morals or giving up dreams. Our family will always be a party of two (or more when we add a dog), and that makes me the happiest man in the world.

"We're perfectly content with being Aunt Jo and Uncle Jack," I say, slipping my arm around her waist. She leans into my embrace.

"What about amending aunt and uncle to godparents?" Abby asks innocently.

"What?!" Jo exclaims. "Are you serious?"

Abby laughs, scooting over in the hospital bed so her husband can sit next to her. "Only if you want to be. We know your stance on having your own, and the possibility of anything happening to us may be far-fetched. We trust you two."

Jo stares at me, a whole conversation passing between us without needing words to explain. She doesn't know Abby called me two weeks ago to run the idea by me. I knew without even talking to Jo she would be onboard with it, but I would never make the decision without her. The silent agreement comes in the form of a watery smile and gleaming, besotted green eyes.

Yes. Of course.

"We'd be honored," I answer, grinning. A sniff comes from beside me, and I use my thumb to wipe away the tears falling on

Jo's face. The noise must have startled the baby because he stirs in her arms, blinking up at us.

"I'm going to love you so much. You can have whatever you want. Uncle Jack will buy it for you," Jo says to the little one, voice sweet like candy.

"Okay, it's time to give the baby back," I say, shaking my head. "Five minutes in and we're already going bankrupt." A shriek causes me to jump.

"Yup. Time to go back to mom," Jo laughs, shuffling toward Abby and passing him off. "We'll leave you three alone. My eardrums are going to take a few minutes to recover."

"Thanks for coming by! We should be home the day after tomorrow."

"Congratulations again, you two. If you need anything, let us know. We'll bring over some dinner later this week so you guys can relax and not worry about food." I give Raul's hand a shake before slipping out of the room with Jo.

"Godparents. That's a title I've never had before," she observes, her hand finding its way back to mine, our palms acting as magnets.

"What do your romance books say about a couple who has no desire to get married or to have children of their own becoming godparents? I'm surprised people aren't storming our front yard with signs and demanding we go to the chapel."

She giggles and the sound warms my blood. "I'm not sure there's been a story like that before. Maybe we can write our own. Any ending with you is a happily ever after in my book. How does our new title sound?"

"I love it. I'm not going anywhere. Not without you. And if that means that we have some added responsibility now, that's fine by me. Bring it on."

"You're going to make me cry again."

"We've had enough of that for the day." I stop us in the

middle of the empty, warm hallway and hand her the other bouquet that's been dangerously close to falling out of my grip over the last 30 minutes. "These are for you."

"Flowers?" she asks, smiling down at the daisies. "But it's not Thursday."

"I guess I'll take them back, then."

"Don't you dare!"

I pull her flush against me. "I love you, Josephine Bowen. You are the light of my life, and I'm so thankful for you."

I've never thought about anyone the way I think about her. It terrified me in the beginning when we restarted our relationship. Was it normal to miss her when she left the room, even just for a minute? Or wonder if she was having a good afternoon? Is it absurd to crave her mouth on mine and want to hear her moan every single day, while simultaneously doing everything in my power to make sure she's constantly smiling?

Over time, I realized this is special. This is a once in a lifetime kind of love.

A great, beautiful, devastating, soul-awakening, earth-shattering love.

The can't eat, can't sleep, reaching for the stars, World Series type of love.

And I'm fortunate enough to be on the receiving end of the magical splendor of her affection.

Not everyone will get the honor of experiencing something of this magnitude. I thought I had this before, but nothing compares to the way she makes me feel. She lights up my life like a supernova explosion, making even the most mundane tasks such as chopping vegetables or doing the dishes a memorable experience, laughter ringing in my ears long into the night.

Yeah, we have bad days. Everyone does. Somehow the bad days don't seem so challenging and daunting when you have someone standing next to you, ready to tackle the demons together, hand in hand, an umbrella nearby in case it storms. For her, I'd gladly get drenched.

We never, ever fight. We challenge each other *constantly,* but our voices never raise and our discussions always end with a hug.

We both go to therapy; me twice a week and Jo once. We never go together, understanding it's our time to be apart and sort through emotions individually. Some days we'll share what we discussed, but most of the time, when we see each other after a session I embrace her, wipe away her tears, and kiss her neck to try and heal the wounds that used to sit there. There may not be any permanent marks on her body, but I don't want her to ever think she carries the weight and pain of her past alone. She'll bury her head in my shirt, rubbing my back in soothing circles as she tells me I'm good enough, *more than enough,* chasing away my deepest, darkest fears.

If I've learned anything from my extensive sessions, it's the people you love deserve to hear the truth. So I've made it my mission to be honest with Jo every single day. She's well aware that I'm an infatuated, lovesick fool. The deviant uses it to her advantage more than necessary. It's cute when she does, because all it takes is a single look and I'd give her anything she wants.

It hasn't sunk in yet, even after almost a year, that I'm blessed to wake up next to her every morning. I can't remember a time before her. It's only After. She brought me back to life in a way I never thought possible.

A couple months after our trip, Jo moved into my house. She also left Itrix to start her own freelance marketing company like she wanted, taking over my old home office and making it her own. No one works as hard as her, and her business is already wildly successful. I send her flowers on random Thursdays, and on Tuesdays I bring her a cup of tea, delighting in the way she lights up at whatever compliment I scribble on the paper.

I also left Itrix, taking on a teaching position at the local community college. It's a bit of a pay cut to start, but nothing beats seeing others learn. I never stay at the campus past 5 p.m., and I don't let my to-do list consume my life. Work is no longer my priority—Jo is. She comes first, in every sense of the word. Always.

"I love you too," she purrs, arms drifting around my waist.

I think back to the first time I said those scary, life-altering words to her.

The girls behind the counter at Beans and Brews giggle as they hand the cups to Jo, and I see her eye them suspiciously.

"What's so funny?" she asks. They shrug, not offering her any insight into their laughter. Jo frowns, walking back to me.

"Everything okay?" I ask nervously, wringing my hands together so I don't reach out and shove the cup in her face.

"Yeah. The girls are being weird. Hang on, I'm not sure which is mine." She looks down at the cups, turning to read the orders written on them. "Wait. What the hell?" Her eyes jerk up to mine and she holds up the paper. I see the words 'I love you' written on one of the cups, exactly like I asked the girls to do. "Is this for real? Or are you having an affair with the twenty-year-old barista? I know you like my age-gap romance novels, Lancaster, but seriously?"

I take a deep breath, gathering all the courage I can summon. My heart is going to beat out of my fucking chest and fall onto the tiled floor of the coffee shop for everyone to see.

"I wasn't sure if I ever wanted to say this again, if I'm being honest. I was afraid of what the words meant and the weight they

held. For the longest time, I thought I would be alone forever. Who could ever want me and the baggage I carry? But then you emerged, Jo, and pulled me out of the cave of despair I have been residing in for far too long. I've always known you were special, and there have been so many moments where I've wanted to tell you how much I..." I stop, swallowing away the fear.

This woman is it for me. There's no one else, and she needs to hear it.

"How much I love you," I continue. "I know it's taken me a while to get here, but I love you so much, Josephine Bowen. I love everything about you and appreciate your patience with me. And I promise to show you every day how thankful I am to have you in my life. I don't need a wedding ring or a legal document. I'll build you the biggest fucking bookshelf. I'll make you mashed potatoes every night. I just need you. That's what makes me happy. It's you and me, for the rest of our lives, sweetheart. And that's enough."

She bridges the gap between us, throwing her arms around my neck and jumping into my arms. Her legs circle around my waist and I'm half tempted to press her against a wall right here, right now.

"I love you too, Jack Lancaster. And I'm so lucky to be loved by you." She kisses me then, hard and powerfully, full of promise and forever.

I huff out a puff of air against her lips, my tongue sliding into her mouth. Her hand threads through my hair, pulling on it, and I hiss, hating how easily the move turns me on. I beg my cock not to stir in my pants and I withdraw away from her, practically breathless.

"I'm trying to poetically declare my love for you, Josephine. This is a grand gesture, just like the sugar trail, thank you very much, and you're making me hard in the middle of a coffee shop in the afternoon."

"It's not my fault you picked a coffee shop in the middle of the afternoon to tell me you love me for the first time," she jokes, and I regretfully slide her down my body until she's planted firmly back on the ground.

"I've wanted to say it for a while now," I admit, my forehead resting against hers. "I think I've always loved you. Since that very first day, every day in between and until the end of time."

"Me, too," she whispers, her palm resting on my cheek. I turn, kissing her hand. "We're keeping this cup forever. It's going in the stack. At the top, I think."

"Infinitely better than 'Insufferable Know-It-All,' I'd say."

"That's debatable. Come on. Let's go home." She tugs me toward the door and I follow obediently, like a lost puppy. I'd follow her to the ends of the world.

***

I've learned over the last few months that love is more than a word used to describe how someone makes you feel.

It's silly names on coffee cups.

It's early mornings, tangled with one another, hearts beating rhythmically in unison.

It's someone who challenges you and pushes you to be the best version of yourself, all while standing by your side.

It's red hair gleaming in the fading sunlight as we walk down the sidewalk.

It's 15 freckles.

It's the joy in every day, punctuated by a kind laugh filtering through our home.

It's warmth and sunshine, brought on by sparkling green eyes.

It's never going to bed angry, and always awakening with a smile.

"Earth to Lancaster," her voice says, pulling me back to the present as I shake off the happy memory. "What are you thinking about over there?"

"You," I reply, and she rolls her eyes. "It's safe to assume I'm always thinking about you, Bowen."

"Suck up." She sticks her tongue out at me.

"Specifically, I'm thinking about the day I told you I loved you."

"The best day of my life. Until tomorrow. It's like every new day is better than the last."

"Now who's the suck up? The sex after was incredible too," I add, laughing as Jo swats my arm. I know she doesn't disagree, though. We didn't make it into the house. As soon as we pulled into the driveway, she was straddling me, dress bunched around her waist, underwear pushed to the side as she sank onto my dick, not giving a fuck who saw us in broad daylight. I've never come so much; emotionally exhausted from the declaration a short while before and sexually satisfied that the woman of my dreams rode me like there was no tomorrow. She's incredible.

"We should do that again."

"My kinky exhibitionist," I say into her hair.

I've always wondered what would have happened if we had hit it off the first time we met. If she kept the elevator doors open for me and I showed up to her meeting on time, not acting like a raging asshole. Then I remember everything happens for a reason, and I don't think I would've had the opportunity to know her in the capacity that I did if our story took an alternative path.

Those small, special moments we got to spend together kept getting tucked away, building into something deeper. The airplane ride when I held her hand. The way she touched my face when it was bruised, a concerned caress. The first time we fucked, exploring each other's bodies in a way I never knew imaginable.

Two years of snide comments, rude behavior, and not getting along might have been wasted time to some. Hell, I'd be willing to bet that most men would have given up on the idea of something happening with a woman who wanted to strangle them on a weekly basis. Deep down, though, I knew I had to be patient. I knew the universe was waiting for the perfect moment to bring us together.

Kids, no kids, marriage or not, we're here now, and I'm happier than I've ever been. We've crafted our own happily ever after. It might look different than the usual definition, but it's ours.

"Come on," Jo says, poking me in the ribs. "Let's go home."

"My favorite place," I answer. She smiles at me and my heart tugs at her beauty. All the adventures we've experienced together have been great, but the best view and most rewarding part is her. She was right all those months ago. She is my unexpected paradise, and I wouldn't change a damn thing.

COMING SOON

Henry's book, *The Companion Project,* will be published on October 11, 2022.

ACKNOWLEDGMENTS

Good grief. Hey. Hi. Thanks for making it this far. First and foremost, I want to thank YOU for reading my book. Whether you loved it, hated it, felt indifferent about it... thank you for taking the time out of your life to read what I created. It means the world to me.

Thank you to Elodie, Dana, Nickie, Mel, Janelle, Emily, Kelly and Katelyn for beta reading a very early version of this story. It looks *a lot* different, but thank you for reading the bones and the encouraging words along the way!

Thank you to Katie, Sarah and Colette for jumping in and reading the new and improved version when I decided to throw everything away and rewrite the entire book in dual POV. Also, thanks for just being awesome hype women. Your reviews have been so kind and I appreciate y'all so much.

Katelin and Haley: Who knew when I asked y'all to beta read months and months ago, we'd wind up becoming such good friends? Thank you for always answering my messages at random hours of the day and night. Helping me finding the right words when my brain doesn't want to function. Telling me what sounds icky and what flows well. I truly could not have gotten to this point with y'all, and I can't wait to read YOUR stuff next. And hug you in real life. I love our chat. I love our spicy fan art sharing. I love you two. So much.

Amanda: Good lord. Where do I even begin? You're the first person I ever shared ANY of my writing with, and the fact that you didn't hate my words gave me a small glimmer of hope it might actually be good. Or, kind of good. I'm so so thankful for you. Thank you for not only being the most supportive reader, but also such a spectacular friend. It's weird that the universe brought us together in a flight attendant training class seven years ago, and we're still in each other's lives. I love it. I love you. I'm glad I have you in my corner. You're the best.

Alyssa and Erin: Hi! I love you both! Thanks for being my buddies! I love that we're all friends who travel together, eat Pop-Tarts in the bathroom when we're jet lagged, celebrate birthdays, and visit Disney parks halfway across the world. I know this isn't ACOTAR, but I hope you like it!

To my mom, dad, sister, Grams and little Riley: I'm the luckiest gal in the world to have you as my family. You could have picked anyone, and you picked ME! Thanks for raising me to always work hard and never give up on my dreams. I love you all!

Sam: Thank you for making my cover dreams come to life. The tears that were shed were 100% authentic, and I can't wait to do the next 472274 books with you. You are SO gifted and talented. Thank you for allowing me to work with you.

Brooke: Thank you for your quick proofreading skills and answering my texts when I don't understand how a comma works. You are always so helpful!

To the Bookstagram community: every like, comment, message, pre-order and share of my writing has made my heart soar. You all kept me going on the days when I didn't want to write anymore. Days when I felt stuck or like what I was putting omg the page wasn't good enough. Because this sure isn't easy. Thank you for supporting me along the way!

Finally, to Mikey and big Riley: You are my happily ever after. It looks totally different from what others might have, but it's ours, and it's wonderful. There's no one else I'd rather eat a whole loaf of bread with or drive me to the airport at four in the morning, barely awake. Thank you for always encouraging me, cheering me on, and not making me get rid of any of the books on the overflowing bookshelves. You're stuck with me forever. I love you guys.

ABOUT THE AUTHOR

Chelsea Curto splits her time between sunny Winter Park, Florida and cooler Boston, Massachusetts, where she's based as a flight attendant. When she's not busy writing, she loves to read, travel, go to theme parks, run, eat tacos, hang out with friends and pet dogs. *An Unexpected Paradise* is her first novel, and she has plenty more in the works.

twitter.com/creadsandwrites

instagram.com/chelseareadsandwrites

tiktok.com/@chelseareadsandwrites

Printed in Great Britain
by Amazon